A Watch in the Night

M.C. MELTON

To the people of Squamish,

Thank you so much for your warm hospitality & your beautiful scenery.

Kind Regards.

M. C. Melton

A Watch in the Night © 2017
M.C. Melton

ISBN: 978-1-925530-95-7 (paperback)

Cataloguing-in-Publication information for this title is listed with the National Library of Australia.

Published by **M.C. Melton** and InHouse Publishing

www.inhousepublishing.com.au

This book is dedicated to

my mother who loved gardens and taught me to trust,

my father who loved books and taught me to search for truth,

and to those whose love has helped me to transcend the dark night!

Published in 2017 it celebrates the 100th anniversary of the manifestation of my father's spirit upon this planet. It is my hope that this story will both entertain and inspire you. For deep within each of us, we have the capacity to draw upon an ever present love, and it is our choice, and ours alone, to somehow create a unique expression of it. I now share with you my humble attempt to do just that! Thank you for choosing to "watch in the night" with me during our short sojourn on earth!

Contents

Preamble

A Watch in the Night evolved from my fascination with the inner world. During its creation I drew inspiration from the Greek legend of *Psyche and Eros* and the famous fairy tale *Beauty and the Beast*, as well as R. Johnson's study of the former work, outlined in his book *She*. Immersing these literary works within the Jungian psychological notions of the inner anima and animus, I created a fantasy of two lost souls struggling to establish trust, find truth, and transcend their shadow selves.

In Ancient Greek mythology, the young maiden Psyche is cursed by the jealous goddess Aphrodite, who does not want her son Eros to wed a human. Thus, she sets Psyche a series of four, near impossible tasks to complete. Psyche prevails until the final task when her efforts are sabotaged by her shadow self. Ironically this apparent failure unleashes Eros' intervention, thus uniting human and sacred worlds through the power of love.

The symbol of an interior castle, first used by the 16th century mystic, Theresa of Avila, to depict the human soul, as well as that of the secret garden made famous by Frances Hodgson Burnett in her novel of the same name, stimulated my imagination to create both the shadow setting of Doomeërie Castle and the harmonious 'Hidden Garden' which the protagonist is driven to discover.

When reading *A Watch in the Night* I hope that you fall further in love with both your human and sacred self, seeing beyond the beast that our fragile human ego sometimes creates, and the false, empty illusions of a materialistic and competitive world. For too long we have forgotten who we truly are. It is time to embrace ourselves and the world with the overwhelming power of consciousness and compassion that abides within us all.

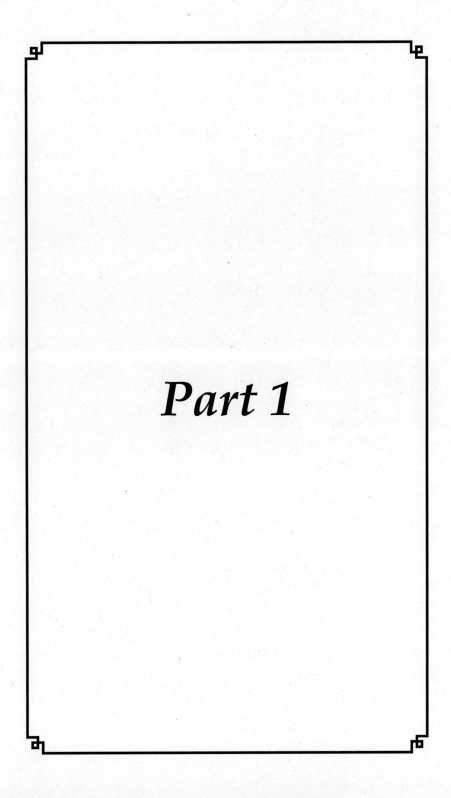

Part 1

CHAPTER 1

Doomeerie Castle

Before the watchman began his first post of the night,
Her soul had faltered and taken flight.

Talitha was floating, gliding, suspended in space. She was weightless; free. Traversing a long stone corridor, an unknown force propelled her benignly onwards. Door after door swung effortlessly open allowing entry; endless, ageless time evaporating. Suddenly, it stopped! The gentle presence lowered her reverently before an imposing, bolted door. She felt the hard stones nudge her into consciousness. Something deep within her counselled her to trust. The doors would relinquish their secrets when the key clicked and the bolt banged … not before!

"Ya alright, missie?" A slightly yellowed, leering grin swam hazily before her. "Ya passed out back there ya did, when that mighty eagle swooped upon yer 'oung friend."

The gaunt, old man gestured towards the rather plain, brown bird that Talitha knew to be Pover, her spirit companion. The tiny creature fluttered uneasily.

"The master saw it 'appen from his study. He came down to 'elp. Carried ya to the well he did … Said ya'd come 'round … to give ya a drink."

He handed her a tin mug. She drank eagerly. Its cool contents spilt lavishly down into her parched emptiness. The world looked more distinct now. She scrambled to her feet, brushing the dust from her long skirt.

"Welcome to Doomeerie!" The bent figure laughed somewhat menacingly, eyeing her up and down through glassy beads that squinted into the diminishing, blue light of dusk.

The great, black castle towered above her, looming forebodingly in the fading light. She turned to look behind her. *Maybe the master was nearby*. Massive, oaken doors halted her gaze, stirring a rambling of recollections in her foggy thoughts. These were the doors in her vision!

"Hello," she said, forcing her thoughts back to her companion. "I'm the new maidservant, Talitha, and this is my bird, Pover." She extended her hand, but he ignored it, picking up her bags.

"Ah, miss. I know ya's. We've been expectin' ya. Come on, we'd best be getting' ya settled inside. I be Marcus … Doomeerie's longest serving worker!"

She stood still, remembering. The journey to Doomeerie had happened surprisingly fast. When she had stepped from the coach, her first sight was a wave of black motion. The bats had been making their evening migration, in ominous ripples. She had watched with growing horror, mesmerised. Amidst the black blizzard, a larger shape had emerged, a massive shadow swooping towards her. Pover had dived for cover. Woosh! The feathery mass had hit her forehead. The force had been powerful. Her world had spun momentarily, and then there was blackness.

"Well, what ya be waitin' for?" The old man eyed her suspiciously.

"What's behind those great doors?" She nodded towards the massive barrier that towered behind them.

"Ah, that be the killin' compound in 'er, miss. Not a sight for a pretty, 'oung thing like yerself. Them's where the animals fight to death for the pleasure and fortune of folk 'ereabouts."

She shivered thinking of her beloved stag, Shiloh. She hoped that she and Pover weren't too late to save him!

He shook his head at the horror plastered upon her features. "You'll get used to Doomeerie, miss. There's a bit of the savage in us all."

As they walked towards the castle, he began to chuckle. "I ain't never seen that before. That there eagle was heading straight for ya or maybe yer little friend there." He nodded towards Pover. "Not that it's a bad omen, girlie. Eagles, folk say, have great sight. What's them say now ... vision ... yeah, that's it, visionary." He darted a sideways glance at her. "They say if you meet with an eagle ya'r on a spiritual quest, a mission or something of the sort."

Her uneasiness escalated. Did he somehow know that she had only taken this position to save Shiloh? The thought that her stag may be dead or maimed tugged at her knotted, worried mind. What if she had allowed Pover and herself to be brought under the curse of Doomeerie for no avail?

"Yep, they reckon that they have perfect timing … perfect timing and … aw what's the word … ya know, ya hit the bull's eye … ac … somethin'—"

"Accuracy," she retorted.

"Yeah, that's it, girlie!" He looked at her shrewdly. *She is a bright, young filly this one*, he thought to himself. *But just 'cause she is good at book learnin' doesn't mean that she can look after 'erself. She'll 'ave to be mighty shrewd if she is gonna cope with the master and his ways.* He continued with his eagle story.

"Perfect timin' and accuracy … the eagle … well it sees its prey from afar and stays watchin'."

The skies were darkening. The yellowish whites of his tired, sunken eyeballs loomed prominently.

"Good advice for ya, girlie, I reckon. Ya jus' mind yer own business, and keep yer mind on yer work, and ya won't come to no 'arm. It's them that don't mind their business that gets into strife."

They entered a great, arched, wooden door. A swirling sense of dread rose from deep within her. Her mouth felt dry, and she swallowed, trying to ease her clamping throat. The cold, dark walls stretched in long, eerie shadows. Their dampness was seeping into her, permeating her with chills of apprehension. *Are they beckoning me on to reveal hidden atrocities?* She nervously tossed the notion about in her mind.

"Now I've 'eard it said that when an eagle swoops ya … yer time's up, but ya'r a bit young for that, so maybe it means stay awake girl, look lively, somethin' grave is about to 'appen." He chuckled again. "What do they say: 'Keep watch like 'em watchmen at night!'"

They arrived at the base of some stone stairs. He cast an interested gaze over her frail, feminine form and shook his head in amusement. A worrying tremor shook his bony skull, and it began to jiggle uncontrollably. Stopping, he put her bag down. His breaths were loud and raspy. She wondered if he was ill and was about to ask if he needed help when he lifted the bag again and began to lumber up the stairs. The tremor stopped.

"C'mon, girlie, I'll show ya where you can rest yer head … and the little chirper too, I guess." He glanced towards Pover.

"The master might insist that ya dine with him tonight, but if yer lucky he'll give ya a night to settle in before he expects ya to attend dinner in the formal hall. Ya never know with 'im. He's a strange one—so moody—still I 'spect he'll be pleased of yer company." He chuckled low. "Someone else he can take his temper out on … Might even be that he'll be less of a brute to me if he has the likes of a young filly to boss about."

The winding, stone staircase spiralled upwards in never ending solitude. Occasionally, Talitha peeped out an opening in the stone wall, catching glimpses of the deep waters of the River Styx in one direction, and the gloomy, encroaching darkness of Nightmare Forest in the other. She wondered where the stables might be. Padyah, her shepherd friend, suspected that Shiloh would be imprisoned there. Nonchalantly, she questioned the twisted figure before her.

"The stables would be over yonder." He pointed to a low lying building a small distance to the north of the west wing of the castle. She followed his gaze a little too enthusiastically. He squinted at her suspiciously.

"Ya be askin' too many questions, girlie," he replied gruffly. "Ya'd be wise not to do that with Master Jockim, especially about the south wing. He won't stand for any busybodies. 'Ere we are!" A long, dim hallway stretched before them. "Damn 'ate those stairs; up and down, all day long! Sure glad that Madame Avileaux and young Anya live 'ere and not me."

"Who are they?" she queried, forgetting the old man's advice.

"There ya go ag'in, girlie. Ya'll get yerself whipped before long. Mark my words! Ah, Madame Avileaux … a kind, old soul. Ya'll like her. She'll look after ya well. But mind ya, she's strict … Won't take any boldness or disobedience. Why even Master Jockim took notice of her as a young lad, and now he just loves her to death. Like a mother to him she was and still is … Brought him up from his earliest years. Yeah, I reckon she was the only love he ever knew; his father being so distant and involved in the affairs of the kingdom. Had little time for the boy he did and fair whipped him to an inch of his life when he upset his plans."

Marcus' exertion had triggered a suffocating pain in his chest. He paused to fill his lungs. There was too much he needed to tell the girl. *She's a pretty, little thing. Shame she has to come to this place of doom. The master will be sure to snatch her innocence away … just like he'd done with the last maid. She was a handsome looking wench that one. This lassie ain't as striking—yet she has an air of kindness about her—something that draws ya' to her. Ah well, it ain't my fault … the evil doings at Doomeerie.*

"You were saying about Madame Avileaux …"

He frowned at her, deciding that it was a waste of time to caution her further. She was just going to have to find out the hard way.

"Madame Avileaux loved Master Jockim like her own … and still does! She never had a son … only Anya, and 'er being such a sickly child, it was just as well. Why, she barely had time to bring up the lad. She was always torn between trying to keep him out of trouble and saving him from his father's wrath, as well as looking after her sick daughter. Ah well, here we are now, girlie."

He rapped loudly on the door. It creaked open. A stout middle-aged woman, with grey, wavy hair caught up loosely into a bun, stood before them. She had a welcoming smile that beamed from her brilliant, blue eyes and the air of one who is competent at duties, down to earth and loving.

"The new, 'oung maid, madame … she's 'ere now. Tal, that's yer name ain't it girlie and the bird, that's—?"

"Pover …" The older woman smiled in welcome. Pover flew instantly into her outstretched hand. "Why you are a cheeky, little rascal, aren't you?" she responded affectionately. "I can see that you and I are going to get on just fine." She let her fly into the room.

"Ah, Tal … welcome, welcome … lovely to meet you. Come on in! We have been waiting for you. I hope that Marcus has been kind to you and not scaring you with silly stories."

With a flurry of happiness, she ushered Talitha into the cosy, fire lit room, throwing her arms about her in a hearty gesture of hospitality.

"Anya!" she called into the room next door. "Our new companion is here. Come and meet her!"

Marcus backed out of the room. "I'll be leaving ya then, ma'am. I'll expect the master will let ya know if he wants the 'oung maidservant at dinner tonight."

He eyed Talitha up and down. "She's a bit thin—but pretty enough—as long as she's wearing skirts I suppose … Was always enough for 'em Deerie men," he muttered.

"Thank you, Marcus," Madame Avileaux snapped. "That will be all for now. You can go. The master has gone out hunting, and he said that he would dine alone when he comes in later."

The sound of movement from the interior room caused them all to turn. A young woman entered the room, propelling herself in a wheelchair. She was about twenty-three, possibly a couple of years older than Talitha. Her confinement in the wheelchair for most of her life had caused her to gain a pleasant plumpness. Far from detracting from her femininity, it enhanced it. She had alert, brown eyes that matched the colour of her hair which was plaited in a practical manner and secured around the crown of her head. Across her friendly, round face, a light spray of freckles highlighted her flawless cheeks. She held out her hand to Talitha in a welcoming manner which was mirrored in her smile.

"Anya, this is Tal … our new help." The old lady beamed happily at her daughter, and the bond between them was obvious. A flicker of melancholy momentarily stole the new found ease that had emerged within Talitha. Their apparent closeness had swiftly magnified the lost and lonely spaces of her soul.

"Welcome, Tal!" Anya beamed in greeting. "How lovely it will be for mother and me to have a new companion. Not to mention the extra time it will give us to be together." A sudden rush of envy stabbed the younger woman's heart.

"Of course, you will be most welcome to join us."

"Thank you," she replied politely, a little embarrassed that her emotions had been so transparent. She scolded herself for her sensitivity. *Surely you must be used to being on you own. Why, you've spent most of your life on the outer. Did you expect that Doomeerie would be any different?*

"I'm sure that I would love to join you." She smiled at Anya who seemed to possess her mother's practical and assertive nature. The tight knots in her shoulders slowly loosened. There was little to fear from these homely companions. Maybe there would even be some friendship.

"Well then," said Madame Avileaux, "you must be so tired Tal, having been through that long tribunal hearing and then the coach journey to Doomeerie. Come and I will show you your quarters. I have left a light supper for you and your young friend." Her eyes softened as she looked at Pover.

Talitha bid Anya goodnight and followed the older woman down the hall into a tiny room. Her eyes scanned the humble furnishings: an iron bed and a scratched wooden table upon which a china pitcher and bowl nestled gracefully beside a plate of bread, cheese, and fruit. Beside the table, stood a carved, wooden chair that was the room's only evidence of elegance. Upon the wall, a somewhat amateurish painting of the falls hung modestly in the now lengthening shadows. She instinctively made her way to the window where Pover had already perched. From there she could see the swirling waters of the River Styx as it made its way down towards the Valley of Loss. In the evening light, it was like a silver, grey ribbon, randomly flung across the rugged contours of the rocky earth.

"It's very beautiful, in a wild kind of way," she softly spoke her thoughts out loud.

"That it is, my dear," the older lady replied. "The River Styx is deep and impassable. It acts as a natural fortress to protect us. Less than a mile south, it falls from a great height into the Valley of Loss ... so named because many a poor soul has lost their life trying to cross above the falls. It is far too swift, and the currents are erratic. The white water is beautiful, but the faint hearted should not attempt to cross it."

"Has anyone ever crossed it?"

"Yes, indeed!" Madame Avileaux beamed with pride. "Master Jockim has, and he alone has survived to tell the story. Still, it protects us well from invasion, and Nightmare Forest is such a dismal place that few venture forth into those marshes. Hence, that protects us on the east. God forbid if we had to defend ourselves these days."

"Why?" Talitha's interest was heightened.

"The castle is not what it was in Jockhein's day ... Jockim's father. Then it was very rich and luxurious. The old master heavily taxed the surrounding people. His ways brought much misery and even death upon them, but ensured that he was able to live a life of luxury and have strong armies." She joined her beside the window and stared out at the satin ribbon shimmering softly in the moonlight.

"I lost my parents and family when Woodlark was ransacked and burnt by his men. Only Fanny, my sister, and I survived. We were brought to the castle to work. I was ordered to care for Jockim. His mother had died in childbirth, and his father had no time or patience for him. With time I met my dear Joe, one of the stable boys. We were married and blessed with the joy of our life, Anya. "

"Has she always been wheel chair bound?" Talitha asked gently, hoping that the older woman wouldn't think her rude.

"Why no, Tal …" Madame Avileaux sank into the chair. "She was a fine, young girl until the age of ten. She used to go up into the mountains to the north with her father when he checked the borders. Then one time they didn't return. The weather was bad, and I feared the worse. Finally, some days later my dear Joe arrived home, carrying Anya in his arms. It seems that her horse had lost its way in a heavy fog that had descended quickly—as it does up there. Over the precipice it had gone, taking her with it. Joe discovered them the next morning. The horse was dead, and our dear Anya could no longer walk. He carried her all of the way back here. His own horse had taken fright and bolted off into the hills."

"I'm so sorry, madame." Talitha sensed the woman's grieving heart beginning to open again after so long. "These past years must have been very difficult for you and your husband."

"Yes, they haven't been easy for me. My dear Joe died of pneumonia not long after returning. He was too exhausted to fight the infection. I raised Anya on my own."

"You also raised, Jockim …"

She wanted to learn what her supposedly harsh master had been like as a boy. Surely, one brought up by such a good, kind woman would not be capable of the cruelty that his reputation boasted of.

"That I did Tal, but you see one woman can only do so much, especially when she is nursing a sick husband and child. The poor lad was only about twelve at the time of the accident … a time when young boys need guidance. He ran wild a lot—mixed with the stable men and the soldiers—saw and learned a lot of life that frightened and hardened him. Not only that, he also watched the ways of his father who became increasingly wicked."

She sighed heavily. "Thank God he has a good heart. I would tell him stories of the ransacking and murders, and he vowed he would never treat his people the same way. He has only asked for minimal taxes over the years, and hence many of the townsfolk are growing in wealth and strength. They spend their money by coming here to bet upon the animal fights. That is how he keeps us alive. God forgive us! I don't like it, and deep down I don't think that he does either, but you see Tal, it's the lesser of two evils, is it not? One has to survive in this world, and the animals would fight each other in the wild. Having it happen here in the confines of the castle somehow satisfies the cruel and nasty streak that flows through men's veins. It also saves us from a life of poverty."

She looked searchingly at the younger woman's angry profile, trying to draw a shred of compassion. Sensing only her strong disapproval and distaste, she quickly changed the topic.

"Ah now, I have talked far too long for our first night together. There will be time enough for us to become better acquainted as the days go by. You must be very tired, and I should be heading off to bed myself. I will see you in the morning." With that she drew Talitha to her, hugging her warmly.

"I'm so glad you're here. I know that we will have some wonderful times together. And now ... get to bed!" She tapped her lightly on the cheek before closing the door behind her.

Talitha looked out the window in the direction of the stables. She must get Shiloh out of here quickly, before he too was forced to fight—that's if he was even still alive! They were so close to being reunited with him again. She hoped that their efforts to get into Doomeerie had not been in vain.

A cloud slid stealthily across the pale crescent of the rising moon. The shadows in her unfamiliar surroundings stretched restlessly. An eerie sense of doom descended. She stared at Pover who returned her gaze lovingly.

"Oh Pover, what a chilling start … Still we've worked hard to get this far! We must keep going—for Shiloh's sake!"

The moon slid out again, seemingly supporting her resolve. It cast a thousand shimmers across the River Styx. "Besides," she said, staring at the turbulent waters as they tumbled and twisted towards the valley, "there's no way out of here. We're trapped!"

A faint shiver slid down her spine. A trickle of the River Styx had somehow seeped into her soul. She knew what folk called the River Styx—the river of death!

CHAPTER 2

The Stable Incident

After Madame Avileaux left, Talitha and Pover headed swiftly for the stables. They managed to open the doors and slip in unnoticed, creating only minimal disturbance amongst the animals. The soft scent of Talitha reached Shiloh's nostrils. He scrambled to his feet, ears twitching in excited anticipation. Balaamine, the old donkey beside him, sensed his heightened state and gracefully lifted her head.

Within a matter of minutes, the three friends were reunited again. Joy and tears followed. Talitha hugged Shiloh, while Pover flitted above. She spoke in hushed tones for what seemed like hours, recounting the events that had unfolded since they had separated. The day had been a long one, and eventually they fell asleep snuggled up close to Shiloh, with Balaamine nearby.

About 11pm, the stable door creaked quietly open. Jockim led in his black stallion, Noble, to be brushed and watered. He worked swiftly with the horse, speaking in hushed tones.

Talitha, who had been in a deep sleep, awoke to sense another presence in the pen next to her. Instinctively, she slid away from the stream of light from Jockim's lantern, catching the first glimpse of her new master. She shivered with excitement and fear as the warm glow played upon his fine looking features, softened by the contentment of caring for his beloved horse.

His eyes were coals of black energy, alert and vibrant to the horse's needs. A shadow of dark stubble upon his lower face brushed up against Noble's neck as he whispered words of praise into his twitching ears. They were a striking pair, man and horse, each so long, lean and muscular—full of life and vitality. Talitha was overwhelmed and not just a little intimidated by Jockim's commanding presence.

She edged her way further into the darkness, intensely aware of the danger of being seen. In doing so, she inadvertently moved into the neighbouring pen. A snort and the vibration of a heavy beast shifting its weight alerted her senses. The hairs on her body prickled in alarm. Danger! All around the heavy stench of the pig pen pressed in. The wild, ferocious bulk was becoming more and more agitated. Furiously, she slid on her belly through the muddy straw to a nearby opening. Suddenly, she felt herself held fast, unable to move. Her long skirt had somehow become entangled in the palings, and without tearing it and creating further commotion she could not free herself.

The snorting became louder and heavier. Around her, the darkness froze in fear. Frantic waves of panic ricocheted through her body, her head swum with dizziness. Spiralling out of control, her thoughts descended down and down, becoming slower and slower, heavier and heavier. *This can't be happening? Surely not!* Shaking uncontrollably, she again tugged at her skirt. It held fast! Tears pricked at her eyes. In the dim light the boar's tusks gleamed sharp, like daggers. She held her breath. It moved closer; its hot breath drifting menacingly towards her. *How could I have been so foolish! There's no way out! It's going to charge!*

Suddenly, a deep voice commanded urgently, "Don't move!"

Next to her, she could just see the outline of two, heavy boots, one of which lifted and planted itself squarely between her shoulder blades, ensuring that she indeed did not move. She felt her upper torso pushed deep into the mud and straw. There was a sudden rush of movement, like a herd bounding down a hillside. Bang! Thud! The entire stables erupted! Creature after creature bolted in panic.

It took a few minutes for the pandemonium to subside and for Jockim to grab his lantern to ensure that the boar was indeed dead. In that time, Talitha vainly tried to free herself but to no avail. He lifted his foot, and she quickly rolled over on her side. Desperately, with tears welling in her eyes, she looked up at the coal, black eyes that were hammering down upon her.

"I ought to leave you caught up there in the shit, you little fool. I've just killed my best boar to save you."

He bent down and drawing a knife, ripped her skirt free. Grabbing her by the arm, he dragged her to her feet. "Get up!" he growled.

She scrambled to her feet, sodden with animal manure and mud. Wet clothes clung to her slender body. For the first time in a long while, she felt keenly aware that she was a woman. A wave of heat swamped her muddied face. Her hands fumbled desperately trying to find the ripped space at the rear of her skirt. Quickly, she pulled the torn fabric across the back of her lower torso.

"And who might we have here, may I ask?" he scoffed, smiling at her sudden rush of modesty. "My new, little maidservant … getting into trouble on her first night in Doomeerie Castle. Let's get you back upstairs where you should be."

With that, he pulled her unceremoniously from the stables and up the never ending, stone stairwell towards Madame Avileaux's door. Rapping impatiently upon it, he stared coldly at her. She realised that it would be futile to attempt to escape. Lowering her head she tried to avoid the darts of anger that shot furiously from his eyes. She was fighting her own interior battle and had no strength to stand up to his ferocity. *Why did I do it? He must think me a proper fool? I feel like a naughty child. Don't cry! I don't want to give him that satisfaction.* She swallowed hard, pushing down her rising self-pity. There was the sound of movement inside and the glimmering of a light under the door, then slowly it opened.

"Jockim, what is it?" Madam Avileaux asked startled, holding a lantern.

"Our new, little maidservant saw fit to spend her first night in the stables. I've just had to shoot the prize boar to save her skin. See that she scrubs clean in the bath will you. And she'll need new clothes."

He smirked, glancing again at the torn skirt that she was still clutching across her body. Then turning his dark gaze towards Madame Avileaux, he added. "I don't want to see her again until tomorrow night. You can send her down to dine with me then."

He strode off and stopping at the top of the stairs, turned to address the older woman. "Thank you, Avie," he said, rather sheepishly. "I'm so sorry to have to disturb you and Anya so late at night." His voice was gentle and genuinely remorseful, as he ran long, lean fingers through his black hair that hung in an unruly manner around his chiselled face.

"It's all right, there's no harm done."

With that he nodded, flashed a somewhat boyish, yet loving smile at her, turned and descended the stairs. Talitha, having held back her tears until now, felt them begin to well in the kindly presence of the older woman. They streamed down her cheeks like a brook that had freed itself from the captivity of a fear filled day.

"Now, now, dear … all is not lost. Come, let's clean you up. It's been a long day for you. Tomorrow will be a new start. The master is not so fearsome. You will see."

CHAPTER 3

Shiloh's Story

Talitha's earliest memory was of the little, stone hut. Life had been good there. She had been given all that she physically needed. However, her heart ached for something more—for companionship, for laughter, for fantasy and fun. If only there was another child afire with the flames of expectation. Her parents were kind but elderly, and her older siblings had long since gone their ways. The days demanded endurance; the nights were loath to provide peace. Pover and she wandered aimlessly through the red, gold autumns that drifted quietly into white winters. Thus, the seasons cycled on and on until finally one, chilly night, something unusual happened.

The wind was wailing, prowling around the hut, tugging at its wooden planks. Talitha lay awake. Gusts of ghostly sighs crept through a thousand, tiny cracks in the walls. She had grown accustomed to their whispers as she lay engrossed in the pages of her favourite book. The pictures of the Hidden Garden mesmerised her. How she longed to go there. There was even a map! When she was older, she would surely discover it. The lantern flickered, protesting that it was late. She glanced up.

Then she heard it—a low bellowing. Forcing herself up, she summoned what courage she could to investigate. *What is it?* Her mind spun like a barrel rolling with possibilities. Her legs were heavy, pumped with lead, as she forced herself towards the door. It seemed to take forever to get there. The strangled air compelled her to breathe faster and faster. *Maybe I should wake Father?* She hesitated, thinking about the elderly man. *No, he's old and frail. I must do it!* Her sweaty palms clutched anxiously at the wooden knob. Dread mounted inside her. The door creaked open slowly at first and then flung back, banging in objection. *What was that, lying on the step? Was it alive?* Slowly, the figure of a fawn, bruised and bleeding, took shape under the shadowy light of her lantern.

He lifted his head, gazing despairingly upon her. The sight of him tugged at her sensitive soul, setting her finer qualities into action. *A fawn!* The thought surfaced in a sigh of relief. *Poor, little thing … he's been hurt.* She carried the broken bundle into the shelter of the shack, cradling him affectionately. Bathing and dressing his wounds, the last shreds of loneliness washed from her mind. *What a wonderful surprise … a charming, little fawn for me to care for! No longer will I be alone. Now, Pover and I have a companion.* She couldn't believe her good fortune! Her usually thoughtful face was awash with affection.

The fawn watched her with wide-eyed wonderment as her soul dived into the pool of his grateful gaze. Finally, he drifted off into a fitful sleep. Had she been privy to his dreams she would have learnt that hunters had secured his mother's untimely death.

So it was that the fawn named Shiloh, fostered within the young maiden new depths of compassion. Indeed, he helped her to forget her misery. With the quiet acceptance and humble knowing that abounds in the animal kingdom, yet often astounds and eludes humans, the little creature trustingly abandoned himself to her care. In such a way, the pair became bonded. Under the watchful gaze of Pover, who mused with delight at how creatures can recreate each other, years passed, during which they grew in strength and wisdom.

Yet, the longing to find the Hidden Garden continued to tug at Talitha. She shared her dream with Pover and Shiloh, and when eventually her parents died, the three companions left the little, stone hut in search of it. After floundering through the forest for several days, they finally stumbled upon a wooden signpost. Inscribed upon it were the words *Hidden Garden via the Valley of Plenty*. Someone however had crossed out the word *plenty* and painted *loss*. Talitha gazed uneasily. Shiloh shivered.

Pover however, felt that they should proceed. Despite the other's misgivings, she flew on. She had not gone far when she turned to see them following. Something in Talitha's heart knew that she could not be separated from her beloved, spirit companion. Shiloh followed reluctantly.

The three friends made their way up a steep incline. They rounded a corner and came to an abrupt halt. There below them was a deep valley. A plush, green carpet stretched between two mountain ranges. These rocky crags were severed by sheer cliffs that forked into a stupendous drop, over which plummeted a thunderous waterfall. It appeared impenetrable. For some time they stood in utter amazement, mesmerised by the sheer magnitude of the scene. Finally, they began to consider how to descend into the valley.

It was then that dissention began to arise. Pover soared high and glided towards the falls, then turned back to encourage the others forward. Talitha, oblivious to her spirit companion's beckoning, crouched low on the ground and began to study the map that she had torn from her book prior to leaving. Pover's incessant chatter about her was annoying.

"Pover, please, I'm trying to concentrate," she snapped. The little bird was not easily dissuaded and continued circling in a frenzy of frantic chirping. Shiloh watched on disheartened.

"I think we should head down towards our right." Talitha stood, pointing towards a rocky path that descended precariously along the cliff face.

Shiloh raised his nostrils, ears twitching nervously. His hide prickled. An innate sense of uneasiness mounted. Talitha started to walk towards the track, encircled by Pover who was still creating a racket. Shiloh turned from them. Unobtrusively, he slunk away, his head bowed. Slowly, he trudged back towards the stone hut, thinking that the others would eventually follow him.

After a time he began to feel hungry. The area was familiar. They had passed this way before. He raised his nostrils to pick up scent. His ears twitched, alert to sounds. There was nothing unusual. He stepped gingerly forward, his sculptured head and stately antlers emerging from a canopy of green. His eyes scanned the surroundings. It was still, save for the light sway of foliage. He entered the clearing. Suddenly, there was a rush of motion! Branches separated! Birds screeched! Something squeezed tightly around his neck. He bolted, but it was too late. He was caught!

Jockim's jaw set in satisfaction. He had the beast. A strange tingling of power surged through his sun-soaked, lean body. This yearling would grow into a fine stag—one that would fight well. After an initial, frantic struggle, Shiloh collapsed in a bundle of exhaustion. He gazed upon the countenance of his conqueror with large, luminous eyes, pleading for pity. Jockim sneered.

He forced Shiloh to his unsteady feet with blows from a switch plucked off a nearby, nettle bush. In the hours that followed, Shiloh somehow managed to stumble forward through bracken and thick undergrowth driven by the harsh sting of the whip.

Finally, they came to a clearing. Before them, dark and menacing, loomed Doomeerie. Shiloh shivered as the scent of the animals hit him in a rush, overwhelming and oppressive. He bolted at the sound of strange cries, attempting to pull away. The whip landed hard upon his hind quarters, forcing him through an opening into a dark stable. It reeked of fear. His eyes scanned the sombre surroundings, searching for a familiar sight. Everywhere there were animals, restless and aggressive, in the confined stench of their cells. The noise escalated. The whip cracked again, its sting causing him to bolt into a cell with an old donkey. Known as Balaamine, she surveyed him cautiously. As their evening meal was thrown in, she stood back, allowing him to have his fill of the sweetest grass first. However, his soulful eyes gently encouraged her to eat. With a hunger driven from hard labour, she moved gingerly forward and after nibbling on the hay for a short time backed off, lifting her chestnut mane to bray a gentle welcome.

Suddenly, the stables shuddered! A bantam cock's shriek echoed with aggressive intent. Before Shiloh, Jockim and several other

27

men formed a circle, like a dark brood of vultures, around two, hostile, bantam cocks. The birds were stalking each other in vicious, repetitive, circular motions. Raucous laughter belched forth from the inebriated men's mouths as they swore bets and tossed gold pieces into two barrels.

The commotion of laughter reached a pitch when the larger cock swooped onto the other, pecking it savagely at the neck. As the fight continued, the two birds tore bleeding hunks of flesh from each other. Shiloh watched, horrified. Finally, the stronger bird, maimed and broken, but still relentlessly clinging to the harshness of life, dragged itself away from a feathery pool of ripped flesh. Shiloh turned away also, too traumatised to watch anymore. Behind him, Balaamine had curled up in a corner, her face averted to the horrors that he had beheld.

That night Shiloh slept poorly. Unaccustomed to his new surrounding, he woke many times. The mournful cries of animals could always be heard, lingering hauntingly within the stable walls.

✳ ✳ ✳

Under the same moon many miles away, Talitha awoke suddenly in a hot, glistening sweat. Pover, sleeping beside her, stirred.

"I have been dreaming of Shiloh," she cried. "He is imprisoned by fear. It clings to what is weakest within him and feeds upon it like a ravenous worm. He is becoming frailer. He no longer believes that he is loveable. He thinks that he only deserves punishment, and he will bring it down upon himself. He will have to fight if he hopes to survive. We can no longer search for the Hidden Garden. Instead, we must set him free!"

CHAPTER 4

The Task of Too Muchness

This choice of too much she cannot bear,
How will she sort? For what will she care?
Like Psyche, she must learn how to choose,
The alternative being, her soul to lose ...

Shiloh's disappearance had been devastating for Talitha and Pover. They wasted many hours blaming each other for it. Still, they did what was within their power to find him. Having followed the young stag's movements, they discovered signs of his scuttle with Jockim. They were about to follow the trail into Nightmare Forest when before them stood two, stately giraffes. They were astounded! Had it not been for the air of wisdom and kindness surrounding the two creatures they would have taken fright.

The taller of them gazed benevolently at the companions. "You are taking the wrong path, travellers. This is not a safe way to go.

One does not enter Nightmare Forest without being equipped with much love, wisdom, and courage. That is still yours to gain, young maiden and humble bird of flight. Come with Medad and me. We will show you a different path by which you can attain such virtues."

"Who are you, and where do you come from?" Taitha wrestled with the giraffe's reference to her lack of courage and wisdom.

He smiled gently, her tone having provided him with a little humour. "I am Eldad, an elder of Padyah's herd, and this is Medad, my wise companion. We have been sent to escort you a different way to recover your young, friend Shiloh. Do not be alarmed, he is still alive, although he suffers at the hands of Jockim, the master of Doomeerie Castle. Yet, it is the path that they are both destined to travel as the stag is the young man's spirit companion. Climb on my back, and your friend Pover can ride on Medad's back. We will cover more ground than if you go by foot."

With that, the regal giraffe gracefully lowered his forefeet to the ground, humbly bowing before her. There seemed nothing else for Talitha to do but climb up. Pover alighted gently upon Medad's back.

As they made their way Eldad told stories of the noble herdsman, Padyah, who would provide them with the means of entering Doomeerie Castle safely, while Medad explained the necessity of Talitha completing a series of tasks to secure the states of trust, truth, and transcendence. Without them nothing could be achieved, neither the recovery of Shiloh, nor the discovery of the Hidden Garden.

Both Pover and Talitha's spirits lightened as they listened to the giraffe's stories. In no time at all they found themselves approaching the rich lands beside the River Styx. Many animals grazed peacefully there, and beside the bank a large tent was pitched.

"Welcome, young friends, to the territory of Padyah," said Eldad with genuine pride and affection. "He is the noble leader of these animals. Creation flourishes in this place although the humans have ignorantly given it the name, *Valley of Loss*. Yes, Padyah is father to all. He plants the seeds from which life springs, and he heals those who have forgotten who they are or have lost their way."

Eldad's description of his master left both Talitha and Pover filled with awe. So it was with some trepidation that they entered the old herdsman's tent. The elderly gentleman immediately sensed the sweet scent of their newly acquired humility. He was happy that love had succeeded in melting a little of the harshness of the ego in his young companions. That there remained quite a large expanse of its iciness he did not doubt, but the fact that the process had begun was indeed encouraging. As for Talitha and Pover, the moment they laid eyes upon his kindly countenance they felt at home.

If the word 'father' conjures all that is strong, noble, and compassionate, then it is an apt description for Padyah. After they had eaten, he sat with them, soaking up the warmth of a coal fire that glowed heartily in the crisp, night air. It was then that he revealed to Talitha her first task.

"At the break of dawn we will make our way down to the River Styx, along which you will find the Trees of Life. From them you must pick twelve fruits of the spirit that you wish to accompany you on your journey. You will need them to enter Doomeerie Castle and to secure Shiloh's freedom."

He stopped and looked into the flames before speaking again. "You must not choose more than twelve as to take too much is death. So, be careful how you decide. There will be many succulent fruits to pick from, and your choice will influence your destiny. What you feed your mind upon is what you become. Your task is to sort from an abundance of colour, scent, texture, and taste. Remember, more than twelve will spell death for your soul."

Talitha caught the concern in his eyes and inwardly prayed for deliverance from spiritual gluttony. However, for one who desired to ascend the spiritual path of perfection so rapidly, it would indeed be a difficult temptation to resist so much goodness.

✳ ✳ ✳

The walk beside the River Styx under the shady veil of the fruit trees the next morning should have been peaceful. Talitha however, was nervous about her ability to sort the fruity delights. What an abundance of scents—tangy and tantalisingly strong! She was spellbound with pleasure as she inhaled them. Bright oranges and deep reds dotted the brilliant, green foliage on the trees, while further along there were shades of lemon and the deep hues of blues and maroons. She couldn't resist running her fingertips over the rough and smooth textures. This further aroused her senses to the joys that awaited her.

Several times she was on the brink of picking a fruit when doubts would creep into her mind. She wondered if she was indeed choosing wisely. She made list upon list, comparing, adding, deleting, and always finding it hard to finalise her choice. Eventually, feeling overwhelmingly confused, she sank down beside a large, oak tree and buried her face in her hands. Pover had been flitting from tree to tree beside her, watching her movements keenly. She alighted gently on her shoulder. Talitha glanced at her friend's frail, brown body. She looked quizzical, with her tiny head tilted on its side.

"Oh, it's too hard," she said. "There are just too many choices and they are all good, but I want to make the perfect choice, and I don't know which combination of twelve is perfect."

The bird looked down at her with a quiet air of compassion.

"How do I know what's right for me Pover? They all seem right." She sighed deeply. "I bet you would know. You always seem to know the way to go." She looked wistfully at her little companion and suddenly her expression lightened. "Can you lead me to make the best choices?"

Pover had been awaiting this invitation. She took off immediately, moving from tree to tree and alighting upon different fruits, at which point she would chirp incessantly. Talitha laughed and scrambled after her plucking the fruits with gay abandon. It was not until her basket was laden that panic gripped her soul. *Oh no,* she thought, *what if I have unthinkingly picked more than twelve!*

She placed the basket on the ground and frantically discarded its contents. To her relief there were only twelve pieces of fruit, however she could not relax until she had checked her count three times. Pover watched her panicked movements, a little saddened at her lack of trust, but knowing her anxious nature, not at all surprised. At the fourth count, Talitha began to study the fruits.

"Why Pover," she announced, "these are the exact same fruits that I chose several times over. Indeed they are the ones that I had on my initial list!" The little bird chirped, acknowledging her discovery. She bent down and kissed her lightly on the head. "Thank you, thank you so very much. Let's take them back to Padyah."

They found the old man at prayer beside the river. His eyes alighted tenderly upon them, and his voice was low and kind. "Ah, my young friends," he said, inclining towards them with the wisdom of a sage, "I have been praying for you. Come, show me your choices."

He carefully lifted each fruit from the basket as if it were the most exquisite gem, cradling it in his bony, old hands. "Yes, you have chosen well … well indeed. Come, let us feast upon them tonight, and tomorrow you will be blessed with their goodness." So, as the sun spilled its dying rays into the River Styx, the three of them made their way back to the campsite, silhouetted in a fading haze of gold.

CHAPTER 5

The Golden Lease

Psyche was commanded to steal the Golden Fleece,
And now Talitha needs to secure the Doomeerie Lease,
How will she do it? Her spirit knows of course,
It will be by courage and prayer—not brute force!

In the days that followed Talitha and Pover enjoyed the hospitality of their valley friends. There were many happy moments spent lazily sprawled out under leafy canopies, watching the herds graze contentedly beneath the protection of peaceful skies. Both she and Pover had regained their energy and enthusiasm for life, and the only thought that marred their happiness was the loss of Shiloh.

It was on a day when clouds wisp their way like cotton wool stretched across a brilliant blue dome, that Padyah joined them under the trees. Sitting on a large stone, he broke the dreamy silence that surrounded them.

"It is good that you chose so wisely with your gifts Talitha because very shortly you will be required to draw upon the states of courage and truth."

She shot up immediately, sitting like an expectant apprentice at the feet of the master. His serious demeanour alarmed her. "What do you mean?"

"The time is right for you to enter Doomeerie. A hearing is to be held at Tribunal Hall. Word has spread that Jockim has decided to lease a room in the north wing of his castle to a new maidservant. We will prepare a case for your employment. That way you will be able to make contact with Shiloh, whom I imagine will be held captive in the stables. Once inside the castle, you will be given direction on how to secure your young friend's freedom."

"What do you mean by a hearing?" Her brows furrowed uneasily.

"It will be like a court case. Others will be there presenting themselves as the best possible candidates. They will try and manipulate the truth to present you in a dubious light, in the hope of turning Jockim's judge against you. However, we will spend the coming weeks preparing you. When you present your case with honesty and courage, he will not be able to resist employing you as the new maidservant"

"But, why am I to do this?" Her shoulders sagged. "Can you not do it for me? You are so wise and brave. Surely he will believe you."

"That is not the way. This is your second task. You must obtain the Golden Lease … not by lies and cunning, nor by brute force, but by truth and courage. Remember when all appears to be lost to remain strong and to believe … for what you believe will come to fruition." He patted her hand gently.

"You are not alone. You have Pover to accompany you, and I will be with you until you leave the tribunal for Doomeerie. All are forbidden to enter the grounds of Doomeerie excepting those who are formally invited. Come, let us go and commence your case now."

With that, he stood and began to stroll towards the tent. Upon entering the dwelling, he opened a chest and pulled out some heavy, brown manuscripts.

"It is time to learn the way of the courts." He looked at her keenly with sharp eyes, alert with the excitement of the new challenge. With a subtle smile of delight, he opened the old books that had not seen the light of day for many years.

For six weeks they worked daily on Talitha's case, and in the seventh week she role played her defence seven times each day. Every possible avenue of incrimination was explored, so that with the coming of the tribunal Talitha had become an orator of the finest calibre. Even so, she was never one to be overly confident, and when she faced the jeering and malicious opposition in the Tribunal Hall she wondered how she would ever cope.

However, she spoke with such a convincing eloquence and calm demeanour that she was quite sure that she must have been assisted by some power far greater than herself. She had barely finished her case when the judge passed sentence in her favour! To the horror and rage of her opponents, she was granted the Golden Lease of Doomeerie Castle. With no chance to say goodbye to their beloved Padyah, who had become more like father than friend, Talitha and Pover were bundled into a coach bound for Doomeerie.

CHAPTER 6

A New Stable Hand

Talitha entered the great hall for dinner. Her heart was battering against her ribs, like a caged creature. A warm, sickly heat swelled into her face. She swallowed hard trying to force the memory of the stable incident from her mind. Jockim was already there—watching her. *How humiliating … to have him force me face down into the slime and then to rip my skirt apart to set me free.* Her stomach churned. She glanced fleeting at him and then lowered her eyes. *Stop thinking about it!* She scolded herself. *You must appear calm and self-assured.* She was at the table now.

"Good evening, Talitha!" His voice sounded deep. "Madame Avileaux tells me that you are frequently called Tal. That's shorter … a better name for a maid. Do you have any objections to my using it?"

"No sir!" She forced eye contact. His dark smirk made her regret her courageous efforts. Quickly, she averted her eyes.

"Please, sit down." He gestured, watching her feminine form keenly as the lower half of it disappeared behind the great, carved table. He smiled in satisfaction.

"Sir ... I ... I—"

"Tell them to serve the meal!" He spoke over her, addressing a young soldier who was pouring wine. "I'm in no mood for lingering on."

Silence descended uneasily. Talitha's rehearsed apology had been squashed. She had wanted to provide an explanation for her foolish behaviour to avert suspicion; to say that she had a great fondness for animals and had gone into the stables to see them, and that she had simply fallen asleep on the soft hay because she was exhausted from the day's journey. There was no lie in any of that.

Strangely enough, Jockim was uncommunicative. He didn't raise the matter of the stable incident. He seemed more interested in scrutinising her. Uncomfortably aware of his penetrating gaze, she sat demurely at the opposite end of the table longing for the meal to finish. When he remarked somewhat sarcastically about her improved appearance, she felt herself blush, much to her own annoyance and his amusement. He couldn't help noticing that she was exceedingly pretty. Perhaps not beautiful like Bess, her predecessor, but she did possess a distinct, feminine charm and grace that was most alluring.

He brushed aside the sense of excitement that stirred within him, remembering that the same sensation had disarmed him the evening before when his gaze had locked into her pleading, desperate eyes. She had reminded him of a frightened fawn. Yes, she may indeed please him in the future, but for now he had to be certain that there would be no repeat performances of yesterday's stable incident. She must know her place. He would need to set a few things straight. Just as Talitha was about to excuse herself, he cleared his throat.

"I'm not going to bother asking why you felt the need to be in the stables so late last night as I know that you won't tell me the truth. However, I will say that as you seem to have such a great affinity for the animal kingdom, I have asked Madame Avileaux to release you from some of your kitchen duties in the late afternoon each day. This time you will spend in the stable cleaning out the pens. I will expect you to eat with me in suitable attire at 6pm sharp every night. If you are late, you will have to put in extra work the next day. Madame Avileaux will oversee this for me. She is your supervisor, and you are to follow her instructions implicitly. Any disobedience or laziness will be reported to me and dealt with appropriately."

He stopped momentarily and drank deeply from his wine goblet. She watched in silence. "You may or may not be aware, depending upon how much of the servant's gossip that you have already listened to, that the livelihood of everybody here including yourself now depends upon the health of those animals. As we have already lost a prize boar due to your stupidity, we do not need to lose any more animals, so I hope that you will do your utmost to care for them. And while we are on the topic of last night's incident, I would like to inform you that that under no circumstances whatsoever are you permitted to enter the south wing."

His cold, dark eyes stared authoritatively. He hoped that she was heeding his commands.

"The remainder of the castle is yours to use in your spare time. You have signed a contract for three years Talitha, so if for some reason you and Pover do not like Doomeerie Castle, you are still required to fulfil that contract. Leaving now is not an option and escape is impossible. To the west is the River Styx which cannot be crossed, to the east is Nightmare Forest, definitely not a place for inexperienced, young maidens to go wandering through unaccompanied, to the north the mountains are impenetrable, and to the south what remains of the castle's army are securing the border. I trust that you have understood all of my instructions. Have you any questions?" He stopped speaking abruptly and stared at her again.

Talitha had tried to control her emotions while he was lecturing her, especially when he had spoken of working in the stable. She imagined that he supposed this to be a punishment; however, she was inwardly delighted at the thought of being able to spend time every day with her beloved Shiloh. She shook her head and did not utter a word lest she gave away her joy.

"Very well then, I shall see you again at 6pm tomorrow evening. You are dismissed."

He stared at the contents of his goblet lost in a sad, lonely world and oblivious to her presence in the room. *Why had Bess left so unexpectedly?* He searched the tortured recesses of his mind again for the umpteenth time. How could she have treated him so cruelly? He would have made her his wife; raised her up from maidservant to mistress of Doomeerie. Was he so damned unlovable, that even she, who had given herself so intimately to him, could not stomach the thought of a lifetime with him? The arrival of this new maid only seemed to make things harder. Was it the same slender frame, the large eyes, the soft tones of her voice? Her presence seemed to hack away at the wound within him.

Talitha rose gracefully from the table and looking straight into his coal, black eyes replied, "Thank you for saving my life last night."

Her disarming response jolted him back into the present. He had not expected that. A slight smile played upon his lips. He watched the red wine swirling in his goblet. "You're most welcome, my dear." His eyes met hers with strong and commanding authority. "However, I do hope that I won't be called upon to make a habit of it."

"I can assure you that you won't. I am very capable of looking after myself," she retorted haughtily, pulling her torso to its full height and raising her pert, little chin a fraction higher.

"Is that so?" He raised his eyebrows. "Might I suggest then that you don't crawl under the barriers of the animal pens when wearing long skirts in the future?"

She felt herself blush profusely and hating him for creating her discomfort, she glared back at his mocking eyes. Turning abruptly she hurried away, her heart pounding furiously and her breath snagged in her throat.

Behind her, the sound of low, deep laughter filled the room. Something about it sounded decidedly sinister!

CHAPTER 7

An Invitation to the North Country

The days and weeks tumbled into routine sameness. Despite this, Talitha began to enjoy her life at Doomeerie. Madame Avileaux although being strict, was a happy, amiable soul, and she loved her and Anya's company. In her spare time, she would sometimes take Anya into the gardens, pushing her wheelchair around the castle grounds. The older girl's favourite spot was under some huge elms beside the River Styx. It was there that they sat chatting one day.

Anya was staring at the swollen waters when suddenly she blurted out, "I wish I could cross the River Styx!"

Talitha looked at her aghast and shivered inwardly at the thought. "Your mother says that no one has survived crossing it, except for the master. Is that true?"

Anya laughed merrily. "Oh yes ... he is a wild one, that Jockim!"

"You love him don't you?" Talitha looked at her strangely.

"Why yes, and you would too if you knew him well enough. He's just a sad, tormented soul, battling with life. I know he seems very harsh, but you know," she turned to face the younger girl in eager excitement, "I do believe that under that authoritarian, master facade he puts on when you are around, he has a soft spot for you. Mother thinks so too!" she added, as though Madame Avileaux's opinion would seal the statement as being truth.

Talitha blushed. "I hardly think so! He still hasn't forgiven me for having to shoot his beloved boar. Anyway even if there was an ounce of truth in what you say, such sentiments are definitely not reciprocated on my part. I think that he is an arrogant, pig headed brute, who thinks that he can control everyone by force. Just like his stupid, old boar."

Both girls laughed. "In fact," Talitha quipped, "he is a stupid bore!" Silence followed as they both became lost in thought.

"Ah yes, boring, my life lacks excitement," Anya eventually asserted dispiritedly. "Don't you wish that something mysterious would happen?"

"Not at all, I'm content with life as it is for the present!" Talitha hoped she would soon be escaping from Doomeerie. That would be exciting enough.

"I don't believe it ... You, who fearlessly crawls into enclosures with wild boars, content with our mundane existence!" They laughed again. Lost in the enjoyment of each other's company, they did not hear the approaching footsteps.

"I believe that you were due to start work in the stables fifteen minutes ago," Jockim addressed Talitha sternly.

She quickly scrambled to her feet; a shot of apprehension stirring her body. "Oh my goodness, I had no idea it was so late. I'm very sorry ..." she stammered, flustered and taken off guard.

Why do I always feel like such a naughty child in his presence? If he wasn't so striking and so damned self-assured I'm sure that I wouldn't appear as ridiculously trivial and insignificant as I do. She'd tried imagining him in all manner of ludicrous situations in an attempt to bolster her self-confidence—but none of them sat well in her mind. She just couldn't imagine him feeling uncomfortable in any situation. It was like he was beyond being belittled.

"Now now, Jockim, I detained her, as she is such good company and was entertaining me. There is no need for any reprisals," Anya interjected.

"You are not responsible for her laxity. She needs to be more aware of the time. She should be earning her keep. We cannot afford to keep staff members who are not vigilant to their duties."

Anya looked up at him, her kind, brown eyes disappointed at his strong reaction. Her expression softened his annoyance.

"You are far too much of a distraction, Anya." He smiled at the woman whom he had always thought of as a sister. "I'm going to have to get Avie to give you a good talking to." They laughed as he took command of the handle bars of her wheelchair. "Come on, I'll take you back upstairs. She sent me down to fetch you anyway."

"I'll see you tonight, Tal," Anya called as the younger woman waved, some distance away now, heading towards the stable.

"Why are you so hard on her Jockim? She's an absolute delight to have around, and she does work very hard, as you know." She turned and looked up at him searchingly. "Why, I think that you are frightened to let her know the real you, aren't you—in case she grows to like you?" Not expecting a reply, she continued on. "Just because you've had a bad experience with Bess, doesn't mean that she will be the same you know."

He interjected sharply. "Enough … I don't want to discuss the past or Bess!" Her eyes mirrored the hurt she was feeling at his cutting response. He checked himself, continuing in a gentler tone. "Yes, she appears to be a good worker, if she can keep her nose out of trouble," he replied, hesitating. "… I don't dislike her by any means, but I'm just not sure what to make of her. Very strange, the affinity she seems to have with some of those animals, particularly that stag and lately the donkey too and then there's that annoying, little, pet bird that seems to follow her everywhere."

He stopped, choosing the less rocky pathway so that Anya would not be jostled. "At least she doesn't appear to be a gold digger like her predecessors. It's definitely not the ambition of becoming mistress of the castle that's brought her here. Still, time will tell … Anyway you don't have to worry about what I think of her, do you?" He looked at Anya implying that the conversation was closed.

She shook her head and sighed. That was Jockim, and there was no changing him.

✳ ✳ ✳

Talitha trudged wearily into the stables. Her shoulders drooped dejectedly, and her head was lowered. Jockim's cold manner had been the stimulus for unlocking painful feelings. She liked Anya and Madame Avileaux, but sometimes when they were together or with Jockim she felt so alone. They shared a common history which she was not part of. There was so much that she still didn't know about them and this strange place. *Will I never find a place where I feel totally accepted, totally at home. As soon as Pover and I get Shiloh out of the abominable place, we must find the Hidden Garden. Surely, I will find happiness there,* she thought.

She had been at Doomeerie for just over two months now, and still there were no signs of how she could possibly escape with Pover and Shiloh. What's more, like Shiloh, she and Pover had also become attached to Balaamine, and she couldn't bear the thought of leaving the donkey behind in Jockim's control. How could she possibly get all three animals away to safety?

Inside the stables, she buried her head in Shiloh's neck and began to cry. The deer nuzzled her gently. Eventually, she drew apart proclaiming bravely, "I will get you out of here Shiloh, I promise you, if it's the last thing I do!"

She was so intent on delivering her proclamation that she did not pick up the warning signals that both Pover and Balaamine were desperately endeavouring to send. The little bird was fluttering around in a frantic state, and the old donkey had begun pawing the ground with her forefoot, clearly indicating her agitation.

Behind her stood Jockim. Feeling guilty for his harshness a little earlier, he had decided to return. Anya was right. He did indeed feel inclined towards the girl. While he still desperately yearned for Bess, he had to admit that when he was in Talitha's company the pain of her departure tended to fade from his mind. This young maid's affinity with animals intrigued him, and her spirited displays of arrogance which occasionally broke through upon her gentle demeanour amused him. In fact, it delighted him to rouse her self-righteousness, as it afforded him greater opportunity to exert his power. Besides, she was damned pretty, in a quaint kind of way, like an intoxicating mixture of a proud little pixie and a gentle, wide-eyed fawn.

More and more he found himself wondering about her, what thoughts danced about in that neatly tied head of auburn, brown hair, which had it been allowed to hang free, would have framed her face in an unruly cascade of wavy grandeur. He yearned to know her kind of love, her way of seeing the world, to touch a little of her soul. For a few minutes he stood quietly watching her slender, feminine form embrace the stag affectionately. Standing not far away he easily overheard her words, however decided to pretend that he hadn't. Clearing his throat, he spoke as though he was just approaching.

"I … um … am very pleased with how tidy you have been keeping the stables. I have been meaning to tell you. Madame Avileaux is also very happy with your work inside the castle." He stopped, noticing her red-rimmed eyes. Then, picking up on her embarrassment, he continued speaking. "I can imagine that you might be a little homesick having been away from familiar places and faces for so long, and I thought that maybe you might like a change of scenery tomorrow. I am heading up to the North Country to check the boundaries. Maybe you might like to accompany me on the journey? Madame Avileaux has indicated that she will manage without your assistance for the day. I am taking my horse, Noble. Perhaps you might like to ride on Balaamine?"

Talitha's immediate reaction was to decline with proud

assertion; however, she simultaneously picked up on the words 'northern boundaries' and thought that this may provide her with an opportunity to discover a possible means of escape. After a moment's hesitation, she replied politely, "Yes, I would like that, thank you."

"Good!" Jockim was pleased. "We'll leave early in the morning, around six. I will meet you down here in the stables then. Madame Avileaux will be able to organise some lunch for us to take as we won't get back until late in the afternoon. I hope that is satisfactory for you." He stared at her with slightly raised eyebrows.

"That will be fine."

Already she was beginning to dread her decision to be alone with him for the entire day. She hated the way she felt unnerved by him. Still, her decision had been made and it would be embarrassing to retract it now. She would have to go and hope that something good would come of the venture.

He turned to walk away and then stopped to look back. "I have noticed that Balaamine and what was that name—Shiloh—their pen is always the cleanest … Funny thing that, isn't it? Perhaps you could put in a little more work in some of the other pens too. We wouldn't want the other animals to become jealous now, would we?" He smiled knowingly and strode off.

CHAPTER 8

The Goblet and the River Styx

How strange that her dream should unfold!
Was it an escape plan that she had been told?
Like Psyche who dipped the goblet into the river of death,
She must drink deeply from the present's holy breath!

Talitha tossed in her bed. Outside the wind had whipped itself into a frenzied roar, and rain began to pelt down in heavy sheets. Maybe the weather would be so bad that she and Jockim would be unable to travel to the North Country in the morning. She hoped so! Sleep did not come easy due to her heightened state, and when it did come, she experienced a most amazing dream.

She was in a boat with Jockim on the turbulent River Styx. The waters were swirling about them, and had it not been for his expertise they would have surely overturned and been carried downstream to certain death. She was hiding an object under her long skirts. She felt guilty for her deception, however she believed that their survival depended upon her doing so.

When he was not looking, she slipped out a sapphire and emerald encrusted, silver goblet and dipped it into the waters, drinking deeply from it. Simultaneously, before her she saw a huge boulder that was shaped like an eagle perched upon a nest. She felt sure that they were going to collide, however with skill and dexterity, Jockim narrowly avoided it. He turned to see if she was alright, his eyes alighting upon the half full goblet in her hand. To her utter amazement, he took it from her and drank what was left.

As he did so, the thunderous, white water began to subside, flowing out into a serene lake. She was overwhelmed with a sense of joy, safety, and freedom. He drew her to him and kissed her tenderly on her lips, still wet from the waters of the river. She clung tightly to him. Seconds later, they drew apart and she saw before her a strange creature emerging; half man, half spirit. Possessing the face of Padyah, the creature smiled kindly at her, saying, "I am the Messenger of Necessity. It is necessary for you to complete the task ahead of you, if you want to attain freedom for yourself and the stag. Do not be afraid, only trust. But remember to follow your soul's guidance, for all is not as it would seem."

She awoke with a start. Where was she? The familiar sensation of cotton and sheepskin reminded her of Doomeerie. The first rays of the morning sun were just beginning to break through the night sky, like light filtering through the cracks of heavy, drawn curtains. She remembered that today she would be travelling up into the North Country with Jockim. The vividness of her dream, still potent in her thoughts, caused a mixed sensation of excitement and fear to flood her mind. *Is there a part of me that is actually attracted to this man?* She hastily squashed the notion. *Surely not! He is an arrogant brute!* She jumped up quickly. He would be angry if she was late.

Jockim was already at the stables with both Noble and Balaamine saddled ready to go when she arrived five minutes early.

"Good morning," he said brightly. "I hope that you slept well. We have a long day's travelling ahead of us."

"Yes, thank you," she replied, feeling uncomfortable at his mention of sleep which brought her dream to mind.

Aware of a sense of uneasiness, he smiled. "Can I help you up?"

He lifted her easily onto the donkey's back. Talitha was happy to have the company of her good friend and with Pover on her shoulder; she looked at Shiloh sending her love. Balaamine swaggered out of the stables.

"I thought we might go up via the cliff face. The scenery is beautiful there. You can see down the river, over the rapids and towards the waterfall. It's quite spectacular and well worth the effort."

"Okay, however I don't think that Balaamine will be able to keep up with Noble's pace."

"No need," he called back, already ahead of her. "It's so steep up there we'll have to dismount and lead Noble and Balaamine. If we get separated, you just follow this path. It leads to the cliff face. I'll wait for you there."

Within minutes, Noble, eager to enjoy the morning's freshness, had taken off. Jockim held him back a little; however, his distance made conversation impossible. Talitha was happy to be on her own with her beloved Pover and Balaamine. She chatted softly to them about her hope of finding an escape route. In less than fifteen minutes she had made it to the base of the cliff where he had dismounted and was tending to Noble.

"Sorry," he said, smiling, "I thought that I'd let Noble get some of the energy out of him so that he's not too skittish on the climb up. Balaamine will be very sensible and hold her own. You won't need to worry about her. I'll lead just to make sure that none of the path has crumbled away. It's quite steep and treacherous in parts, so let me know if you want to stop." He looked at her showing genuine kindness.

"I'm sure that Pover, Balaamine and I will be just fine, thank you."

He laughed at her somewhat arrogant tone. "Yes, I'm sure you will be!" *What lies ahead will no doubt test her little display of bravado,* he thought.

As they ascended the hill, the pathway became narrower and narrower so that they had to go single file at a slow pace, watching their every footstep. Eventually, all sign of vegetation disappeared, exposing a sheer cliff face below them. It dropped off dramatically in sharp, red and brown rocks that the wind and flooded waters had sculptured into eerie shapes.

"This is what is known as the Eerie Cliffs. The castle takes the final part of its name from them. At one stage, it was known as Eerie Cliff Castle." Jockim called back to her over the sound of the wind that was beginning to pick up.

"Why did its named get changed?" She was awe struck by the natural beauty that flooded her senses.

"Something to do with legend, I can't quite recall." He sounded somewhat evasive. "Earlier occupants of the castle were so treacherous and cruel that all who lived in the shadow of the cliffs and the castle were said to be doomed … or something like that … hence Doomeerie. You know what folklore is like. There is always some mysterious and gruesome twist to it. How else would we remember it?" he scoffed.

"Well, you don't seem to have remembered it very well at all, especially as it's about your own ancestors." She was beginning to feel exceptionally vulnerable on the rocky ledge and was annoyed that he had exposed her to such danger.

"The past is past … I prefer not to delve into fairy tales and folk lore. My time is better spent overseeing the concerns of castle life in the present day."

The wind flared up in a mighty gust as if to object to the truth of his statement. It caught her skirt up in a flurry, like sails upon a ship. Instinctively, her hands went forward to prevent them from rising, and she felt her balance swerve. She quickly regained it, but her nerves were raw and edgy.

"Damned skirts," he ranted. "I'll swear they'll be the death of you yet. I suggest that you rein them in tight with one hand, so that you can see where you're walking. Use your other hand to steady yourself against the rock face. Let the donkey's reins go. She'll manage better on her own." The wind roared past them.

She blushed at his outburst but could not move, frozen in space. She clung to the reins in sheer terror. There was no hope of stepping forward. Far below her, the red-walled precipice descended in steep, foreboding shapes, plunging into the grey waters that slide serpent like around the cliffs. A dirge was drumming in her ears. She could feel herself sinking into the swollen waters.

"Tal! Let the reins go, listen to me. We're almost there."

Balaamine moaned low and deep, endorsing his command. Pover flew in front to encourage her gaze up and away from the thought of death. Instantly, the spell was broken. She felt the reins drop from her hand. The sight of Pover leading her on filled her with new courage, and balancing herself against the rock wall she lifted her skirts, edging forward on the track. They rounded a bend onto a safe ledge about a metre wide. Nestled at the back of it were bushes, which covered the entrance to a path that led inland. Talitha, pleased to be out of the gale, sank to the ground in exhaustion. Jockim watched her closely, a mixture of anger and relief flooding over him.

"If you don't heed my commands willingly, I make you do what I say one way or another in the future. You think that you would have learnt your lesson about skirts by now. I've a damned mind …" His words trailed off as she looked up at him visibly shaken.

His expression softened. "Are you okay? I'm sorry. I had no idea the wind would gale up so quickly. Usually it's not like this of a morning, and there was no indication that it would be today, or else I wouldn't have come this way." He crouched down on his haunches at her level. "Well, now that you're here," he said, smiling to encourage her, "why not look at the view. It's what we came for."

She swallowed hard and looked beyond him down the gorge. The sheer beauty of the treacherous wilderness was breathtaking. "It's magnificent!" She gasped, knowing that her words fell far short of the wild, untamed grandeur that swept before her.

"Yes that it is!" Pride bubbled up in his tone.

Little by little, she tried to take in the magnitude of the scene before her. Red, sculptured cliffs rose in dramatic contrast to a brilliant, blue sky. Far below, white and grey fountains of water sprayed over the boulders, eventually plummeting over a sheer cliff face.

"The *Valley of Loss* lies beyond the waterfall. I suspect that you would know that area?" He stopped momentarily for her to comment, but she made no reply. "Originally the castle's land spread right down to the valley, but over time much of that valuable, grazing land has been lost in battles. Now it only lays claim to the wild, inhospitable places like Eerie Cliffs, Nightmare Forest and the River Styx, as well as some of this North Country which we are soon to traverse. It's not very productive land for growing, but there are the animals which bring us some livelihood."

She looked at him, ready to denounce the morality of this practice but decided against it for the present. She did not have the energy to argue. Besides, it was obvious to her that he was also trying to keep a hold on his own anger at her for endangering them on the cliff face.

"What is that clump of rocks near the centre of the river, just prior to the waterfall called? It is so dramatic … Has it a special name?"

"I expect you're referring to Eagle Nest Rock. If you're up closer, it looks just like an enormous eagle perched on a nest. Eagles do in fact nest there among the rocks. It's a safe place to raise their young. Legend also has it that if you venture too close, an eagle will swoop upon you, causing you to plummet to certain death."

She drew her breath in quickly. Eagle Nest Rock—it was in her dream! Instinctively, he picked up on her excitement. "Does it mean something to you?" He looked sharply at her.

"No, not at all, just an unusual name that's all, and the thought of being swept to one's death over the falls is horrific. I'm told that you alone have crossed the river." She tried to change the subject.

"Well now, let me guess who told you that—Avie or Anya?" He laughed. "Yes, you could say that, but I'm quite sure you're not in the mood to hear me boasting of such antics at the moment. I wouldn't want to *bore* you too much." He emphasised the words hoping that she would pick up on his reference to her description of him. Sure enough, her pale cheeks coloured. She realised that Anya must have told him of her less than flattering comments.

"So, where does the track go from here? She turned, knowing full well that it led inland behind her.

"The ladies want to press on, Noble." Jockim patted his horse's mane. "Shall we proceed? We'll let you and Balaamine go first for a while now. The track widens out and moves away from the cliff face." He gestured with his hands in a gentlemanly fashion. Mounting Balaamine, she headed into the scrub.

For the next few miles, they took turn in cantering and walking to try and keep the animals as fresh as they could. Noble was a little impatient of Balaamine's pace, so Jockim kept him occupied by cantering ahead at times and then circling back to meet them. He tried to strike up conversation, but she was guarded in her replies. Eventually, he decided that such a course of action was only going to increase his frustration and her secretiveness, so he just relaxed into the moment. Sensing his change in mood, she also began to let down her guard.

They soon discovered that two people can be very different when they are out of their normal surroundings. Indeed, Jockim seemed so much more considerate when away from the castle. He treated her with respect and she no longer felt like he was imposing his authority upon her. As a result her shyness melted and she found herself talking about the Hidden Garden and the stone hut. She was careful to omit any mention of Shiloh or Medad, Eldad and Padyah.

"Yes, I have heard tales of a beautiful, walled garden, but I thought that it was just a mystical place. I have been in that part of the country a few times, but I have never come across it or a stone hut. I assume that you must have travelled through the *Valley of Loss* to be able to speak at Tribunal Hall then?"

"Yes, I have been there."

"Legend holds that the fruit trees have special powers in that area? Did you eat of them?"

"Yes, I did, so beware as I may turn you into a toad if you are mean to me!" She laughed.

"I think that I would prefer to be a frog. Then you can perform the necessary action to turn me into a prince."

She smiled at his words, both flattered and a little apprehensive of their suggestion. A shy glance fluttered alluringly in his direction.

"Better still," a cheeky grin spread across the shadow of stubble on his lower face, "I think that I would like to be a stag so that you will risk your life to come down and sleep beside me on your first night in a strange castle that is feared by all." He looked at her steadily, waiting for a reply, aware that he was treading on sensitive ground.

"I love all animals. I just happened to end up in the stag's pen that night."

"Hmm, and I guess that it just so happens that in the space of a few short weeks that same stag has stolen your heart, so that now there is no creature dearer to you … except maybe this little, chaperoning bird. Indeed, I suspect that your affinity with him goes back a little further than you are prepared to say Tal, and that his friendship is your reason for coming to Doomeerie."

"You can suspect what you like, Jockim," she said, marvelling at the ease with which she had used his name. He had asked her to do so at dinner the evening before. "It doesn't mean that your thoughts are correct."

"Ah so, he is a fine beast, Shiloh. He will be a good fighter one day, just as you are a good maidservant."

He knew that his words would destroy their momentary sense of closeness. Still, if she was not willing to trust him with the truth, he was not willing to afford her any special privileges. So the rest of the day wore on heavily, with both of them feeling out of sorts. They finished their surveillance of the boundaries and came back via a different path. Talitha had totally lost her bearings. Discouraged, she allowed Balaamine to lag behind.

There is no way that I could escape through this rugged country. What a wasted day! She sighed, staring at Jockim's straight back. *He is such a strange man. I feel drawn to him at times, and yet his arrogance annoys me no end. My mind is such a mess around him. For a while there I felt he was actually attracted to me, and now he is treating me like a tiresome maid. Why do I even care what he thinks of me? A man of his looks could have any woman he desired. It is foolish to think that he finds me the least bit interesting?*

Mirroring her emotions, the weather changed, and a heavy fog began to descend like an oppressive blanket shrouding out the surrounds.

"We need to get back as quickly as we can." Jockim sounded alarmed. "Otherwise we will be spending the night out here on the cliffs. Can't you get that damned donkey to go any faster?"

He picked up his horse whip and struck Balaamine across the rump. The jenny moved away quickly. Again, he galloped up behind her and struck her, causing her to gallop faster. This he repeated a third time, when suddenly she stopped dead in her tracks refusing to move. He rode up close and repeatedly laid the whip down hard upon her rump.

"Move on … you stupid ass!"

Talitha could stand it no more. "Stop it!" she screamed. "You will kill her!" Dismounting, she stood between him and the donkey.

"You'll strike me before you do her again!" She stood her ground firmly.

"Just as you will, turn around and start walking. It matters not to me whether I strike your rump or hers. I only care about getting back to the castle before we are caught in this fog."

She stared at him angrily, abhorred at his response. How could she have ever entertained any thoughts of romance with this beast? She didn't care if he whipped her to the ground, she would not leave Balaamine's side.

Jockim was lost at what to do. He had ensnared himself into a corner. He did not want to strike her, but at the same time he did not want to lose face.

"Damn you, Talitha! You'll be punished for this insolence. There is no point in going any further now anyway, the fog is too heavy. We'll just have to camp here for the night. I hope that you can withstand the cold. I only have the one tent so we'll have to sleep inside together for the warmth. I hope that this teaches you a lesson!"

He dismounted quickly from Noble and set about undoing his pack. She watched on dismally, not sure if she was more afraid of his temper or of what the night ahead might bring!

CHAPTER 9

Finding Jenobay

Morning dawned with a cold, crisp brilliance. Talitha opened her eyes to gaze at her surrounds. She was alone within the tent. She lay still, remembering details from the evening before: the ghostly fog, the freezing temperatures, and waking at one point to find that she had unknowing edged her way in next to Jockim to get warm. It had been so cold that even the hot anger that simmered between them was not able to keep them apart. Sheer survival on the mountain top meant that they needed bodily warmth. She looked down to see that he had placed his heavy coat over her, yet even so her body was aching; her fingers and toes numb. She forced herself up and out of the tent.

Jockim was crouched next to an open fire, cooking. He looked over when he saw her exit the tent and watched her make her way behind a rocky outcrop before heading towards him. The mist had lifted and to her amazement, they were camped within a metre or so of a steep cliff face. She felt sick at the thought of how close they had come to death the evening before.

"Come over and get warm," he called.

She made her way to the fire, wrapping his coat around her. Noble and Balaamine were nearby, patiently waiting for the first rays of sunlight to melt the frost. It clung stiffly in glistening icicles to the stubborn tufts of patchy grass which dotted the bereft landscape.

"Good morning … Get close to the fire. You must be freezing. I've made some tea. Would you like some?" He lent over the fire that glowed warmly in the soft light of dawn, looking fresh and relaxed. She felt safe and grateful for his resourcefulness.

"Yes, please." She stared in fascination at the dark shadow of stubble that lined his jaw. It somehow seemed to make him look even stronger.

He handed her the steaming cup. "I know what you're thinking. We're lucky to be alive. I owe both you and your stubborn, little friend an apology. I'm sorry that I lost my temper last night. I was worried about losing our bearings in the fog. Thanks for saving my life." He added with a distinct note of humility.

"You're welcome however I do hope that I won't be called upon to make a habit of it."

"Touché!" he quipped, throwing his head back and laughing heartily. She could not help but join in. "I guess that makes us even now. Don't worry, there won't be any punishment awaiting you back at the castle for your little display of obstinacy. In fact, I think both you and Balaamine deserve a reward."

He walked over to the donkey and patted her mane. "Balaamine, behold your new mistress!" he said, gesturing towards Talitha. The old donkey lifted her head and looked dreamily at her.

"Oh, thank you!" She jumped to her feet and threw her arms around his neck, kissing him lightly on the cheek. He looked pleasantly surprised. She felt her cheeks redden.

"Oh, I'm sorry, I shouldn't have done that. It just kind of happened." The words tumbled out in a rush, and she quickly looked away.

"Well, I'm glad that it just kind of happened. It's a good start to the day." His smile flashed mischievously.

A good day it was too. They enjoyed each other's company and the fresh mountain air. There was a sense of freedom and newfound intimacy in riding totally alone together in the mountains. Talitha was pleased with herself and the courage that she was developing with each new challenge. He also seemed to have regained his earlier interest in her. She could sense that he was indeed attracted to her, a thought that she found to be flattering and exciting. *Perhaps there is another side to this man?* she wondered as she watched him handling his horse so adeptly. *Maybe Anya and Avie are right, and I have been a little hasty in my judgements!*

On the road home, she asked him a little more about Doomeerie. He shared freely stating that three previous generations of Deeries had lived in the castle. He had closed down various sections of it, including the ballroom and south wing to help reduce maintenance costs, especially since he had chosen to decrease taxes to a bare minimum.

"Tell me about the south wing," she said. "Is it closed purely to ensure that it is maintained in its original state? I would love to view it. What was it originally used for?"

"I'm afraid not, Tal. I have informed all the castle occupants that it is not to be accessed, and an infringement of this rule could cause serious harm. Besides, there is nothing of interest to you there—just some old, family artefacts. My mother used that part of the castle before she died. I'm sure you've heard that she died in childbirth … something that my father never forgave me for … and rightly so." An edge of self-loathing crept into his tone.

"She was an amazing woman I have been told, truly beautiful, not just physically but also in her ways. It seems that she alone possessed the courage and power to rein in my father's greed and cruelty—at least for the few, short years that they were together. The townsfolk loved her. She improved their lot so much."

He rubbed his hand affectionately down Noble's shiny, black neck. "After she died Jockhein, my father, reverted to his old ways with an increased savageness. He ransacked the town, tripled the size of the army, and extended the castle's borders. Eventually, he made me … the son he despised … the leader of one of his battalions." Again, his long, lean fingers caressed the shiny, black mane.

"So, you see, my dear," he turned to look at her with a wry smile on his face, "there are many who have suffered at my hands, and those who oppose me in the future will also suffer. It's in my blood. At Doomeerie rules will not be broken without retribution. The scales must be balanced. Any breach of contract will be met with reprisals. Such it is written to ensure that the castle and its occupants aren't destroyed."

He stared at her commandingly. He hoped that she was heeding him as he did not want to force such a punishment upon her. She shivered inwardly and looked away, endeavouring to maintain her outward composure.

"When Jockhein was eventually killed in battle, I decided to stop advancing and to maintain what we had gained. I gave freedom to all the soldiers who wanted to leave. Understandably, there were many who desired to reclaim what had once been theirs and indeed to take back more. With the castles forces reduced to a third of their original size, we could only keep the area around Doomeerie that the natural elements make impossible for invaders to penetrate."

He glanced up towards the mountains. They stood stark and white; majestic against the clear, blue sky. "Legend maintains that there is a pass between those mountains to the north, so I regularly keep an eye to the borders up here." Then with emphasis, he added. "To this day I have never found it, even though I know this country like the back of my hand, so it would be very foolish for anyone to try and escape that way. It would mean certain death."

She feigned indifference. The hopelessness of her situation lodged heavily in her thoughts. Her spirits were dampening.

"Well, the rest you know. Nowadays we make our livelihood through the animals fighting. Although it's not perfect by your standards Tal, it means that cruelty is no longer inflicted upon the townsfolk through harsh taxes which they cannot pay."

"I do not understand," she retorted indignantly. "Nobody is forcing you to punish them if they cannot afford their taxes."

"You're right, you don't understand … You have not felt the curse, and I hope that you do not bring it upon yourself. Generation after generation, oath after oath, bloodbath after bloodbath, and then it runs through your veins; it is part of the Deerie Dynasty—always has been and always will be." Sensing her disapproval, he stopped. "Anyway, such things are of little concern to a maidservant."

They rode on quietly for some time, his closing words having once again reminded her of the futility of questioning his ways. The path began to weave closer towards the dismal border of Nightmare Forest. Suddenly, Jockim's eyes narrowed. "What the hell ... What's that?"

He kicked Noble lightly in the flanks causing him to break into a cantor and head for what looked like a bundle of flesh, slain and deposited on the edge of the forest. Talitha followed behind, knowing she would have no success in trying to force Balaamine to keep up with the young stallion.

Jockim dismounted. At his feet lay a slain tigress, huddled in a mass of bloodied flesh. He checked her, confirming that she was dead. Not far away, crouched in the tall grass was a highly agitated, young cub. Jockim raised his rifle to shoot the abandoned beast. Behind him, a frenzied scream shattered his concentration.

"Don't! ... Please spare her!" Talitha was running towards him.

He turned to face her and stared. What was wrong? His face was hostile. Quickly, he raised the rifle before her. Psst... bang! ... The world exploded! She screamed, lunging to the ground. Nearby there was a moan, then a heavy thud. *What's happening?* she thought. She lay dazed, frozen in space; breathless.

He ran past and rolled over a portly, male body that was lying on the ground, not far from her. Assured that any threat was gone, she watched him quickly survey the scene, backtracking down the path. "Stay down!" he called.

She laid still, every nerve in her body tightened. Would she need to spring into action? In a few minutes, he returned. It seemed like hours to her tightly coiled muscles. He was carrying a sack.

"Get up! It's clear I think. There was only one of them."

He began furiously searching the dead man's pockets for some form of identification. Pulling out some papers, he read them emitting a low whistle. "Ah indeed, the general is back," he muttered. "I wondered how long it would be before he arrived."

"What do you mean?" Talitha demanded, rattled.

"Our podgy friend here is a deserter from the army, General Kofra's battalion. Konfra was the chief general in my father's forces. He is back in the area. I suspect that we will find his battalion at the castle. It's not a good omen … Means that there is trouble brewing on our borders. This coward must have slaughtered the tigress when they happened upon each other. He just had time to escape into the forest when we came along. I suspect that he was going to use you as a hostage, to force me to hand over Noble and Balaamine. The animals would have assured him of an easier escape."

She felt her knees weaken. "Thank you, I thought that you had shot me."

He smiled wryly. "The thought has entered my head on the odd occasion."

Then looking at the corpse, he opened the sack. "Thieving bastard," he cursed, "making off with the castle's Holy Grail!" He drew out an elegant, silver goblet encrusted with sapphires and emeralds. "He'd fetch a good sum for this."

Talitha gasped, recognising the goblet to be the one from her dream. Jockim looked sharply at her. "Yes, it's beautiful, isn't it?

It's probably the single most valuable piece in the castle. I don't know how he would have got it, especially as it was locked in the south wing. Come on, we'd better get back as soon as possible. I think that we are going to find a very different Doomeerie to the one we left."

He moved to mount Noble and turned to see if she was following. She was walking towards him with the cub cradled in her arms. All at once he was struck by her pure innocence and beauty. She walked with the grace of an angel and looked almost surreal as she pressed the small creature close to her breasts. Long strands of auburn hair fell below her shoulders, blowing gently in the breeze, and with doe-like eyes that tugged at his soul, she pleaded, "We can't leave this creature to fend here in the wilderness. She will die!"

"Exactly," he replied, trying to force the loveliness of her expression from his mind, "which was why I was about to make her death quick and painless."

"We can care for her at the castle."

"She has no mother to feed from Tal. It will not work."

"I will be her mother." She lifted her chin with determination and feminine beauty. He felt something inside him soften and break apart with compassion.

"Alright, as you wish. Put her in the sack. I will tie the goblet to the saddle."

Her eyes beamed with gratitude and despite his disapproval, he couldn't resist smiling. "And what are you going to name your new charge?"

"Jenobay ... She has a strong, independent spirit. I can see it in her eyes."

Jockim looked into the cub's tantalizing eyes. "Indeed she has. I suspect that you will be a good friend to Tal, Jenobay. You will stand by her and be there for her when she needs you after you have attained your full strength." He stopped for a minute, seeming to be immersed in thought. "I also suspect that in caring for you, little cub, she will simultaneously learn to care for that little tiger that I see hidden deep within her … that tiger that needs to be tamed." He looked at her in a manner that hinted he would make her yield to him yet.

She felt a spark ignite deep within her. He sensed her momentary flicker of attraction and smiling, turned his attention back to the cub. Speaking softly, he caressed it gently around the ears. Then placing it in the sack, he mounted Noble, looking down at Talitha. Her eyes had misted over and were gleaming with the soft shine of new found love.

God, she's gorgeous, he thought. He wanted her so badly. It was burning within him now. That urge that he had been grappling with for months, ever since he first dragged her muddied and helpless from the stables. It had been so long since he had felt the soft curves of feminine flesh feverishly ignite his body. Why had he let his temper get the better of him last night? He might have been able to have his way with her. *Damn it,* he thought. *I have lost the opportunity. There will be no chance now … not now that the general and his daughter are at Doomeerie.*

Pulling Noble's reigns roughly he cantered off, disgruntled. He had a strong sense that only trouble awaited him back at Doomeerie!

CHAPTER 10

The General and His Daughter

Doomeerie was a hive of activity. Everywhere soldiers were attending to duties of one manner or another. Talitha received not a few glances from the men as they were unaccustomed to the presence of a pretty, young woman. Jockim left quickly to meet with the general while she and Pover hurried off to attend to Jenobay and Balaamine and to see Shiloh again. The foursome were happy to be reunited and quickly befriended Jenobay. Talitha was able to introduce the cub to a young tigress that had recently given birth to a litter in which only one had survived. After some initial nervousness, the young mother allowed Jenobay to suckle her.

Old Marcus was tending the stables as she settled the tigress down. He shared with her what he knew of the battalion's recent arrival. It seems that Jockim's estranged cousin, Andor, had assembled forces and was planning to invade from the south. The general wanted to join with Jockim's men to halt their advance. Apart from this he did not say a great deal, except to remark that the animals were all restless, having attuned to the pitch of human excitement.

As the afternoon wore on, Talitha made her way to the north wing to prepare herself for the evening meal. Madame Avileaux, Anya and herself had been invited to dine with the newly arrived guests that evening. There was an overwhelming sense of anticipation as the castle had not seen such distinguished visitors for so long. Anya chatted incessantly about the general's son, Vadio, and his daughter, Rose, who had resided at the castle years ago when she was a child. Indeed, it seemed that the children had done a lot together in those early years. Every few years since, they had revisited, and she had kept correspondence with Vadio whom she was particularly fond of. It was now over five years since they had all been together.

Anya's emotions were heightened. She fussed so much about her appearance and became so bossy that her mother eventually sent for assistance from her sister, Fanny, the chief kitchen maid. She had always had a soft spot for the girl.

"I need to get away for a while," she explained when Fanny arrived at the door. "I'll take over your kitchen duties for a time if you'll help Anya get dressed."

"Oh, Avie, it's just the nerves of young love you know." Fanny winked at her elder sister who shook her head in exasperation.

Certainly, all three of the young women glowed with the beauty of youth and anticipation in the soft candlelight of the dinner table. Talitha however, felt considerably underconfident in the presence of the general and his family. She fidgeted with her napkin, unfolding and refolding it, glancing up every so often to assess her companion's characters. The others seemed so self-assured and at home in the great hall. One would have thought Doomeerie Castle was their own.

The general, who was a stout, heavily built gentleman of middle age, paid her little if any attention. She thought him loud and arrogant, and was irritated by the way he fussed over his daughter, Rose. She was an extremely beautiful woman with a voluptuous figure, who was alluringly clad in a manner that accentuated her feminine charms. Her large china blue eyes, brought out by the hue of her soft, silken gown, were constantly fixed on Jockim. Her flaxen hair fell loosely around her bared shoulders, like a golden veil in the dim light. Talitha, feeling the first stings of envy, began to regret having braided her own auburn, brown glory. Even Anya had let her usually neatly tied head of hair fall loosely around her shoulders. Vadio's attention was constantly captured by her. Unlike his father, he was of average height and build. His features were chunky, and his broad, open face was pleasant and agreeable.

Talitha was surprised at what a charming host Jockim could be, especially as he had been so rude and uncommunicative to her on her first evening in the great hall. The general seemed quite fond of him, and Jockim was energised in his company. He was exceptionally bright, witty and attentively attuned to the needs of Rose, who like a purring cat was delighted by his responsiveness. *I wonder if they know of his dark temper and sullen moods,* she thought. *He is certainly putting on a fine performance for them all tonight!*

She sat demurely, wide eyed and watching, unsure of what to say.

The conversation increasingly focused on past common experiences at Doomeerie. Occasionally, she ventured to join the frivolity by adding a comment. These remarks drew embarrassing silences. Madame Avileaux interjected to relieve her discomfort. However, the experience was so humiliating that she decided that it was perhaps better to say nothing at all. Eventually, one of the maids, looking highly uncomfortable, whispered something in Jockim's ear. He nodded gravely.

"I'm extremely sorry but the cooks are not used to so many guests and are requiring extra assistance. We have insufficient staff to wait on our table this evening as Fanny our chief maid has just taken ill. I'll—"

Before he had a chance to finish, Madame Avileaux stood up. "Why Jockim, it would give me great pleasure to serve all of my old friends."

"Not at all, madame," the general bellowed. "Your place is at the table here with us. Might I suggest we make use of the young maidservant?" He looked over at Talitha, paying her attention for the first time that evening.

She felt herself flush as Rose smiled sweetly at her. Her beautiful, ice blue eyes washed away the final trace of Talitha's confident facade. "Of course," she stammered. "I'd be happy to."

Jockim nodded silently and turned his attention to his guests. She entered the kitchen slowly, her gait lacking enthusiasm. A few, angry cooks and scurrying, kitchen maids bustled about her. Steam was rising from various pots, whose lids were bubbling in objection to their intense heat. A strong, beefy smell filled her nostrils, and she felt overcome by the heat and pungent odour. Commands were yelled across the room with an urgency fit for battle, and everywhere tempers frayed.

An older maid threw an apron at her and yelled, "Look lively girl! You're here to work, not to play ladies. Don't think you'll be given any special privileges from Master Jockim now that Mademoiselle Rose is 'ere. He made use of ya for a bit of company when there was no one better about, but now ya'll know yer place like the rest of us!" She smirked over at her. "Only hope ya didn't give away too many of yer favours up on the mountains last night. You'll be sorry if ya did."

Talitha ignored her prying innuendos and went about trying to juggle the plates of soup on a large tray that had been thrust at her. She amazed herself at her ability to carry so many to the table without spilling them. Thinking that it would be socially appropriate to serve the general first, she carefully placed a steaming bowl in front of him.

"You're serving from the wrong side, woman," he stated impatiently, "and ladies before gentlemen." He gestured towards his daughter, Anya and Madame Avileaux.

"I'm very sorry, sir." Her voice shook slightly.

Jockim interjected rapidly. "Talitha has not had a lot of instruction on table serving. She has been involved largely in working in the stables since her arrival at the castle. She has a wonderful way with the animals … unlike anything that I have ever seen before." He smiled encouragingly at her.

"That may be so, Jockim," the general replied, "however as a woman I think that she would be more appropriately put to work in the kitchen, especially now as we have many soldiers to attend to the animals, and you seem to be short on kitchen staff."

"Perhaps, we shall see." Jockim drank deeply from his wine refusing to submit to the general's suggestion.

"Oh dear," Rose interjected, a little put out that Jockim seemed to be taking Talitha's part against her father. "I do hope that she washes her hands after cleaning up the animal droppings on the stable floors."

Silence descended. No one could think of a reply to Rose's somewhat spiteful comment. Talitha gingerly lifted the soup bowl from in front of the general and carefully placed it before Rose. In the process of doing so, she inadvertently upset the balance of her tray which resulted in the plate's contents spilling onto the table. She quickly grasped the tray with both hands to steady it and watched in dismay as thick, soupy, brown liquid, laden with chunks of beef and a colourful array of vegetables dispersed like lava over the tablecloth, trickling down into Rose's silken lap. There were cries of dismay from all.

Rose jumped to her feet yelling, "You stupid little fool! Watch what you are doing!" She snatched at a serviette and began mopping up the mess that had settled on her ice blue, silk gown. "This will ruin my dress!"

"I'm so sorry," Talitha exclaimed, placing the tray on the table and attempting to help.

"Don't touch me!" the girl hissed. "Who knows what your hands have touched."

Madame Avileaux moved rapidly to assist. "Now, now, dear, it's alright, we can fix it up!" She glanced at Jockim who was attempting to hide an amused smile behind his serviette.

Clearing his throat, he suggested, "Avie perhaps you can help Rose change into something else. We'll skip the soup for tonight … I didn't feel much like it anyway. If everyone lifts their cutlery I'm sure that we can have this cloth replaced in a minute. Tal, would you mind returning the soup to the kitchen and bringing us a new tablecloth."

Thus, without much ado the table was reset by the joint effort of those present. However, the evening progressed painfully slowly for Talitha. Rose returned in a new, crimson gown displaying fresh composure and grace. She even showed civility towards Talitha. Aware that her previous caustic tone would do nothing to enhance her femininity and Jockim's interest, she was careful to present herself in a much fairer disposition. Eventually, without further mishap, the meal was over and the general, Vadio and Jockim sojourned to the study for discussions on possible impending battles, while the ladies retired early after what had been a big day for all.

Talitha was already crying as she undid her braids and laid her soft hair upon the pillow. What had started as such a wonderful day with Jockim giving her Balaamine had ended in disaster. It was clear to all that Rose was inclined towards Jockim, and the latter was doing nothing whatsoever to dissuade her advances. In fact, he almost seemed to be taking pleasure in the fact that she fancied him. The mere thought of it flushed Talitha with hot anger. *How dare he lead me on to abandon me at his first encounter with another woman? Why did I ever allow myself to become so infatuated with him?* She vowed to erase him from her mind forever, but try as she would, she was unable to do so. The amused, playful grin that flashed upon his face when she was angry, and his penetrating stares that lingered on her body when he thought that she was unaware, remained stronger than ever in her thoughts, mocking her futile intentions.

She was just beginning to doze off when there was a soft knocking on the door. Grabbing a shawl, she gingerly opened it a fraction. In the dark, she heard Jockim's voice. "Tal," he whispered, "it's me. Can I come in for a minute please? I need to talk with you."

He entered carrying a lantern and a sack. A long, dark cloak hung loosely around his shoulders, acting as a shield to cut out some of the glow from the lantern. "I'm sorry to have to wake you," he said, noting that she was already in her night attire, "but I felt uneasy about how things went tonight. I just wanted to let you know that I was aware how you must have been feeling, and I'm sorry that I couldn't have made things better for you."

"It's alright." She pulled her shawl tighter around her shoulders. "After all, I am the maidservant—as you continually remind me."

He placed the lantern on the table and gently lifted her pert, little chin up so that he could stare deeply into her doe-like eyes.

"I have wanted to tell you for some time now that you are much more to me than just a servant girl. You've added so much more to my life since you've been here. I wake up in the mornings now wanting to face the day because I know that you are a part of it, and as the evening draws closer, I look forward to being with you at dinner. I don't know how to say this, but I've discovered that I become quite fond of you and somehow attached to your troublesome, little ways." He laughed softly.

She stared up at him incredulously, hardly daring to believe what she had just heard. The pupils of her eyes seemed to expand ever outwards in a troubled sea of desperate hope. *Does he really mean what he says?*

Sensing her scepticism, he continued in an effort to secure her belief. "From the night I first saw you in the stables, I knew that you were destined to be a significant part of my life. Now I couldn't imagine living without you."

His words sent an electric current burning throughout her body, and she felt decidedly delirious. The closeness of his body, his self-assurance and masculine bearing made her feel exposed, yet excited. Somehow, she had to remain calm and in control. "I'm sure you'll manage just fine, especially now that Rose is here to keep you occupied."

"Now, now, my dear ..." He tried to sound stern. "Jealousy doesn't sit well with you." Then looking at her tenderly, he added. "I know I haven't been the easiest of masters by any means, and I can't promise that the future will be any better. I'm going to have to play their little game. We're heading into troubled times. Heavy forces are advancing to take over from the south, and if we don't form a coalition with the general and his army, we will all be slaughtered and the castle destroyed. Think of that ... your beloved Shiloh, Balaamine and Jenobay killed ... not to mention our constant chaperone, Pover." He smiled as the tiny bird raised her head to look at him.

"Not to mention that you won't enjoy every minute of dancing to Rose's every whim." She appeared unswayed by his explanation.

He leaned forward and drawing her to him kissed her tenderly on the lips. For a moment the gesture took her by surprise, and she dropped her defences allowing herself to easily be taken over by the passion that immediately welled within her. Sensing her pleasure, he held her even tighter, kissing with increased vigour. Her shawl dropped to the floor, and the soft curves of her breast were full and intoxicating beneath her cotton nightdress. Feeling vulnerable beside the sheer, physical strength of his body, she pulled away. He must not have any more power over her sensuality.

"Always the determined little miss ... with a will of her own," he said mockingly. "You're still not convinced by my words or my actions are you? You keep your heart very guarded, but I can assure you that you have already stolen mine. If my words can't convince you then perhaps this will."

He pulled at the leads on the sack to open it and drew out the silver goblet that Talitha had dreamed of the evening before. The sapphires and emeralds twinkled in the soft light.

"I'm giving it to you for safe keeping. It's the castle's most prized possession, the Holy Grail. It was a gift from my father to my mother, Miriam ... now in your hands. I don't believe that it will be safe in its usual hiding place, especially now that it has already been stolen, but I do trust it in your hands. Consider it to be symbolic of the love and trust that I place in you. Hide it where you will. I won't even ask where you put it. I want you to use it to remind yourself that I really do care for you, even though there will be many times ahead that it will not seem so to you or to others. To keep General Konfra on side I will have to be attentive to his daughter, at least while they are residing here in the castle. I'm sorry that it has to be like this for the present; however, our survival depends upon it. Do you understand?" He looked searchingly down into her wide eyes which had misted over in emotion.

"Thank you," she said, her gaze captured by the twinkling gems. "Thank you ... You have given me a great honour. I will do my best to keep it safe for you." She seemed lost for words at the enormous trust that he had bestowed in her. Her thoughts were dancing with joy at the prospect that perhaps he really did feel for her.

He smiled fondly at her, convinced that she was beginning to take his sentiments seriously. Leaning forward, he gently kissed her on the forehead, cupping her head tenderly in his hands. "Good night, sweet maidservant." He smiled cheekily as he made his way to the door.

She closed it softly behind him, and he crept down the hall, unaware that another door had silently opened behind him. Madame Avileaux caught sight of his dark cloak as he turned the corner to descend the stairs.

So, he has developed feelings for the girl, she thought. *Surely this will only lead to trouble ... just like it did with Bess!*

CHAPTER 11

The Opening Game

Waiting on the table at dinner became part of Talitha's routine. She always approached these evening meals with mixed emotions; excited by the opportunity of seeing Jockim, but loathing having to watch him bestow his attentions upon Rose. Frequently, their eyes would meet, but he would always remain guarded, addressing her as a servant. The only exception occurred if one of the guests complained about her, in which case he was supportive, thus ending the matter quickly.

Madame Avileaux had monitored their initial, secret meetings. She was fearful that the newfound alliance with the general could be destroyed and spoke with Jockim sternly about lavishing his attentions upon a servant girl whose quarters he should not be visiting at night. Jockim lost his patience with her; something that he regretted. He was so fond of the older woman. Eventually, he relented, realising the wisdom of her words. To compromise, he asked if she could possibly arrange some secret *rendezvous* for them.

These meetings however became less frequent as they had to be chosen at private locations and at times when Madame Avileaux was free. Increasingly, they were spent arguing, the topic of contention being Jockim's attention to Rose. Despite Talitha's diminishing trust in him, Jockim kept to his word and never asked her of the whereabouts of the goblet. He secretly hoped that it would be enough to remind her of the love and trust that he had placed in her.

It was obvious to everyone that Talitha was becoming deeply discontented. She ruminated over why she had ever bothered coming to this dark and dismal place. Of course she knew that the answer was to free her beloved Shiloh. More and more however, she began to wonder about the nature of the third task which Padyah had said would be asked of her, and how this could be tied in with her saving her animal friends.

She frequently discussed her dream about the silver goblet with Pover, saying that she believed that this third task involved drinking waters from the goblet which needed to be scooped up near Eagle Nest Rock in the River Styx. Her spirit companion was not at all sure that this was what was required of her to free Shiloh. Talitha tried to convince her by outlining how strange it was that she should become aware of the existence of Eagle Nest Rock and be given possession of the goblet so soon after the dream. Life seemed to be leading her in this direction.

Hence, she became increasingly consumed with the thought of how to get to Eagle Nest Rock. Not wanting to destroy Jockim's trust, her plan was to drink deeply from the goblet filled with water taken from around the rock and then return to the castle leaving it in Madame Avileaux's possession. Next, she would escape at night with her beloved friends. She was convinced that consuming the river's waters would somehow ensure a safe and successful departure. It was only the thought of leaving Jockim, and the difficulty of getting to Eagle Nest Rock that held her back in executing this plan.

Her mind was preoccupied with these intentions one evening when she was asked to set an extra place at dinner for one of the general's officials who had recently returned from abroad. This young man, known as Raybet, was clever, not just intellectually but also in an emotional sense. Indeed, many described him as 'a shrewd fox'. He was of slight to average build with razor sharp features and darting, pale, blue eyes that rapidly assessed any situation, formulating astute plans devised to advance his purposes. He was most charming to all of the ladies, Talitha included, and went to no lengths to treat her with great respect whenever he came across her. It wasn't until later that she was to learn that he was actually the general's adopted son. The old gentleman was certainly very fond of him and very proud of his remarkable ability to devise successful, battle strategies.

Talitha noted with not a little distaste that Rose was beginning to flirt with him, as well as Jockim. Without a doubt, she was in her element surrounded by attentive men. Raybet returned the attention with an ease and charm rivalling that of Jockim. Indeed, everyone at the table seemed to like him except for Jockim, who was distant and a little sarcastic in response to his remarks. Talitha secretly wondered if this was because he resented Raybet competing with him for Rose's flirtations. Anya was also aware of Jockim's cold manner and reprimanded him on more than one occasion for it. Jockim, for his part, believed her to be blinded to Raybet's true character. Knowing that she was a woman in love, he considered her opinion to be naïve and skewed. Raybet, on the other hand, was well aware of the underlying emotions that simmered between Talitha and Jockim, for although the latter was very veiled about his feelings, Talitha's eyes gave away the secrets of her soul.

Raybet had been joining the dinner parties for a couple of weeks when one evening he decided to escort Rose to the great hall. She was dressed becomingly in pale gold and after sweeping his gaze over her, he flirtatiously complimented her on the exquisite gown. Delighted with his remark, she smiled back alluringly, allowing him to take her arm to escort her down the long hallway.

"You really do grace our little, dinner party, Rose … and what an enmeshed little group we are."

"Whatever do you mean by that?" she purred, flashing him a seductive smile.

"Surely, my dear you have noticed the entanglement of emotions present at the table. Why, the general and Madame Avileaux are the only ones present who are not besotted with someone else in the room. Anya and Vadio have only eyes for each other. I am forever endeavouring to impress you, my little, adopted sister. Unfortunately, we have been parted for too long due to my overseeing ghastly, war manoeuvres for Father! And our dear friend, Jockim, is torn between your beautiful self and our petite maidservant."

"Why, Raybet," she remarked, a little annoyed at his final comment, "I do believe that you are reading more into Jockim's emotions than is present. The girl is nothing more than a servant to him. Any remark said about her in defence is only an act of kindness. Jockim is short of servants and needs to get the most out of those that he has."

A fleeting sense of uneasiness arose within her. She dare not fail to secure Jockim's hand in marriage. It was what her father wanted for her. Yet, she couldn't help also feeling strangely excited at the thought of Raybet finding her attractive. After all these years, were his feelings for her becoming more than that of an adopted brother?

"Perhaps so my dear, but have you watched her when their eyes meet? She flushes and is decidedly very self-conscious. And have you noticed how he jumps to her rescue should anyone reprimand her for the slightest error? I do believe that she is quite a bit more than a maidservant to him. Watch tonight, I will show you. I will arrange things so that she is criticised on some minor detail. Observe how he immediately speaks in her defence."

"A little entertainment, Raybet ..." She giggled softly. "I will look forward to it then." Her sparkling, blue eyes shone with devilment as she eyed him with admiration. Raybet was always so astute and amusing.

Seating themselves at the table, Raybet checked that they were alone and then stealthily lifted the starched serviette placed beside the general's silver cutlery. He rubbed it along the sole of his boot and returned it to its original position, with the soiled section face down.

"Really Raybet," Rose remarked, sounding animated, "are you going to poison poor Father?"

"Not at all, Konfra is very observant. He will not use anything that is dirty, and he's just the right person to upset. He holds all of the power at the present moment. Jockim needs him here to protect the castle. You and I can be innocent onlookers, my dear. Sit back and enjoy the entertainment. The opening game is about to commence!"

At that moment, Jockim, Vadio, and the general strode into the great hall together. They were deeply involved in conversation and looked somewhat grave and at odds with each other.

"I daresay that Andor has talked his younger brother, Tyrone, into joining him in the planned attack on Doomeerie!" Vadio was heard remarking.

"Yes and old Aunt Charlotte would be financing the whole venture with jewels taken from here when she left with her brother, Brody, after Jockhein inherited the castle. No doubt she has been filling her nephew's minds with hate towards you, Jockim," the general stated.

"Well that wouldn't be too hard to achieve, especially as father killed Uncle Brody in his failed coup many years ago."

"I might remind you lad, that it was I who killed Brody and not your father, although I'm sure that he would have done so if I hadn't."

"No doubt of that! The hatred between Jockhein and Brody was embedded in them from the earliest years. Indeed, I'm sure that old grandfather Lachlan encouraged it."

"Yes, well the old man certainly knew how to play one against the other … that's for sure. Still your father was the eldest son and the more likely candidate of the two to inherit the castle … when one considered his nature and his bearing."

"A suitable heir for a castle named Doomeerie, no doubt," Jockim mumbled.

"Well, enough of the past and present fighting. Let us enjoy a meal together," Vadio interjected on a lighter note, smiling at the others.

Seating themselves at the table, they all greeted Rose and Raybet, each remarking how beautiful the former looked. They had only time to engage in a few minutes of light pleasantries when they were joined by Madame Avileaux and Anya. The younger woman's eyes shone with eager anticipation as she smiled sweetly at Vadio, who jumped to his feet to take over from her mother and wheel her to the table.

A young soldier generously filled their crystal goblets with swirling, red wine. A few minutes later, Talitha entered the room to serve the soup. The pleasantries of conversation had begun to flow freely as the gentlemen relaxed with the taste of the wine, and the ladies succeeded in diverting their thoughts from war manoeuvres. The group prepared themselves for their first course when suddenly there was an outburst from the general.

"What is this, girl?" He flashed the filthy serviette up for all at the table to see. "Have you been using the serviettes to clean the stables now?"

There was a soft giggle from Rose, barely audible above the general's booming voice. Talitha felt red, hot emotion flood her face. She quickly snatched the serviette from the general.

"I'm so sorry, sir. I had no idea that the serviette was soiled. I'll get you another one immediately." She hurried out of the room, head down.

"I swear that this girl is not bright enough to do more than one task at a time. I've said before and I'll say it again Jockim, you need to get her out of the stables and concentrating solely on domestic tasks. Maybe she will be able to do at least one thing properly then. Her work in the stables is no longer required now that the soldiers are here. Besides, she does very little apart from play with that tiger cub and groom the old donkey and young stag."

The general's rage continued. "Whoever is her overseer should be informed of this misdemeanour and punish her for it. I'm sure you don't need me to remind you of the curse of Doomeerie Castle— all transgression must be dealt with. Your father would have seen to it long before now!" Konfra's face grew redder and redder until it seemed that he would explode.

"I'm sure I don't need to remind you that I am not my father." Jockim's voice was sullen and laconic.

There was an uneasy silence in the room as both men stared at each other, each refusing to be dominated by the other. Talitha, returning to the room, felt the tension grip her tightly. She carefully placed a clean serviette before the general, wanting to melt into the background.

"Who is your overseer, girl?" the general barked.

"Madame Avileaux is my supervisor for domestic castle duties, sir."

"Madame Avileaux, I suggest that you take the matter into your hands, and see that this young woman is taught a lesson about setting clean linen. Maybe an extra couple of hours in the laundry each day would teach you a lesson, girl."

"Yes, sir." Talitha kept her eyes lowered so as not to meet the seven pairs of eyes that stared at her around the table. The heat was rising again. She hated to feel it flushing over her face. It somehow made her feel exposed, naked, and vulnerable.

Madame Avileaux broke the silence. "Perhaps you could advise me as to an appropriate course of action later, after dinner, Jockim," she said calmly, hoping to diffuse the situation and allow Jockim a chance of letting the poor girl off when the matter had settled and everyone had forgotten about it.

Jockim looked directly at her. "I'm more than happy to advise you now, Avie. It is my understanding that Tal has not been involved with the laundry yet. Is that correct?"

"Yes, that is so, Jockim." Madame Avileaux was beginning to wish that she had not spoken at all.

"Then there is no need to follow up with any action whatsoever. Let's begin our meal, folks, otherwise the soup will become cold. Thank you, Tal." He looked up at her, speaking gently. "That will be all for now."

She curtsied and hurried from the room, relieved to be free of the uncomfortable surroundings. For several minutes, there was silence. The tension hung thick. They settled on focusing upon the soup. It was hot and hearty; a pleasant diversion from the stifling atmosphere at the table.

Finally, the general spoke again. "I hope you are aware of your circumstances, young man." He stared down the table at Jockim. "At any time I may choose to remove my army from this castle, in which case you and all of its occupants would not stand a chance against the invading armies. I therefore expect some respect for my position and advice in certain matters."

Jockim looked up, carefully placing his spoon back in his bowl and wiping his mouth with his serviette. An awkward silence descended once more upon the edgy, little group.

"You most certainly have my respect for all advice regarding war matters, sir; however, I would have thought that the occasional harmless mistake from a minor maidservant would be of little consequence to you who surely have much graver concerns to handle." He spoke calmly with an air of both respect and authority.

"As long as that is all she is to you—a minor maidservant. I would be most disappointed to think that you could have your mind focused on such a pitiable, little creature."

Jockim leaned back in his chair and laughed heartily. "Now, Konfra, if my mind was ever occupied on such a pitiable little creature, it would only be to treat her with kindness for her pathetic physical endowments and to ensure that she performed her duties generously for me. Good help is hard to come by these days. If she provided me with a little amusement in the past, it was purely because there was an absence of any fairer company. I would hardly choose to pluck a humble, little wildflower in preference to an exquisite rose." His eyes darted in the direction of Rose who smiled smugly.

"Well then, I'm glad that's settled." The general laughed loudly. "Come on, girl, you can take my plate now. Stop hovering there in the background."

Jockim turned sharply to see Talitha standing behind him. Undoubtedly, she had heard every word. Although they were lies, he knew that a part of her would wonder if there was any truth in them. *Still,* he thought to himself, *I must not look concerned for her, or else I will give our affections away.*

"Thank you, Tal. You may tell the cook that it was most enjoyable," he said quickly, finishing off his last, few mouthfuls. "I think we are all ready for the second course, so you may serve it."

"Yes, sir," she replied; her soft voice barely audible. The words felt like they would choke her. She dared not look at him least he see the pain in her eyes. Madame Avileaux fidgeted uncomfortably with her cutlery as Talitha removed the plates, while Anya desperately tried to change the topic.

Whatever was said from then on was of little consequence to either Jockim or Talitha. Both were preoccupied with their own thoughts, and Jockim wanted to depart from the scene as quickly as he could. He excused himself before dessert and headed for the balcony beyond the ballroom. He stared out at the night sky hating the situation which circumstances had thrust upon him. He must see Talitha as quickly as possible to assure her that his words had been lies said to protect them all.

Engrossed in his dark thoughts, he didn't notice the movement behind him until he caught sight of a soft gleam of gold under the evening sky. Almost simultaneously, the sweet scent of roses wafted towards him.

"Why, Jockim …" the feminine voice purred, "all alone? Is everything alright?" Rose tenderly laid her hand on his arm to reassure him.

"Yes, quite. I just wanted to catch a bit of fresh air. It has been a long day."

"I'm sorry that you and Father quarrelled tonight, especially over a servant girl. You know I am very fond of both of you, and it upsets me to see you angry with each other."

Her sweet scent lingered temptingly around him. Glancing down at her, he was overcome by her physical beauty. Every angle and curve of her body was so perfectly proportioned. Her skin was flawless, and her long, golden hair was like silk falling softly about her pale, bare shoulders. She could easily turn an army.

"I'm pleased to hear that you are very fond of me," he replied, endeavouring to direct the conversation away from Talitha.

"Perhaps it would be improper of me to inquire if my feelings are reciprocated?" She met his gaze, mirroring his dark eyes in her large, blue ones.

"You know they are. What man wouldn't be attracted to a woman as beautiful as you, Rose?"

"Quite the contrary, I know nothing of the sort. A woman requires physical evidence to know that she is cared for." She edged closer to him, rubbing her hand gently on his angular cheek bone.

Taking his cue, he leaned forward and kissed her gently on the lips. She nestled in closer, feeling warm and soft against his body and returned the kiss, allowing her soft, wet lips to linger on his, while her hand gently caressed the stubble on his cheek.

Suddenly, the door behind them was thrust open. There before them stood Talitha! Her face aghast, she looked almost as surprised and shaken as they did. Instinctively, they drew apart as she blurted out, "I'm very sorry to interrupt. Raybet said I would find you here Mademoiselle Rose, and he asked me to give you this." She quickly curtsied and thrust a sealed note into her hand. Without any further words she turned and almost ran from the balcony.

The hallway blurred before her eyes. Warm, wet tears caressed her cheeks. She could not stand this way of life anymore; being thrown crumbs of attention and affection from Jockim when they could steal a few moments alone together. It was all a farce!

I was only ever an amusement or diversion for him, when there were no other eligible women in the castle, she thought, wondering why she had been so gullible. *What an idiot I've been … thinking that I could ever be desired by the master of Doomeerie Castle! I am nothing to him … just an insignificant maid! How can I ever hope to compete against a woman of Rose's calibre! I am making a complete and utter fool of myself!*

She turned the corner wildly, running into Raybet who was leaving the study where he had been drinking with the other men. He quickly assessed her emotional state, but was clever enough to pretend that he hadn't.

"Ah, Tal," he called after her as she went to hurry on, "did you manage to give my note to Rose?"

"Yes sir." She turned briefly to face him.

"Was she on the balcony as I anticipated?" he inquired, walking up beside her.

"Yes sir!" Again, she went to move on, but he stood in her pathway.

"I am wondering if you know that an animal fight has been organised for tomorrow evening for the soldiers. I believe that they are pitting the Rottweilers against each other. Everyone will be involved with it. I daresay it will be of little interest to you however?" He raised his eyebrows waiting for a reply.

"Not at all, sir," she replied, hating Jockim for allowing such cruelty to take place as entertainment, yet simultaneously feeling a tug of guilt. She, like the others, shared in the food that the death of the animals provided.

"Then we are of the same sentiments. Perhaps you will join me for an evening stroll around the castle grounds while the others are involved with their gambling and betting?"

"Yes, I would be happy to sir, as soon as my duties finish after dinner," she replied, grateful for his invitation and attention, as well as an opportunity to have a diversion to the animal fighting. Already it was the talk of the castle, especially amongst the soldiers.

"Good then, I will meet you down by the river pathway as the fighting begins. It will be a full moon tomorrow night so we should have ample light to stroll by."

She nodded wondering if it was a wise choice to go walking with him. Still, the decision had been made. "Good night," she replied. He stepped to the side to allow her past.

"Good night, Tal. I will look forward to tomorrow evening." His smile had a lingering sense of seductiveness about it. She felt anxious but also rebellious. It would be good for Jockim to realise that other men were also seeking her company.

He hummed softly to himself as he made his way up the stairs to his quarters. From his room, he could see a light burning softly in Rose's room directly across the courtyard. He poured himself a port from a crystal decanter and stretched back in a large armchair, a smile beginning to hover about his thin lips. He was imaging Rose sitting in her night attire, looking seductive; her long, golden hair falling softly over the feminine contours of her breasts as she carefully opened the letter he had given her. He could almost see the amusement play on her beautiful face when she read the words that he had scrolled.

"Opening Game; successful!"

"Game Two … about to begin!"

CHAPTER 12

Game Two is Set in Motion

Talitha awoke early feeling decidedly miserable. She knew that Jockim had knocked on her door late the night before. However, in her anger and misery she could not bring herself to open it. Instead, she rolled over in bed and fed her mind upon the guilt that she could cause him by refusing to allow him to give her an explanation. She half hoped to see him throughout the day, but he had left early for military training and was away for the entire day. The evening meal passed routinely with her refusing to make eye contact with him, while he carefully played his role of master.

After her duties were completed, she threw a shawl around her shoulders and headed down to the river pathway. Raybet was waiting there and greeted her warmly. She was pleased to have his company. The sound of merriment escalated by alcohol could be heard. Already, the soldiers were beginning to congregate in mindless masses, eager to watch the brutal battle. Talitha shivered at the fascination that it held for them. Perhaps it was a way of relieving some of the guilt that they felt when they slaughtered their fellow man. She wanted to get as far away as possible from the ugly scene.

The animals in the stables were also in a state of agitation. They instinctively knew what was about to happen. Talitha had asked Pover to be with Shiloh and Balaamine to comfort them while she walked with Jenobay close by her side. The tiger cub frequently accompanied her and was daily growing in strength and size. It loved her like a child.

Raybet took her hand and kissed it lightly in greeting. "I see you've brought your young friend with you," he remarked, a fraction uneasily. "She's growing up and will be quite a formidable ally for you soon. You'll have to watch that she doesn't do any harm. Maybe it would be wise to let her into the wild before too long."

Talitha sighed. "Ah yes, I know that the time is soon coming when I will have to let her go. This is no place for her—the prison that it is. If I kept her here, it would only be a matter of time until one of the general's men suggests that she provide amusement for them all and fight to her death. No, she is destined for a better life. She was meant to roam free."

She watched the young creature lovingly. Her movements were gracefully stealthy in the soft moonlight. The large, chunky paws stepped softly beside her.

"The fighting is abhorrent to you, isn't it?" He stared at her, hoping that she would reveal something of her inner self to him.

"If I had my way, I would see that all the animals were set free." She pulled her shawl closer about her.

"And the deer and the donkey would be the first to go, I dare say," he quipped with a twinkle in his eye.

"Why sir, I believe you know me a little better than I thought you did." She had to admit that she was a little flattered by his obvious interest in her.

"That I do, and what I see I very much like." He reached out and took her by the hand, directing her attention to the full moon which lit the river like a mass of cascading diamonds.

"It's very beautiful, isn't it?" He hoped that the magnificent sight would fill her with joy and contentment in his presence.

"Yes, it is … Like a proud stallion with a flowing, silver mane, daring you to ride on its back … if you're brave or foolish enough." She was silent for a minute lost in her thoughts.

"I dare say it could be done."

"Do you really think so?" Her reply was so eager that he immediately picked up on a hidden agenda.

"Why yes, of course. Why do you ask? Have you a desire to cross it?"

She retreated a little for fear of giving away too much. "Oh it's just a whimsical notion of going out to that peculiar rock. I believe they call it Eagle Nest Rock. I would love to stand out there, safe and free with the waters cascading around me."

"What a strange woman you are, Tal! Still everyone has their dream. Perhaps I can make yours come true for you." He glanced at her shrewdly.

"You mock me!" she replied, hoping that he was in earnest, yet doubting his words were plausible.

"Not at all, my dear … My soldiers are trained for all kinds of feats. I could have one of them transport you in a boat to that point if that is your heart's desire." He smiled quizzically. "But surely that is not your end destination? Is it that you want to cross the river completely to the other side?"

"And what would be the point of that?" She looked searchingly at him, beginning to wonder if she should have trusted him with her thoughts. "How would I survive in the wilderness over there?"

"Let's be honest with each other, Tal." He turned to face her, looking directly into her eyes. "I've seen into your heart. There is nothing here for you anymore is there? Whatever interest that this castle once held for you is gone. Your heart longs for new horizons. Jockim would have you believe that this place is impenetrable, and that the river is a formidable barrier, but it is not unable to be traversed. The land on the other side is not like Nightmare Forest. Neither is it the mountainous terrain of the north. Beyond the forest that you see, is beautiful pasture land dotted with farms. You would find a new way of life there—I am quite sure of that."

"I desire only to go to Eagle Nest Rock and then to return to Doomeerie," she insisted.

He smiled, hiding his disbelief. "Well my dear, if that is your heart's desire I will organise it for you. When the next animal fight is on three weeks from now, I will have a boat and soldier waiting for you. The others will all be involved in the fight as they are tonight, so you will be able to travel to Eagle Nest Rock unnoticed. I will arrange it with one of my most skilled men and let you know where to meet him."

He looked down at her, noticing the apprehension in her doe-like eyes. "You do trust me, don't you? After all, you are doing nothing wrong … only travelling to Eagle Nest Rock and returning. However, I know that you would like to keep your little adventure a secret, and I can promise you that it will remain so with me."

"Thank you." She scanned his sharp features. A strange mixture of excitement and apprehension began to swirl in the pit of her stomach. It was like some smoke signal that she was incapable of reading.

Above them the moon shone brilliantly, bathing Eagle Nest Rock in its soft light. Deep inside her, the smoke signal heralded evil. Yet, she felt drawn towards Eagle Nest Rock. Was she being drawn to her death?

CHAPTER 13

The Third Task Begins as the Second Game Finishes

The evening of the next animal fight was much darker. Heavy clouds obscured the sky. Talitha was forced to carry a lantern, as well as the sack with the silver goblet in it. Clutching the goblet under her cloak, she made her way carefully down to the appointed spot where she was to board the boat. Fear clung tightly to her shoulders and neck in a metal embrace. In the pit of her stomach, sickening, green smoke began to swirl in a foreboding brew.

She and Pover had debated this course of action many times over the past weeks. The bird was certain that it was a poor decision. She suggested that Talitha wait for a period, until she was surer of Raybet's intentions. Talitha, knowing that war could break out at any time, wanted to act now while the opportunity was presenting itself.

She tried to obscure the light from her lantern as best she could. The rocky, river path held nothing of the beauty that it had a few weeks ago when she had been with Raybet. There was only a heavy sense of doom. Somewhere in the shadowy trees nearby Pover hovered, keeping a lookout.

Talitha's thoughts went back over the events of the past few weeks. Jockim had met her one day down near the stables. She had refused to open the door to his knocking at night, so he had managed to get Madame Avileaux to watch out, so that he could speak with her alone. She was cold and cruel to him. She hated herself for acting in such a manner, but she could not bring herself to believe that he truly loved her, especially as he so rarely showed her any attention. His insistence that circumstances determined that he must attend to Rose could not dissuade her deep founded belief that she could never be truly loved by him. Still, she was not a thief, and after drinking from the goblet, she was determined to return it to the castle. There she would wait for the appointed time of escape, which she believed would come.

In the distance, she heard the rough and coarse swearing and yelling of the men as they whipped themselves up into a frenzy of excitement over the fighting animals. "Soon, dear Shiloh, dear Balaamine, we will be out of here," she whispered. Rounding a curve, she emerged from behind a rocky outcrop that was the landmark for a small cave hidden amongst bushes. It was here that she had been told to wait for further instructions. She entered the cave. Apprehension mounted. She was not sure what frightened her more—the thought of travelling out over the raging waters, or the possibility of being caught trying to leave the castle.

It must have been twenty minutes or more when she saw Pover flying frantically towards her. Grabbing her lantern, she searched for a backward exit. Nothing! Only black, stone walls surrounded her on all three sides. Suddenly before her appeared two soldiers, rifles raised, poised to shoot. From between them stepped Jockim, tall and menacing.

"Well, what have we here," he growled. "Planning a *rendezvous* with someone, my dear?" He strode forward and, taking the lantern from her lest she should decide to throw it, noticed something else hidden beneath her cloak. Grabbing her arm roughly, he pulled out the familiar sack and drew from it the silver goblet. With a smouldering stare, he sneered at her. "Planning on taking a little booty were you, something to help finance the journey?"

"It's not what you think. I was only going to Eagle Nest Rock … to drink from the waters there, and then I was going to return it to the castle." She gasped for breath.

He laughed in a dark, menacing way. "Ah, so my dear … and I suppose you would have me believe that the waters have some magical quality, which would ensure that we all live happily ever after. You don't think that I'm that gullible do you? For sure, I've been a fool regarding you but not anymore, Talitha. We play the game by the rules now—the castle's rules."

Turning to address the soldiers, he thundered his orders, "Bind her and take her to the dungeon. She can spend the night there. It will give her a little time to ponder her betrayal. Tomorrow morning, I will let her know her fate. Good evening, gentlemen." He strode out of the cave taking the lantern, goblet, and sack with him.

The dungeon floors were dark and damp. Talitha laid her head down on the cold, hard stone. Clang! The iron gates shut. She began to sob. The blackness was so intense that she could not see her own hand. The place smelt foul, and she did not know where to recline so as not to become contaminated. She coiled her petite body into a huddle and hugged herself tightly, shuddering with sobs that wrenched from deep within. Not only had all her courageous efforts been wasted, now her dream had also been destroyed.

Knowing that Jockim believed that she had deliberately betrayed him crushed her spirit. Part of her knew that she had. *Why didn't I speak to him of my plan?* She berated herself. *But I couldn't let him know that I was freeing Shiloh. He would not have allowed it. He wouldn't have understood?* She sighed. *What does it matter now anyway? I have hurt him deeply after he trusted me.* She hated herself—her very existence. How could she have treated a friend so disrespectfully? Not even the soft down of Pover, who rested next to her swollen cheek, could relieve her agony.

Outside, the heavens burst open pouring down torrents. The blood of the animal fight washed deep into the soil, and the swollen carcass of a half dead stallion was washed clean. In the ensuing hours, it relinquished its life into the sodden earth. The men trudged back to their quarters, angry that their fun had been stopped so prematurely. Those that were too drunk to know their whereabouts were either pulled to shelter by their friends or left to face the elements.

Morning dawned in a grey drizzle, and the dungeon walls leaked wet with a soft sheen. Talitha awoke. Her body ached, protesting about her cold, stony bed. Her dress was covered in mud and slime from where she had inadvertently laid in the darkness. In the dim shadows, she could see it was morning. Pover flew through the bars, her feathers glistening with evidence of the dismal day. It was hours before she heard the familiar sound of iron gates being unlatched, and the same two soldiers entered her cell. Her heart plummeted with dread.

"Blimey, it stinks in here! Com'on girl, he wants to see you now. Hope he enjoys the stench." They both sniggered and bound her hands behind her, pushing her onwards.

He was standing with his back to her when they entered the study, staring out from a large, bay window which overlooked the grey River Styx. He turned slowly to face her, eyes like steel, and barked at the soldiers to wait outside. For what seemed like an eternity he said nothing, his right palm raised clutching his chin, deep in thought.

"You stink! What have you been sleeping in?" he blurted out suddenly. She blushed deeply making no reply.

"Well, what am I to do with you?" He strode across the room. "It seems that the general has found out about your rash escapade last night ... and the fact that you tried to make off with the castle's silver! It leaves me little scope to save you—you silly, little fool. Now we will indeed have to play it strictly by the castle's rules. The punishment for stealing is public whipping to dissuade others from a similar course of action and attempted desertion demands banishment to Nightmare Forest." He stopped and stared at her, smiling in a sad, sinister way. She swallowed hard, unable to comprehend the full extent of misery that was about to befall her.

He marched across the room again in the other direction and

clearing his throat continued. "I have however, after extensive discussions with the general and much persuasion, been able to get him to agree to not removing his forces, if I apply a lesser punishment. Due to the heavy storm last night, the animal fighting was cut short. The men are disgruntled, feeling like they have been cheated from their one and only entertainment. The general has sent his men out to find another stag, and as soon as one is caught, Shiloh will fight."

"No," she shrieked, panic surging into her voice. "You can't do this. I would rather have the whipping and the banishment."

"You seem to forget Talitha that I am master of this castle, and I can do whatever I like," he stated calmly. "The stag is of an age now that it needs to fight. It would be doing so in the wild. If it doesn't fight soon it will never have the skills to survive, which is what you've always wanted for it, isn't it?"

He glared at her with smouldering, dark eyes. "And seeing that you're so keen to have a whipping, I can tell you that you will not be disappointed. The general has insisted that you are to be driven out with whips before the roaring crowd to watch the spectacle from a front row seat. Of course if you run fast enough you'll avoid the lash and no doubt add to their amusement." He sneered, enjoying her dismayed reaction.

She glowered at him, no longer frightened, as anger welled up inside her. "You're not human. You have no heart or soul. You are less than any beast." The words were almost spat at him.

"No, my dear, it is you that have no heart or soul. Let's remember who the real betrayer is here." He walked up close to her, so that the words stung in her ears.

"After the fight, if Shiloh wins, you will be banned from ever having contact with him again. You will no longer be able to work in the stables. I have persuaded General Konfra that we require your assistance here at the castle because we are so short of female staff. You will become maidservant to Rose in the mornings and work in the kitchen in the afternoon. Jenobay is of an age to be released to the wild, and I have already ordered that this take place this morning. It goes without saying that Balaamine will remain yours, because I don't go back on my promises!" He lectured with emphasis and sarcasm. "However, you will not be able to spend time with her, unless of course Rose requests that she rides her, in which case you may accompany them during your morning service to her."

Talitha could bear no more. All of her closest attachments were being stripped away. She collapsed in a heap on the floor, weeping.

He watched her for a few minutes and then ordered sharply, "Get up! You've been spared your life and a full on whipping. You should consider yourself fortunate indeed that I was able to secure as much as I have for you."

She ignored him. Lost in her misery, she continued to sob. He strode over and taking her roughly by the arm, pulled her to her feet.

"Why did you do it, Tal?" he asked, for the first time his voice breaking. "Why? You only had to trust me, and now you have destroyed everything."

He drew her to him and kissed her roughly on the lips. She was like a limp doll in his arms, all sign of hope drained from her. He pushed her savagely away, his momentary weakness quickly contained.

"I cannot believe that you were foolish enough to succumb to

Raybet's suave and cunning ways. He would stoop to any deception to win favour with Konfra by paving a smooth path for Rose. Couldn't you see that he just wanted you out of the way? You fell blindly into his little game … like a deer caught in a trap."

She made no reply, continuing to sob. In disgust, he strode to the door, thrusting it open. "Take her back to the dungeon," his voice thundered. The soldiers rushed to attend to their orders quickly, hustling her out. "And have Madame Avileaux clean her up. And get that filth washed out of her damned cell!"

CHAPTER 14

The Wounding

"Hey missie, they've caught another stag. The fight will take place on Friday. Should be quite a spectacle," one of the guards said sniggering, "seeing that you are going to open the proceedings." He smirked at Talitha. She turned away disgusted and terrified.

Over the proceeding days, Pover brought reports of the new stag; a young, virile beast that was as frightened as poor Shiloh, but equally determined to fight for his life. On the day before the fight, the soldiers bound Talitha and escorted her out to the death compound. The great oaken doors were unlocked, and she was shown the path which she must run towards her front row, viewing seat, beside Jockim and the general.

"You'll be wise not to take your time missy, or else you'll feel the sting of the whip. You'll need to run yer hardest. That's what they want to see ... someone else being punished. Makes 'em feel better about themselves you see—watching others get what they think they deserve. Especially if it's a woman—makes 'em feel stronger and more powerful!"

Every muscle and sinew tightened at the thought of what lay ahead of her. On the way back to the dungeon, she was aware of the passing gaze of the soldiers; most of them amused leers, but a few compassionate glances. The hours passed like days, brooding heavy with fear. All efforts to control her thoughts and emotions seemed futile. Nights provided no relief. Instead, the darkness pressed its shadowy dread upon her. Visions of Shiloh dying and herself reeling before a mocking crowd haunted the little sleep that she was able to snatch.

On the evening prior to the event Jockim secretly summoned Matthias, the soldier whom he had carefully chosen to drive Talitha around the compound. He instructed him that he was to take all possible measures to avoid striking her with his whips. When he considered it necessary to make contact with her body, to ensure that the punishment appeared genuine, he was to strike lightly, as one would a child, while simultaneously cracking the other whip upon the ground. That way the drunken crowd would be fooled into believing that she was indeed being chastised. Jockim was adamant that the whips were to be used only to frighten and humiliate her. In no way were they to cause her physical harm.

Knowing his men well, he was confident that if anyone could make it appear like she was being punished, Matthias could. He had a skill with the whip like none other and was often chosen to execute such proceedings, on the infrequent occasions when they occurred. His dexterity assured that the target was hit with the exact amount of force that Jockim ordered. He often wielded two whips with an amazing precision, making public whippings as much a spectacle to frighten onlookers and thereby deter them from similar misdemeanours, as a punishment for the accused prisoner. On this occasion, his skill would indeed be tested, as it was not an easy task to strike so lightly while simultaneously making it appear harsh.

Jockim paid him a generous sum, swore him to secrecy, and promised more after he had witnessed that his directions had been executed. Matthias proceeded to leave the study struggling to hide the smug curve which tugged at his lips. The thought of his heavily laden pockets pleased him greatly.

Jockim was still ranting as he reached the door. "Provide her with a pair of britches from one of the soldiers or stable hands to put on prior to the whipping. I don't want her tripping over her skirts as she runs around the compound. The crowd will wonder why you don't take the opportunity to strike her severely if she falls."

As Matthias closed the door, a faint curse reached his ears. Jockim shoved his chair back impatiently. He did not have the desire or tolerance to concentrate on the details of his recent takings from Doomeerie's merchant ships. The chair toppled unsteadily upon its carved oaken feet as he began to pace the room.

The day of the fight dawned like any other to all those whom its events would have little impact upon, but for Talitha and Shiloh and those that loved them, it seemed to drag on mercilessly, with ever accelerating tension. By midafternoon Talitha lay crumpled with exhaustion in her cell. She wondered how she would ever summon the energy to walk, let alone run. Her thoughts were fixated upon Shiloh.

At 7pm sharp, the soldiers came. Her heart dropped like lead as the gates whined open. In the shadows of a lantern, she changed into the shirt and britches that were thrown into her. The soldiers eyed her up and down leeringly as she moved to the darker confines of the cell to get dressed. Then, after binding her hands, they hauled her to the death compound that was already a hive of drunken activity.

"Listen to me, girlie." Matthias drew her close to him and whispered in her ear as she felt her legs give way beneath her. "When ya 'ear the crack of the whip … it means ya bolt—like a frightened filly. Ya run the course as fast as yer legs will carry ya. If ya dawdle you'll feel my whip upon yer arse, but if ya keep movin' I promise ya I'll not strike ya … only the ground near ya. The soldiers are already so drunk that they won't know whether ya'r being hit or the ground is … So long as they 'ear the whip cracking and see ya running they'll be satisfied. Do ya 'ear me?" He peered sternly down at her, his smelly breath hot upon her face.

"Yes, yes, I understand." She spluttered, fear choking her words.

With that, the doors flew open, and cracking the whip with the skill and strength of one much practised, Matthias yelled, "Run!"

She felt her legs take off beneath her, and sprinting as hard as she could, Talitha made her way around the dusty compound. Raucous laughing, jeering, and mocking spurred her on. Rotten fruit, vegetables, and eggs, exploded in a cascade of rancid force about her. Sometimes hammering her body with painful blows, they covered her in a garment of putrid filth and shame. Shouts of 'thief' and 'traitor' reverberated in her ears admidst whistles and cheering. "Bring her to her knees! Strike her hard!"

Behind her, every few minutes she felt the unrelenting vibration of the strong whip belting the ground skilfully close to her body. Her heart drummed. Her chest was tight, her head exploding in pain. Jockim watched, churning with anxiety. Yet, to the crowd he appeared emotionless and detached.

Finally, she was there before him. She looked up. Their eyes met. His dark coals momentarily softened with pity. Distracted by them, she halted. Matthias, keen to keep up pretences, lightly struck the whip across the rear of the britches that fitted snugly to her hips. The sting of its contact, and the swish and clap of the second whip which cracked open the dry earth, propelled her on. The crowd cheered in a frenzy of delight as she emitted a cry, more from surprise and shame than pain.

Jockim's eyes hardened into steel as he watched her sprint forward. The gate yielded before her. Two soldiers grabbed her and escorted her to where he stood in full view of the crowd. She collapsed into the vacant seat next to him, burying her head in her lap. He held his hand up, and silence descended upon the gathering.

"Let the fight begin!" he decreed loudly. The two stags bolted into the compound amidst a mighty roar.

The general pulled at Talitha's hair, forcing her head up. "Watch now, lassie. This is all for you. I'd hate you to miss out, especially as you've just provided my men with such fine entertainment. I've been waiting a long time to see you get a good whipping. It's a damned pity that you can run so fast."

Jockim clenched his fist tight but remained calm, allowing the general to satisfy his cruel urge for fun. Before them, the two stags were pacing nervously in circles, bellowing low, their eyes rolled back in heightened tension. Almost simultaneously, they charged. Their antlers locked in fierce determination. They tugged back and forth, eventually swinging their strong heads free. Again and again, the heavy rush of hooves resounded amongst the raucous excitement of the compound. Each time, it was followed by the clash of antlers, shattering the suspense. The stag's bulging necks strained to break free. All of a sudden, Shiloh turned quickly and butted his opponent in the torso. The other stag bellowed loudly and swung to return the strike.

Talitha, overcome by the spectacle, lurched forward in a frantic effort to climb over the barricade. She felt Jockim's strong hands grasp her by the collar and the seat of her britches. He pulled her back towards him roughly. She squirmed, thrashing about like a frightened child. With ease, he clenched her arms around her chest tightly, holding them down with his own strong arms of steel. Hoisting his knee up between her legs, he steadied his foot on the seat in front. She sat poised like a doll, legs dangling either side of her human perch.

Kicking with all her might, she screamed, "Let me go!" He held tight, her futile attempts to break free causing a low chuckle to escape, releasing the tension that had built up like a dam of emotion within his body.

"If you don't stop kicking like a spoilt brat, I'll put you over my knee rather than on it," he said, threatening her. The general smirked with satisfaction.

So it continued—swirling stags—blood dripping, suspended in floating, dust particles and the drum of pounding hooves on the ground. Then, with bellows that indicated they were struggling for life, both stags collapsed almost simultaneously with a heavy thud. There was strained silence as everyone watched and waited. After several minutes, Shiloh's opponent staggered to his feet. A mighty roar resounded in the arena.

The victorious animal was quickly lassoed and taken, stumbling, out of the compound. Talitha did not see the young soldiers come to lift Shiloh's limp body onto a stretcher. She had already collapsed, a dead weight, in Jockim's secure hold.

CHAPTER 15

The Birth of Atonement

With time, she will learn the mystery,
That the wise behold in suffering's history.
The bitter seeds bring much growth,
Yet we harvest them with loath.

Jockim slipped away quickly, making sure that he was lost in the crowds of drunken men, escaping to a secret stable just inside the boundaries of Nightmare Forest. He had ordered his trusted men to take Shiloh there. He decided to ride Noble and take Balaamine, in case the horse spooked and would not enter the forest at night. In which case, he felt certain the donkey would not lose her composure. In the confusion of the aftermath, it was relatively easy for the men carrying Shiloh to leave without suspicion. Those that saw them thought they were merely disposing of the stag's mutilated body.

Having ordered that Talitha be placed into Madame Avileaux's care, Jockim was free to assist Shiloh. He had grown to love the stag. Days earlier, he had sent an envoy of trusted men to the border to explain circumstances to Padyah and to ask the old man to come should Shiloh be gravely injured. He hoped that all had gone to plan. Although he felt ashamed to meet the old sage, there was also an eager anticipation and much hope within him.

Having left Noble tied to a tree near the forest entrance, he entered the darkness riding Balaamine. As they neared the stable, he sensed the presence of something tall watching them and raising his lantern beheld Eldad and Medad, who gracefully lowered their necks to greet him.

"Welcome, Master Jockim, welcome Balaamine," said Eldad. "The old man is waiting for you both inside the stable, but take off your shoes before you enter."

Jockim looked up at the giraffes unsure of what to do. He was not accustomed to taking orders from anyone.

"You are about to step onto holy ground and it would be appropriate to acknowledge this," Medad replied softly, in gentle welcome.

Jockim did as he was asked and entered the stable taking Balaamine with him. The old man was crouching over Shiloh smearing his wounds with a potent smelling ointment and praying reverently. After chanting several words that Jockim could not understand, he raised his sad, kind eyes and focused them on the wearied travellers.

"Ah Master Jockim … you have come for healing too." He smiled sympathetically. "And you've brought Shiloh's dear friend, Balaamine. That is good. The donkey must stay with him, as her presence will assist his healing."

"Alright, I'll leave her here with you both. But I need no healing myself. I am not injured. I've come to see if the stag will live."

"That depends on the Great Spirit." Padyah sighed. "I have done what I can—but do not fear. The spirit will manifest what is best for all."

He walked to the back of the stable, placing the herbal mixture on a small table there. Turning to face Jockim, he looked at him searchingly.

"As to the matter of your state … I am not so convinced that you would not benefit from healing too. Let us say healing of a different kind to our young friend, Shiloh?"

Jockim's gaze met the old man's. It penetrated the pain that permeated his soul. He ran his fingers through his unkempt hair, not knowing what to say.

"Healing of the soul perhaps?"

Laying his rifle down, Jockim felt the full extent of his misery descend upon him. "I have destroyed my very soul, Padyah." He looked over at the young stag. "Not only that, I have also destroyed the woman I love—all for a castle—a castle of doom. How could I have done it?" His voice began to break under the strain of heavy guilt and sorrow.

"A deep sadness swells within you, a betrayal from the young maiden who has come to mean so much to you. Her actions have turned your heart to half malice, half grief." He gazed at Jockim kindly. "She did not come into your life to betray you but to show you another way … to teach you compassion and wisdom."

"Then I have failed both her and myself miserably, for I have acted with cruelty and selfishness. I have destroyed both of us to save the possessions and values of Doomeerie."

"So it may seem, but the story has not yet been fully told. Your shadow self will redeem you, just as hers will redeem her. The atonement has yet to be manifest, and when it is, Talitha will develop both humility and strength; the qualities she now lacks. You have unwittingly laid the seeds for them to sprout within her if she chooses wisely, which I am sure that with time she will. She, in turn, has caused you to question your values, the selfish and merciless ways of your ancestors."

"Perhaps so old man, but even if she could ever bring herself to forgive me, which I very much doubt, I could never do the same for myself. I am doomed to live forever with this hideous beast that I have become."

"It will be hard—a long road back—but you have great, inner strength. You must channel it towards the force of love, not condemnation. What price are you willing to pay to regain your soul?"

"Whatever it takes," Jockim replied soberly.

"Then you must set her free. Show her the secret way out of Doomeerie. She has shown great bravery attempting to complete the third task allotted to her, the drinking of the waters of the River Styx from the silver goblet, but she had not drunk deep enough from her experience at Doomeerie to learn true humility, courage, and trust. She needed to relinquish her pride and fear. The events of tonight will help her to do this."

"If giving her up is what is needed to restore her and to reclaim my soul, then what choice do I have, even though it will truly break my spirit?"

"Take her to Eagle Nest Rock and drink deeply from the Holy Grail with her, so that your souls are forever entwined, even though your immediate destiny will lead you down separate paths."

Jockim regarded the old man wretchedly. "There is no other way my friend … you must trust. She is being called to move on to complete her fourth task; the most difficult of all … Yes, there are few indeed who journey down that path—into the underworld."

He laid his hand gently upon Jockim's shoulder. "And you must tarry no longer because I fear that a great evil is about to befall Doomeerie, and you, are the one who is destined to overcome it."

CHAPTER 16

Escape from Doomeerie

Leaving Balaamine at the stable with Shiloh and Padyah, Jockim rode as fast as Noble could take him back to the castle. He had lost time getting out of Nightmare Forest on foot. When he arrived back at Doomeerie, the first shades of dawn were beginning to lighten the morning sky in soft apricot and golden hues.

The castle was in chaos. Dead bodies were humped in piles. Everywhere wounded soldiers cried out in pain, while their drunken comrades wandered around trying to assist them. They had been attacked not long after he had left, and although they had initially suffered heavy losses due to the inebriated state of the men, the general had quickly rounded up the sober soldiers and managed to drive back the forces.

Jockim wasted no time in getting to the north wing where he found Madame Avileaux with Anya. Talitha was asleep in her room.

"How is she?" he asked.

"She's been sleeping a long time. The attack did not seem to alarm her. It's as if she's lost all heart and soul now that the stag is dead." The older woman was distressed. She looked away to avoid Jockim's gaze. "I know that you had to punish her Jockim, and that this was better than banishment and death, but it breaks my heart to see the despair in her eyes."

"The stag is not dead yet. I have had him taken to the old herdsman, Padyah, who is caring for him. I want to get her out of the castle now, via the south wing passage. You and Anya must go too. I can drag Anya along the passage under the waterfall."

"No, I will not go," Anya cried frantically, "not without Vadio, and he has gone with the general to the front line. I will wait until he returns!"

"There may be no time then, Anya. Go now, with Tal and Avie. I will stay and tell him of your whereabouts."

"Where are we to go, Jockim?" Madame Avileaux grabbed him by the arm. "Have you thought of this? Even if we make it to the other side of the river through the waterfall tunnel which is highly unlikely for Anya—there is nothing there for us—we will just perish in the wilderness. No, I am staying here with Anya ... If our forces don't prevail and the castle is taken at least we will still be together."

"Then I will take Tal, now," he replied, shaking his head at their decision. "Hopefully, there will be time for as many of us as possible to get across at the end, if the castle is to fall. I must hurry. I need to get back to assist Vadio and Konfra."

Thrusting the door to Talitha's room open, he crouched beside the bed. She stirred and opened her eyes, looking up at him.

"Shiloh is still alive," he announced immediately. "I have taken him and Balaamine to be with Padyah. You must trust me now, and come with me."

She swung her legs over the side of the bed as Madame Avileaux threw a shawl around her shoulders. Pressing her close to her body, she hugged Talitha tightly, tears welling in her eyes. "I love you, Tal. Please forgive me any hurt that I have caused you."

"You have caused me no hurt. You always did your best. I love you too. I love you so very much. You have been like a mother to me. Thank you for everything."

Then looking at Anya, she hugged her too. "Goodbye, dear Anya. I love you too."

"Hurry," Jockim insisted. Grasping her hand, they made their way quickly to the south wing with Pover flying beside them.

The south wing had a decidedly haunting, almost dream-like quality about it. They hurried along a long, dim corridor, opening door after door. Finally, they came upon a great, oak panelled door, almost twice their height, which was bolted. Jockim pulled a chain from his pocket and revealed an ornate, cast iron key. He turned it in the lock, and the door yielded before them.

Entering the room, its humble ambience shocked Talitha. Assuming that it had been his mother's bedroom, she had expected it to be ornate and expensively decorated, but apart from a bed, chest, table, and chair there was no other furniture. Four, magnificent, stained glass windows, almost the entire length of the wall, dominated the room, and in the far corner a mirror the size of a door, was adhered to the wall. It was encased within a golden frame that depicted a series of miniature, sculptured stories. At the end of the room, stood a circular stone column, which could be entered by means of an unassuming, narrow, wooden door.

Talitha stopped, unable to take her eyes off the beautiful, glass windows. Morning rays of coloured light permeated them. Each window depicted a slightly different scene involving young women. The first showed a swarthy, young woman carrying a tiger cub in her arms and entering into a shadowy, underground cave, while the second depicted a maiden with flaxen hair walking through the forest accompanied by a donkey. In the third, a pale, dark eyed woman with flowing, black hair was caressing a white stag in the snow drenched mountains, and the final one showed a red haired maiden releasing a beautiful, white bird to freedom. Her eyes widened as she took in the details. She was immediately struck by their similarity to the bonds she shared with her animal friends.

Jockim nodded, understanding her thoughts. "I don't know why," he said. "It's uncanny ... I keep forcing the similarity from my mind as it unnerves me—especially this one." He pointed to the woman carrying the tiger cub. "I didn't want to believe that it might somehow involve you."

Talitha's heart skipped a beat, and she drew her breath quickly. The cave seemed to lead into the darkness of the underworld.

"The tiger ... Padyah spoke of it in connection with your escape. It embodies courage; mastery of one's inner fears and demons. He seemed to indicate that you must travel underground with the creature to forge your own personal power ... But there is no time ... We must keep going if we're going to get you out of here safely."

He unlocked the door that opened into the stone column, and they headed up some stairs to a tiny balcony. From there they could see far out to the sea. On the distant horizon, Talitha could just make out the twinkle of lights.

"That is Edgewater and Southport," he pointed in the direction of the light, "where Padyah suggests you go. You will be met by one of his men in that vicinity. He will explain what you must do. I will get you across the River Styx, and then you will be on your own. Follow the course of the river. There will be no armies there, so you should be relatively safe. Here are a few provisions."

He thrust back the bolt securing a tiny, rustic cabinet and pulled out a bag of provisions set aside for a quick escape, along with a sack that she recognised to be the same one that held the goblet. Her eyes lowered in pain. He took her chin in his hand and gently raised her face so that their eyes met.

"It's alright. Padyah has explained. Forgive me, my love, for the hurt I have caused you." He kissed her on the lips, not wanting to draw apart. Tears fell softly down her cheeks.

"Why is it that we always come to the truth too late?" He released her reluctantly. Grabbing the bag, he turned to descend the stairs. "Come, we go down now." He held out his hand towards her.

She clasped it and followed him down what seemed like a never ending, stone stairwell that led into a murky, underground tunnel. This became dimmer and narrower until they were lying prone, pulling themselves along in darkness.

"Don't be frightened," he called back. "It opens up soon to a series of caves that are actually under the river's rapids."

The noise of water crashing over rocks could be vaguely heard. It gradually became louder and louder until it was almost deafening. Suddenly, the tunnel ended abruptly, widening into a small cave hidden from view by the cascades that crashed over its opening.

"Above here is Eagle Nest Rock," he yelled.

Taking the goblet from the sack, he held it out to catch some of the water from the falls. The contents quickly filled, spilling their crystal droplets over the sides of the goblet. He handed it to her to drink. The cold, fresh water revitalised her, and having consumed half, she gave it back to him to finish. He looked into her misted eyes. Sensing it may be the last time that he would be with her, he was filled with despair. He drank the remaining water and drew her to him, holding her soft, warm body close.

"Go safely, my love." His voice was barely audible above the plunging cascade. "I can go no further. I must return to help the others. If you follow these series of caves, you will not get lost. They go to the other side of the river. My love remains with you wherever you are, whatever you face. Take the goblet to remind you that we have both drunk deeply from our time at Doomeerie. This experience will bind our spirits together forever."

He held her tightly, kissing the tears from her cheeks.

"I love you. I'm so sorry. Please forgive me." She choked, overcome with sadness.

He eventually pulled her from him, knowing that her safety and that of many others was at risk if they delayed. With a final glance that wrenched at the emptiness deep within him, he turned and re-entered the tunnel. She found herself alone once more. She was deep under the mysterious waters of the River Styx—the river of death.

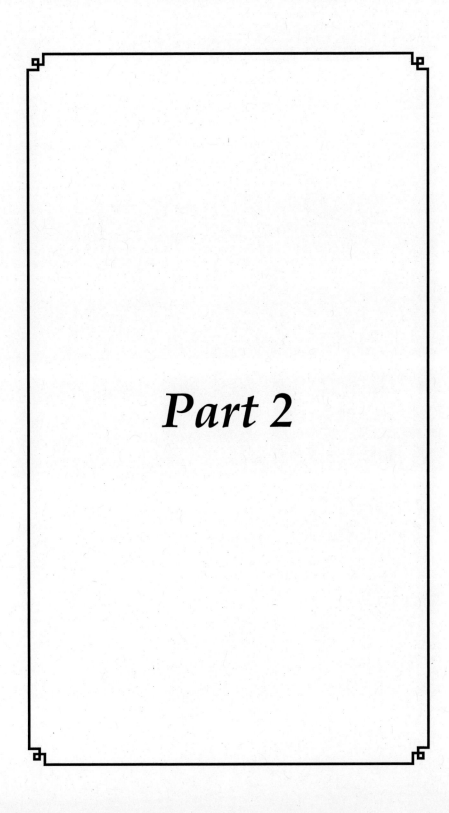

Part 2

CHAPTER 1

The Golden Cage

Talitha was finally free. Yet a sense of sadness hovered around her. A multitude of misgivings were continually crawling into her mind. *Will I ever see Jockim or Shiloh again? I have failed— completely and utterly. Shiloh is badly wounded … He may die … I have betrayed Jockim. Why, oh why did I ever do it? Why didn't I wait like Pover wanted?* Guilt grasped her thoughts and twisted them into hideous dimensions until she could bear no more. The only means of escape was to blame Jockim, and so she spat out her self-hate upon him. *He didn't have to make Shiloh fight. What kind of friend subjects the one they love to such cruel humiliation? He thought more of saving Doomeerie than he did of me!* Thus, her mind spun pendulum like in its own inner hell, and even Pover was unable to save her from the hideous spaces where her soul wandered. Still, she forged on, not knowing what else to do. This must be the way she was meant to go. Padyah had indicated that to Jockim. Perhaps she would eventually be led to the Hidden Garden.

As they made their way south along the bank, she took care to stay out of sight. The rambling river forged ever onwards, each bend rounding to a view similar to the last. Once out of the earshot of the thunderous waterfall, the booming of distant canons could be distinguished—a dirge that drummed on into death. With each explosion, Talitha wondered if Jockim stood or fell. Eventually, as darkness descended, she decided to camp for the night.

Exhausted from the tumultuous events of the preceding days, sleep came easily and heavily, lasting for several hours. Suddenly, the sound of swishing saplings seeped into her consciousness. Too late! A lined, leather face leered down. A tug ripped away her shawl! Gaping, yellow teeth chuckled in amusement at their new found treasure.

"Get up, girl!"

A sturdy, middle-aged man dragged her to her feet. A strong, sweaty smell overcame her. Beside him, a wizened, old woman and a motley group of companions crowded in upon her like beady eyed crows. Likened by their dirty and dishevelled appearance, they stared at her suspiciously. Talitha's throat constricted trapping her voice. She stared wide eyed in terror at the group. Pover flew stealthily into a nearby tree.

"We'll take 'er wit' us. She's probably a castle wench," the middle-aged man commanded. "Jockim may pay a pretty sum for 'er after the fightin's over."

"Why take 'er wit' us, Markam?" the old hag hissed. "She's jus' anotha' mouth to feed … Let's jus' strip 'er of 'er stuff, and leave 'er 'ere to fend for 'erself."

"I'm wit' 'at," a swarthy, young male answered, "but, we'll 'ave some fun 'fore we leave 'er!" A chorus of agreement arose from the men.

The old hag turned on them. "Watch yerselves. Ya don't need to upset yer women folk, ya mob of fools!" She spluttered through the gaps in her teeth. "She ain't worth the effort."

"Shut up! She's commin' wit' us," Markam broke into the chorus of dissention, silencing it, "at least for now."

Picking up her sack of provisions, he prodded her ahead of him, drawing a knife from his pocket. Forced on, Talitha stumbled through the forest while Pover followed hidden in the foliage. Eventually, they entered a tiny clearing, spoilt by the effects of human occupation. Old barrels and tins littered the ground that was barren from the effects of continual fires. Upon its dusty surface, dirty children ran and fought. Women, crouching like giant, hairy spiders, fussed about the business of preparing food. Talitha was shoved into the circle of their activity. They eyed her up and down like they were about to consume her as prey.

"Where did ya get 'er from?" one squealed.

"I'd say she's from the castle," Markam replied. "Dono' how she got across the river but let's see what she's got wit' 'er." He opened her sack, sprawling the contents onto an old mat that stretched in colourful weaves across the ground.

"Not much worth keepin'. We'll have it done 'ith in one sittin'."

"Perhaps ya girls would like to share 'er pretty clothes?" One of the young men moved in upon Talitha lifting her skirts with a stick to reveal her cotton petticoat. She froze, knowing that she had hidden the goblet in a secret pocket in her undergarment.

"Get yer eyes of 'er, Moko!" the old hag hissed, pushing him away.

Swallowing hard, Talitha inwardly breathed a sigh of relief. Again, Markam, the man with the knife, stepped forward.

"Where're ya from girl? Speak up … Ave ya lost ya tongue?"

Talitha's mind raced. She didn't want to put her castle friends in danger. "Please, you can have the food. I meant no harm. If you let me go, I'll not cause you any trouble."

Markam threw his head back and laughed heartily. "Aye, that be sure. Ya won't be causin' us no trouble 'cause I won't be lettin' ya go. Bind 'er up Flynn, and take 'er inside the single wench's carriage," he ordered a red-haired man. "It's time to eat, and I'm hungry. We'll question 'er tomorrow. She can tell us 'ow she got across the river. She might 'ave a boat. There could be others and more stuff. We'll take 'er to Kyriedor later and see what 'e makes of 'er. When she's hungry enough she'll talk. Any man who lays a 'and on 'er in the meantime, will 'ave me to answer to." His eyes circled the group in a menacing swoop. Glancing away, the men began to back off, one after another, muttering obscenities.

Flynn roughly bound her hands and taking her by the upper arm led her into a brightly coloured cabin at the far end of the campsite. It was adorned by an array of charms and trinkets. Bells tinkled as they pushed their way through a tattered, crimson scarf that afforded the only privacy to its entrance.

Becoming accustomed to the dimmer light, Talitha's eyes perceived a beautiful, turquoise hummingbird staring at her from behind the bars of a golden cage in the corner of the cabin. The soft odour of sweet musk and human sweat filled her nostrils.

"There's ya bed." Flynn nodded to some dirty cushions on the floor that had been roughly embroidered by womenfolk. "Angie and Margie also sleep 'ere, so mind you keep ya space. Angie will 'ave to attend to 'er little un' throughout the night," he pointed to a fair headed boy of about three or four years who was asleep in the corner, "so you'd be best to rest over this side." He gestured towards the corner where the golden cage was lodged on a hook, part way down the wall. Looking her up and down he made no further comment and proceeded to leave. As he raised the tattered scarf, he stopped, turning around.

"We're not bad folk ma'am … only seems that way. The rest of the world don't like us … They don't understand us. Our ways are different. We can't live by 'eir fancy ways. That's why we choose to live away from 'em, in the forest. We don't do nobody nay harm, unless they 'urt one of us, and then we'll look after our own. You treat the women folk well, and they'll get to like ya, ya'll see." He sighed, scratching his red head. "We're just different that's all, and the world don't like ya if yer too different. It scares 'em." He chuckled and descended the small steps that exited the cabin.

Talitha instinctively went straight towards the golden cage. The striking bird looked melancholy and under nourished, in spite of an abundance of seed, carrot, and apple in the cage.

"Hello," she said kindly. "I'm Tal, what's your name, beautiful one?" The tiny creature stared at her silently, lost in a lonely world of its own. "You are so beautiful!" She admired the brilliant turquoise of the creature's soft down. "You are the colours of a turquoise gem. I'm going to call you, Gem!" She smiled at the bird that stared silently.

Assuming that the creature's sadness was caused by its imprisonment, she awkwardly slid the ornate, golden door open with her bound hands and spoke softly to encourage it out. Still, the bird remained fixed like a statue upon its perch. Only the slight movement of its sad eyes assured her that it was indeed aware of her presence.

"She ain't gonna come out." A twangy, feminine voice accompanied a slight shaking of the carriage. A young, red haired woman climbed inside.

"Hello!" She smiled at Talitha. "I'm Angie, Flynn's daughter and that there's Toby, fast asleep." She pointed to the child, encircled in a cocoon of cushions. "He's me boy. Father said ya'd like some company. Thought ya might be lonely. Don't be scared of us. We won't hurt ya. Here, let me take that rope off yer hands." She reached for Talitha's wrists and removed the bonds.

"Won't you get into trouble for untying me?"

"Naw, they won't care—especially now that they've begun to drink. They'll just wanna have fun. But yar' best out of their sight, when the men get drunk, being pretty and young as ya are."

"I'm Tal." She smiled stiffly, gazing into the young woman's vivid, blue eyes.

Outside, the sound of merriment elevated. The glow of an open fire filtered in through the scarfed entrance. Angie nodded towards the gaiety. "That's 'ow young Toby came to be … 'Appened on a night like tonight. Tye, me man, took a fancy to me. Never did get to see his son. He was shot some months later trying to thieve some 'orses. I was dreadful upset at the time, but ya keep goin', and I got me dad 'ere to 'elp me with Toby. Us folk, we stick together and look out for each other … 'Ere, I've brought you somethin' to eat."

She handed Talitha a piece of dry bread and some roasted chicken. "I thought you'd be hungry!" She grinned, as Tal hastily began to consume it. "Not like our little friend 'ere … Won't eat nothin' for us … She's fadin' away. We've tried to get 'er to come out and even left the door open for a long time in the 'ope that she would fly to freedom. That's what I call her … Freedom, because she wants it, but when the doors left open, she won't fly off. Na, she wouldn't be able to survive out in the wild anyway. She ain't got the strength to care for 'erself anymore."

Talitha stared at the fragile creature. "Where did you get her? She is very beautiful and so is the cage," she said, admiring the bars that were woven exquisitely with a decorative, leaf pattern. She was almost sure that it was gold and would be worth a costly sum.

"A wealthy magician at Southport gave 'er to us in exchange for some stuff." Angie glanced shadily at Talitha. "Daresay this cage was 'is prized possession … Probably thought more of the cage than he did of 'er. She used to fetch 'im quite a lot of money I 'eard. Besides being beautiful, she 'ad the most lovely of songs … Folk would come from near and far to 'ear 'er sing, I believe. He'd make 'em pay to 'ear her. But then one day she jus' stopped singin' and 'er song ain't never been 'eard since. Strange thing, ain't it?"

Talitha couldn't take her eyes off the exquisite bird. "Did he stop feeding her because she wouldn't sing?"

"Nup, she jus' stopped 'erself. No one knows why. We can't sell 'er, being so sickly. We thought of settin' 'er free and selling the cage. Fair thing to do—birds shouldn't be in cages—but she won't leave. It's like she's under some magical spell or something. Maybe she feels safe in it. So now we can't sell it until she dies because town folk'll probably kill her and put a healthy bird in there. That's the way them folks in towns and cities are. Only want to show off things that are perfect, don't they? Wouldn't do to 'ave a sickly bird in a fancy cage now would it?"

She began to rearrange the cushions and make herself comfortable on the floor. "Ah well, Tal. I'm really tired. I might 'ave to get up to young Toby 'ere if 'e 'as nightmares, so I'm gonna sleep." She chuckled. "Don't go out during the night. If the men don't get ya, the wild animals will—plenty of 'em in this part of the woods. There's a chamber pot over there if ya need to go." She pointed to a china bowl on the table. "The men that are on night duty board up the door when we're all tucked in … That's in case they fall asleep … which 'as 'appened a few times … Probably 'ad too much to drink …"

Her voice started to trail off in disconnected phrases. Soon she was asleep, her long, golden, red hair cascading in a blaze of feminine glory around her oval face and high cheek bones. Despite her slightly unkempt appearance, Talitha couldn't help marvelling at her wild, untamed beauty. It was clear that the lad was hers. Their jaws were set with the same proud and determined fashion.

Talitha looked around her again, dismayed at the thought of being locked in a confined space with others. Freedom stared back, offering no comfort. Deciding that she would be unable to escape at present, she opted to try and get some sleep. She tossed and turned, her mind preoccupied with thoughts of Freedom and her escape. It was not long before she heard familiar chirping near the cabin's entrance. She lifted the scarf to let Pover in.

Spying the cage, the little, brown bird flew up to the bars. Freedom had fallen asleep lying on its base. She was too weak to hold herself upright on the perch. Talitha opened the door to the cage, whispering, "She's sick … She won't eat or fly out. Maybe you can help her, but you will have to be careful not to get locked in. I will leave the door ajar."

Pover flew inside and pecked gently at the soft, turquoise feathers. Freedom raised her head. Pover nestled in next to her, allowing the frail bird to rest her head on her soft body. Instinctively, the smaller bird relaxed.

Talitha, touched by the scene, smiled. Tears welled in her eyes. She thought of Jockim, Shiloh, Balaamine, and Jenobay. How long ago her life with them now seemed to be. Who would have thought that within the space of a few hours she and Pover would be prisoners? She held within the gaudy confines of an old caravan and Pover within the delicate bars of a golden cage.

CHAPTER 2

White Cliff Castle

"Ya'r from Doomerie, aren't ya lass?" Markam scrutinised her as she consumed the final mouthful of steaming porridge. Talitha didn't reply immediately. She wanted to consider what would be the most advantageous answer for herself and Pover.

Nervously, she surveyed the little group of gypsies that surrounded her. The same two men who seemed to have authority within the group, Markam and Flynn sat opposite her, eyeing her up and down suspiciously. They were both middle aged, possessing a presence of power, although Flynn's face was etched with lines of compassion around his eyes; something that the other man lacked. Angie sat beside her father, serving Toby porridge and diverting her attention between ensuring that the boy ate every mouthful and watching Talitha keenly.

"If ya want to live and see ya young friend live, I'd tell the truth lassie." Markam glanced towards Pover who sat trapped within the golden cage. Someone had closed the door, and in the morning Talitha had been unable to open it.

"Ya friend will be freed if ya talk to us … otherwise she's ours, and ya can fend for yerself out there in the wilderness. Ya won't get far without supplies, and I won't be stopping me men from a bit of fun once ya away from the campsite. What their women folk don't see won't hurt 'em." Markam said blatantly.

Flynn shuffled his feet uncomfortably and looked towards Angie who rolled her eyes in disgust. Markam spied the gesture and reprimanded her.

"Leave us woman! It's time you got a man 'ere. No good ya livin' on yer own with the lad and the half-wit girl. Ya'r too high and mighty about who ya want, that's yer problem. Weren't that way the night ya shacked up with the boy's father? Withholding yer favours is only makin' the men edgy."

"That's enough!" Flynn broke in protectively. "Leave us please Angie an' take Tobias wit' ya."

Angie's eyes were searing hot, blue flames as she stared haughtily at Markam. She searched for some tattered shoes amongst the pillows, shoved them on the boy's feet, and lifting him onto her hip, tossed her golden, red glory over her shoulders. She left the cabin without saying a word.

"Okay girl, speak up … Are ya from the castle or aren't ya?" Markam demanded.

"Yes, I am. I was a maidservant there."

"So why did they let ya go?"

"I tried to escape, and the soldiers caught me. Jockim banished me to Nightmare Forest for attempted desertion." She stopped, realizing that she had already lied and surprised at how easily the words had slipped out.

"Go on girl … so how did ya get the supplies, and how did ya get across the river."

"I promised my favours to a young soldier if he'd leave the supplies hidden just inside the boundary of Nightmare Forest." Considering Markam's previous comment, she thought that he'd accept this explanation as plausible.

"How did ya know where to find where he'd hidden them?"

"It was the same place where we'd met." She paused again. "You know, when we were together."

"And how did ya get across the river?" He prompted further, keen to discern if she was lying.

"I went to the enemy lines via the covering of the forest, and I surrendered. I said that I would give my favours freely to the soldiers in payment for transport across the river, down further, away from the rapids."

Markam stared at her. "Why should I believe ya, girl …?"

She stuck her pert, little chin up in an act of defiance. "Why shouldn't you believe me? I am no liar."

He raised his hand and struck her across the face. "Ya don't talk to me like that! Ya'r only a woman … and not much of a woman at that!" he said savagely.

She fell back upon the cushions. Tears erupted. Her cheek pulsated with throbbing pain. Inside the cage, Pover leapt forward in a flutter of fury clinging to the bars. The sudden rush of movement caught Markam's attention.

"Fond of ya, that little urchin ain't she?" He smirked. "Ya'r right about the punishment for desertion being banishment so that makes yer story partly true, but I'm not so sure about ya being willin' ta give yer favours away. We'll see what ya'll do to survive and keep yer little bird friend livin'. Time will tell if ya'r true to yer words." He turned to address Flynn. "Tell Moko to come in will ya. I owe 'im a favour."

Flynn stood up and walked to the door. He called out for Moko. Within a few seconds the same coarse-faced, bulky, young man, who had raised her skirts with a stick the evening before, appeared at the cabin entrance.

"Ya want me, Markam?" he said, his eyes feasting on Talitha who was now looking like a trapped animal.

"Ya've served the clan well lately, Moko. I wanna reward ya with a bit of petticoat. Da ya fancy this one at all?" Markam lent forward. "Open ya mouth girl. Comm'on smile. Show 'im yer pearly, white teeth."

Terrified, Talitha forced a smile to her lips.

"Ain't seen anything like that for a while 'ave we, except for our Angie? What do ya think Moko?"

"She'll do jus' fine, Markam." He strode towards Talitha and proceeded to pull her to her feet.

"Not jus' yet, Moko … Ya'r heading off for yer trip up north tomorrow. We want ya to be in good nick. She'd be the prize waiting for ya when ya return. I'll promise ya no other man will lay hands on 'er, till ya've had yer way wit 'er." He chuckled at the disappointment showing on the young man's face and seeing the relief on Talitha's added. "Give 'er something to look forward to, hey. She can spend 'er days thinking of the joys to come, and if she should happen to refuse, then that little friend of 'ers will make a nice stew! What do ya reckon?" He winked at Moko, and they both chortled heartily. "Com'on now lad, I'll help ya wit' yer supplies for the journey."

They headed out of the cabin, Moko smiling broadly at his good fortune. Flynn stared silently at her for a few minutes until the men were out of hearing range.

"Why did ya lie, lass? It would 'ave gone better for ya if ya'd told the truth. Ya ain't never been wit' a man, 'av ya?"

"What makes you think I lied?" Talitha replied, gently rubbing her swollen cheek.

"Gypsies are masters at lying. They know when someone ain't tellin' the truth. Markam knows. He's jus' tryna scare you into tellin' the truth by promisin' that Moko has his way wit' ya. Ya tell him the truth and he'll not force ya to be wit' Moko … but if ya don't, mark my word, it won't go well for ya."

She said nothing, and he shook his head in dismay. "If ya can't tell Markam or me, talk wit' Angie, she 'as a good heart."

He looked at her sadly and scratched the crown of his red head. He didn't know what to do to help the poor creature. She reminded him of his daughter.

"Still, if ya've been at the castle it's a wonder Master Jockim hasn't had his way wit' ya— pretty, little thing that ya are. But then again maybe he cares for ya, and that's why he ain't takin' advantage of ya. That would make sense … him wantin' to get ya out of the castle now that the fightin' started. They say that he's different to 'is father, Jockhein … more of a gentleman, so to speak."

He headed for the entrance, not expecting her to reply. Lifting the scarf, he turned to look at her. She eyed him back suspiciously.

"Is Konfra there?"

"Yes, how do you know the general?"

Flynn threw his head back and roared with laughter. "Everyone knows the general. He's the most powerful man on the island, lass. Are his sons with 'im?"

"Yes, Vadio and Raybet are fighting with him alongside Jockim for the castle."

"Loyal to the end to the Deerie clan ... Old Konfra will end up dying for Doomeerie and taking his sons to 'eir graves along wit' 'im."

He shook his head again and without another word, he turned and left the cabin. Talitha ran to the golden cage and tried to unlock the door, but it held tight. It was only a few minutes before Angie re-entered the cabin.

"Ya won't be able open it," she said nonchalantly. "There's a secret to it ... only Flynn and I know." She flung herself down on the pillows and threw her hands behind the golden, red halo that framed her face. "Toby's out playing with some young 'uns, so I thought I's come an' chat wit' ya."

Talitha looked down angrily at her and said nothing.

"Why did ya lie, Tal?"

"Who says I did? And how do you know what I said anyway? Were you listening?"

The same, shady look that had been on Angie's face the evening before when she spoke about the golden cage, drifted momentarily across it again.

"Couldn't help but 'ear some of it," she answered unabashedly, "and when I saw Moko leaving the cabin grinning from ear to ear, I knew what would 'ave happened. When 'ave ya gotta be wit' 'im? Now or when he returns?"

Talitha looked away, her eyes filling up with tears. She crouched in a bundle on the floor and began to shake with pent up emotion. It was too much for her: the imprisonment, whipping, Shiloh's fight, leaving Doomeerie and Jockim, and finally being captured by the gypsies and promised as a whore to save Pover's life. The sobbing wrenched freely.

Angie walked quietly over to the cage and unlocked the golden gate. Pover flew out and landed on her arm.

"I'm sorry, Tal." Angie placed her hand on her shoulder. "I truly am, but Flynn and I can't 'elp ya till ya tell us the truth … only then can we get Markam to change 'is mind."

Between bouts of sobbing Talitha blurted out her story: her efforts to save Shiloh from Doomeerie, her feelings for Jockim, her punishment when found trying to escape, and finally, Jockim setting her free. She was careful not to divulge the secret entrance to the castle via the south wing, as she did not want to place her Doomeerie friends in any kind of danger. Instead, she made up a story that Jockim had sent a trusted, young soldier to get her across the river.

Angie attentively asked questions here and there, trying to make sense of Talitha's disjointed tale. She then set about arranging a fresh bed for her and told her to sleep while she tried to sort out things with Flynn and Markam. It was several hours later and almost dark when Flynn re-entered the cabin with his daughter.

Angie woke Talitha and presented her with a light meal of soup and bread. While she ate, Flynn talked.

"I hope ya'r feelin' a bit better, lass. Angie has told Markam and me of yer tale. Quite an adventure ya've had … No wonder ya'r so tired." He stopped waiting for her to reply, but as she said nothing, he continued.

"Seeing ya told the truth, Markam 'as said that he 'as told Moko that he can't have 'is way wit' ya. The lad will not force himself upon ya now that ya've spoken out. When folk are true to us, we return the favour. Ya'll be safe for the time being, an' we'll make sure that ya'll come to no harm. Yer pet bird can come out at day but will 'ave to be locked in at nights. That way we know ya won't try an escape. Do ya understand?"

"Yes, thank you." Talitha was grateful for the promise of protection, at least for the time being until she could figure out a way of getting herself and Pover out of the camp.

"Righteo, it's all settled!" Flynn kissed his daughter goodnight.

"Love ya, dad." She giggled, patting his red head softly with the palm of her hand. "Ya'r a good father and a great pop too. Toby and I are lucky to 'ave ya."

He smiled warmly back at her and stood to leave. "I'll leave ya girls to talk. Get some time together before Margie turns in for the night." He turned to Talitha and smiled. "I'm glad that Angie 'as a new friend. She needs some woman company who can talk about things that interest 'er. Margie's more of a child than a friend. Good night, Tal. I'll see ya in the morning. Rest assured … ya'll be safe tonight. Ya've me word."

Angie grinned at Talitha after he had left. "Don't know what I'd ever do without 'im. He's saved me skin many a time."

"What from, the punishment for lying?"

"What da ya mean by that?" The red headed woman sounded slightly put out.

"Oh come on, Angie, I know you haven't always been truthful with me either."

"What da ya mean?" she repeated, feigning astonishment.

"Last night when I was asking you about Freedom and the cage, I saw the look on your face. You gypsies stole it from the merchant didn't you?"

Angie looked sheepish. "Alright ... yeah we did, but if ya ever leave this place, which I doubt ya ever will cause Markam will wanna keep ya 'ere so that he has some bargaining power wit' Jockim, ya mus' na say so. It could mean big trouble for us."

"Why, surely people are used to gypsies taking stuff. That's what they do, don't they?"

"Ya'r startin' to sound like 'em high an' mighty town folk, Tal," Angie retorted hotly. "Jus' remember the big favour that's been done for ya."

"I'm sorry; I didn't mean it that way. It's just that it's only a bird cage, even if it is made of gold."

Angie looked at her, deep in thought. "Ah, I guess there's no harm tellin', ya'r not likely to be goin' anywhere, and ya've been clean wit' me."

Talitha stared at her, not knowing what to say.

"Have ya 'eard of White Cliff Castle, south of Shulam? The cage an' the bird come from 'ere."

"No, I haven't ... I thought that Doomeerie was the only castle on the island."

"That'd be right—Doomeerie folk think the world starts 'n ends wit' 'em." Angie smirked. "White Cliff Castle is on the west coast, south of the place they call Shulam—long way from Doomeerie." Her blue eyes flashed intriguingly. She was about to divulge a strange secret. "Issac White, 'e never had much to do wit' the Doomeerie clan. Kept to 'imself 'e did. 'E 'ad no need to, I guess. He 'ad everything anyone could ever want for, livin' out there on them beautiful, white cliffs overlookin' the ocean. Suppose e'd also 'eard of the Doomeerie curse an' didn't want to get caught up wit' it, but 'is luck changed for 'im after 'is first wife died givin' birth to 'is daughter, Anita."

She twisted her long, lean body on its side, curving her femininity around a shabby, old cushion. "He loved 'er so much that 'e was heartbroken an' in spite of 'is wealth 'e never had the sense to know a good woman from a bad one. He married quickly ag'in to a woman from the Oge clan. Ebony was 'er name, or should I say, is 'er name … She still lives wit' him out there."

"Who are the Oge clan? Are they gypsies?"

"Hell no … ya ain't 'eard of the Oge?" Angie sprung up in surprise. Talitha shook her head.

"God forbid girl, I would 'ave thought that Padyah would 'ave warned ya about' em!"

"What about them?"

"The Oge are clans scattered over the west side of the River Styx. They are evil folk. They become friendly wit' ya an' twist yer mind so that ya think ya'r doin' good, when really ya'r doing badly! Then they twist yer mind back ag'in, so ya see how bad ya are, an' ya hate yerself … Ya can't live wit' yerself, so ya turn into a zombie, an' they feed off yer brain!"

"What do you mean, 'feed off your brain'?" A creeping sensation had begun to crawl across Talitha's flesh.

"Jus' what I said … They take all the energy from yer thoughts. Make ya hate yerself so much that ya don't wanna think, so ya become an empty shell of a person jus' walking around eatin' and workin' without thinkin'—like ya'r a moron." She lent close to Talitha. "Not like Margie," she whispered. "She's jus' slow witted. Those that the Oge get control o'er, 'em folk," she shook her head, "they are creepy … like the walkin' dead."

Talitha shifted uncomfortably as a tingle of fear shuddered down her spine.

"Yeah … after he married Ebony 'is luck changed. Wild storms came from the west, and waves the size of mountains hit that coast. Damn near took most of them white cliffs away out to sea. Strangely enough the castle was left standin' on a rocky outcrop, with a land drawbridge barely the size of a horse dray leadin' out to it."

Angie's blue eyes widened, mirroring the wonder of her description of the uncanny occurrence. "Isaac lost all 'is ships in them storms and couldn't afford to get supplies sent out to him, livin' way out there on the west coast. He wanted to move back in closer to the towns, but Ebony wouldn't 'ear of it. At least that's what they say. She talked 'im into leasing the beautiful hummingbird to a merchant at Southport, in payment for food and money. They say he didn't wanna part wit' the bird." She looked dreamily at Freedom.

"Legend holds that it came to the castle the night Anita was born and sung the most exquisite song. The girl kept the bird as a pet, and when it was sent away, she wouldn't talk or eat. She would run into the forest lookin' for it, an' one day she got lost an' was never seen agin. Ole

Isaac was broken hearted and the bird they say stopped singin'. 'Bout that time, us gypsies came across it and took it 'cause that merchant had done us wrong in some dealings. Wish we hadn't now. I reckon the damn thing has been cursed in some way by the Oge."

"Was the child ever found?"

"Yeah, some travellers told us that they 'ad 'eard that she was found by poachers. She couldn't talk an' tell 'em who she was, so they took 'er to the east coast and gave 'er to some folk to care for. That's all I know. Isaac and Ebony never did get 'er back. Nobody ever said they 'ad seen 'er, even though Isaac travelled to the east to ask about 'er."

"That is sad ... No wonder Freedom doesn't sing anymore."

"Yeah, well I reckon that golden cage is bewitched."

Talitha looked at it, gleaming beautifully under the soft light of the lantern. It was exquisite, but only its occupants held any interest to her. Once again, Pover lay on its floor with the turquoise hummingbird resting upon the soft down of her body. The sudden shaking of the cabin jolted her thoughts back to the present. Her eyes scanned the door. The tubby figure of Margie emerged from behind the shabby scarf.

"Why is she wit' us ag'in tonight, Angie?" she whined, eyeing Talitha sullenly. "I wan 'er to go."

"It's alright Margie. Tal is gonna be our friend."

"Ya'r me friend Ange, not 'er ... I don't like 'er!"

"Ya will wit' time, Margie ..." Angie tucked her in under a grubby blanket. "Good night now."

Talitha turned her body to the wall. Her eyes were beginning to fill with tears, and she shut them tightly. Once again, she longed to be back at Doomeerie.

CHAPTER 3

The Return of Jenobay

If Talitha had learned anything from her time at Doomeerie, it was to trust, embrace the present and wait for the appointed time for change. The silver goblet was a continual reminder for her that she must drink deeply from the present before moving on. So, knowing that escape from the gypsy camp would be impossible for quite some time, she set her mind to getting to know these earthy, yet kind folk.

It was not hard to build friendships with both Angie and Margie. Neither of them had partners as the number of young women in the gypsy camp far outnumbered that of the men. Angie's life was devoted to her boy, and she showed no interest in developing any kind of romantic relationship, despite the fact that her wild beauty would have made her highly desirable. She had been loved and abandoned once, and she was not the kind of woman to repeat mistakes in life. Despite her down to earth nature, she had a keen spirit for adventure and when roused, a fiery temper that did justice to her mane of red, gold hair. Any of the men who might have considered taking advantage of her thought twice as she knew how to stand up for herself. Besides, Flynn was always there to keep an eye out for her. The group held him in high esteem for his kind and wise ways, and when Markam was away, Flynn was the undisputed next in charge.

Margie, the cabin's other occupant, was a simple soul, slow of wits and speech. She had a dumpy solid frame, with a moon-like face, punctured by hazy, blue eyes that stared somewhat dully from under heavily, folded lids. Although she was very happy most times, she could become extremely obstinate and upset when events occurred contrary to her wishes. Angie was pleased to have the company of Talitha, as Margie was so immature. Many times, she felt like she had two children to care for. However being a kind, generous soul, she was happy to attend to her needs, along with Toby's.

The other women were not so friendly towards Talitha and often eyed her suspiciously. Her pretty features and slender body posed a threat to them. Many did not trust their menfolk, especially after they had been drinking. They, like Markam, were well aware of the trouble that she could cause in the camp and took pains to keep her away from them. She spent her days helping with the domestic tasks and caring for the children. Sometimes she, Angie, Margie, and Toby, would venture forth into the woods to explore. Pover remained close by her side on such occasions and was well loved by her cabin companions.

Pover also spent a lot of time with Freedom, trying to encourage her to eat. In fact, both birds became inseparable, and

Freedom did appear to improve a little. Every night Pover would lie on the bottom of the cage, allowing her to rest her frail body on her huddled feathers. Talitha fancied that Pover's brown feathers were becoming lighter, but it was difficult for her to tell with any degree of certainty.

They had been in the camp for some weeks, when an incident happened that finally earned her trust from the entire clan. She was in the forest with some gypsy women and children collecting berries, when they heard Margie begin to scream. Dumping her basket, Angie quickly scooped up Toby. She and Talitha bolted in the direction of the commotion. The other women and children hurried along behind.

Angie's lean, athletic frame ensured that she was first to arrive. She stopped dead in her tracks. Margie, crouched up against a cluster of rocks, was screaming hysterically—a tigress advancing stealthily towards her. Within seconds, Talitha was there beside Angie. Their sudden movements caused the animal to spring into action. She bounded towards Margie with remarkable speed. Talitha's mind locked into the past.

"Jenobay, no!" she shrieked.

To everyone's utter amazement the tigress stopped. She turned to face Talitha. Instinctively, she bounded towards her. The others watched, horrified. With a playful leap, Jenobay tossed Talitha gently on the ground and began licking her face.

Struggling to her feet, Talitha briefly outlined her and Jenobay's shared history. The entire group stared, dumbfounded. As the terror slowly subsided, they all took turns at petting Jenobay, although Margie could not be coaxed to do so. Staying well back, she stared at the others, especially Talitha in a state of sullen shock. Her feeble mind grappled with the event. She whispered suspiciously to her closest companion, "How does Tal 'ave power to stop the tigress? Maybe she be a witch or somethin' of the sort?"

After some time the women left. Talitha stayed on with Jenobay. She was overjoyed to be reunited with her friend. They played together for hours. Towards dusk, Angie arrived back with some rabbit for the tigress and encouraged Talitha to come back to camp. She reluctantly headed back.

Back at the camp, she was bestowed a hero's welcome. One and all embraced her. She was given pride of place at the evening meal. Everyone wanted to know about Jenobay. The group decided that, should the tigress appear again, they would feed her, as she may well afford them protection in the future.

Jenobay did indeed stay close to camp, and the gypsy folk always kept aside a share of their catch for her. In the evenings, Talitha and Pover could sense her presence lurking in the shadows behind the trees, and in the morning, the food that had been laid out for her was always gone.

Regularly, they would meet her when out gathering nuts or berries. Angie, in particular began to forge a special kinship with the tigress. Their spirits seemed to be one and the same, so wild, adventurous and courageous. Talitha was happy knowing that should she ever leave, they would be there to care for each other.

Such times helped to make her and Pover's stay a lot happier. Indeed, thanks to Jenobay's presence they were now in the hearts, as well as the home of the gypsy people. Having lost the friendship of those at Doomeerie, it was easy for Talitha and Pover to stay on with the gypsies. The thought of moving onto Southport and Edgewater had now drifted from Talitha's mind and only arose periodically. Nonetheless, she frequently dreamed of Jockim, Shiloh, and Doomeerie, and she even wondered about returning. How could she ever hope to be reunited with any of them by going further away?

News from the gypsy scouts who travelled further up the river was that the battle was still raging, but none could say which side had the advantage. There seemed no point in Talitha trying to return. She reasoned that if she stayed nearby, she may one day go back. The weeks drifted into months. Finally, a day dawned that would stay etched in her mind forever. She was invited to accompany the elders to see the enigmatic Kyriedor, the one that the gypsies believed to be a great prophet. Some even called him son of the Great Spirit.

CHAPTER 4

Kyriedor's Cabin

I t was not far to Kyriedor's cabin. Indeed, Talitha had unwittingly been that way many times before. She had never seen the entrance as it was well hidden behind a dense clump of bushes. Only those who wanted to discover it or who were led to it, could find it. The cabin backed into a large cave. One entered via a crevice in the rocks into a smaller cave and then clambered through further rocks into a larger, interior cave, which in turn opened into Kyriedor's cabin. The latter was well hidden by a huge, circular outcrop of heavy boulders.

Talitha immediately warmed to Kyriedor. He was a lean, muscular man, in his late twenties, somewhat taller than average, with a humble air of quiet confidence. His tanned, sculptured face was bearded, and lined by wavy, dark hair that hung loosely to his shoulders. He had the kindest, most pleasant face that she had ever beheld. However, it was his eyes that captivated her. These deep, soulful pools filled with compassion the moment they gazed upon her. Immediately, she eased into his presence, drawn to him in a way that she had never before experienced. In fact, she had the sensation that they had met before, maybe in another lifetime. He seemed to possess the most intimate knowledge of her spirit, yet despite knowing her darkest secrets, focused solely upon her finest qualities. In fact, for the first time in her life, she felt truly respected and esteemed. It was a warm, homely feeling that swelled benevolently into her hollow, lonely spaces.

The sensation filled her with such peace that her eyes brimmed with emotion when she was introduced to him. Embarrassed, she quickly brushed away the moisture. He pretended that he hadn't noticed and after welcoming her in his warm embrace, went on to do the same with the eleven other members of the gypsy clan who had accompanied her.

They sat down around a rough, wooden table, animated in his presence. He insisted on waiting upon them, despite their protests. Angie, Talitha, and Margie, rose to help. The atmosphere was unpretentious and laughter reverberated in the cabin. The jovial spirit continued for quite some time, until the gypsies settled and began to discuss their concerns. They were furious that one of their scouts had been killed in the crossfire for the castle.

"Will t'eir damned fightin' nair stop?" The intense edge in Markam's voice dampened any trace of frivolity which remained in the room. "We've lost 'nuther man. Moko was killed last week when scoutin up t'ere. T'eir greed is destroyin' us, an' I for one am tired of sittin' back watchin' innocent lives lost an' crops an' livestock destroyed."

"'Ere, 'ere!" The men's voices resounded around the table.

"Thank God old Liza died last winter … rest 'er soul. It would 'ave destroyed 'er to see 'er only son killed."

"Yes, an' they say if Andor takes over the castle, he'll be worse than Jockim."

Kyriedor shot a quick glance at Talitha as Markam continued. "He'll not jus' 'ave the animals fight. He'll tax the town folk heavily again, and there'll be 'ard times ahead for us all. Us gypsies 're likely to be rounded up 'an taken t'ere to work as slaves for the Doomeerie folk."

"We must do something, Kyriedor? What would ya 'ave us do? Now's the time! We must rise up. We'll do whatever ya say."

There was silence around the table. They waited for him to speak. He bowed his head for a few minutes and then looking steadily at them he spoke calmly, the confidence in his inner convictions shining through his simple statements.

"The fighting will not last forever. To join in would only worsen the situation. It would mean further loss for your people, Markam. Just wait! The castle folk seem bad because we do not know them, but they too have hearts and souls just like ours. They have lost their way that is all."

"'Nd while we wait for 'em to change, we put our own people in danger." One of the younger men broke in impatiently.

"Trust, Babus!" Kyriedor lent forward placing his hand upon the other man's shoulder. "You gain nothing but your own death by fighting against your brothers. Our father, Padyah, is in that area. He is not taking up arms, nor instructing the wild beasts to attack. We must do as he does and trust that the Great Spirit has a plan in this. Trust that peace will come for those at Doomeerie and for all of us."

He looked searchingly at them all, his eyes pleading for a hint of compassion. "In truth I tell you, it is not the men of Doomeerie that you must be fearful of but rather the Oge. A little of their ways has infiltrated us all."

Ignoring his final remark, Markam spoke out impatiently. "There is no good in sitting back an' waitin' for peace to jus' 'appen. By 'en it may be too late for our folk."

"The one who will help to take Doomeerie to peace is already in our midst, Markam," Kyriedor replied quietly, his gaze resting lovingly upon Talitha.

Eleven pairs of eyes stared at her in shock. Not Talitha? Not the slip of a maiden whom they had stumbled across in the forest? How could she possibly change fate?

An uncomfortably long silence followed. Angie cleared her throat. "Well she 'ad power wit' the tigress, who knows what she could do at Doomeerie," she said, trying to convince herself as much as anyone else.

Flynn grunted in agreement. The others said nothing, while a couple of uneasy sniggers followed. Margie joined in the laughter, thinking that it was a smart thing to do.

"How's she going to do anything?" Jariot, one of the more learned of the gypsies, scoffed.

"Padyah has sent Talitha to you not to fight against the castle forces," Kyriedor replied, "but to lead them to peace and true understanding. She will do that by finding it herself first. She has known for some time that she is to make a journey, and the time for it has now come."

He smiled encouragingly at her. Rising from the table, he walked to an old chest, opened it, and removed a leather bound manuscript. He held it reverently, affording it great respect.

"Something for you to study my young friend before you commence on the journey that you are required to take."

She reddened a little. *Kyriedor must be the man that Padyah intended me to meet.* Her mind raced on. *Does he realise that I have deliberately postponed travelling further south to prolong my comfort and security?*

For his part Kyriedor had long since prayed for the compassion to stop judging. He therefore made no outward sign that he was aware or disapproved of her delayed actions. "You know in your heart my friend that now is the time to set out. This manuscript will help you understand what to do."

"Thank you." She took the thick book feeling a sense of excitement and fear. The others remained quiet, eyeing her sceptically as he continued to explain its contents.

"There is much that you will not understand in it. You are welcome back to discuss its contents any time that you like. I am very familiar with the material in it and can only strive to live it out. I sense that there are many challenges ahead of me, but the time to begin teaching publically has not yet been made manifest to me."

He paused for a minute lost in his own thoughts and then continued. "In the meantime, I meditate upon its meaning and await my instructions. One of which has been to pass on *The Tao of Trust* to a young maiden named Talitha, who desires to keep watch in the night."

"I feel this task is too great for me," she mumbled, weighed down by her fears. *Surely, there is some mistake. It could not be me who is chosen.*

Sensing her anxiety, he continued on encouragingly. "You will indeed be embarking on your hardest journey yet, a journey to the underworld, your fourth task. There are few that choose to go there in their lifetime, but the rewards are enormous. Such a journey will assist you to remove all barriers to love in your life."

She looked down at the leather manuscript. Hope and dread simultaneously drenched through her mind, leaving her confused. She did not know what to say. The honour that had been bestowed upon her was far too great, and the sheer responsibility of it had already begun to weigh heavily.

Kyriedor smiled supportively. "You only need try. With each new challenge, you need only to try once more. You will have relapses. That is part of the journey." His eyes held a great tenderness. "We never get there perfectly in our bodily state, but when you have travelled far enough, you will be lifted out of the confines of flesh, and the spirit will make up for what cannot be attained by the body."

He stopped and silence hung heavily in the room. All eyes were upon her. She felt the intensity of their ignorance and disbelief boring into her heart.

"There are many ways to attain peace, but they all take the course of trust—a wild and windswept way. You have already experienced much undoing, I sense." Speaking tenderly, he took her hand into his. "There have been many painful changes in your external world, but you have not yet recognised that all changes are helpful. You must transfer your trust to all situations." He looked at her intently, and she sensed his uncompromising belief in her.

"What is stopping you from travelling on, Talitha? You must ask Spirit to guide you. Trust you will be given the light of true understanding. Learn to lay your own judgement aside. You will find that the Holy One's will is your way in every circumstance. Then and only then, will you experience real tranquillity."

Silence settled upon the cabin. Kyriedor had a way of making everything appear shining and new when he spoke. His charisma convinced others that anything was possible for the one who believes. Yet Talitha's mind was a bustling marketplace of misgivings.

"If you desire to be reunited with Shiloh and to obtain inner peace, you must trust this way."

The gypsies stared at her, sensing the deep struggle that was arising in her life. They knew that Kyriedor was encouraging her to follow his counsel. However, they did not understand the deeper losses that this would entail for her.

How can I leave the security of the gypsy camp which I have only just found? More and more misgivings kept tumbling into the troubled stream of thoughts that was trickling into her mind. *I may never see Jockim again. At any time, I can return to Doomeerie. If I journey to the underworld, I might never be able to come back. Will I ever have the chance of seeing Shiloh and Balaamine again? Have I only just been reunited with Jenobay to say goodbye? Surely, this is not meant to be. It is so unfair, after all that I have already been through. How much more, can be asked of me?"*

Still, the look of love and encouragement in his eyes beckoned her forth. He stood and bowed before her. The others seeing him do so instinctively followed. Then he laid his hands upon her shoulders, saying, "Do not fear for your gypsy and castle friends. They will be here when you return. You must entrust them to the Great Spirit, whose care for his creatures is beyond your understanding."

He leaned forward and breathed softly upon her, whispering into her ear, "Talitha, trust your truth … transcend!"

She felt her spirit fill with an abundance of love and peace at the sound of his voice and the sensation of his warm, gentle breath. So profound was the experience that it burst forth from her features in an affluence of joy. "Thank you," she whispered. "Yes, I will try."

He smiled at her so tenderly that she wanted to melt into his arms, losing herself in his loving embrace forever. The sensation lasted all the way back to the camp. Her friends, noticing that she was very quiet, assumed that she was preoccupied with the seemingly monumental task that awaited her. They respectfully left her to the privacy of her own thoughts.

Stepping back into the gypsy cabin, she placed the manuscript on the table. She glanced towards the golden cage and saw Pover and Freedom nestled together. Suddenly, her newfound peace was torn asunder. She realised that Kyriedor had meant that her little companion from the beginning was not to go with her. Pover's place for the present was with Freedom. The immensity of her task suddenly broke through into her consciousness, descending upon her with savage force. She collapsed in a huddle on the floor sobbing wretchedly.

This journey is far too much to ask of anyone, she thought, *let alone me. I do not possess this level of trust. How can I release my very soul to the great unknown?*

CHAPTER 5

A Legend That Lives On

"Do you know of the legend of Doomeerie?" Talitha eagerly questioned Kyriedor. She had grown so close to him over the past few weeks as they had studied *The Tao of Trust* together. Surely, he would not deny her curiosity like the others at the castle had. She felt that no question was too trite or personal to inquire of him.

"Hasn't anyone at the castle told you?"

"No one, Kyriedor, I suspect that they were ordered not to repeat it, for whomever I asked either said they didn't know or would cleverly avert the topic."

"Ahh, Master Jockim wants no part of it I gather and yet his actions towards you and Shiloh would indicate that it still plays a very real part in his thoughts." He went quiet. Talitha looked at him intently. "Yes ... a strange place Doomeerie ... full of uncanny happenings ... I'm not surprised at all that Jockim doesn't want it

173

repeated. The men in his family don't have a great reputation. No doubt he wants to disassociate himself from them."

He leaned back in his chair, bequeathing himself the required comfort to commence a long tale. After a deep breath, he began the strange story.

"The legend of doom that befalls the castle occupants began many years ago in the era of Jockim's great grandfather, Joab Deerie. He was a fine man who had built the castle at a young age and had two sons. He loved them both dearly, and the boys grew up happily enough together. Yes, they were competitive and eager to prove themselves as boys are, but character and temperament took them in different directions."

He looked tenderly towards Talitha, pleased that she felt some peace in his presence. Her eyes widened delightfully as he continued.

"The younger son, Lachlan, was a keen traveller. He made quite a bit of money for the castle by selling the island's produce abroad. Back then, almost three quarters of the island belonged to Doomeerie. They were prosperous times indeed! The sale of the cargo made enough for the family to live lavishly, as well as provide for the folk on the land. In fact, the castle was known as Deerie Castle ... an affection name for the place which was well loved by the islanders. It came to be known as such, not just because of the Deerie Family name but also due to the large numbers of deers located in the then known Night Forest ... now called Nightmare Forest, which borders the castle on the eastern side, as you know."

"But I thought Jockim told me that it had been called Eerie Castle after the cliffs that the River Styx fords?"

"Yes indeed, that is so, but that name came later."

He immediately picked up on her impatience. A wave of compassion swelled within him. Such eagerness may well be the cause of much trouble for her. Yet, they still had ample time to study *The Tao* before she returned to Doomeerie. He quietened his concern.

"Now, where was I. Ah yes, Lachlan was a shrewd business man and always ensured that he got good prices when abroad. However, the older of the two sons, Luke, was more favoured by the town folk. They knew him better. A humble man, he worked with them and helped them cultivate the land. Back in those days, the Valley of Loss, then known as the Valley of Plenty, was a heavily cultivated area producing more than enough food for the island's occupants. It had such an oversupply that Lachlan was able to sell it abroad."

Talitha studied his sun-soaked features. She had grown to love their angles. What fortune had brought her into the home of this wise and compassionate soul? Surely she was undeserving of it?

"Luke fell in love and eventually married a young woman named Clare, daughter of the local rector—pretty little thing. She was working as a maidservant at the castle. You never saw any paintings of her at the castle?" He smiled at her inquiringly. She shook her head. "I guess that they've all been taken down. She was a kind soul and never forgot to care for the town folk even when she became mistress of the castle. Legend goes that she would often be seen visiting the sick or needy at the town. Anyway, shortly after their marriage she became pregnant, but sadly the baby was still born."

His features hollowed a little, being no stranger to sadness. He had seen what the Oge could do to men. Those at Doomeerie had suffered much by yielding to their persuasive powers. Still, he must continue. If Talitha was to assist with the freeing of Doomeerie folk, she had to know the truth surrounding its past.

"Meanwhile around that time Lachlan brought home a bride also—an exquisitely beautiful woman from abroad. He had hardly been home with her for long when he decided to leave again to make more money and was away for several months. The poor woman was very lonely, especially as being a foreigner she couldn't speak the language. Legend has it that she would often be seen walking along Eerie Cliffs, staring at the river making its way down the gorge, or standing at the summit of the waterfall, a solitary figure with her beautiful, dark hair blowing in the wind. It must have been hard for her, with her new husband away, living in a strange land. Clare was kind to her, but she had her own family and friends, and she was still recovering from the death of her son, so this woman, known as Sarai, was left alone a lot. It was not long however, before she too was seen to be pregnant." He shook his head sadly, preempting what he was about to reveal.

"Well, Lachlan arrived home before the confinement date and was shocked to find Sarai with child. For whatever reason he refused to believe that the child was his own, and he began to throw suspicion upon his elder brother. Luke vehemently denied the accusation; nevertheless, it created great upset in the family, especially between him and Clare. Indeed, matters became so bad that it began to divide the kingdom between those who supported Luke, and those who believed Lachlan."

"Some reasoned that Lachlan had lied in a deliberate attempt to destroy his brother's reputation, so he would lose popularity. That way his father would be forced to hand the kingdom over to him to ensure peace. This was a reasonable assumption as Clare was well loved by the town folk, and if Luke had cheated upon her they would never have been able to forgive him."

A slight movement nearby drew his attention. He stood and peered through the stone framed door. "Jenobay," he exclaimed affectionately, "you've come to join your mistress!"

The tigress stared up at him, the fire in her eyes softening. She slumped effortlessly to the stone floor beside Talitha, feline and fluid in motion. He gently massaged her neck, meeting the flame behind her eyes with a deep love.

"An ancient power—you emanate the self-possession of the spirit, my beautiful tigress." He stroked her admiringly. "Soon you will bequeath our young friend, Talitha, a little of your courage, but for the present, lie by her side."

His eyes attuned to the momentary fear that flickered through Talitha's expression. *What does he mean by that?* Her mind scurried quickly in a dozen, different directions. Reading her apprehension, he quickly drew her back into the present.

"Now, where was I?" He stretched out casually on the stone floor beside them, resting his head into his arms. Staring up at the thatched roof, he continued. "Oh yes, the mystery surrounding Sarai's confinement. Well, others felt that perhaps Lachlan was telling the truth, for although Luke was a good man he had an eye for pretty women, and there was none to compare with the beauty of Sarai. At times, Luke and she had been seen walking the cliffs together. Whatever the truth of the matter was, no one will ever definitely know. Sarai could not throw any light upon the confusion as she was unable to understand or speak English. Luke maintained his innocence. He was devastated that he had lost his child, and that his relationship with his young wife had been permanently damaged. Lachlan was furious at his older brother, believing him to have seduced his wife."

He stopped again, and she wondered why. His glance had fleetingly alighted upon her. Just what was the enigma that it held? If only she could understand him better. He seemed to be able to read her so well, yet he was so deep, so mysterious at times. Again, she was struck by the notion that he was about to request something of her, but instead he continued.

"Not surprisingly a rift developed between the brothers that caused much sorrow to their old father. This rift only worsened when Sarai died giving birth to a son, Jockhein, Jockim's father. Lachlan could not be consoled, and he blamed his brother for her death. Not long after this, Luke's body was found dead in Night Forest. He had been stabbed and left to drown in the marshes. Suspicion of course fell to Lachlan, but no proof could be had. The news was too much for their old father who passed away about six months after that."

He sighed with a deep heave of sadness. The utter waste of it all sank heavily upon him. A flickering spark of uneasiness shot through her. It lodged in the pit of her stomach, expanding into a sickening sense of guilt. *Why? I was not part of this madness. Yet aren't the same emotions of bitterness and anger festering deep within me too?* She dismissed the notion quickly. *That is not true. I was a victim. It is only natural that I should sometimes feel hostile towards those who hurt me—after all they are to blame, not me. I was righteous in my actions, only attempting to procure Shiloh's freedom.* She forced her mind back to the story. Kyriedor was speaking again.

"So the castle and land naturally went to Lachlan. He took Clare for himself, and she bore him three children, a boy whom he named Brody and two daughters, Charlotte and Catalina. He was a bitter man, confused and twisted in his dealings, siding first with one son, Jockhein, and then with the other, Brody. He could never decide if Jockhein was his first born son or not, but he was naturally drawn to the boy because he looked so much like his mother, Sarai, while at the same time having the manner and ways of himself. The other lad, Brody, grew up with Clare's colouring and complexion and was drawn to farm life and the town folk. Over the years both lads developed an intense jealousy of the other and were always unsure as to who would inherit the land and the castle."

Again he stopped, staring at her abruptly and intently. "Watch your thoughts and feelings, Talitha! They are the flames behind your eyes. They can destroy the world or set it alight with wisdom. You must stay awake and keep watch in the darkness of your mind. Douse the flames of hate and fear, but not before you have listened to what they are asking of you. They speak of a hidden unmet need, deep within you. You think that they are private, but their energy forges on with a force mightier than Doomeerie Falls, carving the landscape of your life." He was momentarily silent and then smiled a little, less serious now. "What was I saying …?"

Within seconds, the story was unfolding further. "In the meantime strange occurrences were observed around the cliffs and in Night Forest. Many claimed to have seen the ghosts of Sarai and

Luke walking along the cliffs together. Some reported seeing Luke riding madly through the forest in a rage, killing all life in sight, while others maintained that Sarai could be heard moaning for her baby around the cliffs at night. Hence, the name Eerie Castle and Nightmare Forest developed. For some uncanny reason the herds of deer moved north out of Nightmare Forest and rarely returned. Stories developed of travellers becoming lost in the forest. Indeed, very few who entered it survived to tell their story, and those that did spoke of being afflicted by nightmares of their greatest fears. These men were never the same again, many of them becoming raving lunatics. The kingdom of the Oge was making rapid advances, yet few were wise enough to discern it."

Talitha felt a shiver tingle its way down her back. Any mention of the Oge always alarmed her. Kyriedor had indicated that it was easy to be taken under their spell; a little laziness of the mind, a failure to try and live one's truth. Thank goodness she was with him. A sense of security settled cosily upon her troubled thoughts again.

"The final tragedy occurred when Catalina, Lachlan and Clare's youngest child, lost her footing and fell into the river. She was playing with a daughter of one of the maids at the castle when it happened. They had ventured too close to the bank. This little girl reached to grab her and also fell in. Charlotte, Catalina's elder sister was reported to have gone in after both girls, but the current was too treacherous. She had no hope of saving them and grabbed onto an overhanging branch. Later, she was pulled to safety. Little Catalina and the other child were swept over the falls; hence the name, Valley of Loss. Poor Clare could bear no more sorrow in her life. She had lost two children. She had stayed in a loveless marriage with Lachlan, where she believed herself to be an object of revenge for Luke's perceived adultery. Sometime later, during a severe winter, she developed pneumonia and not having the strength of body or will to fight it, she passed away. Many began to call the castle 'Doomeerie', saying that those who occupied it were doomed to pay dearly for their sinful ways."

Jenobay yawned and stretched her superb stripes across the stone surface. Talitha fancied that the tigress had heard it all before, that she somehow knew it in her heart. Yet, she did not seem at all perturbed. Kyriedor patted her again, continuing his tale.

"Jockhein grew up with such stories, and it was not surprising that after his father died he wanted to throw off the curse. He became strict to the point of merciless, and everyone who transgressed in any manner was severely punished. Brody could not stand for his ways, and he eventually left the castle taking Charlotte with him. They went to live with the townsfolk in Woodlark. Times were hard. Jockhein could not manage the castle as well as go abroad like Lachlan had once done, so he was forced to tax the townsfolk. Successive seasons of bad weather witnessed less and less produce, and heavier taxes were imposed to cover expenses." He sat up shaking his head sadly. The tale was a long and unsettling one. He eyed Talitha carefully. Was it too much for her? Still, it was important that she know.

"General Konfra was one of Jockhein's finest commanders. He was devoted to him and managed to bring in a little from the much smaller fleet of merchant ships. On one trip, he brought home a beautiful, young maiden who had been orphaned at a young age. The childless couple who had raised her had both died, and she was forced to find work to survive. Her name was Miriam. She was tall and slender, not unlike Sarai to look at, with flowing, dark locks that fell about her shoulders in soft waves. However, her features were of European descent, not Arabian, and her skin was fair. With eyes like a doe that stole deep into your soul and a gentle, caring manner, she captured Jockhein's heart. He loved her deeply. During the time that they were together, his ways softened, and the town folk even began to accept him. However, she died giving birth to Jockim and the rest you know."

"Oh, how sad," Talitha intervened. "Yes, Jockim did seem to have a strange sense of guilt and self-loathing about his mother's death."

"I daresay his father blamed him for it, from the earliest of ages. Jockhein was broken hearted and believed that the curse of the castle had befallen him. He sunk into greater debt and had to tax the townsfolk more and more. The people turned against him, and forces from the south under the leadership of Brody, rallied and attacked. Jockhein lost much of his land, to the extent of that which exists today. Brody was killed in battle, but his eldest son, Andor has stepped forward to avenge his father in the recent resurgence of fighting at Doomeerie. And so you see Tal, the war had nothing to do with your having attempted to escape, although the general, knowing the legend, would have had the soldiers believe otherwise."

"Poor Jockim …" Talitha sighed. "No wonder he never wanted to discuss his ancestors."

"Yes, indeed … He has had a difficult life. Jockhein blamed him for the death of Miriam, and he was harshly disciplined as a young lad. If it had not been for the presence of Madame Avileaux, who was a motherly influence on him, as well as a fair share of his dear mother's compassionate ways, God knows how he would have turned out."

Kyriedor stood up. His story had come to an end. Talitha sat in silence, trying to digest all that she had learnt.

"So Tal, there is little more that I can tell you. I suspect that you have a very significant role to play in the lives of many people, not the least of which is Master Jockim. One is to hope that he will come to the realization that his future life is not determined by his past. He has the power of choice and blaming will only lock him further into life's prison of doom."

He stopped momentarily and looked at her intently. "What about your life, Tal? We've been studying the sacred sutra for some time now. You've always known that you have yet to complete your fourth task." Sensing her fear, he crouched before her, taking her hand in his. "Dear Tal, your task is to go into the dungeons of your mind and to free those whom you have locked away as prisoners, for only then will you be free."

Her eyes filled; a sadness that had been silently swirling through the spoiled cistern of her soul. How did he know her so well, even better than she knew herself? She was frightened of opening that cistern, for fear that she would drown in its foulness. She looked away.

"Jenobay will accompany you. She will imbue you with her courage," he whispered.

The tigress growled. Her name had been spoken. She nudged Talitha. With watery, fractured vision, Talitha watched the orange and black goddess slip her secrets stealthily into her soul. Suddenly, she found herself murmuring, "Yes, I am ready, Kyriedor."

He stared into her eyes, admiring the faint flicker of fire that was beginning to emerge in their ever disturbed depths.

CHAPTER 6

A Sacred Adversary

Jenobay and Tal rounded yet another corner of the boulder maze that hid Kyriedor's cabin. The rocky, narrow crevices went on forever, and she was convinced that she would be unable to find her way back to the cabin on her own. They had zig zagged and climbed boulders, crawled between rock crevices and scrambled down strange, step like indentations hewn into the solid rock walls. She was pleased of the tigress' company, as Kyriedor had insisted that she make the journey without him, although he had assured her that she was safe with Jenobay, and that his spirit would be with her to strengthen her. Silently she recited the words of the sacred sutra. They somehow helped to ease the never ending anxieties that strangled her thoughts.

Just where is Jenobay leading me, and what will await me? Her tortured mind fumbled with a frightening spectrum of possibilities. Kyriedor had said that she needed to see with fresh vision, with fire in her soul, and that it was best not to give her any information as this would lead to judgements and make the journey harder for her. 'Just trust!' he had counselled.

If only I had his courage and strength of character, she lamented, allowing herself to wallow in a comforting pool of self-pity. Her momentary self-preoccupation caused her to lose footing. She lurched forward. The jagged, rock corridor tore angrily at her forearm as she attempted to steady herself, but too late, she had landed in a bog.

Jenobay stopped and looked back nonchalantly. The tigress seemed bemused by her awkwardness. Talitha pulled herself up roughly, chiding herself for being so foolish and trying to ignore the discomfort that she felt at Jenobay's gaze. Her mind flooded with memories of how Jockim had lifted her from the muddy manure, on her first night at the castle. How ridiculous she must have looked. A nauseous sense of shame swelled inside as she felt the heat rise in her cheeks. Jenobay moved in closely and gently licked her reddened forearm.

"Oh Jenobay," she said, "how much further?" As if heeding her question, she bounded behind a rocky outcrop and then appeared back in front of her growling softly.

"Oh alright …" She eased her tired body up and attempted to restore some dignity to her now filthy dress. She brushed lightly at the tears that were erupting, unaware that she was blurring her face with warrior like paint.

Following close behind Jenobay, she entered what appeared to be a cave. The coolness upon her wet clothing sent a shiver shuddering down her spine. It smelt musty. *So dim,* she thought, straining to make out what seemed like a soft glow of light ahead of them. Then she saw it ... the silhouette of a man. She stopped still, fear clamping every sinew into a tight contortion.

"Oh God!" she whispered. "No, not you ..."

Raybet! How could Kyriedor do this to me? The one soul she had hoped never to lay eyes upon again stood before her. Her throat thickened. Her head began to reel. Her frozen thoughts refused to move! What should she do? How to escape? Instinctively, she backed towards the entrance. To her horror, Jenobay stood in her way, snarling with ferocity.

"I think she wants you to stay, to confront your enemy face on, Tal." Raybet spoke softly. "I promise you I won't harm you. Besides, you know I wouldn't stand a chance against her if I tried to do anything! I'm too exhausted." He collapsed onto a hammock strung between two, jutting boulders. "Kyriedor has been caring for me ... saved me from the Oge." He closed his eyes and added wearily, "He said you'd come. That meeting with you would assist with my healing ... body and spirit!" He sniggered. "You didn't know I had a spirit worth saving, did you?"

She ignored his remark. "What do you know of the Oge?" she snapped.

"A little more than you I think, my dear, considering that I've been under their power for the last few months. I managed to escape with Rose and Father a few weeks back, but Konfra is gravely ill from his war wounds. I decided to leave him and Rose with some farm folk while I travelled south to get assistance from the gypsies if I could. I need horses and supplies for a new start. The Oge attempted to overtake me yet again at one point, but Kyriedor's men assisted me and brought me to him."

"And what makes you think that the gypsies will want to help you?"

He sighed. *Maybe she was right. Maybe he was too despicable even for the gypsies, for anybody except Kyriedor.*

"Anyway, what do you want with me?" She impatiently interrupted his self-condemnatory thoughts. "And what about Jockim …? Is he—?"

"Yes, my dear, you will be pleased to know that he is alive and well and has full possession again of his precious castle. How many lives have been ruined for that abominable place … yours, mine, Roses', Avie's, Konfra's and that's just the start of the destruction."

Talitha stared at Raybet with loathing. His once dark hair had begun to show the first signs of grey, and his face was now lined with the creases that fear edges so deeply. His eyes however, were still the pale blue that they had always been—the smooth, silken lights that had lured her into a trap.

"The past is over. What do you want of me?"

"My, you have grown up … so much more assertive than the little handmaid at Doomeerie." He dragged his body up and looked directly at her, his tone softening. "Forgiveness Tal, I want your forgiveness for my betrayal."

She said nothing. Her throat tightened in disgust. Inside her an angry knot began to swell, tight strands of hate rising to choke her thoughts, so strong that she could feel them bursting at her temples to escape. After his cruel and cunning betrayal, did he think that he could just calmly request her forgiveness, and she would gladly hand it over? What kind of a fool did he surmise her to be?

"I know that I am undeserving of it, however if you could forgive me, I might have the courage to tell the truth to a dying man … a man whom I have loved since he took me into his family as an adolescent lad."

She stared at him and swallowed hard. "I don't understand what I have to do with you and the general."

"Konfra always wanted Doomeerie for one of his children. He had fought long and hard for Jockhein and did not agree with Jockim's decision after his father's death to disband the forces and stop taxing the village folk so heavily. He had always wanted Rose to marry Jockim and to become mistress of the castle, but being dismissed as he was there seemed to be no hope of that occurring, until Andor's forces started to assemble and prepare for attack. That gave Konfra the perfect opportunity to set his plan in action: to save Doomeerie for Jockim and to reunite him and Rose in matrimony. I'm sure that the plan would have worked very well if a certain handmaid had not come on the scene. Konfra was too embedded in his illusion to believe that Jockim had other interests."

He laughed bitterly. "Yes, the old fool didn't even know that I had loved Rose for most of my adult life. Still, I can't complain. He has been good to me. Taking me away from my background of poverty and raising me as if I was his son."

He stopped, deep in thought, muttering, "What kind of a son tries to murder his own father?" His barely audible ravings floated insidiously into the silence. Unaware that he had even spoken and that she had heard his sinister self-talk, he continued. "That's why I had to get you out of the picture, however I didn't reckon on Jockim's loyalty to Doomeerie being so strong. I knew that he would never banish you to sure death in Nightmare Forest. However, I counted on him pretending to do so and leaving with you. In which case yours truly would be in the perfect position to marry Rose and take possession of the castle. I'm quite sure that Vadio would not have stood in my way, being so damned loyal to Jockim as he is, he would never have felt comfortable in taking over his castle. But you see my dear, I was not born into money, nor was I ever handed such power on a silver platter. I had to work hard for my power, and that I did. Konfra rewarded me by making me his top commander."

He paused briefly in deep thought again. "There are two types of people in this world. Those who are born lucky and those who have to work hard to get what they want. I fell into the latter category, and I wasn't going to let the opportunity of using a pretty, little handmaid to help me go by. So you see I had to betray you."

"Yes, I see very clearly. But, what I don't understand are your words, 'what kind of son tries to murder his own father'?" She was still aghast at what she had heard him mutter.

"Did I say that?"

"Yes, you did, just now! What did you mean by it?"

He stood and shuffled away from her, picking up a flask and drinking deeply from it. A faint odour of whisky wafted through the cave.

"I suppose if I want your forgiveness I should tell you the whole story. It's a small price to pay for what I've put you through."

She said nothing, staring at him stonily.

"When Jockim didn't go ahead and leave the castle with you under the guise of your banishment, I had to take matters into my own hands. I took charge of the forces, as at the time Jockim was nowhere to be found. Of course, he was off trying to save your stag, Shiloh, but in the confusion everyone assumed he was with his men. I knew he would fight for his castle because he had been unwilling to give it up for the love of his life."

He turned in time to see the pain cross her face. For some reason it seemed to make him feel even more miserable. "So I sent his battalion into the heat of the battle, where I knew there would be the greatest losses. Unbeknown to me, Konfra chose to lead that battalion, and so you see my dear if he dies, as I fear he may, I am responsible for his death."

Raybet stopped and sinking to the ground on his knees leaned forward placing his head in his hands, "What have I done, Tal? I have destroyed so many lives … yours, Rose's, Konfra's, Jockim's and my own. I cannot forgive myself."

"Did Jockim realise your murderous intentions?" she demanded, impervious to his emotional pain.

"He surmised, although he said nothing at first. After we had defeated Andor's forces, I knew that he would interrogate me, so I decided to take my chances and rallied forth some of the men in a coup to take over the castle. There were many who believed that his failure to banish you had resulted in Andor's attack, so they had lost confidence in him." He smiled a little sadly. "The old Doomeerie curse continues to have a stranglehold on the men's minds."

Her lips twisted into a snarl. He hadn't changed. He was still able to manipulate people through his cunning inferences.

"Vadio of course sided with Jockim, and we were outnumbered. We suffered heavy losses, and eventually I was forced to leave by the secret passage under the falls. Rose was waiting safely on the other side to learn whether we had taken possession of the castle or not. She is a brave and loyal soul. She could have gone back. She wasn't implicated in the coup. But instead, she chose to stay with me. Later, we came across Konfra, who had been captured by the Oge. We surrendered to them, on condition that we could attend to him and prevent his death. Rose was able to nurse him back to a state where he was strong enough to escape from them, but the venture took its toll. We realised that we would have to separate if I was to secure help for us all to move on. He needed more time to recuperate. That is why I travelled on alone, leaving them at the farm house."

He stopped and stared at her. What else could he say? That was it. That was him. He couldn't change the past even though his days had been clouded by grief, and his nights had been lost to nightmares of guilt.

What a pitiable figure of a man he is, she thought. Yet, she could feel no sympathy, harsh thoughts screaming in her head as they were.

"You deserve to feel pain—nothing but unquenchable agony for your appalling, atrocious actions!" She wanted to spit the words at him, but instead she pushed down hard upon the heat, turning it into frozen spite.

"I can do nothing for you. You have made your own choices." She turned to leave.

"Wait … please, wait Tal, I'm sorry. I am so sorry!"

"I will not wish you death Raybet because that would be to sink to your level of abasement. But, I wish you no peace, not now … not ever! I hope you rot in your own misery!"

She turned and fled outside. Tears blurred her vision, but the sight of Jenobay's orange and black splendour safely led her to Kyriedor's cabin. She thrust the door open wildly, not stopping to knock. He looked up, his eyes softening at her appearance and then clouding with concern.

"How could you do that to me … after all my hours of studying the sutra, working with you? I thought you cared about me, but you tricked me just as Raybet did?" She flung the words angrily at him.

"So it would seem," he replied gently.

"So it would seem." She mimicked him sarcastically. "Is that all you can say for yourself? I hate you—despise you. I wish that I had never laid eyes upon you. I …" The look of compassion in his eyes disarmed her. She stopped momentarily, and then feeling the hurt heave her into action, she stooped down and lifted the nearest item, a sacred relic given to him from Padyah, hurling it through space like a spinning missile.

Clang! It landed at his feet and snapped into two pieces, rolling across the floor. She stared at it, mesmerised. What had she done! It was precious to him, and now it was in pieces, discarded like rubbish. This couldn't be happening!

He bent down and picked the pieces up laying them gently on the table. She froze, feeling the full measure of her actions. "Oh Kyriedor … I'm sorry." She spluttered as a wave of remorse engulfed her. "I'm so sorry. I never meant—"

His arms were around her before she could finish. "It's alright … I understand." He held her tenderly; a safe space for her rage to vent after eons of restraint. "There's no harm done."

"Oh … but there is!" She sobbed, her body heaving in despair.

"I've destroyed what is most precious to you."

"I'm holding what's most precious to me, Tal." He smiled down at her. "Give yourself permission to feel your pain. It won't last forever if you stay with it for a while and don't force it down as you have done for so long. It's okay to be angry … Folk have desecrated you—knowingly and unknowingly—but you have the power to restore yourself and with time, you will. Why, even now your tears are washing away that warrior paint that's been smeared on your pretty face!"

Her fingers lightly touched her face. She hadn't realised it was dirty. Raybet had not said anything. *Oh what does it matter anyway? I am with Kyriedor … He always accepts me just as I am! Why should I be any different?* There was a certain sense of peace in standing authentic, instead of attempting to be good. She laid her head on his shoulder. The feeling was rare; a gem of quietude, a hushed silence that breathed harmony. It was like knowing that in spite of everything, life was still sacred, even in the midst of betrayal, like some strange rhythm that kept beating calmly, consistently, compassionately, in spite of all the pain that had been hammered into it.

CHAPTER 7

Journey to the Underworld

How will she endure the journey to the underworld?
Like Psyche, her courage must unfurl.
She must forgive the past and its betrayal,
For the ego will always err and fail.

"Don't be afraid," Kyriedor counselled, as he helped her down into the underground cave. "Remember even though you may not see me, I am there with you." She was silent, intent upon what lay before her. "Follow the stream … it will lead you to the boatman."

The water that flowed from the underground stream lapped around her ankles. It was cold, harsh, and brittle. She entered the gloom of the cave alone and stepped out of the stream onto the bank. *It's so dark!* She held the lantern up. *I hope that this is the right thing to do. Maybe I shouldn't have let Kyriedor talk me into this!*

Shadows stretched eerily along the walls of the dank cave. The stream was flowing downwards, gaining in strength and momentum. She crept forward, each step demanding the force of resolve. The rock walls eyed her menacingly. A thousand, bony faces stared, sculptured into their stone crevices. The sound of water rushing was heightening, the stream was widening and soon there would be no embankment, only sheer rock walls passaging the underground stream. *This is madness … utter madness … I must turn back!* The glow from the lantern captured movement up ahead. She lifted it higher, her heart battering wildly within the confines of her chest. She swallowed hard. It was the boatman. Slowly, trembling with fear and cold, she approached the hooded, black figure. He stood tall and foreboding, awaiting her, the dark folds of his garment obscuring his face in sinister shadows. As Kyriedor had counselled she knelt before him, struggling to say the words that she had rehearsed.

"Greetings boatman of the Underworld, I have come to travel down the underground stream … to learn the secrets of my soul. Like the sages and masters who have come this way before me, I desire to sail into the unchartered waters of my soul—to learn its truth. Please take me into my Cave of Unknowing."

The hooded figure moved stealthily, drawing a knife from under his cloak. She gasped! He reached forward and with skeleton like hands grasped a lock of her long hair. Swiftly, he severed it with the knife and threw it into the stream. She watched horrified as a section of the water began to take on a strange, brackish hue and flow off to the west. With a foreboding aura, he gestured to step into the small boat. "We journey to the pool of ripples and reeds," he replied hollowly. "Prepare your soul."

The bony, sinuous hands released the rope that held the small vessel, and it propelled forward with a flash of momentum. She clasped the sides, knuckles white, her nails scouring into the wood. The blackness speed past. They were going down, down at an ever accelerating pace. The black waters heaved about her, threatening to toss her into their shadowy abyss. *This is death! I will drown in the bowels of the earth!*

"Stop it!" she screamed. "Turn us around! We will die!"

The hooded, black figure turned his head momentarily but made no other sign to indicate that he had even heard her. Suddenly, she felt the boat lift and leap forward over what appeared to be a cascade of water. They jolted abruptly into a deep, underground pool. The force of the landing sent a sudden thud of throbbing pain up her spine. She cried out! The water went suddenly stagnant, and the boat was still. She frantically held the lantern up to survey her surroundings. They seemed to be in some kind of underground cave.

"Now we must wait." The hooded figure spoke solemnly.

"Wait for what? What is this place?"

"It is the cave of ripples and reeds," the sombre reply echoed.

She held the lantern over the side of the boat, trying to assess the depth of the water. Suddenly before her, it appeared to be draining away. The boat was lowering. A rushing, gurgling noise echoed throughout the cave.

"What's happening?" she asked frantically.

"The spirit is preparing your soul to be enlightened." The figure lowered his head reverently, shadowy folds disappearing into darkness.

The water kept descending. It was waist deep, knee deep. She watched fascinated, her fear slowly ebbing away. Now it was ankle deep.

"Step out of the boat," the boatman commanded. "Prepare to be washed in the waters."

She looked up at him, confused. His face remained hidden by the hood.

"I don't understand how can I be washed? There is hardly any water now."

"Step out of the boat and into the water," he repeated, sounding hollow like a booming gong resonating its warning. "Some of the souls from your life's journey will soon enter the cave of ripples and reeds. You must be ready, waiting."

She gingerly climbed out of the boat and lifted her skirts. The water felt strangely warm and comforting. Then looking up, she gasped. Spectres like figures were entering the cave, and she knew them! There was Avie and Vadio and Anya—Anya walking! She couldn't believe her eyes. She called out in a frenzy of delight, but they appeared not to hear her. Gliding past, they made their way into the darkness of the cave and disappeared.

The ripples from their movement floated gently across the water and caressed her feet warmly. She smiled. It was so wonderful to see them again. Her heart swelled. It felt like it would burst with gratitude. Why had she been so afraid? This was delightful. *If only they could hear me … If only they would stay!* She started towards them, but stopped. There was further movement. More figures were coming. The waters were stirring and rising. Little waves were tumbling towards her. There was Rose. She felt something strange entwine her ankle, and now Konfra! A larger wave rushed in upon her.

The water had risen to her thighs in a matter of seconds. She made to climb back into the boat but something was stopping her! There were reeds, hundreds of them coming towards her in the now chilled waters, like slimy, green serpents, twisting and curling their vibrating coils around her legs. Panic gripped! She couldn't move!

"Help me ... I can't move ... Help me, please!" she shrieked desperately.

The boatman remained still and dark. Suddenly, a mighty wave crashed into the cave. From behind it emerged Raybet.

She screamed. "No ... no ... get away from me ... all of you ... get away!"

The water was at her breast now. Frantically, she tried to pull the reeds away with her hands. The slimy, serpent coils latched faster and faster. She couldn't move. The brackish water kept rising. Now it was at her shoulders, her neck. She struggled violently. Another wave and she was under the water—her lungs exploding, a world of tiny, green and blue suspensions floating surreally past her, in slow motion. The serpent reeds swam in circular masses, lodging themselves in her nostrils, her ears, and now her mouth. Her heart dislodged, falling forward and now back again. Then, before her Raybet appeared, his features watery and magnified. He was coming closer and closer. Now he was right up next to her face. His mouth was opening and the serpent like reeds were reaching out to her. Tiny, black bubbles flowed from his mouth, hitting her in the face.

"Welcome to the world of traitors, Tal." His voice was distorted, sounding haunting, like a gurgling echo. "What you see in me is what you behold within yourself. Free me, and you free your own spirit. We are trapped in the illusions of our minds and hearts and have forgotten our true selves. Remembering is the way home!"

The reeds were choking her. She could utter no reply. She stared frantically at his surreal face, fear gripping her throat. The world turned black, and she drifted silently—her mind floating along a watery abyss. A deep sense of compassion welled within her. Now she understood why Kyriedor had wanted her to meet him. In forgiving him, she would also be releasing herself. She surrendered herself into the void. She was ready to let go of all the bitterness that had been festering within her, no longer desiring to harvest raw, abrasive hurts. She wanted only to be washed free of them.

Suddenly, she sensed the pressure ease from her arms and legs, and the water began to recede just as quickly as it had risen. Through the bleary recesses of her mind, she saw the boatman reach down and lift her effortlessly back into the vessel. She watched herself pull the slimy, wet reeds off her face and body and discard them into the water. Slowly, they dissolved in the receding stream—a blurred memory of a moment of insight.

✹ ✹ ✹

Talitha opened her eyes. Kyriedor was leaning over her. Somehow, she was safe, back within the homely confines of his cabin.

"You have showed great courage, young maid." He spoke lovingly. "Like the masters and sages of the past you have travelled down the path of truth, and your soul will be strengthened."

She stared up at him, grateful that she finally was free. Warm, wet tears began to well in her eyes; tears of gratitude. She was returning to her true self. No longer were her senses strangled with fear and hate. She could breathe freely again, knowing that she was sacred and innocent. She had been mistaken for a while, lost on her journey home, but now she was returning—returning to a better place. Maybe she might even be a step closer to her sacred Hidden Garden!

CHAPTER 8

The Holy Grail Changes Hands

A sudden ramming on Kyriedor's door sent a shudder ricocheting through Talitha. She glanced nervously at Raybet.

"Kyriedor isn't expecting anyone is he, Tal?" he whispered urgently.

She shook her head. "I'll answer it. Quick hide outside. If it's safe, I'll call you back in."

He looked concerned. He had grown fond of Talitha over the past six weeks. She had helped him such a lot. Not just by assisting Kyriedor to nurse him back to health, but more importantly by extending him her forgiveness and compassion. Her kindness had astounded him, and there wasn't a day that went past that he didn't give thanks for having met her. He couldn't bear the thought of her coming to any harm, especially because of him.

"Hurry," she insisted. "I promise you that I won't open it to anyone I don't know." He nodded feeling more assured and moved stealthily out the back entrance. Anxiously, she slid the eye window of the door open.

"Oh Ange …" She laughed, relieved. "You scared me! I thought it might be the Oge. Your knock was so urgent. Hang on, I'll unlatch the door. Is Kyriedor with you?"

"No, it's just me, Tal. He's still back at the camp tending to the sick."

The door squeaked open. Angie entered in a frenzied rush of anxiety, red hair spilling unkempt in a blaze of glory to her waist. She was breathless.

"Oh, I couldnu' wait for Kyriedor. I needed to see ya straight away!"

"Why, what's wrong?" Talitha's fine, dark brows furrowed. Her friend seemed so agitated. "Has Toby taken a turn for the worse?"

Angie nodded her red, gold splendour slowly. "Oh, he's in a real bad way. Kyriedor says there's nothin' more that he can do for 'im. He thinks the only way of savin' him is to take 'im to Padyah." Tears pricked at her eyes. "I know 'em birds aren't ready to travel yet, Tal, but please, ya gotta 'elp us." She glanced furtively at Pover and Freedom. Talitha had moved them to Kyriedor's cabin to speed Freedom's recovery. "Promise me ya'll get Jockim to let us into Doomeerie, so that Padyah can save me boy. Word has it that he is at Doomeerie."

"Of course I will, Angie." She scooped her friends trembling hands into her own. "I can go without Pover. She'll come back to me when Freedom is well … I know she will." A soft chirping from the golden cage seemed to be reaffirming her promise.

"Aw, Gad bless ya!" Angie threw her arms around her friend hugging her tightly. "I knew ya'd 'elp me."

She was so lost in the wave of relief that engulfed her that she didn't hear the back door open quietly behind her. Raybet stood transfixed, staring at her.

Talitha laughed softly. "I'll do whatever I can. Oh, Raybet …" she announced, spying him standing statue-like, "come in and meet my dear friend, Angie."

Angie spun around to see the stranger. She froze. Her face drained white and her hand instinctively reached for her throat. "Oh my Gad …" she whispered, "it can't be … surely not?"

Her startled words breathed life back into his motionless body. "Angie … my little Ange … I had hoped but never dared to dream …" He was beside her now, scooping her up in his arms; his face breaking into a thousand creases of joy.

"Raybet," she squealed, "I don't believe it. Raybet … Is it really you?" She melted into his embrace, shrieking with delight.

Talitha edged back dumbfounded, watching the scene unfold before her. She dared not say a word. It seemed too sacred, too strange, like she was watching a hallowed event in their lives. Eventually, they drew apart laughing, and then he clasped her again and spun her around in his hands.

"Look at you … Just look at you!" he exclaimed. "You're beautiful … What happened to that little tomboy in the gypsy camp."

"She became a woman!" She beamed back at him. He drew her to him once more, hugging her tightly. They separated again. Her blue eyes sparkled mischievously. "And what brings General Knofra's best commander to Kyriedor's cabin, Raybet?"

He shook his head. "Yes, you always had to be 'in the know' didn't you, Ange. You haven't changed much." He matched her brilliant smile with a laugh.

Talitha began to wonder if they even knew she was still present. She cleared her throat tentatively. "I can see that there is no need for introductions." She smiled questioningly at them.

Angie threw her arms around her again. "Oh, Tal, how long have ya been hidin' me long lost half-brother 'ere in Kyriedor's cabin and not tellin' me?"

"Half-brother …" She repeated the word, sounding like there had been some mistake.

"That's right, Tal." Raybet beamed, unable to take his eyes off Angie. "Konfra took me from the gypsy camp all those years ago. Is Flynn …?"

"Aye, he is for sure." She instinctively knew he was asking about their beloved father. "Aw 'ow grand it'll be for 'im to see ya. He ain't talked of ya much … Didn't wanna make me sad, I reckon. But, I remember 'im sayin' one day when I was frettin' … 'Ya'll see 'im ag'in lass … don't be cryin'. I've a feelin' that ya' ma is goin' work things out up there in 'eaven. She'll make sure that ya'll see 'im ag'in … mark me words she will. Yes, Cathy'll make sure!'"

They both laughed at her attempt to mimic Flynn. Raybet shook his head, his eyes beginning to brim. "It's been so long … so very long. Too many nights dreaming of you and Flynn, and too many days wasted fighting when I could have been," he went silent, and then grabbing her again he lifted her off the floor and into the air, "carrying my little sis' around on my back the way I used to."

"I'd be too heavy for that now!" She giggled. "Besides, half the time ya'd be cartin' two of us around—me and Toby. Tobias, he's me boy; son of Ty, me man. But he be dead now, and Toby … well …" Her eyes immediately began to fill.

Raybet directed her to a seat. "Tell me about Toby, Angie. I gather that he is very ill."

She nodded and burst into a deluge of tears. It had all been too much: the bad news that Kyriedor had given her about Tobias that morning and now meeting her half-brother again after so many years. Through bouts of sobbing, she managed to relay to Raybet that Kyriedor had been treating Tobias for some time now for a mysterious illness. However, he was not getting better, in fact in the last twelve hours his health had deteriorated badly.

"Oh, but now ya can 'elp too. Ya can take us to Doomeerie. Ya've fought for the castle. Jockim would surely repay ya by lettin' us in to see Padyah." A new light danced in her eyes as she glanced quickly at Raybet, then Talitha, and then back to Raybet for confirmation.

Raybet shook his head. "I'm so sorry Ange. I've no sway with Jockim or any of the others at Doomeerie. In fact, they despise me." He sketchily related the events that had led to his leaving the castle.

She nodded sadly. "I can see ya ain't forgotten yer gypsy ways, Raybet." Trying to hide her disappointment, she smiled brightly. "Good on ya … Na gypsy brother of mine takes orders from Jockim Deerie and 'is kind. Ya worth more than all 'em Doomeerie folk put together!"

They laughed, and she suddenly remembered Talitha's feelings for Jockim. "Oh, I'm sorry Tal. I shouldn't say such things about Jockim sees I've n'er met the man. They say he's much better than 'is father was." Her cheeks coloured a little, and she smiled sheepishly.

"Oh, that's alright … Under the circumstances I can quite understand how the gypsy folk feel about the castle folk but truly, they aren't so bad. They're just like the gypsies really … wanting to love and be loved … only their wealth has filled them with fear. They think that they have to punish anyone who does wrong or else they will lose everything!"

Angie nodded gravely. "Ya'll still go for me won't ya? Havin' this scoundrel as me bother won't change ya mind will it?" She winked at Raybet.

"Of course not … I'll go! I only hope that I can be of some help." Talitha was determined to assist her friend but doubted if she had any chance of persuading Jockim to allow gypsies into the castle. Did he still love her? It had been so long. Had he ever really loved her? A melancholy mood began to settle over her. She had longed to see him for so long, but now, as the time for their reunion approached, she began to doubt herself. An unsettling notion kept nagging, stripping away her tenuous sense of hope. If he had loved her, why hadn't he left Doomeerie with her, as Raybet had expected he would?

"I don't know, Tal," Raybet replied warily. "Jockim is such a strange man … so moody. It's hard to know where anyone stands with him. They say he had the last handmaiden banished because she stole some of his mother's gems. I don't want you to come to any harm." He took her hand gently. "You've been such a true friend to me. I don't know if I can stand by and watch you re-enter that castle of doom … but if Toby's life depends on it …" His voice trailed off as he watched his half-sister's anguished face.

"I've got to try," Talitha insisted. She couldn't bear to see the desperate look that tortured Angie. Her friend's trembling lips smiled back sadly. She didn't want to put Talitha's life in any harm, but her son was dying. She was her only hope of saving him.

Raybet still seemed unconvinced. "There must be some other way." He rubbed his fingers repeatedly across his brow, but his thoughts were heavy and confused. Too much was happening. He had found his half-sister and her son and now it seemed that he would soon lose the latter. Surely, there must be something that he could do? Again, he entertained the idea of approaching Jockim, but it seemed a fruitless course of action. He would kill him before he had a chance to even ask for help for the lad. Raybet's brain had shut down. He could see no other option than hoping that Talitha could sway Jockim.

"I'm going and that's that!" Talitha stood up decisively. "I'll leave first thing in the morning. If I am successful I will get a message through to you." They nodded in unison. "And if I fail," she swallowed hard, "you must use this to negotiate your way into the castle, Raybet." She lifted her skirt and produced the silver goblet.

Raybet gasped, turning pale. Now his head was beginning to reel. "No, Tal … you must keep that!" he interjected sharply.

She shook her head. "We need a back-up plan. Jockim failed to save me and Shiloh once before. I cannot know for certain that he will help me now. I hope that he still loves me and will see reason, but we cannot be sure. It has been too long. If he agrees to you all entering the castle, you can give it to me, and I will take it to him. If not, it is the only way that we will be able to save Tobias' life. Either way, he will have it returned to him because I trust you to save Tobias."

Raybet looked troubled. "Dear Tal … you would trust me with this after what I have done? You are an amazing woman—a truly honourable friend."

Angie looked uncomfortable. She reasoned that Raybet must have been Talitha's betrayer. What a noble friend she was to put the past behind her to help Tobias. Her son's life was at stake. She held her breath.

Talitha smiled. "I trust you," she replied softly, knowing that she had truly forgiven him. A warm feeling of wellbeing flooded her body, filling her with love. It seemed like it would burst from her in a wave of joy.

Raybet lowered his head humbly in an effort to avert the moisture that kept building up in his eyes. "Then we have a pact!" He smiled, placing his hand over hers as she handed him the goblet. "Thank you … I am humbled by your trust."

Angie's blue eyes glistened gratefully. "Thank you … oh thank you, Tal!" The tears softly contoured their way down her swarthy cheeks as she laid her hands over Raybet's and Talitha's.

"Aye, we 'ave a pact!" She darted a mischievous look at them. "May the 'Oly Grail of Doomeerie grant us all our 'eart's desire!"

The door swung open. They looked up. Kyriedor was there before them. He smiled broadly.

"Ah, I see you two have been reunited at last."

"You knew about our relationship, Kyriedor?" Raybet looked surprised.

"Flynn confided in me about Konfra taking his son some years ago. I put two and two together when I met you Raybet, especially as you were travelling with Konfra. Not too many men called Raybet, and you were the right age." He smiled at Angie. "You know he has been harping on visiting the gypsy camp for weeks now. I was holding off a little to ensure he was well enough, physically and mentally … but under the circumstances, it is good that you are reunited. Raybet will support you."

"Aye and he can help me transport Tobias to the castle so that he can be tended to by Padyah."

Raybet nodded. Kyriedor looked at him. They both were wondering what sort of reception he would be given by Jockim.

"Oh, don't worry, Kyriedor." Angie intercepted, reading their concerns. "Tal has agreed to act as go between; to go in first and to persuade Jockim to let us all in."

Kyriedor placed his hessian sack on the table in measured, thoughtful motion. He looked up slowly, a grave expression on his face.

"I'm not so sure that's such a good idea. Tal has a lot more study on *The Tao* to do yet. She is far from having mastered it. I fear that the dark forces at the castle will overpower her while she is still vulnerable. She is only just beginning to make progress, and Pover will be unable to accompany her—Freedom still requires her company. It is not wise to enter such dark places without one's spirit companion."

"But, surely Padyah will be there to help," Raybet interjected.

"Yes, that is so … if Jockim permits Tal to see him." He sat down at the table and lowered his head in thought. Angie fell silent, her golden, red hair drooping lower. Raybet placed his arm around her sagging shoulders. Tears began to fall softly.

"Oh please, Kyriedor … There is no one else … You yourself said that I was the one to change the folk at Doomeerie," Talitha pleaded.

"Yes, but that was to be when I sensed you were strong enough … There is much more work for you to do." He glanced over at Angie and felt his heart plunge. He could not let Tobias die. *Perhaps she is right,* he thought. *There seems to be no other reasonable course of action. I am just going to have to trust that the Great Spirit has some power and purpose in this change of events."*

He stood up decisively. "Alright … under the circumstances I can see no other way. Go and see if you can persuade Jockim to save the boy. But Tal," he walked over to her and took her hands in his, "promise me these things …"

Her face was awash with joy. "What Kyriedor?"

"You will take the time to tend to your own emotional and spiritual needs. I cannot stress the importance of this enough. You will need all your inner strength to stand up to Jockim. Although he has been with our father, Padyah, I fear that dark forces still have a mighty grip on his heart. You must not practise kindness indiscriminately, for it is imperative that you have the energy to attend to your own needs …" He sighed, and a faraway look came into his eyes. The words he spoke seemed to come from beyond him, from some ancient, mystical source. "Do not try and save the imprisoned, dead man, nor the woman who breaks the spinning needle, nor the lame man with the donkey and sticks."

She looked at him curiously. *What a strange thing to say.* "Yes … of course … if you say so … Then I have your blessing to go?" she inquired hopefully, eyebrows raised in expectation.

He nodded, and she hugged him. He laughed, drawing her close. "I will keep the birds until they are well enough to travel. Then I will have them fly to Sanctusis, the holy hermit at the lake country. He will send them on to you at the appointed time."

"Oh, thank you, Kyriedor ... thank you!" Her heart was dancing, her spirits soaring.

He kissed her lightly on the forehead. "Remember ... I love you ... Take counsel from Padyah if you are able to meet with him. I too will be with you in spirit. Pray when you need assistance, and look after yourself."

He was desperately hoping that she comprehended the full gravity of the situation, but she had already left. She was embracing Angie and hadn't even heard his final warning.

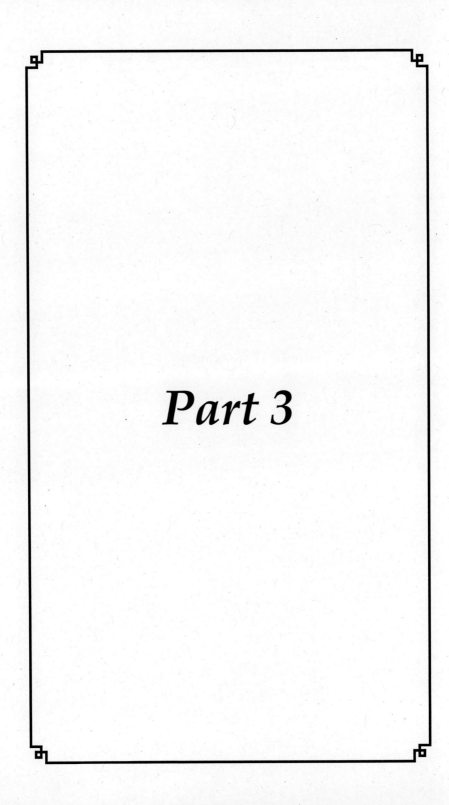

Part 3

CHAPTER 1

Anya and the Alcove

It was strange to be back inside Doomeerie Castle. The past flooded through Talitha's mind. The stain glass windows had not been damaged in the battle. For a time she became spell bound by them again, engrossed in their beauty and their uncanny resonance to the events in her own life. Eventually, noises from outside nervously shattered the silence. Clang! The heavy door was unbolted. Quickly, she hid behind the little door in the circular, stone column.

"Master Jockim arrived back from his short trip to Nightmare Forest early this morning, ma'am," a female voice remarked. "He's instructed me that he won't want to see anyone until this evening. I'll set an extra place for him at the dinner table. I expect he'll tell you his news then."

"Very well, Fanny." Talitha recognised Anya's voice immediately, and her heart began to pound excitedly. "What type of a mood was he in? Could you gauge at all?"

"He was fairly uncommunicative … didn't seem to want to discuss his business. He did inquire after your health though. I suspect he's tired. He must have ridden all night and arrived here in the wee hours of the morning. And you know ma'am, it is a taxing experience being in that forest … It is so creepy. I swear I don't know why he is drawn back to it all the time. You'd think that he'd had enough of it after being there for the past year. Some say he's going a bit crazy like Master Luke went years ago … looking for that stag … You know the one that fought when Talitha was here."

"Now, now, Fanny … I'm sure that he has a perfectly legitimate reason for returning to the forest. I hope that you're not getting caught up in servant gossip and superstition."

"Not at all, ma'am … however he does scare me a little, Master Jockim … especially when he gets angry."

Anya giggled. "You're not alone there. Can you braid my hair for me this morning please? Vadio has promised to wheel me by the river, and it is so windy today. I don't want it to get all knotted."

"Of course, now Master Vadio, you are very lucky to be married to him. He is such a good and kind man—and so placid too. I daresay he's a wonderful husband."

"Indeed, he is! I *am* very lucky to be married to him. He has been an absolutely wonderful support since mama passed away. I would have been devastated without him. He has helped me such a lot."

"Yes, he has been kind to us servants too. I'm so glad that he and Master Jockim get on so well. It's good that Master Jockim trusts him and leaves the castle under his authority when he travels.

It must give him great peace of mind to know that Master Vadio is keeping an eye to things?"

"I'm sure that it does. Vadio is like his father, Konfra. He is very loyal to Jockim, as Konfra was to Jockhein."

"Ah yes, the old general, I think of him sometimes. I wonder where he might be and if he is still alive. What a terrible thing those battles were ... destroyed such a strong and capable man and his beautiful daughter, Rose. How sad he would have been to know that she eloped with that scoundrel, Raybet. Why you know us servants always thought that Master Jockim and Miss Rose would end up together. They would have made such a handsome couple; him being so tall and dark and she so fair and beautiful. Still, it was not to be."

"Thank you, Fanny. That looks lovely." Talitha imagined that Anya was admiring her braided hair in the mirror as she had seen her do when they shared castle quarters.

"What dress will you be wearing today, ma'am. I'll fetch it for you."

"The pink one I think, with the black trimming."

"I'll get it then, ma'am. Is there anything else that you'll be requiring?"

"Not presently, thank you."

The servant woman's heavy tread nosily departed. Talitha decided to remain hiding until after she had finished dressing Anya. She sat quietly within the tiny alcove. Presently, she heard the great, oak doors creak open again and Fanny's familiar voice addressing her mistress.

"Here we are, ma'am. Let me help you into it. I'm just going to lift you now and you can pull the dress through under you. There we go. Don't you look lovely? Pretty as a picture you are. Master Vadio is lucky to have you too, I daresay."

Outside the clouds were rolling across a darkened sky. "It's such a bleak day. I've brought your black shawl in case you need it down there by the river. Is there anything else now, ma'am?"

"No, thank you … When Vadio comes in from his early morning chores can you let him know I'm here in Miriam's room? I'm just going to read while I wait for him."

"Alright then, ma'am, I'll leave you in peace while I attend to my morning duties."

Her footsteps receded as Anya called out, "Thank you, Fanny." Creak! The door closed with a loud bang. Talitha waited but a few seconds and then stepped nervously from the alcove. Anya glanced up startled by the sudden movement.

"My God, is that you, Tal?"

The younger woman ran towards her. They embraced fervently. Tears streamed down Anya's cheeks. "I can't believe it. You are finally here beside me after all this time. Surely it's a miracle." She laughed, searching for her hanky.

Talitha giggled. "It's so good to see you. I have imagined this moment so many times over the past months."

"My goodness won't Jockim be beside himself when he knows that you are back. Where have you been all this time? What have you done?"

"Just a minute …" Talitha walked to the door and stood silently for a minute gesturing to Anya to remain quiet. She bolted it.

"No one will come until about an hour's time, then Vadio will arrive to take me for a walk by the river. Come …" She patted the bed, beckoning her friend to sit beside her. "Come and tell me your story."

Talitha sketchily related the events of her life since leaving the castle, being careful to omit any reference to her meeting with Raybet, as well as Angie and Tobias' plight. She had decided that she could not tell anyone this news until she had first spoken with Jockim. Anya was amazed at her courage and endurance.

"Dear Tal, you have certainly shown great bravery. I always knew that you had tremendous courage, right from when you went into the wild boar's pen on the first night in the castle." They both shook with laughter.

"Didn't that make Jockim furious!" Another burst of laughter resounded in the room.

Anya shook her head lovingly. "Oh, he will be so happy to see you. He has missed you dreadfully. You know that he hasn't been here much. For many months he searched for you, and now he spends a great deal of time in Nightmare Forest. Some say he is still searching for Shiloh so that he can give him back to you."

"I don't expect that he can undo the past. I have come to complete the contract that I began with him two years ago. There is now only a year to go before that time is up, and I will honour my word."

Anya placed her hand over the younger woman's lean fingers. "You are such a good, honest soul." She looked deeply into her eyes again, shaking her head once more. She could hardly believe that her friend was with her again.

"But look at you. You look like a gypsy girl—hair all matted and in a filthy dress. We will have to get you back to your beautiful self before Jockim sees you. Go to our chambers, first floor down. You will recognise our room as it has a tapestry of the castle completed by mama on the wall beside it. Bathe and change into one of my dresses. I'm sure that you will find something to fit, especially if you draw the waist in with a sash. When I come back from being with Vadio, I will awaken Jockim and let him know the good news. You will have plenty of time to get ready by then. Hide now while I ring for Sophie to arrange the bath. We don't have many servants these days. They are all kept occupied on the ground floor with tasks for the entire morning, so you won't be disturbed."

Talitha, sensing the urgency of the moment, smiled and quickly kissed Anya. "Thank you dear Anya. I knew that you'd help me!"

CHAPTER 2

Talitha in a Tight Spot

The warm bath was soothing. Talitha stretched lazily back. The waters calmed every sinew in her tired body. For a time, she closed her eyes and allowed herself complete respite. The image of little Toby dying nagged her thoughts. How helpless and distressed Angie must be feeling. She must not tarry any longer. Rising, she heard hammering on the door. Quickly, she hid behind the dressing screen. Her heart sank as she realised that she had left her towel on the bed. Crouching low, she hoped that the intruder would not enter.

The door burst open, the sound of its sudden swish muffled by heavy boots. Bang! Bang! Bang! Several drawers were opened and shut in haste and then a loud crash! Lavender! Its ambrosial wave wafted throughout the room.

"Damn it! Where the hell does she keep it?" An angry voice cursed. Recognising it to be Jockim's, her heart missed a beat.

He crouched low and began to collect the pieces of broken china. A soft, almost imperceptible movement roused his senses. He glanced at the screen. A woman's, wet feet stood behind it, in a pool of dripping, bath water.

"It seems I am not alone," he said slowly, annoyed that one of the servant girls had been so bold as to use her mistress' room. Then, considering the awkward situation that the unfortunate creature was caught in, he decided that it would be amusing to prolong her discomfort. *Why not have a little fun*, he thought, standing up. *A suitable consequence for such brash behaviour!*

"Well now, who have we here? Must be a bold soul indeed, to have the audacity to use her mistress' room to bathe? Come out and show yourself?" He laughed low and teasingly.

Behind the screen Talitha swallowed hard and wished that she could disappear into the stone wall. She was not game to speak or raise her head for fear of being recognised and hoped that he would abandon his request and leave.

Jockim looked around the room and noticed that a towel had been thrown carelessly on the bed. Sensing the opportunity for further devilment, he continued, hoping to make the poor soul squirm in heightened discomfort.

"Well now, why so shy? You must be beginning to feel a little cold hiding behind there, but I'm happy to wait and make your acquaintance."

He chuckled softly again as the feet shuffled uncomfortably.

Finally, a timid voice arose. "The towel please, sir. If you would kindly throw the towel over, I'll come out."

Jockim could not believe his ears. The voice sounded like Talitha. He must be going crazy. Quickly, he grabbed the towel and threw it over the screen. The hidden occupant on the other side caught it deftly, and a few minutes later, there standing before him wrapped in a towel, was Talitha.

Had she not felt so miserable, she would have laughed at his expression. His jaw plummeted in disbelief, and he stared at her with incredulity. She cleared her throat and said politely the only thing that she could think of. "Hello, Jockim. It's nice to see you again."

"My, my … you certainly do have a way of making entrances, don't you?" He leaned back on the dresser and folded his arms beginning to shake with laughter. "I don't believe it!" He shook his head in amusement. "I just don't believe it. For months I've been searching for you and then one morning I get up, and here you are standing naked before me in my own home."

"Well, not quite," she replied testily, "and if you would kindly remove your presence from this room that Anya has thoughtfully permitted me to use, I might be able to get dressed."

"Still, the spirited little madam I see." A smirk spread across his face.

"And you're still as rude as you always were," she retorted back, regretting her words as soon as they had tumbled out. This meeting was not going according to plan at all. She had lost her composure and was feeling very vulnerable.

"Mmm … the lady is feeling embarrassed and uncomfortable, I gather. I would have thought that you might be used to that after all these years, Tal. You seem to have a habit of getting yourself into somewhat awkward situations."

He smiled cheekily at her. She stared stonily back at him, unable to share his amusement.

"Well," he ran his long, lean fingers through his dark, unkempt hair, "I'd better be the gentleman and do the right thing. I'll see you in my study in fifteen minutes. I trust you remember where it is?"

He smiled and, taking one last look at her now freezing body which was beginning to shiver from cold, strode out of the room laughing and shaking his head in disbelief.

Talitha quickly bolted the door to ensure that there would be no further intruders. She dressed in one of Anya's garments barely noticing what she had chosen. She was furious with herself for having been so careless. Anya however, had insisted that she would not be disturbed. Now she had lost all of her confidence. How could she convince him to allow Raybet to enter the castle with Angie and Toby? Already, she was starting to feel very much like a powerless maidservant once more.

CHAPTER 3

So That's What She Really Wants

Flustered, Talitha knocked on the study door. She hadn't had the time to soothe her rattled emotions. Her cheeks still felt warm when she pictured herself hiding naked behind the screen. *How embarrassing! I cannot believe that just happened,* she thought. It seemed an eternity before she heard the door begin to open. He gestured for her to enter.

"Well now, let me formally welcome you back to Doomeerie, Tal. Come and sit by the fire. It is such a bleak day, and I would hate you to catch your cold." He grinned, glancing at her attire. "My, that dress suits you. You look almost as lovely as you did a few moments ago."

She ignored his remark, gracefully lowering herself into the heavily brocaded armchair, next to the crackling warmth. Despite the chilly weather, her face was burning. Amused to notice her flushed complexion, he continued.

"Well, what brings you back to Doomeerie after all this time?"

"I have come to complete my contract to you. I wish to honour my word," she replied dutifully.

"Oh?" His eyebrows rose as he poured a small brandy. *Such a formal reply! She's obviously still very uncomfortable about being caught naked.* "Would you like a little bandy to warm you up?"

"No, thank you."

"Well then, I hope you don't mind if I partake of a nip?"

She shook her head as he sat down in the chair opposite and stared at her. Her eyes were wide and troubled, unable to hold his gaze.

"I have taken the liberty of ordering some tea for you as I thought that you would prefer that."

Smiling, he looked down at the amber contents of his glass as they took on the soft glow of the firelight. Minutes passed in silence. Finally, he stared back at her again, his eyebrows slightly lifted in expectation. She felt increasingly uncomfortable in the prolonged silence. She squirmed a little in her chair. Her cheeks took on yet another wave of crimson.

"Well, I ..." He laughed, feeling slightly awkward. He just wanted to embrace her, hold her close, but she was obviously still suffering from heightened sensitivity about being caught bathing. He placed the glass down and reached forward taking her hands in his. "It is truly wonderful to have you back at Doomeerie, Tal. I have missed you greatly." He smiled to see her stiffness ease a little. "I looked for you for such a long time. Where have you been?"

"I've been living with the gypsies and studying with the spiritual master, Kyriedor," she replied enthusiastically. He sensed the ice beginning to crack. She glanced up shyly. "I too have missed you, Jockim." Another flow of pink coloured her complexion. She quickly looked down. The memory of her near naked encounter was still sabotaging her poise.

He smiled. She was lovelier than he had remembered. "Did the gypsies hold you captive?" He seemed concerned.

"No, not at all!" she replied with animation. "Oh well at first they did, but then Jenobay came to my rescue, and they welcomed me into their hearts." She laughed, briefly relating the incident with Margie.

He listened attentively. *Why had she stayed with them so long? Why hadn't she tried to come back earlier?*

A knock at the door jolted him back to the present. "Come in!" he called.

Fanny entered. "Your tea, sir …" She stopped aghast, staring at Talitha.

"Hello Fanny." Talitha raised her hand in greeting as Fanny laid the tea tray down.

"Well I'll be … after all this time. Hello, Tal." She took the girls hand, shook it, and then placed her hands on her hips. "We could do with extra help in the kitchen."

Jockim laughed. "Well, we'll see, Fanny. Thank you for the tea."

Fanny curtsied. "You welcome, sir. Will that be all or would you like me to stay and pour it?"

"No, we'll be right thank you." Jockim replied kindly.

"Yes, how silly of me," Fanny retorted. "You've a maid with you to attend to it." She eyed Talitha up and down disapproving, wondering what she was doing wearing one of Anya's dresses. "I leave you then, sir."

Jockim waited until the door had closed and then spoke quietly. "Fanny is in charge of the servants now. You may not know that Avie was killed in the fighting."

"I had heard ... I'm so sorry, Jockim."

"It's been especially hard for Anya." A familiar sense of hollowness floated through him as he looked at her. Doe-like eyes were filling with compassion. He didn't want this to be a sad time. He continued quickly.

"Fanny does an amazing job." He smiled, beginning to pour the tea. "However, she rules with an iron rod. I'm afraid that all the kindness in that family must have been given to Avie, her older sister at birth—poor Fanny missed out. Let's just say that you don't need to get on the wrong side of her." He handed her the china cup. "Still, underneath her harsh exterior there is a heart of gold, and I would never intentionally upset her. She has been most loyal to me, and when all's said and done, she is Avie's sister."

Talitha felt uncomfortable. Should she have offered to pour the tea? This was so awkward. Fanny had reminded her of her servant status just when she was beginning to feel that she could open up to him and explain the situation surrounding Tobias. She would have to say something soon while they could still talk in privacy. She took a deep breath.

"Jockim," she said timorously, "there is another reason why I came back."

He held the glass tighter. His heart jolted quickly. *Was she going to say that she still loved him?*

"Yes, go on …" He smiled at her encouragingly.

She began to explain. At first, he just listened, the smile fading slowly from his face. Then, at mention of Raybet, his face darkened and his brows knotted. She felt herself becoming confused, breathless; the words seemed to be tumbling out the wrong way. Was she making any sense at all? His jaw set tight. *What is he thinking? Does he understand that this means life or death for Tobias?"* More and more, she was beginning to feel like a naughty child who was confessing her misdemeanours. She desperately wanted him to know how much Raybet had changed, how much she trusted him, how she even felt safe leaving the silver goblet with him.

"Well that's it … Now you know everything!" She stopped, her hand shaking as the china cup clinked into the saucer.

"Indeed, it would seem that I do, but perhaps I just need a little clarification on a couple of matters."

He positioned the empty glass down carefully on the table, crossed his legs and placing his hands on both of the chair's arm rests stared straight at her.

"I believe that you have given away the silver goblet that I gave to you in love and trust to the man who betrayed both you and me? Is that right?"

She looked at him, sensing his rising anger. She did not know how to answer.

"I also understand that you would now like me to allow this man who attempted to kill both myself and Konfra back into Doomeerie, with his gypsy half-sister and her child?"

Again, she knew not how to reply.

"I further comprehend that you believe me to be so consumed by money and the love of valuables, that I would put everyone's life at risk by trusting this man, just so that I can get the Doomeerie goblet back?"

She continued to remain silent. The way he had interpreted things filled her with shame. She lowered her head like a chastised child and stared sadly into the fire. Her attempts to try and make him understand had failed.

"Answer me!" He raised his voice in a loud and commanding fashion. "Is this your little game of bribery and manipulation? You give your sweetheart the silver goblet so that Jockim will do anything, including sell his very soul to get it back?"

"Jockim, please," she leant forward, looking into his eyes earnestly, "try to understand. Perhaps I have explained matters poorly, but a child's life is at stake. There are no romantic feelings between Raybet and myself. I merely have forgiven him for the past, and now I am trying to help his half-sister who is also a very dear friend to me. I thought that you would trust my discretion; that you would know that I would only give the goblet to one who could be trusted; and that this would be proof enough for you that Raybet is a redeemed man!"

He sighed despondently; the weight of her words sank heavily. He had hoped to be holding her in his arms by now, but instead he was desperately trying to contain his anger towards her.

"Oh, I understand Talitha … only too well. Raybet has succeeded in deceiving you yet again, and I am furious that after everything that has happened you are *still* so naïve that you trust him."

She fell silent, not knowing what to say. He stood up and began pacing the floor. Watching the restless motion made her stomach churn. He had done the same thing the day that he had told her that Shiloh must fight. It had been in the study then too. Her left thumb nail clawed at the ridge of her ring fingernail. It felt uneven. She sensed it beginning to break under the pressure. She stopped. Her left knee began to shake up and down in rapid movement, a tense, nervous motion. She became aware of its jiggling and forced herself to stop, clasping her hands together tightly. Finally, he turned to stare at her, just as he had that day.

"Alright," he said sternly, "because you are requesting it of me, I will give the matter some thought. I am certainly not promising anything. In the meantime, you can take up your old duties. I will tell Fanny that you are here to finish your contract. We will discuss this matter again later, at my convenience. You may go."

She stood up and walked towards the door. It seemed such a long way away. *What a mess I made of that!* she chided herself. *Oh well, at least he is considering it ... Yet, I feel that I have lost his trust and affection.*

"Oh, Talitha," she turned to face him, "you can have Avie's room. If you have any belongings, leave them there. Fanny will provide you with the necessary uniforms. And, by the way, as you already know Padyah is staying here at the castle at present; however, you will not be permitted to see him. I will also inform him that he is not to approach you ... And Tal," she looked up at the wounded expression that shot fleetingly through his eyes, "it is good to have you back ... despite all this Raybet nonsense!"

"Yes, sir, it is good to be back." She surprised herself at how easily the word 'sir' flowed from her mouth. A few minutes before, she had been calling him Jockim. Her shoulders began to sag. Her head lowered as she exited the room. He waited until she was gone and then ran his hands through his hair in frustration.

"Damn you Raybet ..." he cursed. "Will she never be free of your suavity and seduction?"

CHAPTER 4

Eating Humble Pie

Tears began to prick at Talitha's eyes. Suddenly, a door slammed below. She couldn't bear the thought of Anya seeing her upset. Stealthily, she headed down the stairs. She knew where to go—the stables. There her beloved Balaamine would be waiting. She had longed to see the old donkey again. The hectic last few hours had caused her to forget this anticipated joy. Quickly, she made her way out of the castle.

The once full stables now seemed lonely and bereft with very few animals in sight. Sure enough in the little pen where Shiloh and Balaamine had kept lodging together, the humble, little donkey lay resting on the hay. Talitha ran towards her. Balaamine lifted her tired neck. Her nostrils quivered picking up her scent, long before her fading eyesight could depict her. Emitting an excited little bray, she scrambled to her feet. Talitha flung her arms around her and sobbed. The little donkey nuzzled gently into her.

"Oh Balaamine, I wondered if I would ever see you again." Snuggling up beside the donkey, she gently stroked her mane and between bouts of sobbing, poured out her distress in broken sentences. They were not long together when Fanny marched into the stable, her heavy form huffing and puffing from exertion.

"I thought I find you here, girl. Get up! You've got jobs to do—starting with the outhouses." Talitha stared up at her, startled by her aggressive entrance.

"Oh, you're a brazen piece of goods, aren't you? Waltzing in here after all this time, taking the liberty to bathe in Mistress Anya's bath and wearing one of her dresses. Who do you think you are? You, with your high and mighty ways! Think you're something special don't you, just because the master has always had a soft spot for you." She threw the servant's attire at her. "Put that on now and take that fine dress off." Talitha hesitated, unsure if she should return to the castle to change.

"Go on ... get to it. Before I take a horse whip to you myself." Her round face reddened in anger. She placed her sturdy hands on her broad hips. "If you were my daughter I would have taught you a lesson by now." Talitha began to unbutton her dress, and slipping it off she handed it over to the older woman.

Fanny eyed her up and down as she pulled the skirt up over her petticoat. "God knows what the master sees in you ... scrawny bit of brazenness. Hopefully, he's finally seen through your cunning, little ways. You'd think you'd have learnt your lesson not to chase after that traitor Raybet, especially when he was responsible for you getting a good whipping and losing the stag. But no, you little tramp, you had to worm your way in with him again. Never mind about Mistress Rose. I suppose you've broken her heart too."

"It's not like that at all, Fanny," Talitha interjected.

"Oh, don't you lie to me. I heard what was said in the study. You've got a hide asking Master Jockim to let Raybet and those gypsy folk into the castle. After all he's done while you've been out gallivanting with gypsies. Why, he's let the animals go free. We're trying to make ends meet through the cultivation of the Valley of Loss again, which the Doomeerie forces fortunately got back in the battle … but it's not easy. When he's here at the castle, he works harder than anybody. He's taken the prisoners out of their cells and is caring for them up in the east wing. He's even got that medicine man, Padyah, living here in the castle to help them. He's worn himself out searching day and night for you and that bloomin' stag, and you return with your high and mighty ways and bargain for some gypsy boy and Raybet to come into the castle, using his own mother's silver goblet that he gave you as a gift!"

She grabbed a bucket and aggressively began to pump water into it. Talitha tied the apron around her fine waist. "I've never beheld such unabashed boldness." She pushed the bucket into Talitha's arms.

"You do not understand. I never intended to bribe Jockim with his mother's silver … That is just how he has interpreted it."

"Oh, be gone with ya!" she replied hotly, picking up a long-handled bristle brush and brandishing it about menacingly. "I'm done with your fancy ways of twisting things around. Get out now and clean those outhouses."

Talitha put the bucket down and stood her ground.

"Fanny, you can at least give me a hearing. What you are saying is not true. I'm not doing any chores until we sort this out. If we are to work together then we should at least show some respect for each other. The things that you are saying are preposterous. And furthermore, what Jockim and I discussed in the study is none of your business. As a servant, you should not have been eavesdropping. Neither should you be giving your opinion on matters that you know very little about."

Fanny's face reddened with anger at the younger woman's obstinacy. She was about to explode.

"How dare you tell me what to do, girl! Who do you think you are, lecturing me about a servant's place?" she retorted angrily, just as Jockim strode into the stables.

His thoughts were still ruminating irritably, escalating into all sorts of scandalous suspicions. "Is there a problem, Fanny?" he inquired looking scathingly at Talitha, who having decided that there was nothing to be gained by extending the conversation with Fanny, bent over to pick up the bucket.

"Nothing that I can't handle sir …" Fanny landed the bristled end of the brush roughly across her extended rear. "Get goin' girl before I take this brush to you good and proper."

"Ohh … Fanny!" Talitha exclaimed, shocked by the older woman's audacity and the ferocity of the sudden blow. Her face flushed with humiliation. She glanced at Jockim who made no attempt to hide his amusement.

"I see that you have matters in hand. Our little maidservant has become even fuller of her own importance since she left. I'm sure that I can rely upon you to teach her some much needed lessons.

Let me know if you require any assistance. I'll be only too happy to oblige." Seeing Talitha mortified sent a ripple of satisfaction flowing through him, stewing as he was over her new found alliance with Raybet. She fled from the stables, hot with shame and anger.

"No, I think that I'll manage just fine, sir. I've seen the likes of her kind before. They speak and act all fancy and think they are above the rest of the servants, but they come around quickly when the right medicine is applied."

He watched as she bustled after Talitha with an air of self-satisfaction. A strange mixture of pleasure and remorse welled within him. *Good on you, Fanny! Bring her down to size. How dare she flaunt back into the castle expecting me to welcome Raybet. I've spent the last two years thinking of no one but her and all she is concerned about is helping him. Well Talitha, I'll make sure that you are down on your knees begging for my mercy before the week is over. A few days with Fanny should be enough to change your ways. What a fool I've been to even think that you could ever love me or to entertain the notion that we might have some type of life together. All this time you've been chasing after Raybet, and now you are trying to manipulate me into helping him of all people … I can think of no one whom I detest more than that sly, suave fox!*

He strode determinedly towards the castle, pushing hard against the sadness that welled up inside him, in a desperate effort to ignore its compelling presence.

Talitha completed the outhouses under Fanny's supervision. The older maid then ordered that she assist her with the washing and starching of the linen. Lunch was taken in the servant's kitchen. There were smirks and sly comments from the other staff who had already heard of the mornings events. Fanny ensured that Talitha was straight back to work after lunch, mopping floors, cleaning the upstairs bedrooms, assisting with the collection and sorting of the washing, and finally helping to prepare dinner. Expecting to wait on the table at dinnertime, she automatically reached for a clean apron. Fanny stopped her.

"Ah, no, lass … The master has said that seeing that you have attended to your duties well, you can sit at the table with the others in the great hall tonight."

Her voice had softened since her earlier outbursts. She was even feeling a little remorseful that she had lost her temper so badly. If nothing else, Talitha was a good worker and a big help to have around. *Maybe the girl is trying to help a sick lad,* she thought. *She always did have a kind heart, even though she is stubborn and proud. Still, eating humble pie will do her no harm!* The older woman quietened her misgivings. *She needs to be put back in her box. It isn't good for a servant girl to think she is anything special—only trouble can come of it!*

Talitha's face brightened. Fanny noticing it remarked cautiously, "I wouldn't be too happy though. He's still mighty angry with you. I haven't seen him this upset since Raybet tried to take the castle by force. He won't be dining in the great hall tonight. He's having his dinner in his room. Can you inform Madame Anya and Master Vadio when you go up there?"

"Yes, ma'am," she replied demurely, folding the apron and placing it carefully back on the shelf. She was secretly relieved that she did not have to face Jockim again.

"Talitha …" Fanny called out after her as she headed for the door.

"Yes ma'am?"

"I hope that you have learnt your lesson today. I know that it has been a difficult day for you. However, if you don't put on airs and graces and act as if you're better than the other staff, they will soon warm to you. And you'll find that I'm just as good to work for as Madame Avileaux was. I won't stand for any insubordinate behaviour though. Neither will I tolerate servants not respecting the master. You had no place questioning my commands this morning. I'm sorry that I had to say what I did, but you needed to hear it."

"Yes ma'am." Talitha hoped that that would be the end of it, but Fanny continued lecturing.

"I know that I humiliated you in front of the master in the stables, but when pride rears its ugly head it needs to be nipped in the bud. The best way to do that is to make the punishment fit the crime. I hope that I won't need to do it again, but mark my words, I won't hesitate to prescribe sour medicine again if it's needed."

Talitha flushed. *How am I ever going to work under this old battle-axe?* Her thoughts were escalating with self-doubt and despair. "I understand, ma'am. I apologise for my disrespect this morning." Even though she didn't mean a word of it, her reply sounded convincing.

Satisfied, Fanny smiled. She had established her position clearly. "Good, we understand each other then. Thank you for your help today. You have worked well. I shall see you at 4:30am in the morning for bread baking. You might as well begin learning straight away. Sophie and Mary deserve a break from the early morning shift. I hope that tomorrow will be a better day."

"Thank you, ma'am … Will that be all now?"

"Yes, you're dismissed. I'll look forward to an honest day's work from you tomorrow … with an attitude that is fitting for a maidservant."

Talitha made her way to the great hall, trying to hold back tears. Anya and Vadio were already seated there. With the slightly flushed complexion and sombre eyes of a naughty child, she quietly joined them at the table. They smiled and greeted her kindly, sensing her dispirited mood. She immediately related the news that Jockim was not joining them.

Anya seemed concerned. "Oh dear, that is not a good sign at all. He hasn't been like this for such a long time." She glanced reproachfully at Talitha. "He told me all of what you said to him this morning, Tal. I am so sorry that it has turned out the way that it has. I know that your intentions for this sick boy are for the best, but Jockim has been deeply hurt by Raybet, as we all have."

Any trace of understanding that had been present in her words began to dissipate at the mention of Raybet. "I can understand why he is so upset with you, and quite frankly," her voice sharpened, "I don't blame him at all. It must have hurt him a great deal to think that you had given Miriam's cup to Raybet—especially after he had betrayed both you and Jockim. I cannot understand what possessed you to do such a thing. To think that Jockim has—"

"That's enough, Anya," Vadio interjected kindly, placing his sunburnt hand over his wife's pale one. "It has been a big day for Tal. She has already received due disciplining from Fanny throughout the day. There is no need for us to add further."

Talitha was well aware that the staff had all enjoyed Fanny's embellished account of how she had dealt with her obstinacy in the stables. No doubt, the news of her chastisement in front of Jockim had spread upstairs too. She blushed at the thought of Vadio and Anya knowing of it. She wondered if it had all been worth it. Even Anya couldn't understand her perception of the events. Indeed, if it had not been for the thought of Toby dying, she would have begun to doubt herself.

"Well, perhaps that discipline was in order considering the circumstances." Anya's reply came harsh, like a slap across Talitha's face. "Fanny has been a good and loyal servant. She is mama's sister. She does deserve some respect. Junior servants need to be put in their place if they defy her authority."

Her defence of Fanny was obvious. Talitha was not surprised, the two had always enjoyed a special friendship and this could have only strengthened since her mother's death.

"Indeed, she does deserve respect," Vadio replied, "and I understand that Tal has learnt her lesson and will not speak in such a manner to her again."

He glanced over at Talitha who was inwardly debating what would have been the better course of action, facing the whispers and sniggers of the servant's table, or being further chastised by Anya.

"That is so isn't it, Tal." Vadio looked to her for confirmation.

She could not bring herself to answer him. Finally, when she did speak, she was surprised at how cold her voice sounded. "My intentions have never been to be disrespectful to anyone, Vadio, since I have entered the castle. If that is how people have interpreted it, then so be it."

Anya huffed with indignation. "What has happened to you, Talitha? You have become so full of your own importance? You are not the friend who I once knew."

Jumping up from the table Talitha made her way swiftly for the door, fighting the tears that were threatening to once again tear away the mask of indignation from her face.

"Talitha—stop!" Vadio's voice held such authority that she froze. "Resume your place back at this table immediately, madame." She hesitated, not knowing what to do. "Either you do as I say, or I will inform Jockim of your ungracious behaviour. It is only by Anya's request that you have been permitted to dine in the great hall tonight. If you walk out in a huff because she has chastised you fittingly, I personally will report your behaviour to Jockim. No doubt he will have you dine with the servants in the future."

Behind her tightened shoulders, she heard Anya begin to cry. "It's alright, Vadio ... please don't say anything to Jockim. It will make matters worse. I'm sorry, Tal. I shouldn't have said that. Please forgive me. I will always consider you to be my friend."

It was more the thought of hurting Anya, than of dining with the servants that tore at Talitha's heart. She turned and walked back to the table, unable to look at Vadio.

"I am sorry too, Anya. I had no intention to hurt you. You are right. I will endeavour to be more respectful to Fanny in the future. Thank you for asking Jockim if I could dine with you."

Anya drew a small hanky from her pocket and wiped her eyes. "I'm sorry that I have been so emotional Tal; it's been all the events of today ... Seeing you this morning was such a wonderful surprise. I have dreamed of our reunion for so long!" A little sob escaped amidst her shaky words. "I was distressed to learn of your disagreement with Jockim, and later I overheard the servants laughing about what had happened between you and Fanny in the stables, in front of Jockim. I was angry that things had all turned out so badly. This wouldn't have happened if it had not been for your request. I have longed to see you and Jockim together happily again as you once were." Her words faltered as she broke down into a fresh bout of sobbing.

Vadio put his arm around Anya. "Perhaps you should inform Tal of your condition, Anya."

Anya looked lovingly up into his eyes. "Yes, I was going to. I just wanted to wait for the right moment."

"What condition?" Talitha asked, alarmed. "Are you not well?"

A smile broke out across her tear strained face, adding to Talitha's confusion. "No, quite the contrary, I'm two months pregnant. Not many know, only Jockim and Fanny." Joy beamed from her eyes.

"Oh congratulations Anya …" She leapt up to hug her friend. "I am so very happy for you. That is wonderful news, wonderful!"

She turned to hug Vadio also. "Congratulations Vadio, I am very happy for you. You will make fine parents!"

"Thank you, Tal. We are both very excited, as we have wanted a child for a long time. Anya has had difficulty conceiving, and we feared that it may never be possible. She has already had two miscarriages." He looked down at his wife proudly. "So you see she is very emotional at present. The doctor says that she is not to overexert herself or to become upset, as it will not help her condition." He patted his wife's hand again. "Forgive me if I spoke sharply to you just now. I did not want to see Anya get further vexed."

"Of course not," Talitha replied, feeling a fresh wave of guilt wash over her. "I'm sorry that my return has caused such trouble within the castle."

Vadio sensed her discomfort. "You must understand that while we sympathise with your concern for this sick lad, we have all been through a great deal of hurt since you left. Raybet not only turned against Jockim, he also almost sent my father to his death, unwittingly I will admit, but all the same he came very close to being killed, all because of his evil plan to have Jockim slaughtered. I cannot believe that he could have put a man who took him off the streets and raised him as his own, in such a dangerous position."

Vadio spoke with a power that she had not noticed in him before. He had obviously become accustomed to his position of authority in Jockim's absence.

"I am happy to hear that both Father and Rose have been reunited, and that Father has given Rose and Raybet his blessing, but I cannot do the same. Not after the way that I saw him act. I know that it is hard for you, and that Jockim is perhaps overreacting a little because he thinks that he has been betrayed, but I do believe that with time you too will see that he is acting for the best."

He winked kindly at her. "Cheer up, the castle will soon stop humming about this morning's events in the stable, and you know what they say: 'Having to eat a little humble pie never hurt anybody.' Jockim will come around. Give him time. I'm sure of it. Why it's only the first night and already he's relieved you of serving duties to dine with us."

"Yes, very noble of him." She struggled to prevent an edge of sarcasm sounding in her voice.

There was an awkward silence for a few minutes. Fanny had

just entered the room and was placing the meals before them. She shot a sideways glance towards Talitha, warning her that her tone and comment were inappropriate. Anya and Vadio looked at each other and fearing further reprisals were about to be delivered, Anya quickly commented, "Let's commence dinner … This looks delicious! We don't want it to get cold. Thank you, Fanny. That will be all for now."

CHAPTER 5

Held Hostage

Later the next day, Talitha was summoned to the study. A roaring fire bathed it in a warm glow. Jockim and Vadio had the castle plans spread out across a large, oak desk. They appeared deep in thought and neither bothered to look up as she entered. Eventually, Vadio said, "I think its better that we reinforce this section, Jockim." He pointed to a specific area on the large parchment.

"Yes, I was thinking the same." Jockim seemed lost in thought. "I don't think that we should be too concerned just yet. The Oge have not long taken over at White Cliff Castle. It will take some time before they infiltrate the east. Still, I'm disturbed that they have killed Isaac White as I had considered forming an alliance with him against them. There will be no chance of that now that his new wife, Ebony, rules over the castle. The folk west of Raven Ridge Range are in for difficult times if they oppose the Oge. I fear for Kyriedor. Thank God we have Padyah here with us."

"Yes, we are indeed fortunate!"

Jockim began to roll up the parchment. "Good, we'll go with that plan then." His face eased into a satisfied expression. Glancing up, he noticed Talitha standing awkwardly in the doorway. Vadio seeing her too, made to leave.

"Well, I'll be on my way."

"No, I would rather you stay please," Jockim replied quickly. "It is all strictly business … just a meeting with one of the servants who has a roll to play in our plans."

He beckoned coldly towards Talitha. "Come here, Talitha."

She approached and stood opposite him, facing the imposing, oak desk that had been carved into a symbol of authority.

"I have given the discussion that we had yesterday considerable thought," he said, looking carefully at her to sense any change in reaction, "and I have decided that in light of the fact that a young, boy's life is at stake, I will do what I can to assist."

Despite great effort, Talitha could not keep her face expressionless. He noted the presence of hope and relief in her eyes, which he quickly aimed to quell.

"However, it will be at a price, which *you* will play a part in."

"What is that to be?" Nothing could be worse than what she had already been through at Doomeerie.

"You will be bound and taken as hostage to Raybet. He will be told that if there is any trickery at all, you will be punished. I will allow him and the woman and her child to enter the castle so that the boy can be attended to by Padyah."

Again he watched her expression. She stifled her emotions.

"Once inside the castle, Raybet will be locked in the dungeon. The woman, whom you call Angie, will also be locked in a room with her son. Her meals will be taken to her, and she will have no visitors apart from me, Vadio, and Padyah. Your part in this affair is only to act as a hostage. You are to have no further communication with any of your three friends. If you take it upon yourself to break this rule, you will force me to execute the necessary consequences."

"And what might that be?"

"You would rather not know." He was annoyed at her little show of defiance and unable to think of anything on the spur of the moment.

"There is nothing that you can do to hurt me further. You already came close to destroying what I loved most before I left last time."

Her words visibly wounded him, and for a brief moment she was saddened, knowing that he had tried so hard to find Shiloh. He quickly covered his hurt with a show of anger.

"I had thought that I would allow you the day off from your duties as tomorrow will be such a big day, but it seems to me that you have not yet learned your place in this castle. You can therefore assist Fanny again today, and you can start by cleaning Anya's bath. A rather brash young maidservant took it upon herself to bathe there yesterday."

Talitha felt herself redden as Jockim and Vadio's eyes met briefly, each of them sharing a common amusement.

"I really must be going." Vadio rose to his feet, scratching his head in an effort to distract from the merriment that was playing about his lips. "I have a lot of chores awaiting me. Good morning Jockim ... Tal ..." He turned to acknowledge them both as he hastily made his way out.

Jockim sat down at his desk and began to write. She waited in the awkward silence, not sure whether to come or go. After several minutes, she summoned the courage to ask, "Will that be all then, sir?"

With an exasperated sigh, he looked up at her coldly. Then opening the bottom drawer of the desk, he pulled out a thick manuscript bound in leather.

"As you can see I am busy writing. While you are waiting, you can improve your ignorance about Doomeerie. Here is the code of conduct outlining rules and suggested reprisals for breaking them. Find the section on giving away castle belongings, which by the way is equated with theft. Read it out to me." He handed her the heavy book.

After a few minutes he stopped writing again and looked up. "Have you found it yet?"

"Yes."

"Yes *sir* is how you address me!" He emphasised the word, staring at her. "Well, read it out to me, *maid*."

"Yes, sir," she replied obediently. "*A servant of Doomeerie is not permitted to give away any item which his or her master, may have given to him or her, for safe keeping or temporary use. If he or she should do so, this is considered to be theft and the punishment will therefore be the same, that is, public whipping. The severity of this will be at the discretion of the master.*"

"Good, do you understand that?"

"Yes, sir …"

"It seems that you never learnt your lesson from the first time, Talitha?" His cold, dark eyes were boring into her, attempting to crack open her controlled demeanour. She did not reply. He scraped his chair back from the table angrily and stood up.

"Have you told anyone else besides me of your generosity to Raybet?" Sarcasm spilt over his curt tone.

"No sir."

She was finding it increasingly difficult to control her voice. It was beginning to sound squeaky and shaken. He sensed her growing trepidation and felt a wave of satisfaction flow through him.

"Good then, I have instructed Fanny not to say anything to any of the servants. Vadio and Anya can be trusted not to speak of it. Fanny gave you a much needed wallop with the bristled end of the brush yesterday, and since I witnessed it and the entire castle is buzzing with amusement about it, we can say that it is public. So let's say that the code has been fulfilled for the present shall we. I will record it as your punishment." He sensed her tightened frame relax a little. She kept her eyes down.

"Look at me when I address you, maid." Doe-like eyes shot up to meet him, ablaze with hate.

"You try my patience, Talitha. It is tiresome having to go through all this again. Turn to the other section that I have marked. It is on disrespect and insolence to superiors."

She opened the book where a folded sheet of paper had been placed. "Well go ahead, read it out loud!"

"*Should a servant be insolent, disrespectful or disobedient to a superior they should be punished as that superior sees fit, either through the inclusion of additional duties or the removal of any privileges. They should also give a formal apology to their superior in the presence of their master.*"

"You were given extra duties yesterday from Fanny, and again you have received them today from me for your rudeness just now. I will also record that. You need to apologise to Fanny now. Read this that I have written for you, so that you will do it well. I will summon her to the room, and when she arrives, you will get down on your knees in front of her and apologise, using sentiments similar to those written. Take the time to familiarise yourself with them now."

He strode over to the bell and pulled it sharply. Shortly, Fanny bustled into the room. "Good morning, sir." She curtsied. "How may I assist you?"

"Morning, Fanny!" He smiled at her in a dark, sardonic way. "Talitha would like to formally apologise to you for her disrespectful behaviour yesterday in the stables." He looked at her; the solemn nod of his head a cue for her to begin.

She knelt on the floor in front of the heavy set woman who folded her thick arms across her bosom; an air of power and pride settling upon her in smug satisfaction. They were both towering above her, one set of eyes filled with eager anticipation, the other cold with anger.

"I am truly sorry, Fanny ..." Her throat clamped but she compelled herself to utter the rehearsed words. "Please forgive me for the disrespectful manner in which I spoke to you yesterday. I am most grateful," again she hesitated and, taking a deep breath, continued, "that you punished me in such a timely and appropriate manner. I wish nothing more than to be freed of my proud and haughty ways and to be a faithful and humble servant to my master." The final words were rushed through as if she could not stomach them, having to expel them as quickly as possible. "If you should consider that I need further chastisement at any time, I beg that you would not spare me, but rather inflict upon me whatever reprisal you consider to be appropriate for the redemption of my wickedness."

She lowered her eyes to the floor, feeling her cheeks burning with humiliation. "As a sign of my sincerity, I will now remain on my knees until you command me to rise."

Fanny felt a warm rush of endorsement run through her veins and looking at Jockim she gushed. "Thank you, sir. I will do my best to try and assist her to mend her haughty ways."

"No, it is I who am grateful. You save me these tiresome jobs with the servants." He smiled grimly at her. "I have some figures to attend to now, so if you'd like to tell me how long you want her to remain kneeling, I will ensure that she does so while you go on and attend to your duties."

"I will leave that to your discretion, sir. You would know how contrite and genuine her words are, more so than me." She curtsied again and left the room, looking smugly at Talitha.

He strode over to his desk and sat down opening some manuscripts that were stacked up on it. Glancing up at her kneeing upon the rug, her petite frame silhouetted by the fire, he felt a sudden tug of pity.

"Damn you, Talitha. Get up off your knees and get out of my sight, before I change my mind. I hope that you've finally learned your lesson. I don't want to lay eyes upon you again today. You're dismissed."

She clamoured to her feet and headed straight for the door, feeling the hot shame burning scarlet upon her face. He called out after her, "Stay out of Fanny and the other servant's sight for about twenty minutes, and if any of them ask you how long I made you kneel, tell them that you think it was at least fifteen minutes. Oh, and by the way, if Fanny gives you a good report today you can take your meal with Vadio and Anya. I will be eating in my room again tonight."

"Thank you, sir," she replied dutifully, turning to look at him.

"Don't thank me, thank Anya. I am only allowing it to please her."

Their eyes met again briefly, spearing darts of spite into each other. She turned and walked defiantly from the room.

✳ ✳ ✳

The bleak, cold weather continued and with the coming of the new day, torrents of rain poured from the heavens. After breakfast, the soldiers came to Talitha's room and bound her hands tightly. Jockim accompanied them, saying that he would escort her up to Miriam's room, and that they were to wait there for him. After they had left, he looked her up and down sternly.

"Reminiscent of old times isn't it, my dear." He sneered. "If you do as you are instructed by my men you will come to no harm. If you decide to put into play some stupid, little, escape plan, you will not only be putting your own life in danger but also the life of your friends. Do you understand?"

She surveyed him coldly. "It doesn't have to be done this way, you know. They would come in peace, not wanting to harm anyone."

He took her by the shoulders and pushing her up against the stone wall kissed her roughly on the lips. Holding her prisoner with the weight of his body, he whispered into her ear. "Yes, and that needn't have been done that way either. I had hoped that I'd welcome you back into this castle like royalty, but instead your actions force me into treating you like a slave. Either way, I'm going to have what I've waited so long for."

He kissed her again, and she kicked him with her foot. The impact made him disengage. He laughed and taking her roughly by the arm, pulled her towards the door.

"Come on … Let's get on with it, shall we."

Arriving at Miriam's room, they found the soldiers waiting. "Shoot twice if the entire group is coming back. We will allow for three quarters of an hour. It shouldn't be any longer even if the lad has to be pulled through on a stretcher. Shoot once if only you are coming back. Make sure that Raybet has the goblet with him." He glanced harshly at her.

"Yes sir."

Taking Talitha by the arm, they hauled her down the stone stairwell to the passage below. The whole expedition went remarkably to plan. Raybet had suspected that she may be held as hostage. He was therefore not surprised when the little group approached the gypsy caravan. He and Angie had packed what they needed and were ready to proceed. The thought of the boy's health was their only concern, hence they were eager to co-operate with the soldiers. Together the group made it back to Miriam's room. Angie and the boy were quickly herded off to see Padyah, Talitha to bathe and change, as she like the others had been drenched by the rain, while Raybet was held at gunpoint.

"Welcome back to Doomeerie, my friend." Jockim eyed him with disgust. "I'm sorry that I can't give you better lodgings than the dudgeon, but considering our parting circumstances, I'm sure that your expectations wouldn't have been too high."

"I only want to see the boy get well and he and the woman leave safely. Do with me what you will!"

"Such noble sentiments, sir ... You may have fooled Talitha with your redeemed soul act, but I am not so easily convinced. Perhaps some time in the dungeon might bring about true contrition. I was pleased to learn that the general has finally recovered from his accident—strange and unfortunate affair that wasn't it?"

Raybet stared back at him remaining silent. Jockim paced around him, struggling to check an urge to knock him to the ground. So many times as a lad, Raybet had skilfully manipulated situations. If there was a fight between the lads, Raybet had only to whinge to Konfra, who would run with tales about Jockim's behaviour to his father. He, in turn, would belt him severely. Now he was back in his castle manipulating the woman he loved. It wasn't enough that he should take off with Rose; he also wanted to have his way with Talitha. Jockim's thoughts continued to rant, whipping his temper into a fury.

"And Mademoiselle Rose ... she finally gave her affections. Shame she missed out on receiving the castle as an added bonus. I hope that you have treated her well. Despite being somewhat misguided, she is basically a good soul—was always so willing to do whatever her dear father advised. I'm glad that the two of them have had some time together. No doubt Vadio will be eager to hear news of his father, as well as of her, and you will have plenty of time to relate every little detail to him over the coming weeks."

He turned to the soldiers. "Take him down to the dungeon. Vadio or I will be down to see him sometime later."

He turned to walk away and then stopped to address them again. "Bring the goblet down to my study will you. I want to look at it."

A few minutes later the soldier in charge entered Jockim's study. He looked concerned. "Sir, I don't quite know how to tell you this."

Jockim looked keenly at him. "The goblet was not there, hey?"

"No, sir ..." He unrolled a length of dark blue, velvet fabric. "On the contrary there were two goblets in his possession!"

Jockim went pale as his eyes alighted on the shining, drinking vessels. Before him, lay two identical goblets; one in gold and the other, the familiar silver. The gold one, incrusted with rubies and diamonds, sparkled brilliantly in the intense light of the fire. Beside it, the silver one, equal in beauty, beamed flashes of emerald and sapphire from its softer sheen. His hands lifted the gold goblet up to the light and his voice, barely audible, muttered, "The lost goblet of Doomeerie ... I had always thought that it was only a legend!"

CHAPTER 6

A Holy Curiosity

Talitha had settled into Madame Avileaux's room. Its familiar surroundings flooded her mind with melancholy. Jockim had insisted that it be maintained in the same state that it was in when she was alive. Avie, as she was affectionately known, had been like a mother to Talitha, and the young woman's eyes filled with emotion as she fondled her brushes and combs on the dresser.

She was tired from the morning's events. Undoubtedly, she felt pleased that Jockim had showed enough compassion to save Tobias' life, but she could see little evidence of him having changed for the better. Had Avie's passing hardened him even more? Why had she wasted so much time longing to see him again? She despised the very sight of him now. She sank onto the bed, heavy and despondent, her shoulders drooping. The last few days had been so unbearably difficult. Humiliation and pain were burying her in a mound of humus; hurt pride festering into a suppressed hostility. The memory of Kyriedor's counsel and the flame behind Jenobay's eyes had slipped silently from her thoughts without her even realising.

Disgruntled and listless, she opened the top drawer. Lightly, she ran her fingers over the small collection of items—a wooden box of pretty, pearl hair clips that spoke of years gone by, and a pair of spectacles that looked lost and forlorn, unable to be of any purpose now that their owner had departed. A gold cross, tarnished and slightly bent, spoke of Avie's unrelenting faith. Finally, her hand alighted upon an old bible, its yellowed pages tattered at the edges, and its cover creased with use. What stories might it reveal of this once brave and homely woman? Sadly, she began to leaf through the pages.

Eager to reveal its long held secrets, the book fell open at a spot marked by a loose leaf of folded paper. Sketched upon it was a drawing of a striking, young woman dressed in colourful, bohemian clothing. Upon her cupped hands, a white dove was nestled. Talitha immediately recognised the sketch to be a depiction of one of the stained glass windows in Miriam's room. Her interest aroused, she turned the paper over to find some reference. On the back, a letter had been scrawled.

My dear Jockhien,

Please forgive me for sending you this letter, but I cannot die without letting you know that you have a son. After your soldiers took me to the gypsy camp, the kind folk made a home for me and our unborn baby. I did not show them the golden goblet that you had given to me for your first born child, as I wanted our child's identity to remain a secret forever. I know that is how you would have wished it to be, as you would not have wanted dear Miriam to have ever known about the child, especially as she too was shortly to give birth to a son.

She was always a wonderful, kind mistress to me, and I never wanted to hurt her by letting her know of our secret love. I am not foolish enough to think that you did not love her, for what man could fail to love such a beautiful creature. Yet, I also believe that I have always held a special corner of your heart too, and that despite the fact that we will never be together again, a part of you will always love me, as I do you.

Our son was born in the early hours of a fine, October morning, and I called him Raybet, a name that I know could in no way ever be associated with your kinsfolk. Although not a strong lad physically, he has shown remarkable intelligence, and I am a little ashamed to say that he has learned some of the shrewd and not so honest ways of the gypsies.

Still, these are good folk, and I have met and married a man named Flynn. He has been a fine father to Raybet and a good husband to me. I have given him a daughter, a beautiful girl with flowing, red hair, not unlike my own. We named her Angelina. We have had a happy life together, but now I fear that my time is coming to an end. I have been extremely unwell for some weeks. I will give the goblet and our secret to Flynn for safe keeping. Being the man that he is, you can be assured that he will never reveal it, save but to secure your son's life.

My final request to you, my first love, is that you honour me in the traditional way of your ancestors. Just as Luke had a stained glass window which depicted Clare and her donkey constructed in the tower, and Lachlan immortalised Sarai with the tigers brought from over the seas, I now ask that you construct a window for me, as you see in this picture with the white dove. One of the gypsies sketched it for me not long after Raybet was born. I have heard from the townsfolk that when Miriam died, you immortalised her in the coloured light of the snow covered mountains with the stag that she so loved. The birds of the forest have been my loving companions on this earth, and I can think of no way to be better remembered than to be shown living free and wild as they do.

Thank you for the love and life that we once shared for a short time. It is my deepest wish that you will someday know your first born son, Raybet.

Forever in love,
Your humble maidservant,
Catherine

Talitha's hands shook as she closed the letter. Her head swam with a deluge of unanswered questions. *Who else in the castle knows this information? Do Jockim and Raybet know? Do Vadio and Anya know? Did Madame Avileaux take this secret to her grave? What should I do?*

Feeling guilty for having stumbled upon such secret information, she folded the picture and placed it back where she had found it. Confused and nervous, she left the room. They would be expecting her downstairs to take up her duties. She made her way down to the kitchens, not remembering how she got there. She would inquire of Fanny what chores would be required of her for the remainder of the day, as would be expected of her. What else could she do? She must not let on that anything of significance had occurred.

Just as she closed her door on the first floor, another opened on the second floor of the castle. Old Marcus shuffled into Jockim's study. He was not at all happy to have been summoned there. Being elderly, he was now incapable of doing much at the castle, and he feared that he would be told to leave. In a desperate effort to present himself as a worthwhile servant he began listing all of the chores that he had completed in the past week, many of which had not been done by him at all, but rather by his sons and their families. Jockim, who was uninterested in such matters, got straight to the point.

"I'm not going to dismiss you, Marcus. You have served my father and me well over the years, so as far as I am concerned you can spend your final years here at Doomeerie, regardless of how much you are capable of doing. I simply wanted to find out some information from you about my father, and seeing that you are the castle's oldest occupant, I hope that you have a good memory."

Immensely relieved, the old man cheered up. "Aye sir, I 'av a very good memory … What would ya like to know about yer father?"

"I want to know Marcus, if he had any mistresses and if they bore him any children?

"Well, that's not quite what I expected, sir. Usually such matters are kept secret, but seeing that ya'r his 'gitimate son and what not—heir to the castle as they say—I guess that I can tell ya what I know. Never told anybody before ya know! I was sworn to secrecy by Master Jockhien, and I didn't wanna get on the wrong side of 'im and lose me job, so I never did tell nobody. But yeah, he had a pretty, little filly on the side … not unlike that little miss that you fancy; the one that got punished just before the fighting started and then mysteriously disappeared. They tell me she's back ag'in … Is that right sir, is she back?

"Yes, she has returned to finish her contract." Jockim was growing impatient.

"Hope she don't bring bad luck on us, sir. Begging yer pardon sir, but she tried to steal the castle's silver and escape. Many of the servants and soldiers think that she should have been banished to Nightmare Forest and because ya didn't, Andor's forces came down upon us."

"I don't think that's going to happen again. She was duly punished at the time … given a public whipping for her disobedience, so justice has been satisfied. Now, what about my father's mistress? Did she have a child by him?"

"Well yes, sir, she did … or so they say. She was yer mother's maidservant, and when she came to be with child he sent her away, as he didn't want yer mother, Miriam to find out about it. The maid was mighty upset as I recall, but she loved yer mother as we all did and therefore was willing to go. We took 'er at night and gave 'er to the gypsy folk to care for. She was too frightened to go back to 'er own town folk, being with child as she was. We never did 'ear any more about her after that. Dunno what happened. Maybe she died in childbirth, or maybe she had a child—no one ever did find out. Cathy … that was 'er name, yeah, Catherine—pretty, little thing—a bit wild and free with long, red hair … I could see why he took to her, I could. She was a looka, but then there was none to compare with yer mother. She was a graceful swan, yer mother; a beautiful, black, graceful swan with her long, dark 'air."

"Alright … Did she take anything from the castle with her when she went, do you know?"

"Why yes sir, that she did … She took a golden goblet not unlike the one that yer young filly was supposed to have stolen. He gave it to her to use for booty in case she needed to support herself and the child. Never did 'ear any more of that either. I guess them gypsy folk made short work of it."

"The child … if it had been born … how old do you think it would be?"

"Why sir, not much older than yerself … Lady Miriam came to be with child but a few months after young Cathy left the castle. I remember because she was so close with her. She was sad that she was unable to share her joy and 'elp 'er with the confinement."

"And you say that no one else knows of this?"

"I've spoke about it to no one sir, I swear … Unless the master confided in someone. But after yer mother died, apart from the general, he had no one that he really talked to."

"Do you think that the general knew of any illegitimate offspring?"

"That I couldn't say … He never spoke much wit' me, the general—only to give me orders."

"Alright, thank you, Marcus. That will be all for now."

"Yer welcome, sir. Glad to be of some 'elp."

"Oh, Marcus …"

"Yes sir?" The old man had begun to rise. His bony hands pressed down hard upon the arms of the chair as he steadied himself. He looked at Jockim, his head beginning to shake uncontrollably.

"Please don't speak about this conversation or this woman Catherine to anyone. It should remain our secret," Jockim requested gently, feeling uncomfortable at the sight of his lolling head bobbing around uncontrollably.

"Of course, sir, I've kept it secret all these years past. Can't see why I would want to tell anyone now. G'day to ya, sir," he replied brightly. The shaking stopped and he hobbled towards the door.

"Good day and thank you."

Jockim stared out at the River Styx for a long time. Old wounds bound up for years began to unravel at amazing speed. He was fourteen years old again, and there was Raybet mocking him with contempt. He remembered the occasion well. He, Vadio, and Raybet had been permitted to accompany the men on a hunting expedition for the first time. Jockhein had organised it, and more than anything else, he wanted to win his father's approval; to be considered a man.

They were in Nightmare Forest. He shivered inwardly as he remembered it being even more foreboding than it now seemed. Within forty-eight hours, the men had shot a doe and bundled her on the back of one of their horses, ready to return to the castle. She had a fawn, to which they gave little thought. There was talk whether to shoot it or let the wild animals destroy it. They decided upon the latter. Jockim guessed correctly that they were suspicious that too much killing could bring bad luck upon them. So they moved on, leaving the little creature abandoned in the forest.

Jockim entered his young mind again, painfully recalling the fawn's soulful eyes looking up at him, like great pools of sadness. Shiloh's eyes reminded him so much of them, especially on the day that he had ensnared him. He ran his long fingers through his dark, wavy hair, pressing down hard upon his scalp, trying somehow to erase the memories.

His thoughts returned to the hunting expedition. The fawn had imprinted his gaze upon his young, impressionable mind, and although he left with the men, he inwardly vowed to return. What had he hoped to do? Bundle it secretly into a sack he supposed and try and slip it into the castle grounds to care for it—something that would have been impossible, but the young are always optimistic.

The next morning he was discovered missing. Jockhein, Konfra, and a couple of the other men, returned to the sight of the killing, where of course they found him huddled up next to the fawn. Raybet, having pleaded to come too, accompanied them. Jockhein was furious with his younger son. He ordered his men to capture the forlorn creature and then to shoot it before his eyes, but Raybet had interceded. Wanting to prove his manhood and always eager to trump Jockim, he requested to be allowed to do the killing. Jockhein approved, and Konfra guided him with the pistol. Just at the point of shooting, Jockim had broken free of his father's hold and lunged at Raybet with fists raised, knocking him to the ground. The pistol had gone off, but the bullet had only grazed the helpless creature that had scrambled free from his startled captor and fled into the forest.

Jockhein pulled the lads apart, and taking a horse whip to Jockim drove him through the forest back to the camp site.

There he proceeded to humiliate him in front of the men. His scathing comments resounded with amazing clarity in Jockim's ears.

"You fawning, little fool. I should have dressed you in skirts." The men laughed at his sharp and cruel wit. "I'll make a man out of you yet," he said, driving him with the whip before them back to Doomeerie.

Back at the castle, Jockim could feel the shame burning within him. Raybet looked down at his torn shirt and reddened back as he dismounted from his horse. He brushed past, eyeing him disdainfully.

"What a girl you are, Jockim! Wait until I tell Rose what happened. She will laugh her pretty head off. She may even let you play with one of her dolls."

Despite his pain, Jockim lunged towards him again. Jockhein brought the swift sting of the whip hard down upon his shoulders. "When you prove yourself a man like Raybet has today Jockim, then you can fight. You have acted more like a sooky, poddy calf."

He planted his boot roughly into the boy's backside, sending him sprawling face down in the dust. Jockim felt his eyes sting with tears as his father yelled at him, "Get up!" Slowly, he staggered to his feet, brushing any evidence of pain from his eyes.

"Take the boy up to Madame Avileaux. She can attend to him. His place is with the women and small children—not the men." He turned and slapped Raybet on the back. "Come, lad … You showed good pistol skills today. Konfra must be very proud to be father to a boy like you."

They turned their backs on Jockim and walked into the castle.

Vadio stopped to assist, but Jockim pushed him away. "Leave me alone," he hissed savagely.

The deep shame that had crashed through him like a wave spread its pain throughout his body and then began to slowly ebb back. Further and further it withdrew, until it rose like a great wall of hate ready to crash its contents over all who entered his life: hate for Jockhein, hate for Raybet, hate for the fawn who had brought such shame upon him. Turning, he picked up the *Doomeerie Code of Conduct* from his desk and threw it with all his might across the room. He collapsed in a huddle on the floor, slamming his tightened fists upon the cold, unfeeling stone, moaning like a wounded beast. There he stayed, adrift on a tidal wave of emotion. Finally, the wave of antipathy could extend no further. With a deep sigh, he stood up. It was time to face his brother.

CHAPTER 7

The Silver Stag

"Welcome to the family!" Jockim smiled sardonically at his half-brother, who stood before him in the study, securely bound. "Quite an illustrious lot we are, us Deeries: murderers, liars, adulterers, thieves, gamblers—you name it—we're proficient at it all. That would account for why those skills come so easily to you, big brother. Jockim eyed Raybet up and down with an expression of disgust.

"No doubt you were thrilled to know that I'm you're blood brother." Raybet smirked.

"It certainly solves a lot of riddles." Jockim acknowledged Raybet's cynical comment. "As to my feelings, they have never been any great concern of yours, have they Raybet—except that is, to do whatever you could to make them as dark as possible."

"Surely you're not suggesting that I should be responsible for your feelings, Jockim?"

"Not at all, bastard brother, but let's face it you always went out of your way to take everything that I ever loved: Jockhein, the fawn in Nightmare Forest all those years ago, the castle, and now, Talitha. It must be so frustrating to think that you were the end result of father's union with a mistress rather than a wife. Just think, all this could have been yours, and you wouldn't have even had to kill for it."

Raybet smiled sadly. "I do regret trying to place you in the heat of the battle to claim the castle, Jockim."

"Say it like it is, Raybet … Trying to murder me!"

"Indeed, I was jealous of you. You seemed to get things so easy in life. Maybe that's why Jockhein wanted to make it so hard for you little brother, so that you'd develop a little of the ambition and determination that he no doubt saw in me. I always sensed that your—our father—loved me, though I didn't realise the connection until Tal gave me the silver chalice. I then remembered seeing an identical gold one in my mother's possession. Konfra had picked me from all the other lads at the gypsy camp that night when he came, and I guessed why. Jockhein had sent him to get me. No doubt he'd paid him a handsome sum to adopt me, so that he could have me nearby … No wonder Flynn didn't have any hope of opposing him! Jockhein would have had the entire camp slaughtered to get me. Flynn spoke about it when I returned there. Poor ole fool, he's suffered from so much guilt over the years, thinking he'd let Cathy down."

There was silence for a few minutes as they both contemplated faded memories of their father. "You're right though," Raybet said. "Yes, I did want to kill the fawn to win Jockhein's approval when we were kids, and I have always wanted the castle, but as for Tal—she was just a pawn for getting you out of the way—initially that is. I figured that you'd banish her to Nightmare Forest, but under cover you'd go with her, leaving the castle for grabs. Vadio wouldn't take it. He's too bloody loyal for that. So it would be available for yours truly. Unfortunately, I overestimated your love for the poor girl. It never entered my head that you'd have her whipped and the stag fight. Didn't think that you had it in you Jockim, but then again, maybe you are more like our father than you think you are?"

Jockim grabbed him be the collar and flung him to the floor, with a ferocity worthy of the years of hate that had forged it.

"Say it like it is, Jockim … The castle meant more to you than the girl … and still does." The pain in Raybet's head had dulled enough for him to speak.

Jockim lent down and pulled him to his feet again, only to smash him to the floor once more with his fist. Raybet groaned lowly and closed his eyes.

"Have you seduced her, Raybet?" he asked ferociously. There was silence and then Raybet started to laugh.

"Seduced Tal … not at all brother … she's too smart to be seduced. If you want her, you're either going to have to get her to love you or rape her. And no, I haven't done that either." He added quickly, fearing that Jockim would kick him senseless.

Jockim stared down at him, not knowing whether to believe him or not.

"She is only a friend; a very true and noble friend. Her forgiveness has saved my life."

Jockim remained silent, still unsure of what to do. Raybet pulled himself up to sit. His jaw ached from where he had been hit, and he felt the sensation of blood dripping from his mouth. It tasted slightly sweet, a little sickly.

"If you want Tal, I suggest that you start treating her with the respect that she deserves. Surely, you've unleashed your hate on her enough already … having her whipped and humiliated … getting the stag to fight. God forbid man, if that's how you treat the woman that you love, I'd hate to see how you treat the ones you hate."

Bringing his bound hands up to his jaw, he wiped the corner of his bleeding mouth against the cuff of his shirt. "Do with me what you will, Jockim. Kill me if you like. I've always known that you detest me but leave Tal, Angie, and the boy alone. They have done nothing against you."

"Killing is too easy an end for you, Raybet. It's not going to be that simple." Jockim marched to the door and flung it open. "Take him downstairs to the dungeon again. Don't bother attending to his wounds. He has always liked to prove how tough he is."

The soldiers hauled him to his feet and hustled him out of the room. Jockim sank down into the arm chair, head in hands, his mind swimming with hate and confusion. His thoughts were torn in a myriad of different directions. There was Avie, Miriam, and Talitha, begging for mercy for Raybet, yet behind them Jockhein's face scorned him as a weak and ineffectual son, a son who had been responsible for the death of his beloved wife. He thought of holding Talitha close to him, feeling her warm, soft body curving gently into his lean, muscular form, filling the voids that had left him lonely and lost for so long. Yet, there she was again staring at him now, with the contempt that he had so often seen written on her face. He wanted to break her proud and haughty spirit: bring her to her knees, see tears come to her eyes, have her beg him for mercy. Perhaps Raybet was right. Maybe she could grow to love him and give herself to him, if he treated her differently. The thought softened him for but a second. No, it was not possible—not after everything that had happened. He stood up abruptly and strode from the room. Just what was he going to do with Raybet?

* * *

In the weeks that followed, it seemed that the curse of doom had indeed struck its full ferocity upon the castle. Punishments for even minor misdemeanours where handed out with ever increasing ferocity. Those who had been there after Miriam had died thought that Jockim had returned to the old ways of his father. He waged war with all he spoke to within the castle walls. Vadio tried to keep Anya away from him and even ventured to talk sense into him on occasion, but to no avail. Jockim had showed him the golden goblet and asked him if he had known the secret, but it seemed that Jockhein and Konfra had kept it well hidden, as even he was astounded to learn of it. Eventually, Vadio confided in Anya so that she did not lose total faith in Jockim. The explanation at least gave a reason for his heinous behaviour.

Padyah tried to approach him many times, but he would have nothing to do with the old sage, and fearing that he would be thrown out of the castle and unable to help the boy, he did not force the issue. Even Fanny was on tenterhooks, making sure that all the maids under her command did not make any mistakes. She bustled through the corridors keeping a vigilant eye, searching for the slightest error which might stimulate his wrath to arise.

Everyone dreaded making contact with him, none more than Talitha. On one occasion when leaving the castle, he had noticed a little dirt on the floor for which she was responsible. She was immediately summoned and ordered to mop it again. He watched her closely as she quickly wiped up the small traces of dust from the offensive, grey slate slabs. Aware of the dark and foreboding stares that scrutinised her every move, she worked hastily to escape their clutches.

As she completed her task, he strode over to where she sat crouched on the floor, gathering the final particles of dirt within the clutches of her cleaning rag. He kicked the full bucket of foaming water and the contents spilled over the rear of her dress. Instinctively, she jumped to her feet.

"Do it again," he yelled. "Get down on your knees and do it again. You need the practice. It will teach you not to miss anything the first time."

The rear of her dress, sodden from the waist down, clung to her body as she crouched on her hands and knees and mopped up the extending puddle. Standing above her, he watched the curves of her body twisting in panic driven motion, remembering how he had saved her from the boar's pen. He had wanted her then, but now his whole body ached with desire for her. The thought that she would never be his saddened him, and when she finally completed her task, his mood had changed from one of lustful anger to dejection.

"Is it to your satisfaction now, sir?" she inquired, rising anxiously.

His sad eyes appeared confused and a little shameful. "Yes, it's fine." His hands ran through his unkempt hair, signalling his distracted state. Picking up the bucket, she turned to leave.

"Oh Tal," he called out. Her heart dropped like a leaden stone. She turned to face him, her eyes shot with fear. His hopes of saying something to lessen the pain that he had caused her plummeted. "Nothing," he said, looking at the brown pools of fear looming large in her pretty face, "nothing at all." The words were little more than a whisper; sad and hollow against the stone walls. She turned and fled, grateful to be freed from his menacing presence.

✳ ✳ ✳

Finally, about a month later he decided to do it. The idea had been continually plaguing him for weeks. He could see no other way out of the situation in which he now found himself. He bound Raybet and rode with him at the dead of night into Nightmare Forest. He tied him to a tree, the same one that had been etched in his mind since the fawn had been almost shot. Raising his pistol, he aimed between his brother's eyes. They were blue and cold, no longer mocking him, but resigned and detached. Indeed, Raybet appeared calm, almost welcoming of the final freedom which death would offer him. Slowly, Jockim laid his forefinger upon the smooth, steal trigger. It was cold and unfeeling. The air was still. Now, was the appointed time; the long awaited moment!

A slight rustle broke into the silence. What was that? The wind sighing to him that it was a witness? Again, he heard the soft swish of movement. He peered into the shadowy gloom. Now he was straining, examining a faint flash of moonlight. Were the flickering shadows reminding him that light was still present in darkness? He lowered the pistol.

A magnificent, silver-white stag stepped out from the shadows. It moved in direct line with Raybet, blocking him from sight. Jockim stared spellbound into the bottomless pools of its eyes. Shiloh, it was Shiloh. Surely not now! Not after he had searched for him for so long. Jockim drew in a short, sharp breath. It expelled in silken, cold vapour. The stag stared straight into his soul, its eyes heavy with a haunting melancholy. Then suddenly, it turned and glided stealthily into the forest, moonlight dappling its stately, graceful movements, amidst the flickers of shimmering leaves.

Sinking to the forest floor, Jockim dropped his pistol to the ground. Raybet closed his eyes and laid his head back against the trunk of the tree. A deep sigh emitted a trail of white, moon dust from his parched, thin lips. His time had not yet come. In his heart he knew that the moment of death had passed, slipped by him stealthily in the stillness of the forest, taken by the stag that had appeared so mysteriously. The stag that looked so much like Shiloh!

CHAPTER 8

A Time for Truth

Jockim returned to the castle with Raybet still bound. Locking him in one of the rooms near the other prisoners whom he had moved to the east wing, he alerted the guard on duty of his presence. Then, still shaken, he collapsed into his own bed. He slept badly. The same reoccurring dream fragmented his sleep into tiny scraps of slumber that he wearily clutched at, causing him to thrash around inside the cotton cocoon that entangled him.

The dream unfolded in its typical fashion. He was in Nightmare Forest. The branches above him stretched their bony, extension like fingers, pointing in condemnation. All around him there was a heavy fog that descended shroud-like over the twisted trees. Every now and again, it would rise to reveal the swampy earth. He trudged on, relentlessly pursued by a brother, an ancient adversary. First it was Raybet, now Lachlan, and next Jockhein. The shadow figure stalked him, plotting his death. It was a hideous murder, lingering and painful. He saw himself stabbed and then left to pull his bleeding body over a multitude of sharp stakes that rose from the muddy depth of the dismal swamp. Eventually, his strength gave way. He lay face down in the mud, drowning in his own grave. The heavens opened to deliver shafts of stabbing rain. They filled the swamps, eager to drown his rotting flesh.

Following this dream, there was yet another. Now he was the villain, committing Raybet to slow starvation in the cellars far below his castle. He peered through the shadowy enclosure of the cell as life ebbed from his brother in the stench and dampness of the dark, stone enclosure; a man-made wasteland, viler than any bleak wilderness which nature could construe.

He awoke startled and covered in sweat. Rising, he lit his lantern. It was three in the morning. He pulled a heavy cloak over his shoulders to lock out the cold that had crept into the morning. Descending the staircase, he stopped outside the locked doors of the prisoners. The soldier who was on duty was not overly startled by his appearance, having become accustomed to him wandering about at night.

"No stirring at all tonight, sir, by any of them," he said in a hushed voice.

"Thank you, Will … When will you be relieved?"

"At four sir."

Jockim nodded gravely. He made to move on towards the kitchen.

"Begging your pardon, sir, I hope you will permit me to express my views. You seem troubled, sir."

"Say what you will." Jockim squinted at him through the flickering shadows of the lantern.

"You should not trouble yourself about them so, sir. They are comfortable and well fed and cared for. Remember they have committed crimes against Doomeerie. The men are starting to say that you are too soft on them, and that their sleep should not be broken having to babysit the likes of murderers."

"It is not their affair, Will. Tell the men that if they want to move on they can. I am not holding them prisoner here." He retorted so sharply that Will was sorry that he had spoken.

Jockim turned with a heavy step to move on and then stopped. "But thank you for what you do. And tell the others that I appreciate their efforts too. I will try and reward them a little in their wages."

"Thank you, sir," Will replied, relieved.

Jockim trudged down to the kitchens. In the solitude of the solidly, reinforced walls, he felt free to make as much noise as he wished. Searching for a brandy bottle, he rummaged through the contents of the pantry. Eventually, securing his comfort, he sank into one of the chairs and consumed his first glass before even realising that he had. His head sank drowsily onto the table. When the kind voice of Padyah alerted him to another presence, he wondered at first if he was dreaming again.

"My dear friend, sleep eludes you yet again I see. May I join you?"

Jockim pulled up a chair in reply. The old man sat down and poured himself a little brandy. "Yet another nightmare. Your shadow companions are not keen to leave you alone these days. They visit you more and more. Tell me what they are saying to you tonight."

"Just the same murder in the swamps ... I die a thousand deaths over and over. And then I commit them to death too."

"You will never put them to rest until you listen to them?"

"I've moved the prisoners out of the dungeons and into the castle, given them access to your healing care. What more can I do?" He looked searchingly at the old man.

"That is not for me to tell you Jockim, for in your heart I suspect that you already know the answer. What of your brother?"

Jockim looked up at him through eyes veiled with pain and guilt. "He is my father's son too ... my elder brother ... son of Jockhein's mistress, Catherine. For so many years, I have longed for some companionship, a brother to share my hopes and concerns with, but this man, this bastard brother ..."

He broke off and drunk deeply, placing his empty glass heavily on the table. "I fear that I am becoming like Lachlan. I am drowning in jealousy and suspicion of him. I cannot rid my mind of the thought that he will not only have my castle, but that he has already or soon will have his way with Talitha. See how readily she believes in him and his innocence after all that he has already done to us. I suspect that she somehow knows of his connection to the castle and is trying to help him secure it. It is just too much to ask of any man, Padyah, too much!"

"What is too much?"

"That I share with my brother all that I have: my castle, my land, and maybe lose to him the woman that I love."

"You never lose anything that you give away, my friend; it is always given back to you. In pardoning him, you pardon yourself. If Talitha is to be with him, then nothing that you can do will ever stop that. Detach from your fears. Let go, embrace the peace that it to be found therein."

Jockim lowered his head onto his arms that were folded on the table and began to sob. The old man gently placed his hand on his back and said not a word, for no words would be able to ease the pain that had been growing for years. Now that the truth had begun to unravel, it was the time to make choices.

Eventually, Jockim lifted his head and propped it against his hand; his elbow leaning on the table. "I tried to kill him tonight, Padyah. I took him into the forest, tied him up to the tree, the same old oak that he had tried to kill the fawn under. I lined the pistol up. I only needed to pull the trigger, but some sound or movement; some passing shadow caught my attention. I looked up and there was Shiloh standing before me, staring into my soul. His eyes were filled with such sorrow that he disarmed me. He stayed but a second and then moved on, but in that time, he changed my heart. I could not bring myself to do it. I brought Raybet home and have imprisoned him up in the castle along with the others. He is in a bad way."

Jockim looked up at the old man, visibly shaken. "Do you think that you could attend to him tomorrow and for as long as is needed to return him to his health?"

"I can and will!" The old man's eyes alighted with the fire of hope.

"I have decided to give him half share of the castle, Padyah. There is no other way out of the curse of Doomeerie—only that or death."

"You have chosen well, Jockim. Now ask for the courage to do it, as a thousand reasons will creep into your mind not to, before you bring it to pass."

CHAPTER 9

The Curse Begins To Crack

When Jockim entered Raybet's room three days later, he was sitting up in bed eating. The dull ache that had lodged in his head, pounding for attention for about a month now had subsided, making it possible for his brain to care about living once again. His body, still drained of energy, felt listless, like an old horse that had fought too many battles and was now begging to be put down.

Jockim pulled up a chair and eyed him in a detached manner. "You're looking a lot better. Padyah has done a good job."

Raybet sighed and laid his head back down on the pillow. He pushed the half eaten food away. It was too much effort to consume it anyway. "What do you want with me brother? To fatten me up and then kill me?"

"Would that help to alleviate some of your guilt?

"What I have done, I have done," Raybet said with an air of resignation. "I know that I have made my peace with God and with Tal. I have prayed for Konfra and Rose. I have tried to do what I could to help Angie and Tobias. I have given you back the golden goblet as an act of reconciliation and returned the silver. I can only ask you for your forgiveness and tell you that I am deeply sorry for my heinous acts over the years, but if you choose not to forgive me, then so be it. It is not my business, and I am happy for you to do with me what you will."

He stopped for a minute. It was such an effort to speak. The words were great, heavy barrels of thought requiring effort to be lifted from his psyche to his speech organs. "All I ask is that you care for Angie, Toby, and Tal. They do not deserve your vengeance."

"It will take me time to forgive you Raybet, and I'm not sure if I ever will, but for now at least I no longer desire to kill you." Frustrated, he stood up abruptly and began pacing about the room impatiently. "I can have no peace of mind with this unfinished business hanging over my head. Why should I believe you, Raybet?"

"I can give you no reason, Jockim. I don't deserve it. I have never done anything to deserve it, but thank God, Rose and Tal believed in me. I would never have changed if they hadn't."

"Well, I'm glad that Tal believes in someone because it's certainly not me anymore ... if it ever was ... especially after she thought I was responsible for Shiloh's brush with death. I should never have allowed Konfra to talk me into that, but I didn't know how else to save her from banishment and sure death in Nightmare Forest."

"She believes in you. Actually, if you ask me, she loves you. You were always on her mind. Her mission was to get back to you, Shiloh, and the Hidden Garden ... whatever the hell that is!"

"I felt that her sentiments had somehow swayed towards you. That you not only sought my castle, but also the woman I love," Jockim remarked tentatively. A faint hope was beginning to emerge from the shadows of his dark thoughts.

Raybet laughed wearily. "Me, are you crazy? She looks on me like a brother and nothing more. In fact, she hated me when we were first reunited. It was only because she had the conviction to act on her beliefs and not her feelings that she forgave me. I owe her a great debt."

Jockim stared at him, still unable to gauge if he was speaking genuinely. He desperately wanted to trust him, but there had been too many deceptions over the years.

"If you didn't have our father's and grandfather's blood flowing through your veins I might believe you." He smiled sardonically. "However, taking into account that womanising runs in this family, I can't help but wonder why she would forgive you unless you had somehow charmed your way into her heart."

"Charmed my way into her heart? Breathed sweet nothings to her as I held her against me in bed? Is that what your suggesting, Jockim? I thought you knew Tal better than that. She's too strong of spirit to be seduced. No, Jockim, if things aren't working in the right way for you with her, look to yourself. Why, you treat the poor girl abhorrently. Who in their right mind would have her working as a maidservant after she came back to them?" Raybet sighed in exasperation at his brother's lack of insight. "You have no understanding at all of women, do you?"

"Well it was her suggestion to recommence work as maidservant, not mine." A little worm of guilt began to creep insidiously into the brambles of confusion that blocked Jockim's mind.

"You didn't have to follow through with it. What else was she going to say? I think I love you, and I hope that you love me too. So, I'm going to tell you this at the risk of you rejecting me and my spirit being crushed."

"Yes," he replied matter of factly. "The truth sounds a damned good option to me."

"And have you told her the truth about your feelings?" Raybet quipped back, looking quizzically at him.

"The right opportunity hasn't arisen yet," Jockim replied defensively.

"Well, my advice is that if you want her you'd better make it arise! She's far too good for you anyway." Raybet laughed wearily.

Jockim looked down at the body which he knew to be his brother's. It looked different, much frailer and not so important. His spirit also seemed different, so peaceful. It held none of the ambition and cunning that had motivated it in the past. Then, it had been a lively and self-centred little fox, full of beguile and shrewdness, always able to catch and consume the prized chickens of his life, which he like a mother hen, had tried to protect.

"If only I could trust you not to take up the pistol against us again," he muttered.

"You punished Tal for not trusting you when you were flirting with Rose to keep Konfra's favour. Why don't you practise what you preach and show a little trust in her discretion about me? She's no fool, Jockim."

"Alright, for the time being you can continue lodging here in the castle. There will be a soldier outside your bedroom door at all times, and you will be under lock and key. At least it will be more comfortable than down in the dungeon. We will talk again after I have spoken with Vadio. If you need anything in your room, let me know."

He opened the door and addressed the soldier waiting there. "If he needs any food, drink or blankets give it to him. Any other requests check with me first. Do you understand?"

The soldier nodded dutifully. "Yes sir!"

✳ ✳ ✳

Later that evening, Jockim joined the others for dinner. It was the first time that he'd done so since Talitha had arrived back at the castle. He appeared calmer, more like he was before Raybet had returned with Angie and Tobias. Towards the conclusion of the meal, he remarked casually that Vadio and he had met and decided to move Raybet up into the east wing of the castle. He added that under no circumstances was he to have any visitors apart from himself, Vadio and Padyah.

"Should he prove himself able to be trusted within a few weeks, I may give him freedom of the castle as I have given Angie today. I invited her to dinner, but she chose to stay beside Tobias tonight. She may join us in a few days if the boy shows further improvement."

"That's very kind of you indeed, Jockim!" Anya remarked, astounded at the sudden change of plans. "But do you really think that that is such a wise idea Vadio, in light of Raybet's past history?"

"I think that Jockim has chosen the best course of action, my love." He patted her hand. "I'm quite sure that everything will be fine." He looked at her in a fashion that only she could read. It had that, 'I'll explain later' ambience about it.

291

"I understand your concern Anya, but the past is over now, and we must look to what is best for all in the present." Jockim pushed his chair back and stood.

"Ah Talitha, I wondered if you might join me for a stroll?" He smiled charmingly at her.

"I'm sorry, sir, I am feeling tired tonight. It has been a big day and I thought that I would retire early, if I may be excused." She was happy to be given an opportunity of refusing him.

"Perhaps I did not express myself clearly." Annoyance bubbled into his voice. "I should have stated that I am telling you to stroll with me as part of your duties."

"Well, seeing you put it that way, I can hardly refuse, sir," she replied, determined not to be intimidated by his manner. She pulled her fine body up to its full height, thrusting her shoulders back. Her long, auburn hair, which she had let hang loose, shimmered lightly in the glow of the table's candlelight. Anya and Vadio quickly stole glances at each other as she exited the room before him.

"He really has no idea how to handle women," whispered Vadio, shaking his head. "Perhaps you could have a word with him … give him some hints. He will never endear himself to Tal if he continues to boss her about in such a manner."

She grinned back at her husband. "I can only try, Vadio. Believe me, he is not an easy man to sway. Perhaps it would be more beneficial to get her to understand him."

Outside the air was cool and fresh. Despite her tiredness, Talitha felt somewhat revived. The moon cast silvery shadows across their pathway, bringing back memories of happier times. Occasionally, it was obliterated by heavy masses of dark, streaky clouds that had been pulled from the sides of the sky's canvas, to remind her of more sinister forces at play. They strode towards the river, the space between them nursing the hurts of the past. Eventually, he spoke.

"I am sorry about the manner in which I just spoke to you in there. I had no right to command you to walk with me. I understand that you would be very tired. If you would prefer to retire earlier, then please feel free to do so."

"Thank you, but a short stroll will probably help me to relax. I may sleep better." She was determined not to be upset in any manner by him. *He is of little consequence to me now*, she thought, feeding upon the angry emotions that simmered inside her.

"I hope so, I … er … I just wanted to have the opportunity to be alone with you. I wanted to apologise for my behaviour over the past month. I'm aware that I have been what you would call 'a beast'. A lot has been happening for me. I've been trying to adjust to it. You know the return of Raybet has been quite confronting for me. However, I am endeavouring to change."

Silence descended upon them momentarily. It was compelling and expectant. She had chosen to make it difficult for him by not acknowledging his feelings. Raybet had said that she had forgiven him. *I'll remind her of that*, he thought, grasping at shafts of hope in the darkness of her silence.

"You have given Raybet your forgiveness … Perhaps you might consider doing the same for me," he asked, quickly adding, "even though I know I don't deserve it." He hoped that a little show of humility may assist to persuade her to let down the cold barrier that was being subtly, yet swiftly erected between them.

"I'm sorry, it's just—"

"It's just what?" he inquired, a little too anxiously.

"It's this whole maidservant thing. I feel like I'm under the curse of the Doomeerie maidservants," she blurted out.

"What do you mean by that?" He looked at her sharply. He couldn't help wondering if she knew of his father's relationship with his maidservant, Catherine.

Realising that she had revealed more than she intended, she started to stammer. "N … Nothing … nothing at all … oh … I don't know." She floundered, trying to think of a plausible reply. "You know this whole master servant thing. I guess I feel vulnerable considering the reputation of your forefathers." Her response came cloaked with circumspection.

"Well, I can assure you that I am neither the ghost of Luke nor Lachlan, which you have no doubt heard about from your stay with Kyriedor. However, I don't feel comfortable either with the thought of holding you here under a servitude contract. You are welcome to leave if that is what you now desire. Although I would much prefer that you didn't."

He stopped and looked up at the castle quietly for a moment before continuing. "I can understand that it's not the most homely of places for a young woman. Nevertheless, I'm sure that the walls of Doomeerie aren't going to collapse about us because a little maidservant has broken her contract. However, to be on the safe side, I could always think of a suitable punishment for you, to prevent any possibility of that happening, if you do decide to leave before your contract is up." He grinned at her cheekily, unable to resist a further innuendo of his power.

"I'm quite sure that you could and would find great delight in doing so however I do believe that I am meant to be here at present. Besides, I have nowhere else to go. All of my closest friends are here, except for Kyriedor, and I understand that he is now living a nomadic life, teaching and healing. Maybe with time, when I have saved enough money, I will search for Shiloh and the Hidden Garden." She was relieved that the conversation had moved on and comforted her fears by clutching on to the thought that Kyriedor had confirmed that her mission was to be at Doomeerie.

"Well, then it's settled. You will stay on ... for the year." He looked at her with renewed animation. "I am very happy, even though you still have not given me your forgiveness." He prompted again, hoping that she would pick up on the hint and assuage his guilt.

She said nothing and the disappointment landed like lead within him. Still, at least she was staying on despite having been given the opportunity to leave freely. That was a good start. Remembering that she had only wanted to walk a short distance and convinced that he would make no further gain with her at present, he stopped and inquired, "Do you want to head back?"

"Perhaps I should," she replied taciturnly, not trusting herself lest she should make yet another *faux pas* in her tired state. "It is getting late."

"I'll walk back a little of the way with you, and then I want to check on Noble for the night."

She looked up at him. "Everyone has told me that you have changed since I left after Shiloh's fight, and tonight I can see that you have. In less than twenty four hours there has been an almost complete reversal of your attitude towards Raybet. What has caused this, sir?"

Her voice was perhaps a little too urgent. Two can play at the same game he thought to himself. *If she is holding out on me, then I too will keep her wondering about my motivations.*

"Now, now, my dear ..." He looked down at her tiny frame. "You don't expect me to reveal all of my secrets in one night do you. Let's just say that your presence here is a good influence on me. And while I think of it, I would much prefer that you addressed me as Jockim, like you used to, rather than sir."

He was pleased to note the subtle curve of her lips. Their softness indicated that his reply had both charmed and intrigued her. She wisely chose not to push the point with him and as they had reached the castle steps, turned to say goodnight.

"Good night, Tal," he replied. "Thank you for walking with me."

He wanted her so much. Every nerve in his body screamed at him to take her in his arms, hold her tightly and kiss her, until she would melt into his embrace and yield to him. Accustomed to disciplining himself, he pushed down hard upon his sensual appetite, promising himself that there would come a time when it would have its full. He tried to focus upon the gains that he had made. It was an enormous sense of relief that she was going to stay on. But even so, he had a lingering doubt that something wasn't quite right.

Just what had she meant by those words 'the curse of the Doomeerie maidservants'? he thought as he headed towards the stables. *I'm quite sure she knows more than she is letting on! If so, is this whole plan an attempt to get Raybet into a position of power in the castle? Does she entertain some sentiments for him after all? Just how much did Kyriedor tell her? And, had Raybet lied about her not knowing of the existence of the golden goblet? Where was Rose? Why had she not sought Raybet out if she and her father were free of the Oge and if she truly loved him?*

Without him realizing it, Jockim's mind had already spun back into a sinister mist of mistrust. In spite of his strong feelings for her, he was caught up in a vicious love—hate cycle. He was losing his way in this swirling fog. It cleared for only minutes, allowing his mind to navigate his bearings, before descending again, like gluggy, cold soup, clinging distastefully to the crevasses of his mouth. All efforts to convince himself that she would ever, or could ever, come to love him, were difficult to swallow. It was going to take more than a little cleansing to free himself from the poison that he had so mindlessly consumed.

A Watch in the Storm

Jockim continued to ask Talitha to stroll with him after dinner, however most nights she refused. He accepted the rebuttals even though he inwardly felt increasingly frustrated. Still, he was determined that he would not let her see his temper again. Anya had assured him that this was the best way of winning her affections. All the same, it took considerable effort for him to smile kindly at her when she announced that she was going to retire early, night after night. He had waited all through the tiresome day to spend time alone with her—surely she could afford him a few scraps of her pretty smile.

Talitha deliberately chose to remove herself from him. He stimulated such a confusing array of emotions within her: excitement, fear, attraction, rejection, vulnerability, haughtiness, and so the list of opposites went on and on. Swaying her back and forth pendulum fashion, these conflicting voices competed with each other for her attention day after day, like naughty children. She was frightened that these wearisome urchins would reveal themselves. She didn't like feeling exposed. It signalled her weakness and vulnerability. It reminded her that she was far from perfect. She wanted to remain calm and in control. It was far easier to squash and deny such painful emotions than it was to attend to them. Fanny kept her busy during the long days, and at nights she tumbled exhausted into bed, forgetting about Kyriedor's warnings and the reeds and ripples.

Tobias had improved remarkably and he and Angie were now joining the others for dinner. The gypsy woman's company energised Talitha, and the two of them would laugh and chat together. The light from their alluring brown and blue eyes danced across the same waters of shared merriment as they recalled happy times. Anya and Vadio doted on Tobias. The lad took to them with equal affection and kept them laughing continually with his wide eyed and winsome ways. They would look at each other in shared amusement, when he would relate tales of smugglers having hidden treasures in the bowels of the castle, or of ghosts lurking in the spiked turrets of its towers. Vadio's hand would instinctively reach out and caress Anya's expanding stomach, assuring its growing spirit that he longed to welcome the arrival of his child.

Jockim frequently felt removed from the frivolity at the dinner table. Tonight, as usual, his thoughts had taken to brooding about Raybet. His half-brother was definitely improving. Before long, he would be restored to full health again. He couldn't risk having him associate with Talitha. That would be tempting fate. No, he would have to keep him locked up. Part of him wished that Raybet would commit some grave evil again, hurt someone, or steal something, so that he would appear justified in continuing to imprison him. However, he certainly did seem to be a redeemed soul. Nowadays, he was content to lie on his bed, eyes closed in saint-like fashion. Every so often, he would arise and force himself to hobble about in an effort to improve his strength.

He was always polite and respectful towards Jockim when he forced himself to enter the confines of his imprisonment. Such occasions left Jockim feeling vaguely guilty and on edge. He was used to respect, the soldiers and staff showed it to him every day, but it was the type born of fear, not of the compassion which now seemed to spring fountain-like from Raybet. How had this man who had been so ruthlessly calculating and greedy for all of his life managed to attain the bearing of a mystic? It annoyed Jockim to think that despite his dogged efforts to recreate his own character, he was still far from becoming the man he wanted to be; the man that Talitha would love and admire. Sure, he had freed the animals, stopped the fighting and gambling, removed the prisoners from the dungeons and allowed them to be roomed behind locked doors within the confines of the castle's comforts, but still he felt tarnished. Deep within him the reptiles of fear, anger, jealousy, hate, and self-loathing, lunged forward every so often, to rob him of a hefty chunk of his self-esteem.

Jockim sat enviously eyeing Vadio's hand caressing his wife's ever expanding stomach. Previously, he had discussed with him the plan of sharing half of the castle with Raybet. He too seemed satisfied that he was a changed man, but they had both thought it better to hold off until his health improved further, before discussing it with him. Besides, Jockim could not bring himself to talk about it just yet. The idea seemed very noble and his heart warmed to it, but another part of him argued against it. Why should he hand half of his fortune over to a man who had competed and fought with him for almost all of their lives? No matter how good he appeared to be now, his past was wicked enough to have had him executed. No one could argue with that, least of all Jockim! It seemed so unreasonable to just forgive and forget in a few weeks, a hatred that had taken a lifetime to fashion into such a delectable delight to savour. Its sweetness made him feel better about himself. He appeared positively monk-like, a holy man, when he permitted the taste of Raybet's past to linger in his mind. No, there was plenty of time to give the matter further thought. No need for any rash decisions, just yet. Tired of rehearsing the same old arguments, he stood up abruptly, unaware that he was rudely interrupting the frivolity at the table.

"I'm going to check on Noble," he mumbled in the dark manner that frequently settled cloak-like upon him. "I think that we are in for a bad storm. I want to make sure that the men have locked the horses and Balaamine down securely for the night."

The others looked up, a little startled. Vadio's offer to assist was ignored as he strode impatiently from the room. Outside, the clouds which had been clustering uneasily in heavy masses of brooding swirls throughout the day, obliterated any light except for the glow from his lantern, which trembled out a warning of what nature intended to unleash. Noble was edgy as he had expected, but he responded well enough to his gentle, commanding voice and settled for the night. Balaamine, always the more placid, did the same.

Re-entering the drawing room, he surveyed an altered ambience. The others were crowded around the table, their faces animated in the light of the candles which flickered blue and brown in their eyes. Angie was deftly shuffling a pack of cards through her long, lean fingers. Her hands moved gracefully with the precision and speed of a skill born at an early age. Her long, strawberry, golden hair was covered by a veil of black lace. Her beauty had an alluring, almost mysterious quality which Jockim's glance didn't fail to notice. Opposite her sat Talitha, eyes alive with excitement; face breaking into lines of pleasure as she watched her friend. Maybe now was a good time to tell her of his plans regarding her possible change of duties at the castle? He strolled over.

"Oh, Jockim," Anya cooed like a mother hen, "come and join us. Angie is reading our futures in the cards. She's about to tell us what lies in stall for Tal."

Jockim pulled up a chair. "An early morning start to bake bread with Fanny," he said rather dryly. "Or if she fails to arise, a good scolding, I would hope." He couldn't help feeling annoyed at their having fun while things seemed to weigh so heavily upon him. "Don't tell me you believe in this rubbish, Vadio?" He shot a scornful glance at Angie, shaking his head in disbelief that his friends could be so gullible.

"Oh don't be such a bore, Jockim. It's a little fun!" Anya chirped. A flash of lightning cracked across the darkened sky, bathing the huddled group in ghostly illumination. "Tonight is ideal! The storm will provide the perfect backdrop!" A delightful thrill of excitement shuddered down her spine.

"Now, now, Anya, don't get too excited. I'll think I'm going to ban you from having a reading, in case you believe it too much … might not be good for our bub." Vadio smiled down at the little bump that was nestled softly under the folds of Anya's dress. Patting it gently, his glance alighted tenderly on his wife's freckled, homely face. "We can't afford to have you get too excited, my love!"

She grimaced back at him. "Oh a little excitement never hurt anyone did it, Tal?" She laughed nervously as the sky boomed out in protest at their proceedings.

Angie eyes flashed blue cinders under her darkened lashes. She closed them and lowered her head reverently like a Grecian goddess, her hair spilling red, gold, moon dust about the feminine angles of her face. Silence descended upon the group as her voice floated out upon the shadowy surroundings, deep and sweet.

"Great spirits of our ancestors, abide wit' us now, on t'is night of shadows, of tempest an' truth. We implore yer wisdom an' guidance."

Jockim raised his eyebrows. *Surely, these words are much practised. They hardly sound like Angie at all.* He eyed his fellow companions thoughtfully. *What fools they all are, taking it so seriously. Ah well, it can't hurt to have a little diversionary entertainment. At least it affords me a little more time with Talitha.*

"Ancestors of the maidservant Talitha, come to 'er now, an' grant 'er wisdom an' guidance as she chooses 'er path for the future."

Yes, Jockim thought. *Let it be with me, bring her to my bed enlightened ancestors and hurry up about it. I'm growing weary of waiting for her.*

The sky bellowed angrily in response. He humorously pictured a thousand spirits of her departed ancestors racing towards Talitha to protect her from his amorous advances. Angie opened her eyes again, enigmatic and entrancing.

"Now choose yer seven cards Talitha, for seven is the 'oly number from ancient times. Blest is 'e who is accompanied by the number seven throughout life." She fanned out the deck in her long, spidery fingers. "Take yer time and pray for guidance. Only choose those cards that ya feel drawn to."

Talitha sat spellbound. The minutes ticked by. If they had not afforded Jockim the opportunity to securitise her pretty features in the soft glow of the candles he would have been frustrated with the time spent. Instead, he was held captive by the doe-like expression in her large, liquid, brown eyes. They melted away his impatience and mockery, leaving him mesmerised. Angie laid the chosen items face up on the table.

"Now," she said, "ya must choose two: one for the feminine part of yerself which is made manifest to the world; the other for yer soul mate, the masculine part of yourself, which ya cleave to, hidden deep within ya. Remember, choose only what ya fancy."

Talitha looked carefully at the cards placed neatly along the table in a row. They stared back at her, each beckoning her into the mystery that they promised to expose. Her eyes were drawn to the fourth card along. It pictured a deep pool into which something had been dropped, creating ever expanding, concentric circles.

"I choose that one!" She indicated with a quick movement, illuminated by a sudden shaft of lighting that spread its ghostly shimmer across the barriers of space. A moment passed. "And I think that one!" Her fingers alighted upon an image of dancing flames that appeared to rise from the card, drawn by the lightning to create a commanding presence. It was the first in line. The sky bellowed again in angry response to having just been whipped apart. Angie scooped the other cards up in a flash.

"The first ya choose is for yer feminine self. There is a great darkness that will befall ya … like fallin into a deep, dark pond wit' no one ta save ya but yerself."

Anya looked concerned. This prediction was unnerving. She shuddered. What effect would it have upon her friend?

"But see the shimmers on these ripples?" Again, the spider spread its legs out across the card to point out the circles of light depicted on the pond. "'Ey are to show ya that the darkness that will befall ya also 'as glimmers of light … only ya must have the eyes to see it. Yer fall into the watery abyss, will bless ya with new eyes. Ya will be able to see 'at there are blessings in yer sufferings, so ya will learn to love 'em for the grace and goodness that they bring ya."

She smiled tenderly at her friend's wide eyed response. "And yer second card … that is for the inner man within yaself … yer soul mate. He mus' be willing to let go of all that he desires to control … free of all 'is emotional hooks. Only then will he come to see the love within 'im. Then love will flow freely back into 'is soul."

A crystallised silence dared anyone to break it apart with futile words. Again, the thunder smashed down upon them, in response to the swift fork of lightning that split the sky, shattering the fragile peace that pervaded. It was Jockim, unable to squash the sceptic within himself, who spoke first.

"A thought to cherish next time Fanny takes to you with the long handled brush, Tal!" He sniggered. "You will learn profound humility from the felt effects of its bristles upon your derriere!" He regretted his dry humour as soon as it had been unthinkingly expressed. Her obvious discomfort spoke of the sting of his insensitive wit.

"Oh shut up, Jockim!" Anya chided. "Why bring that up again. It's in the past. We've all forgotten about it." Her words fell unconvincingly upon all present, who were trying to avoid making contact with the doe-like eyes shimmering in shame. "Why don't you pick cards, seeing that you have so much to say?"

"Yes, why not?" he replied with a forced element of merriment. He could not think of anything more ridiculous, however it might take some of the heat out of the moment for Talitha. "Shuffle again, Angie!"

Again, the spider scurried to line them up neatly in front of him upon the table. He decisively chose the seven cards that appeared most prominent to him. It was a simple task to choose two from them.

"That one!" he said, quickly pointing to a stick-like figure that resembled a man. "Yes … that one too!" He chose a more rounded design, almost heart shaped, like a leaf that had been dissected by its stem.

His eyes glanced at Talitha to check if her embarrassment had diminished. Diving into her doe-like pools his discerning spirit immediately picked up that they were still shimmering with deep shame. Quickly, he averted his glance.

"Well now, Angie, tell all. What are the deep secrets of my soul? Now is your chance for revenge. Make me squirm with shame in front of my friends." He laughed mockingly at her. Again, the night boomed out defiantly at them. A gust of unprecedented wind shook the windows with its fury.

"Sir, do not mock me or the cards. Evil will befall ya. Ya do not understand the power of yer ancestral spirits. The departed Deerie clan possess dark powers!"

The tension heightened. A moments silence lingered hauntingly while she paid respect to the dead, trying to assuage their anger which he had aggravated. Mysteriously, she continued.

"Yer first card tells of yer masculine self that is made manifest to the outer world. It shows that ya have indeed begun the journey within, but that ya still 'ave a long way to go. Ya need to focus on yerself, because ya'r the most important thing in yer life. Don't be frettin wit' what to do about others. Sort yerself out first."

Jockim instinctively looked towards Vadio who raised his eyebrows, a slight smirk curving his lips. "The second," she said, "shows the inner woman, deep within ya, yer soul mate."

"Yes, what of her?" Jockim couldn't resist the temptation to look at Talitha.

"She needs to take responsibility for 'er emotions, sir … Not to be lookin' to blame others for the situation that she finds 'erself in. She has made 'er choices, and now she must deal with the emotions that they cause to bubble up within 'er. She is trying to deny 'em, escape from the attraction and desire for love that she feels, because they make her feel uncomfortable, messy. She doesn't like that, sir. She likes to be perfect, and these emotions are fraught wit' such darkness and strength that she fears they will drown 'er."

Angie words were like hot pokers to Talitha's ears. Jockim's eyes immediately shot towards her, holding her gaze in a tight embrace. A helpless doe caught by the noose of his penetrating stare; she was unable to release herself. A flood of hot, red blood surged into her face. She imagined that all at the table could hear her temples beating, bursting to be released. Her hidden feelings for him, those that she hated to admit even to herself had been exposed. She was standing naked before them all!

"Indeed, she does," Jockim exclaimed softly, almost under his breath. The barely audible words seemed to shout across the table at Talitha, as the lightening illuminated all present as to their underlying meaning. She jumped up, hot and flustered.

"Well, that is enough conversing with the spirits for me. Good night, everyone. I think I'll head off to bed. I have an early—"

Boooom! Another bellow stomped heavily. Crash! The nearby window cascaded into hundreds of shimmering shafts strewn wildly across the unyielding floor. Cries of shock escaped around the table. Now was the time! Everyone's attention was stolen by the shining spectacle. Talitha hastened to escape!

Simultaneously, the wind howled its way through the window of opportunity. In one final act of defiance, nature extinguished the candles in a sigh of curling smoke. They were plunged into darkness. Talitha kept going, eager to escape. Suddenly, the space changed before her! She felt her shin hit against something hard. The shadows moved position around her. "Oh!" A little cry escaped from her, shocked that she was no longer standing upright. Now she was on the cold, stone floor and her body ached in protest, but it was her leg that screamed out at her the most. The pain shot up it, blocking out thought of all else.

Lightning exploded momentarily into the room again, to be followed by the heavy drumming of a deluge of shafting, stinging rain. Minutes passed and the candles were relit. They tenuously clung to their gentle flames, fighting to maintain their presence.

"Get someone here to border up that window, Vadio!" Jockim was already beside Talitha. "Are you alright?" he asked, demanding an answer from her in spite of the pain that drew her attention inwards.

"My leg, the pain … it's so bad!"

Angie ran to him with a lantern. He scooped Talitha up tenderly. "Thank you." He grasped the lantern. "Can you get Padyah immediately? Tell him to come to Tal's room."

Angie nodded. Vadio lit another lantern. The candles had already relinquished their tentative claim to the light. Another blast of wind rattled through the space in the wall.

Within minutes, he had her on the bed. He lifted her skirt and petticoat up to her knees, pulling up the left leg of her pantaloons so that he could better see her lower foot. She had no desire to resist. The pain was screaming its way up her leg and into her hip. Within minutes, Padyah was there beside him, his long, cool fingers touching the throbbing limb.

"No, she hasn't broken it. Only a sprain I think. A couple of days in bed should suffice, followed by no more hard labour and plenty of rest. She needs to mostly sit. A little bit of walking now and again, slowly, and not much at first. Then gradually build it up. She'll be alright." He nodded with satisfaction.

"Here take this, Talitha; it will help with the pain, while I attend to your foot."

He handed her a distasteful greenish, black brew. She forced its bitterness down her throat despite its objections. Anything was better than the pain searing up her protesting leg.

"You're going to have to stay off it for a few days. No more work in the kitchen or the laundry for you for a couple of weeks."

Jockim looked at her lying helplessly on the bed, concern easing from his face. A mixture of relief and excitement flooded over him. "She can help me with the bookwork in the study when she's up to it. I've wanted to have her there to assist me for a good while now, but Fanny wouldn't hear of it. Don't like upsetting Fanny too much, so I didn't push for it. She will just have to accept it now."

Padyah couldn't help smiling as he picked up on their opposing emotions. There was a definite air of jubilation in Jockim's voice. Fate had finally worked in his favour, delegating him with his heart's desire. The pain had subsided enough for Talitha to understand his words. She was about to be plunged into the bubbling cauldron of her emotions, into a pool of hot pride, to face the powerful whirlpool that pulled at her within.

Padyah looked compassionately down at her. He lent forward and taking her hand spoke softly, "I will have to leave the castle soon, dear Tal. My work is all but completed here, and I am wanted elsewhere. Jockim will take good care of you, but you must also care for yourself. Take a little time now that you are unable to work to sort out the thoughts and feelings that are troubling you. I am sure that Kyriedor would have advised you to care for your emotional and spiritual self. Now, more than ever, you must be vigilant and watch into the night."

CHAPTER 11

My Poor, Proud, Little Maid

"If you struggle, I'll put you over my shoulder and smack your derriere!" Jockim quipped brightly as he lifted her from the bed a few days later to carry her to his study.

Her cheeks flushed at the thought of his threat. She shot a sideways glance at his amused face. Was he likely to carry out his threat? He most definitely would and it would give him great amusement to do so. No, the better course of action was to remain calm and composed, to pretend that she didn't mind being transported in his arms to work in the study. She sighed in an effort to smother her rising frustration.

"That's a good girl. I always knew that you had a quick brain to sum up the situation. Besides, I thought I'd get in first before you scratched my eyes out!"

Upon arrival in the study, he lowered her gently into the chair on the opposite side of the desk. "Your place of work my dear, for

313

the next few weeks anyway." He smiled charmingly down at her. "I do think that I've covered your ever need. Morning tea and lunch will be brought up to us, and in the afternoon, you can rest up again. Well, for the next week anyway. When you want to relieve yourself just let me know. I've placed a commode in the adjoining room. I can carry you in there." A look of horror stole the sullenness from her face. "Fanny will assist you in there if needed." He smiled knowingly. She looked away, angry at herself for having so readily given away her independence and the subsequent humiliation it was now going to cost her.

"Come now, Tal." He crouched down on one knee, taking one of her hands tenderly in his. "It's not so bad is it? Just remember that every cloud has a silver lining or something like that. That was the general gist of Angie's fortune telling card that you chose wasn't it? Who knows, you and I may even grow to like each other a little, now that we are working in such close quarters."

She stared sulkily into his amused gaze, refusing to lighten up. He let go of her hand, slapping his palms down jovially upon his upper thighs.

"Ah well, let's get started, shall we. Padyah tells me that I must give you a little practise at walking with support each day. Best thing to do it first in the morning when you are fresh, he says. I'll lift you up, and you can support yourself by putting your arm around my shoulder. I'll place mine around your waist to stop you from falling." She appeared unresponsive and looked away.

"Look lively, girl, now's not the time for sulking!" He lifted her to her feet. Immediately, the pain soared up the offending limb, and she felt her legs give way under her. He grabbed her tightly around the waist supporting her to stand.

"Please can we leave it?" she snapped. "It hurts too much."

"Not at all … You're to do as you are told. You are just going to have to endure a little discomfort if you want your leg to heal properly."

Defiantly, she allowed herself to go limp in his arms in an effort to force him to lower her to the seat. He loosened his grip just enough so that he held her in standing position, but simultaneously allowed her to take more of her own weight. She whimpered.

"Jockim, it really hurts," she pleaded, tears springing to her eyes. "Please, put me down."

"I know," he replied, a strange mixture of annoyance at her sulkiness and sympathy that she should have to endure such pain, struggling for supremacy within him, "but you've got to try. Enough of this stubbornness! When you show me that you are willing to try I will support you more, taking some of the pain from your foot, but at the moment we both know that you are being extremely lazy, not a usual trait of yours, Talitha."

She sniffed, the tears now erupting like a hidden spring behind her eyes. "Alright, I'll try, but please can I have a hanky."

"Yes, you can, but only after you've walked to the armchair with me and back to the table again. It's not far, only two metres."

The anger surged up within her having the effect that he had hoped for. She hated him seeing her so broken, it crushed her pride, her fierce pride that held her together. Even more, she hated him having such absolute control over her every move. Sniffling, she ferociously wiped away her tears and forced herself to move forward. Immediately, he tightened his grasp upon her, supporting her more so that the pain lessened. She leaned heavily upon him, grateful for his strength. They shuffled along together. He thought that he would feel exuberance at holding her so close, but to his surprise, her discomfort only wounded him. He was wise enough however to know that he couldn't show any sign of sympathy, for she would be like a wild cat, tearing him to shreds if given the slightest opportunity.

"Good girl," he coaxed, "keep pushing, don't give up yet. Not much further now."

She collapsed into the chair, relief spreading over her face. He handed her a handkerchief and she snatched it roughly from him, wiping her eyes ferociously and blowing her nose hard. She no longer cared about being genteel in his presence. The better plan would be to revolt him so that he would leave her alone. He laughed at her crude attempt at coarseness, sensing the intention behind the behaviour that emanated so uneasily from her. There was no way that a doe could become a hog!

"Now that wasn't so bad, was it?" His boyish grin brought a fresh bout of sulkiness to her face. He ran his hands through his hair. She was going to be even harder to tame than he had anticipated.

"Let's have a look at your tasks shall we. Focus on something a bit more positive." He moved her chair in and opened a manual. "I will need you to read through these takings and scribe them again under headings. For example: vegetables, livestock, wine supplies, timber and so on, as I have listed here. That way I can get a better understanding of where our expenditures and sales are actually going.

We can plan for the future then. Things are improving and I want to get the most that I can from the exports over the coming year. There's a lot to do!" He flicked back through the hastily scribbled manual. "It should take a few weeks. When required, I'll get you to update the discipline manual that outlines misdemeanours against Doomeerie and their delegated punishments, but I'll explain that then, prior to proceedings."

His body was close to hers as he lent over her. Its long, lean form stirred some primeval sense of excitement deep within her. Its urgency made her feel out of control.

"Alright, I understand," she replied hurriedly, in an attempt to make him move on.

"Good!" He beamed down at her.

She ignored him and placed her head down, commencing work. He positioned himself in his seat opposite her and smiling opened the latest manual to study. Silence descended upon the room. He found it hard to concentrate. She looked so damned cute. Why didn't she talk? How could he break the ice? He decided to leave things as they were for the time being. Shortly, Fanny arrived with morning tea. The most delicious pastries that Talitha had ever beheld sat royally upon a silver platter, along with fruit and biscuits.

"Your tea sir ..." She entered the study briskly, looking slightly annoyed. "Cook said that the pastries took quite some time to bake." Jockim picked up quickly on her agitated attempt to rescue cook from any further efforts which they both would have considered to be a waste of time and energy.

"Shall I pour the tea for you?" The edgy voice continued, undaunted by his lack of response to her previous innuendo.

"Thank you, Fanny." He smiled charmingly up at her, and she softened a little. "Will that be all then, sir?"

"Yes, for now Fanny, thank you." He nodded appreciatively. She made to leave. "Oh, please tell cook that I am very grateful for all of her efforts."

Fanny huffed a little, nodded, curtsied, and bustled out of the room a little less annoyed than what she had been when she came in. The rose, china cups sat daintily upon the desk, holding their steaming contents gracefully.

"Please," Jockim's hand gestured, "help yourself!"

Talitha reached out and gingerly lifted the fragile china to her lips. It looked so exquisite that she hardly dared to spoil its gold edged rim with the stain of tea. She sipped it slowly, revelling in its warmth that slid slowly down her throat, enlivening her depleted energy. He insisted that she try a chocolate éclair and succumbing to the temptation, she chose a small one, chewing each mouthful ever so deliberately, mindful that it was indeed a rare treat. Being unaccustomed to such delights, she was at pains to prolong the pleasure. He watched her carefully, satisfied that the food and beverage seemed to be softening her mood, even though she was still loath to chat.

She felt considerably uncomfortable, like royalty, mistress of the castle, yet ashamed and unworthy of such delights, especially as she had been in such a cantankerous mood. Thanking him politely, she settled down to work again. Slightly disappointed that the tea had not loosened her tongue, he followed suit. A half hour went by. Suddenly she was aware of discomfort. *No*, she thought, *I don't want to go*. She shrugged off the sensation. Again it returned, this time more insistent than the last. She swallowed hard. There was no denying it. She needed to visit the lavatory. This was so humiliating. She would have to ask him to lift her there.

"Jockim ..." She glanced uneasily up at him.

"Yes?" His eyebrows rose, shocked that she was actually addressing him. Then catching her shy expression, the content of the conversation dawned upon him. He was about to save her the discomfort of disclosing her awkward sentiments, but then checked himself. *No,* he thought, *let her ask. She has hardly spoken all morning to me. It may well break the ice.* He stared back at her expectantly.

"I think I need to ... would you mind ... can I trouble you take me to the commode, please," she stammered, flushing deeply.

He smiled back at her, amused at her obvious discomfort. "Why of course, I'd be pleased to."

He scraped his chair back and walking around to her, pulled hers away from the table. He lifted her gently and carried her into the room next door. A screen was set up towards the side wall and behind it a commode had been modestly placed. It looked stark and prominent. She wished that she would somehow disappear in a puff of smoke like she had seen pictures of fairies do in children's books. He lowered her gently upon it.

"I'll call for Fanny. She'll come fairly quickly, I'm sure. She usually does. Tell her to call me when you are finished, and I will carry you back. I'll be working in the study." He strode out of the room.

A few minutes later, he was back with her, Fanny having taken the used chamber pot with her. "Ready to go ...?"

She couldn't bring herself to look at him. Lifting her up

tenderly, he carried her back to the study. She whispered a polite expression of appreciation, still unable to meet his gaze. Grateful to be returned to her chair and the diversion of work, her head lowered itself into the privacy of the bookwork once more.

A few minutes later, he heard a slight sniffle. Looking up, he saw that she was furiously trying to wipe away tears that refused to be ignored. Fighting her efforts, the independent, little droplets were determined to escape and streamed triumphantly down her furrowed cheeks, army like, intent upon invasion.

"What's wrong, Talitha? Does your leg hurt again?" He stood and walked to her side of the desk. Turning her chair to face him, he crouched down in front of her.

"No." She shook her head. He lowered his eyes, knowing full well what the problem was. His brain thought quickly for a diversion that might pull her out of the dark place where her thoughts were lingering.

"Poor Anya, she has been like this for years, and I cannot stand even a few hours of it," she spluttered. "I am already tired of the humiliation that my dependence upon others causes me." A heavy sigh escaped from within her body to be followed quickly by a sudden sob that jerked out unceremoniously. "I am so angry at myself for having been so careless as to fall over." The words tumbled out messily amidst sniffles and sighs.

He took her hand in his and drawing another handkerchief from his pocket wiped the troublesome tears away. "It might be enough for one day! How about a walk in the garden? Maybe Anya will let us borrow her chair for a period? Let's see!"

She watched him walk over to ring for Fanny, so confident and self-possessed in his stride. He pulled the bell lightly. Now he was facing her, smiling brightly.

"Fanny's on her way!" The sobbing continued a little less vehemently. He ran his fingers through his hair again, at a loss as to how to console her. Returning, he crouched before her again, smiling mischievously.

"My poor, proud, little maid … it is indeed hard medicine to swallow. Nevertheless, you will be all the better for it." At the sight of his boyish grin, a tingle of attraction riveted through her body. She tried to ignore it. Looking up at him through doe-like eyes, he thought he caught the faintest flash of it, if only for a second.

Fanny bustled in again, obviously annoyed that her chores had been further interrupted. "Sir … you rang for me?" She huffed, unable to keep the annoyance out of her voice.

"Fanny, would you mind asking Anya if she would allow us to use her wheelchair for about a half hour? Talitha is not feeling well, and I thought that a bout of fresh air might assist." He smiled a fraction sheepishly at her, thinking that a display of remorse might soften the older woman's growing frustration.

"Master Vadio is presently strolling with her beside the river. If you like I can ask that she shorten her walk for the likes of the servant girl!" she replied; disapproval and annoyance spilling out over her curt words.

"No, that won't be necessary, thank you all the same, Fanny." He smiled back, unaffected by her obvious display of displeasure. "I'll carry Talitha downstairs." The older woman looked over at the girl unable to contain her irritation.

"Very well, sir," she chipped in reply. "Will that be all?"

"Yes, thank you, Fanny. My apologies for the interruption again; I understand that you would be very busy downstairs, especially as you are without your best worker." He smiled over at Talitha.

Fanny turned and marched out of the room, ignoring Talitha. Her head and shoulders were thrown back in soldier like fashion, intending to indicate that she could manage quite well without the girl. Jockim waited until the door closed and roared with laughter.

"Well I do believe, my dear Tal, that you have finally succeeded in getting your revenge on old Fanny."

He lifted her carefully from the chair. The look of amused devilment lit up his face and flitted lightly into her consciousness, creating comic scenes of Fanny huffing and puffing like an old witch whose latest spell had just backfired upon her. The laughter broke loose from deep within her, and she couldn't stop it. Flowing freely, it relaxed her rigid body, so that she melted lightly into his arms, feeling safe, secure, and cherished. She was a child again, cradled in the strong arms of love, but somehow it was more than that, she was also a woman, desirable and alluring in her own way. The strength and proximity of his presence made her acutely aware of her femininity. For a moment, she tried to pull away from the strong sensation, and then the sight of the trees swaying lightly in the breeze, the leaves free falling around them, and the cool brush of air upon her cheeks, allowed her to relax into it. She nestled contently into his arms, happy to let things be, just as they were … at least for the present!

CHAPTER 12

A Matter of Timing

"Begging your pardon, sir …" Fanny bailed Jockim up in the hall a couple of weeks later. "I wonder if I might have a few words with you in private."

"I am rather busy." Jockim scanned his mind to think of a suitable excuse to evade the forthcoming lecture.

"It will only take a minute of your time, sir. I believe that Miss Tally has not yet entered the study for her day's work, so might I speak with you there now?"

"Oh alright, Fanny …" He had already postponed this requested conversation for the last two days. Might as well get it over and done with he thought, turning and making his way to the study.

The door was hardly closed when Fanny began. "I would like to speak frankly, sir, if I may do so." She continued, not waiting for his approval. "It is in the best interests of yourself and all concerned, that I speak so. I believe that my dear sister, Avie, would have already spoken to you about this matter herself if she was still here, and in her absence I feel that it is my duty to do so."

"Go on." Jockim sighed. *Here it comes, the matron's lecture about morals and the need not to cause any more scandal at Doomeerie, but I will hear her out, after all, she is Avie's sister.*

He turned his back on her and settled to staring out the great, panelled, glass windows. The River Styx was looking decidedly greyer, mirroring a more sombre sky. *Perhaps we're in for rain,* he thought.

"Miss Tally is walking reasonably well now, sir. Yes, I know she has a bit of a hobble still, but I think she should join me back in the kitchen and laundry for duties. I will make sure that she does not have an extended stay on her feet, and we are very much in need of her additional help."

"I understand that you are hard pressed for good workers, but I still require her assistance to help me here with the bookwork," he replied, not easily swayed.

"It is not good for her moral constitution to be alone up here in the study with you for so many hours, sir!"

Jockim turned and stared at her raising his eyebrows. She stiffened her body, pushing her large and prominent breasts forward in a manner to suggest that she would not be easily intimidated.

"I hope you don't think me out of line, sir, but it is obvious to everyone in the castle that she has grown increasingly fond of you over the last few weeks. I know that you have always been a little partial to her too. However ..." she cleared her throat in an effort to provide herself with additional time to think of appropriate wording, "things will come to no good if they should progress any further. She is not of the calibre to be a wife, and I hardly think that you need to be tied down by a mistress at present while we are still setting matters aright at Doomeerie after the war. If there should be a child, well, the servants will be all affright about the prospect of the Doomeerie curse befalling us once more."

"A child …" He threw his head back in laughter. "God forbid, you must think me a proper philanderer. Things have hardly got to that stage. You obviously don't know Talitha very well." He tilted his head on the side, running his fingers through his black hair, white teeth gleaming in amusement and eyes alive with merriment at the thought of her suggestion.

"I do not need to remind you, sir, that the last maidservant you got close to left stealing jewels from the castle," she replied sourly, "and I might add that you can't fool me. I see the way you both draw apart on the settee when I enter the room. You are no doubt kissing her, sir, and a woman of my age knows how quickly one thing can lead to another."

Jockim flashed a boyish grin which confirmed her suspicions. "Alright Fanny, yes, I have kissed the girl on the odd occasion, but there has been little more than that … more's the pity. Tal is not one to give away her charms easily."

"All the same, sir, folks around the castle are starting to talk. If you do care for the girl and not just your own pleasure, you are best to have her finish up in here and return to the kitchen." A sudden knock on the door signalled that Talitha was waiting outside.

"Alright, I'll take your counsel into consideration," he replied, wanting to put an end to the discussion.

"Thank you, sir. I wouldn't take too long thinking about it either," she added with a note of warning. "A young girl's heart opens very quickly like a rose once it is plucked."

He smiled at her use of simile. Talitha fitted well with the garden imagery.

"Thank you, Fanny. You're dismissed. Oh, and you can tell Tal that she can come in on your way out." He successfully stopped the smile that wanted to capture his lips, just as the knock on the door was repeated a little louder.

Fanny brushed past Talitha, casting a withering look that would have wilted even the strongest of constitutions. She entered the room and her crushed spirits lifted at the sight of Jockim standing staring out towards the river. He was deep in thought and she was hesitant to interrupt. Just what had he and Fanny been discussing?

She is right of course, Jockim was thinking. *There is no way that I can continue this work arrangement indefinitely. Her reputation will be in tatters.* He sighed heavily. *Oh, be damned with them all! Who cares what they think! I've a good mind to release her from her contract this very morning and make her my guest … with time I could propose. Now, that would set the tongues wagging. If only I could be sure of her sentiments. What if her feelings for me are not as deep as I hope? Then I would appear a fool when she up and leaves. No, give it a little time … I need to be sure. I'll tell her she's to go back to Fanny at the start of the coming week as that may prompt her to be more open with her feelings towards me. Better still, I'll make clear my feelings about her first and then maybe she'll open up and respond similarly. If so, I will then release her from her contract. If not, I'll return her to Fanny and see what eventuates from there.*

He felt pleased with his plan. It would protect him as well as giving her the time she needed to sort out her emotions. He hoped that she would open up to him and declare her love again. If she didn't it would be difficult not having her beside him. She had brought such pleasure into his life—beyond his wildest dreams. Why, he was a changed man. He could feel himself being renewed daily. Only yesterday he had summoned the courage to tell Raybet of his plans to share the castle with him. Although he still couldn't grant his half-brother freedom. Maybe it would be easier if Talitha didn't keep bringing him up in their conversation. It happened too frequently, as if there was some hidden agenda that she wanted to discuss but just couldn't bring herself to say openly. Surely she couldn't feel for Raybet, not after the way that she had acted with him over the past few weeks. Other women would be capable of such deception, but not Talitha. He turned to see her looking at him, a little dispirited.

"Is everything alright?" she inquired demurely. "I sensed Fanny's disapproval of me just now. Have I done something to displease you or her?"

"Not at all, it's just Fanny. We are both fighting over who is to have you working for them?" He decided it better to inform her so that she would not be too disappointed if arrangements did have to change.

"Oh … and who won?" She looked up at him in that doe-like way that always disarmed him.

"Me, of course," he said decisively, taking up his seat and gesturing for her to do the same.

"Oh … I'm pleased." A stray lock of hair fell softly over her temple. She seemed even more vulnerable than usual today.

Fanny was right about one thing. He did have a responsibility to protect her.

The grey waters from the river had somehow flowed into his eyes, giving them a troubled expression. She tried to brush aside the sense of disappointment that had crept into the room with Fanny's departure. Opening the manual, she prepared herself to commence work. Something wasn't right … Something was worrying her. It was the thought of Raybet.

How can he keep his own brother locked up in a room? If he can't show respect and equality to Raybet, how can he ever give it to me? She felt certain he knew that Raybet was his half-brother, and yet he kept him prisoner. *Even if their relationship had been troubled in the past, surely he would want to try and amend it now? Or does he not want to do so because he fears sharing his fortune. I am certain that Raybet would be open to atonement.* The man whom she had grown to care for at Kyriedor's cave was not a man filled with hate and revenge. *How can I ever trust that he will truly love me as equal if he cannot even make his own brother a free man?* Padyah was right, she could not struggle with these thoughts any more. They were tearing her mind into shreds. She was just going to have to discuss it with him.

"Jockim …" She faltered, feeling apprehensive.

"Yes …" He smiled at her. "What is it?"

She placed the quill down carefully. "There is something of great importance to me. I just have to discuss it with you. I have to let you know my feelings …"

His heart began to quicken. *This was it! Finally, she was going to proclaim her love for him!*

A hammering upon the door signalled urgency. They both looked up.

"I'm so sorry, Tal." He sounded annoyed at the pressing interruption. "Can it keep for a couple of minutes? I'd better answer it. It sounds urgent?"

"Of course ..." She smiled sadly. She had only just summoned the courage to broach the topic, and now she would have to hold back.

"Come in," Jockim commanded.

Noah, the chief commander of the soldiers entered briskly in response to Jockim's bidding.

"Good morning, sir!" His expression was grave.

"Morning, Noah. What is it?"

I have some unfortunate news to report, sir."

"Go on then, what is it?"

"Your horse, sir, Noble ... he has had to be put down." Noah shuffled uncomfortably.

"What! Why?" Jockim rose up quickly, his expression dark. "What has happened?"

"The hunting expedition into Nightmare Forest, sir ... We have not long returned to the castle with a couple of does, shot one fawn, the other got away amongst the brambles. The men were disappointed. That young lad, Jeremiah Morris, you know Christian's eldest son, Marcus' grandson, well he came with us for the first time. The lad took your horse last night and headed back into the forest. We suspect that he was trying to prove himself. He also took a rifle with him. Probably hoping to find the other fawn and shoot it. He wanted to be a hero, no doubt. You know what it's like at that age, sir. Well ... something happened. The horse took fright. Went crazy he did and fell down a precipice. The boy was lucky to get away with his life. He wandered back into camp just on dawn. A group of us followed his directions back to Noble."

He stopped and swallowed hard, genuine sadness etching kind creases into his face. "I'm sorry sir, he was a fine horse, but we had to shoot him. His leg was broken, and he was lying amongst the marshes in pain."

Jockim's fists clenched and his face contorted into a fierceness that froze upon his features. Talitha felt breathless, her head was swimming, her temples beginning to pulsate, drumming a warning that his fury was soon to explode.

"Send the boy to me!" His words were stark and brutal in the silence that followed.

"Yes, I'm sorry, sir." Noah clipped on his heels and left the room.

Jockim opened a desk drawer and pulled out a coiled whip. He stared ahead of him into dark oblivion. Talitha swallowed hard.

"I'm sorry, Jockim. He's just a boy. It was an accident."

He hadn't even heard her. Noble, his pride and joy; Noble, a magnificent stallion, the prize of Doomeerie, his faithful companion—gift from his father for his bravery, destroyed all because a foolish boy wanted to prove himself to be a hero. He paced the room, whip coiled in his fist. Noble, killed because the boy wanted to shoot a helpless fawn, just like Raybet all those years ago, trying to be a hero, at a helpless creature's expense. The rapping on the door jolted him back to the present.

"Come in," he barked.

Noah gave the lad a slight shove into the room. The boy tumbled in like an unsteady colt. He couldn't have been more than twelve or thirteen, tall and gangly for his age with a curly mop of strawberry, blonde hair. His blue eyes were wide with fear. They focused on Jockim and then on the whip, and he swallowed hard.

"Well ... Jeremiah," Jockim eyed the lad with contempt, "what am I to do with you? Destroyed my prize stallion, have you?"

"I ... I'm sorry, sir," he stammered. "I was trying to help the men get a better catch for the hunt. I didn't mean ..." His blue eyes were drowning, thrashing about helplessly in fear as he glanced from the coiled whip ready to spring to life, to Jockim's face, stony and unrelenting.

"What do you think the punishment might be for thieving Doomeerie's most prized stallion lad?" Jockim thundered.

The boy swallowed hard and said nothing.

"Answer me, boy!"

"A whipping, sir," he mumbled, head lowered.

"Shame you didn't use your brains as much last night boy, hey."

He strode up to Jeremiah and grabbing him by the scruff of the collar pulled him off the ground eye to eye with him. "So you want to be a man, do you ... to kill and to maim?"

"Sir"

"Are you prepared to take a man's whipping across your bare shoulders, or would you prefer that I paddle your bottom like a child?"

"I'll take the man's punishment, sir," the boy whispered.

"He's barely twelve, sir," Noah interjected, stepping forward.

Jockim stared at him coldly. "He's on the brink of manhood. Maybe a decent whipping will be a good initiation for him. Something he'll never forget."

He turned to look at the young commander. He liked and respected Noah, but he was not going to have him interfere.

"That will be all thank you, Noah. You may leave us."

Noah's jaw clenched. "Sir," he replied stonily and exited the room.

"Take your shirt off and brace yourself, arms up against the mantel piece." Jockim uncoiled the snake; slender and black, eager to strike with its venom sting.

Jeremiah started to shake. He fumbled with the buttons on his shirt, his blue eyes losing their battle to stay afloat, sinking slowly beneath the tears that welled in them. Jockim watched him mercilessly. Behind him, Talitha's voice floated with urgency across the room.

"Jockim, for God's sake … the boy didn't intend any harm. It was an accident!"

He turned and sprung at her viper like. "Stay out of this woman. It is not your affair."

Jeremiah laid his shirt on the couch and turning raised his arms up so that his hands grasped the mantel piece. His bare back was scrawny and pale, jagged bones trembling under the film of taunt skin. His heart pounded within his chest, threatening to burst free at any second. He must be man. He had brought so much shame to his father already. He must be a man now, be brave, no matter what the cost.

Jockim brought the whip down hard upon the floor, and the lad's body flinched. He smiled grimly in satisfaction. He waited until Jeremiah's muscles had relaxed again and then raising the whip landed it across the seat of his britches, avoiding his bare flesh. Jeremiah let out a yelp, his muscles tightening again.

"You're not worthy of a man's punishment, son. You've showed no bravery. Your actions are akin to a silly girl's. A good paddling across your bottom should teach you a lesson … No glory or honour for you son, only shame." He brought the whip down again across the boy's britches.

Talitha jumped up from the table. "Stop this, Jockim! That is enough!"

Jockim appeared not to even hear her. His eyes were boring into the boys back; his jaw set in grim determination. In his mind Jeremiah had become the adolescent Raybet who had attempted to kill his fawn all those years ago.

"Jockim stop! Please!" She was beside him now, tugging like a child on his arm, doe-like eyes pleading with him.

He turned to look at her. The pain in her eyes disarmed him. The energy drained from his body, leaving him depleted and confused. Suddenly, the lad was no longer a memory of Raybet; he was Jeremiah, a silly, rash kid who had tried to prove he was a man. He sighed heavily, dropping the whip from his hand.

"Get out of here, Jeremiah. You're more trouble than your worth. I'll deal with you later." He threw the boy's shirt at him.

Not waiting to put it on, Jeremiah rushed past Jockim like a frightened colt, awkwardly diving for the door. He flung it open with wild abandon, landing into the arms of Noah who was waiting outside.

Jockim strode over to the door and addressed Noah. "I will advise you as to some extra chores that the boy can do for further punishment later on this morning. Take him to his parents. I've done with him."

Closing the door behind him, he strode over to Talitha. She stood frozen in space, staring up at him wide eyed and distressed.

"Well, you have saved Jeremiah from his misery. Can you save me from mine too?" His voice sounded hollow, his face chiselled in despair.

She swallowed hard, not knowing how to answer. Her face was flushed; her lips slightly open. Suddenly, he desperately wanted to kiss them. He gingerly lifted his hand and slid the top buttons of her blouse open. She did not resist, but stood staring, diving into the sorrowful depths of his eyes. His hands moved reverently as if he was touching a precious artefact. Gently, his fingers traced their way across her soft, pale shoulders, pondering the bones that protruded under their silken ivory. His eyes were drawn to the tiny cavity at the base of her neck. It was so fragile, so vulnerable, so enticing. Lightly, he placed his fingers into the soft hollow. Then sliding his hand behind her neck, he lifted her head and kissed her as if her love could in some way cleanse him of his sorrow. She returned his kisses, wanting to erase the pain that she too had felt crashing through her at the thought of his loss. Eventually, they drew apart, and he sank onto the settee, drawing her down beside him. His body was humped and tired. He held his head in his hands.

"I'm so sorry," he said. "I totally forgot myself. I was in another lifetime."

She nodded. "Your father—"

"Yes … something like that," he interrupted, not wanting to return to the thought of Raybet. *How had matters got so out of hand?*

he ruminated sadly. *I hoped it would be another good day. It started out painfully with Fanny, but then Tal had been going to confide her feelings to me. What was she going to say before Noah knocked?*

He turned and smiled at her. "I'm sorry." He took her hand in his. "You were going to tell me something before all of this commotion. What was it that you wanted to say, Tal?"

"It's of no matter, Jockim. It's been a disturbing morning for you. We can discuss it another time." She had not the heart or fortitude to raise the topic of Raybet now.

"No," he pressed, "I'm alright. Your concerns are important to me. I want to know."

"Truly Jockim, it can wait. It's not urgent."

"No, Talitha, I insist. If something is not right for you, I want to set it straight. There are to be no further secrets between us. I have something that I want to tell you too. But tell me your concerns first." He smiled kindly at her.

She hesitated. Her gut squirmed, advising against it.

"Come on!" He nudged her playfully with his elbow. "Surely you can trust me by now? I want what is best for you."

She lowered her head. The queasy sense of uneasiness began to heighten. She glanced into the fire. The flames were leaping—like the light behind Jenobay's eyes. She must claim her self-power, advocate for her needs; she couldn't keep putting it off.

"Well, it's about Raybet—" She stopped mid-sentence sensing his body tighten.

His spirits plummeted. *Not bloody Raybet again! Will she never be free of her obsession with him? Why can't she just let things be? Leave him out of our lives?*

Suddenly, his thoughts swung back to Noble, galloping proud and free, the wind rippling through his beautiful, black mane. Grief and anger flooded through him. He was grasping desperately, trying to hold onto his depleted energy, trying to hold his anger in check.

"I'm sorry, Talitha," he interrupted rudely, "you were right. I should not have pressed you to disclose your thoughts. I am in no frame of mind at the moment to discuss Raybet." His words were terse and cold.

"We'll let it be then," she replied, regretting that she had not listened to her intuition. "What did you want to tell me?"

He ran his fingers through his hair, preoccupied by the thought of his dead horse. "Oh, it was nothing much … only that you'll be reporting back to Fanny for kitchen and laundry duties as of Monday."

It was out before he had even given it a thought. He wasn't even conscious that he hadn't disclosed his feelings towards her as planned. He unwittingly had given Raybet power over his psyche to sabotage him yet again!

"Oh … I see." She gently removed her hand from his. *Why did I ever think that things could be different between us? These last few weeks have given him a few moments of pleasure and distraction … nothing more.* A deep sense of sadness welled within her. She pushed down hard upon her feelings, forcing them from her mind. He must not see her cry. She hurriedly buttoned up her blouse.

He had risen and was walking towards the door. "I won't be working in the study any more today. There are things to sort out. I've been in doors for too long over the past few weeks. Will you be right to go ahead and finish as much on the books as you can?" he inquired absentmindedly, not caring about her reply.

"Yes Jockim." Her reply came feeble and half-hearted.

He picked up the whip and threw it back into the drawer. "Enter Jeremiah's punishment in the Doomeerie Code of Conduct," he said, shutting the drawer sharply. "No, wait a little. There's another matter I need to see Noah about with regard to that lad."

She didn't answer. He looked over at her frail figure, crushed with despondency. The sight of her made him feel even more miserable. The pain was suffocating. He had to get out. He strode towards the door. She heard it slam as he pulled it behind him. She was alone, a prisoner to her own shattered psyche.

CHAPTER 13

Rendezvous with **Raybet**

"One thing I'll say for ya, missie, is that ya'r braver than any handmaiden we've ever 'ad at Doomeerie before." Marcus lowered the bale of hay that he was carting into the stable, his head still shaking mercilessly. "Standin' up for young Jeremiah in front of the master the way ya did. There's not too many around 'ere who'd 'ave the courage to do that."

Talitha smiled at the old man. News of the incident had spread swiftly amongst the servants. All had greeted her kindly. She remembered when she had been rejected and ridiculed by the castle staff; now she was now shown genuine affection and respect by all.

"Anytime ya want a favour ya just ask, girlie. Christian and Rachael are indebted to ya for helpin' the lad. They'd do anything for ya."

He sidled the bale into the corner, twisting his old, broken body back and forth to ease the mass into place. His head stabilised again. "The master's makin' up for Jeremiah's missin' lashes by givin' 'im extra duties. Got the poor lad gettin' up in the middle of the night to empty the chamber pots in them prisoner's rooms. Takes him full on an hour by the time he does 'em all, cleans 'em out and returns 'em. It's up and down 'em stairs that's the killer and in the dark of night. Fair frightening for the lad, it is. Ya know there's always been talk of ghosts up 'ere at the castle. Master Lachlan and Lady Clare are said to wander about when there's an ill wind. The boy's terrified of 'em."

He shook his head in dismay, leaning back against the bale to catch his breath. "Master knows it too. That's why he's given 'im the job. Say's it'll teach 'im how to be a man." He shook his head again, worrying it back and forth like an old crone. "Oh, he's got a cruel twist in 'im young Master Jockim—just like his father. But thank God it only comes out every now and ag'in, when things really upset 'im."

"I'm sorry, Marcus." Talitha looked over at him. She had been brushing Balaamine. Stroking the old jenny's coat always calmed her. There was something rhythmic and focused about it that gave her space and time to marvel at the soft, brown markings on her back that patched together the brighter, chestnut ones. "That must be so hard for Jeremiah. He would be tired and anxious."

"Ay, he is, girlie. His mother says he can't get to sleep at nights thinking about it, and then he's expected to be up performing his duties early the next morning. Jockim's got Noah checking that he does everything just so. Poor kid! He's paid his wages for his disobedience, but he's learnt 'is lesson," he said, pushing his old cap back from his leathery forehead, "and he's only got to do it for one more night."

"That's good!" She stopped her stroke abruptly in the middle of Balaamine's back. The donkey twitched her ears back, alert to her change of touch.

"Marcus, do you think I could have a word with Christian sometime about the boy. I might be able to help him?"

"What ya thinkin' up now, missie. Don't ya be getting' yerself into more trouble on account of the boy. Ya've already done more than what would be expected of a scrap of a girl like ya." He eyed her suspiciously.

She threw her head back laughing generously. He couldn't help noticing how pretty her smile was, something ever so gentle and kind about it. No wonder she had a way with the master. *She'd melt any man's heart she would*, he thought.

"Not at all, he may even be able to help me!" she replied enigmatically.

"Alright girlie, I'll see if I can find 'im."

"Thank you!"

He turned to shuffle his bent, tired body out of the stable door.

"Oh, Marcus …"

"Yes, girlie?"

"Please don't tell anyone, will you?" she asked, an edge of disquiet hovering in her voice.

"Course not, Miss Tally. Ole Marcus is dam good at keepin' secrets. You can mark my word on that score!" His twisted, scarecrow body shuffled out of sight.

Talitha returned her attention to Balaamine. "Oh Balaamine, what should I do?" She gazed into the donkey's deep, liquid eyes. "I feel a moral obligation to let Raybet know the truth about his past. It is not right that I should be privy to such information and yet withhold it from him. I would not like someone doing that to me. Should I ask Christian if he'll let me accompany the boy on his chores to the prisoner's rooms tonight, so that I can give the note to Raybet?"

The old donkey looked up lovingly at her. Talitha fancied she could see a hint of trepidation ripple through her eyes. Confirming her suspicions, Balaamine snorted and shuffled nervously.

"I know ... Jockim—what effect will it have on him? I've been wrestling with that for weeks now. It's that, plus the fact that it's so hard to get access to Raybet that has stopped me."

She sighed and pulled up a little stool beside the donkey. "I wish I had been able to broach the subject with him before the day Noble was shot. He was so kind and caring then. Maybe he would have been receptive to discussing it? After all, he did seem to be softening a little towards Raybet." She wistfully laid her head against the donkey's flank. It felt warm and safe. Tears sprung to her eyes.

What should she do? She felt deceitful withholding the truth from Raybet. It was awful to feel like a coward. She should stand up for her principles. She would have no self-respect if she didn't.

Damn you, Jockim, she thought. *Nobody is going to dictate to me the type of person I am to be. I will choose what I think is the right thing to do. I will be who I want to be, and if that upsets you, so be it. What have I to lose? You have taken Shiloh from me. You cannot take Pover, she is safe with Sanctusis, and I know that you won't harm Balaamine.* She stroked the donkey's flank again. *Especially now that Noble is dead.*

She hugged the donkey and quickly left the stables. Had she stayed too long? Would Fanny be annoyed with her? She was so preoccupied that she almost bumped into Marcus rolling another bale of hay into the barn on her way out.

"Hey, careful there, missy … Ya'r in a mighty hurry."

"Sorry Marcus." She smiled sheepishly. "I wasn't looking where I was going."

"So I see." He smiled at her. "Oh, by the way," he lowered his voice a little, "Christian's up in the animal fightin' compound doin' a job for the master now. He's by 'imself. It might be a good time to see 'im. Nar body 'ill see ya in there with 'em high walls."

"Thank you!" She smiled nervously and hurried on. He stopped to watch her hurrying to the compound. *Just what is she up to?* Lifting his cap up, he scratched his head. *Jus' as well I donno … There's sure to be trouble come of it, and I don't wanna be no part of it. I've 'ad more than me fair share of whippins' at this damn castle of horrors.* His head began to wobble worriedly again as he bent over to edge the bale into the barn.

The deal with Christian was sealed within a few minutes. She would accompany Jeremiah to the prisoner's room that night, dressed in soldiers clothing. They would say that Jockim had ordered that Jeremiah be given assistance. She left the animal compound feeling ill with fear. She assured herself that it was just the location that was making her feel nauseous. She hated the killing compound. Memories of her shame and humiliation flooded her mind. *Why, oh why was I ever so foolhardy and rash to trust Raybet back then and get myself into such a terrible predicament?* She stopped. *What am I doing? I am putting myself in danger for the same man. It's all going to happen again, just like it did the first time!*

Tears blurred her vision. She hurried on. She couldn't be late for Fanny. *He's not the same man—he's changed. The old Raybet is dead—gone.* She assured herself, again and again. *He has a right to be told the truth. Everyone has a right to the truth. Oh God,* she thought in desperation, *how I wish Pover was here to guide me. I feel like I am going blindly.*

She rushed into the kitchen face flushed, and washed her hands. Quickly, she pulled her apron from the hook and began peeling potatoes, head down. Fanny said nothing. She knew the girl was ten minutes late, but the look on her face indicated that she was very upset. Had she been scolded for her tardiness by the master? *That must be it,* she thought, noticing that Talitha was trying hard to hold back tears. *Oh well, enough has been said and done,* she concluded. *I'll let her tardiness go this time.*

✳ ✳ ✳

At midnight the faintest shaft of a moon struggled to break free of the clouds that clung to it with grasping, sinuous fingers. Jeremiah and Talitha pulled their cloaks around them, using the soft light of a lantern to cast away the eerie shadows that danced about the halls. At every turn the dark, shifting shapes gathered up their cloaks and floated towards them. Was it Clare, wanton and willowy, gliding past them on the breeze of a shifting curtain; or Lachlan, poised and erect, hiding behind the heavy, ornate furniture, eager to lodge a dagger deep between their bones? A cold shiver clung to Talitha. Any amount of reasoning could not shake it off. Her throat was dry, her skin creeping with tiny tremors.

Beside her Jeremiah swallowed. It was so hard trying to be a man. He was a tall lad, already just outstripping Talitha. He had always been proud of his height, but it also brought with it a price; the curse of responsibility, of always having to act older than what he was. It made him place pressure on himself, more pressure than a young boy should take on. Unfortunately, his emotional maturity hadn't kept up to his rapidly growing height. Hence, he often placed himself in unsafe predicaments in order to prove himself, and when he failed because the odds were stacked against him, he lost his confidence and felt even more miserable than he had before he started. Still, it was good to have a companion tonight. He only hoped that they didn't get caught out. He was terrified of Master Jockim and his whip.

They reached the top of the stairs and Will looked at the pair strangely. Talitha, heavily cloaked, kept her head down.

"Jeremiah reporting for duty, sir," the lad announced bravely. "Master Jockim has ordered that I be given some assistance by Carter tonight." He nodded towards Talitha. "The men often miss the mark in the dark of night, and there are puddles to clean on the floor. Carter and I will take it in turns to mop the floor, while the other takes the pots down, sir. It will shorten the time a little."

On cue Talitha presented the bucket of frothy water which gleamed silvery lathers in the lantern's light. A scrubbing brush bobbed up and down within it, partly submerged by foamy bubbles. A white rag clung wearily to the end of the brush.

"Alright Jeremiah, I thought that it was too big a job for one lad. We'll start down this end of the corridor first tonight, shall we?" He opened the door and Jeremiah and Talitha stole a glance at each other. Raybet's room was the second last down the hall if Jeremiah had remembered correctly.

The work was exhausting especially lugging the chamber pots down the stairs to the outhouses, scrubbing them clean and then returning them upstairs. No wonder Jeremiah was depleted. Finally, they were at Raybet's room. Talitha's heart had lodged in her throat, ready to cry out at the slightest provocation. Jeremiah had taken the pot as planned to allow her time to talk with Raybet. She tried to steady herself as she gently shook him. What if he was startled at her presence and called out.

"Raybet," she whispered. "Raybet, it's me, Talitha."

A soft moan emitted from his lips.

"Raybet," she whispered more urgently, "it's me, Talitha, wake up!"

Rose was suddenly leaning over him, her soft voice purring in his ears.

"Rose!" He bolted upright urgently.

"Hush … not Rose … Talitha! You're in the castle. Be quiet. Someone will hear us."

"Talitha! …" He rubbed his eyes as she quickly lowered the hood of her cloak so that he could recognise her.

"Talitha," he repeated, a note of joy resounding in his voice, "it's been so long since I've seen you!" He threw his arms around her, drawing her close to his chest and holding her tight.

"Indeed, how charming!" The voice from the door, unmistakably Jockim's, reached their awareness at the same time as the light from his lantern alerted them to his presence. Instinctively, they pulled apart. Talitha's heart dropped like lead, a never ending fall gathering momentum as it plunged deeper and deeper.

Jockim had been restless. The thought of what had occurred in the study continually nagged him. Had he been too hard on the boy, expecting him to work in the dead of night? And Talitha, had he sabotaged all the gains that he had made with her over the past few weeks by returning her to Fanny? He hoped not. He had got up and decided to check on the prisoners. Maybe he would tell the boy to go back to bed. He had been given enough punishment—after all, he was only a lad.

Now there was Talitha before him in Raybet's arms. His worst fears had come to fruition. His heart plummeted as they sprang apart. Almost instantaneously, he felt it resurge, drumming with anger and hate.

"Oh, please, don't let me stop you. It was so touching to watch. What was planned next Raybet? We're you going to slide over and ask her to get under the covers with you?"

"Please, Jockim, I can explain. It's not what you think," she protested.

"Then start explaining, madame." His voice was remarkably controlled, despite the dark lilt of menace that underscored it.

Where to begin? How to explain? Raybet and Jockim stared at her.

"Oh come on, Jockim!" Raybet made light of the situation. "She has just come to visit an old friend. Good God man, you've had me tucked up in here for so long, not allowing anyone into see me. I'm a dead man imprisoned to the rest of the world!"

Talitha shivered! She didn't know why. Perhaps it was Raybet's morbid reference to his predicament. Jockim stared at her waiting for a response. It was too complicated. She would have to show him the letter. She dug deep within her trouser pocket and pulled out the note from Catherine.

"I found this in my room some weeks ago. I wanted to show it to you but the time never seemed right. You were always so angry at first and then, well, I didn't want to spoil the moment over the last few weeks. It's about Raybet's heritage."

Jockim snatched the note, frowning at her. "Will," he called for the young officer's assistance.

"Yes sir!"

"Keep a pistol to them while I read this note."

"Yes sir ... Move Miss Tally and I'll have to shoot Raybet."

Talitha swallowed hard and sunk down again sitting on the edge of the bed. Her heart had picked up its familiar drum. She watched Jockim's face. It grew tighter and darker. His eyes flitted from one side of the page to the other. Then suddenly, he looked up at her viciously.

"You conniving, little vixen ..." His body loomed over her. "What gives you the right to meddle in other people's affairs? Why bring this letter to Raybet and not me? Surely you should have brought it to me first to deal with. I'm the master of this castle, and it concerns me first and foremost."

"Why give it to you first? It is his business before anyone else's." She stood up to face him. "Of course if I gave it to you first then if you didn't like its contents you could destroy it and all evidence of the truth would be lost!" She flung the words back at him accusingly.

Raybet glanced quickly from one to the other, wondering about the contents of the note.

"Is that what you'd think I'd do after all I've done for him and Angie and Tobias? You have no trust in me whatsoever. My, you are the precious little heroine, aren't you?"

He grabbed her by the arm and thrust her onto the bed next to Raybet. Go on, get into bed with him and plot behind my back. I'll be damned if I care. You're not worth it."

He turned to face Will who was now clutching onto Jeremiah's arm. "Miss Talitha would like to talk to the prisoner. Give her half an hour privately with him, and then bring her out and lock the door again. By that time it will be change of shift, and you can bring the key back to me. I will be in my room."

"What would you have me do with the boy, sir?" Will tightened his grip as Jeremiah began to struggle.

Jockim eyed him viciously. "Send him back to his father. I'll let Noah know his fate in the morning. He can sweat on it in the meantime."

He turned on his heels and strode out of the room. Will pulled a now subdued Jeremiah out of the room and locked Talitha and Raybet inside. Shattered, Talitha broke into tears. Raybet put his arm around her, comforting her as they sat on the edge of the bed together.

"Hush now, Tal. I'm so sorry. He's a bastard—an utter bastard!" He held her close as the sobbing subsided.

"Poor Jeremiah and Christian, I have got them into more trouble." She sniffled.

"His wrath may cool off a little before morning," Raybet replied unconvincingly. "What was in the letter, Tal? Who was it from?

She quickly explained its contents, and a shadow of disappointment drifted over his face. He would have longed to have seen his mother's handwriting, the way she had strung the words together, how she had described him. He sighed heavily.

"Dearest Tal, you have been through so much to bring me the truth, but I already knew this information and so does Jockim. Vadio and Anya do as well, I suspect. I'm surprised that Jockim hadn't told you yet. It was his intention to."

Aware that they only had a short time together, he quickly explained to her about the two goblets, and the discussions that had occurred between himself and Jockim since his arrival.

"He told me that I could have half of his castle a few days ago. I asked that we not let others know until I had spoken with Rose and decided if that is what she wants—to live here in the castle with him and Vadio and Anya again. It is her choice too. I didn't want everyone to know, lest she not desire that now after everything that has happened."

He stopped and looked sadly into the dark, brown pools of emotion that were swimming with despair beside him.

"Hence, we decided to keep it as a secret until she and Konfra arrived, and I could speak with her. To assist in doing so we decided to keep up pretences that I was still prisoner. However, I also secretly suspect that Jockim wanted to keep me away from you as much as possible, as well as making sure that I continued to pass the test of time regarding my changed ways. You see Talitha, you may not want to hear it, but he is utterly besotted with you my dear. He is highly jealous of anyone whom he thinks may have won your trust and affection."

She sighed in dismay, shaking her head. "Not anymore Raybet ... not after the events of the last few days. I have thoroughly disillusioned him."

The door flung open. "Okay, miss," Will's pistol was aimed at them, "time's up. My replacement is here. Master Jockim has instructed me to lock you in your room tonight and to unlock it in the morning. I'll accompany you there now."

"Thank you, Will." She sighed, tears moistening her eyes.

"I wouldn't be too concerned, miss," he said once they were outside the room. "The master said that it's just for the one night."

He accompanied her down the dark hallways. The shadows had lost their ghosts. They simply hung dismally now, witnessing that her world was filled with dejection.

"Good night, Miss Tally!" He shut the door as she entered her room.

She waited until she had heard the key turn and then tested the door. Sure enough, it held fast. She collapsed in a heap upon the bed. It was all too much for her to comprehend. She had put herself through so much turmoil for Raybet's sake and as a result had damaged her relationship with Jockim even further. She could not even begin to think how to mend things, tired and confused as she was.

She slept heavily that night and awoke late. Lying still for a few seconds, she stared at the familiar surroundings about her, while the events of the previous night began to tumble rapidly into her head. She jumped up to test if the door was locked. A quick turn and it relinquished its hold. Will must have been up and unlocked it, and she hadn't even heard him. Hurriedly she dressed, trying to think of some way of apologising to Jockim.

Arriving late at the table, she noticed that he was not yet there. The atmosphere was heavy and subdued. How much did the others know she wondered? Was he planning to hibernate again as he had at other times when he was angry with her? Fanny began to serve, eyeing Talitha up and down as she did.

"Shouldn't we wait for Jockim?" she inquired, looking at the others. There was silence.

Eventually, Vadio spoke, "He's gone, Tal. He's left the castle. He said that he didn't know when he would be back." He cleared his throat. "It could be weeks, or months, or even years. I'm so sorry, I thought you knew. He said that he'd had a *rendezvous* with you last night and that you would understand."

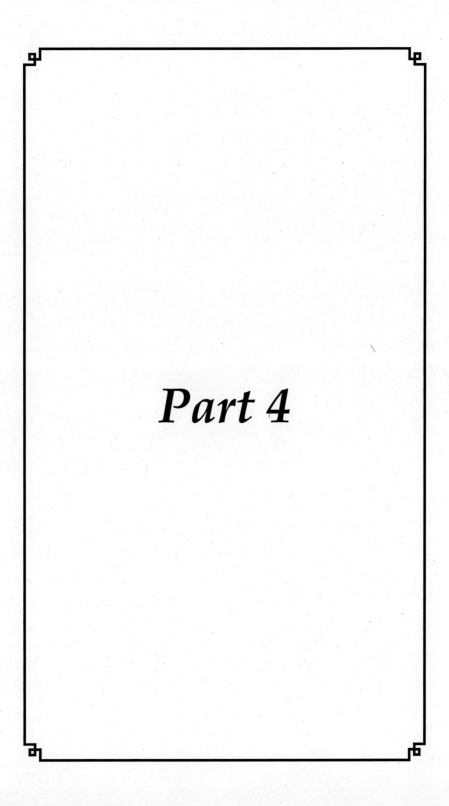

Part 4

CHAPTER 1

The Doomeerie Code of Conduct

Jockim had departed early that morning. Leaving a note for Vadio to ask him to manage the castle in his absence, he stopped in to see Noah before going. He felt guilty about the boy. Despite his actions having resulted in the death of Noble he was only a child, and he knew how important it was for a lad of that age to prove his courage.

"The boy is to have no further punishment," Jockim instructed a bleary eyed Noah. "Does his father know the contents of the letter Talitha gave to Raybet?"

"I don't believe so, sir. He said that Talitha wouldn't tell him. Said that it was better that he didn't know in case things should not work out as planned." Noah pulled his shirt on.

Jockim nodded. "Do you think he is telling the truth?"

"Yes sir, I do. He's a good man. He was only trying to repay Talitha for having cut short Jeremiah's whipping." He emptied a pitcher of water into a large basin and splashed its sharp coldness upon his face. "And Talitha, sir ... are there any instructions to follow? Fanny will be sure to ask."

Jockim thought for a few minutes. Noah waited in silence. Picking up a towel, he dried his dripping face. He hoped that the punishment wouldn't be too harsh. She was a brave lass, albeit a little too interfering in what should be men's business.

"She is to spend two hours of her free time once a week studying the *Doomeerie Code of Conduct*.

"Might I ask, sir, where you are going—in the event that we may need to find you?"

"I can see no reason why you would need me. Vadio will manage well in my absence, but initially I will head for the lake country. After that I don't know where I will go as yet." He looked at Noah sternly. "That information is strictly for yourself and Vadio. No one else is to know."

"Of course, sir ... travel safely. News from the outside is that there is a lot of unrest. The Oge are on the increase and heading slowly towards the east." He hesitated and then decided to express his thoughts. "We want you back, sir. You're a good man. It's not easy running a place such as this."

Jockim smiled, placing his hand upon his shoulder. "Thank you, Noah. Thank you for everything." He picked up his pack. At the door he stopped once more, turning to say, "Oh, and by the way, the prisoner, Raybet, may be released. The others are to stay where they are for the time being. We don't need my dear cousin, Tyrone, and his men causing any further problems just yet."

Noah nodded and both men smiled. As Jockim closed the door, Noah sunk back down onto his bed. *He is such a tormented soul ... always roaming the countryside looking for something. Was it the stag again? Why did it distress him so? Or was it the girl, and the fact that he suspected that she fancied Raybet? Who knows?*

He shook his head. The first shafts of light were already greeting him through the smudged window of his quarters. He'd best keep moving. He would need to supervise the men. But first, he would drop in and see Christian, to tell him that there would be no reprisal for Jeremiah.

✳ ✳ ✳

Talitha opened the thick manual. The black letters loomed heavily before her, *Doomeerie Code of Conduct*. Her emotions plummeted.

"This is your second hour of study for the week, Talitha. You can record it in the book now or in an hour's time when I tell you to finish up. The master will want to check on it when he arrives back." Fanny's voice was strident as it had been since the day Jockim left. "Make sure you use the time wisely. There's a lot to learn, and we don't know when he will be back."

She scrawled in the date and time beside the record of her punishment. Dispiritedly, she flicked back through the section of the manual entitled *Record of Misdemeanours and Punishments*. It went on and on. Some were silly, trifling punishments like cleaning the master's boots; others were more sinister, like the ones listed under Jockhein's era. She glanced through them quickly.

Matthew Stillus—Public whipping of fifty lashes—Punishment for stealing food and refusing to follow orders.

Thomas Clifton—Heavy labour for a month—Punishment for involvement in drunken brawls.

Jockim Deerie—No dinner for a week—Punishment for disobedience: refusal to give up his chair at dinner for General Konfra's younger son, Raybet.

Oh, I wonder how old he was then, Talitha thought. *He must have disliked Raybet even as a child.*

She glanced on. A few more lines and then his name appeared again. *Jockim Deerie—Thrashing with the long-handled, bristled brush—Punishment for disobedience: refusal to allow the general's son, Raybet, to use his horse.* Her finger continued to run down the names. Again she stopped, her eyes alighting on Jockim's name. *Jockim Deerie—Public whipping—Punishment for attacking the general's son, Raybet, during a hunting expedition (administered by Jockhein Deerie).*

Goodness, she thought, *the lads certainly seemed to have fought a lot. Yet, there were no entries of chastisement for Raybet. Had Jockhein favoured one son over the other … the son that he was unable to claim publically as his own?*

She sat staring at the grey walls closing in around her. *What a place of doom and gloom this castle was and still is,* she thought. She wondered where Jockim might be. Was he still angry with her? Maybe he was looking for Shiloh again. Her hopes raised a little.

"Talitha, what is the punishment for idleness?" Fanny's strident voice broke into her thoughts.

"I don't know, ma'am."

"Well then look it up girl and read it out to me."

She flicked through the manual finding the correct location. "Idleness is to be punished by an increase in work as to what the supervisor should see fit, ma'am."

"Good, you've just gained another half hour of study for sitting there dreaming. Record it in the manual!"

She scrawled her name in again under her previous entry. Fanny was part of the furniture at Doomeerie. She fitted in perfectly; heavy and brooding, stifling life, squashing it down into a manual of misdemeanours. Always looking for what should be punished rather than what could be praised. It was going to be a long night.

✳ ✳ ✳

Jockim had trudged on relentlessly throughout the day. Finally, Lake Serenity stretched wearily before him. Exhausted, he lay down under the cover of his cloak, hidden by the dense greenery along its shores. He would easily make Lake Sanctuary tomorrow. Sanctusis, the holy hermit would be there. He would help him. Somehow he would find the inner peace that eluded him, the harmony that he had tried to take from her doe-like eyes. He had come so close to making it his own. Yet, life had ruthlessly snatched it from him once again. But tomorrow things would be different. There would be Sanctusis and possibly even Shiloh himself!

CHAPTER 2

Arrivals and Departures

Kyriedor had been teaching in the coastal towns in the south. There was talk of folk being healed. Many followed him, yet opposition to his compassionate ways was strong, especially amongst the Oge. Sanctusis spoke tirelessly of him. He feared that his time was limited and that if he was killed his sacred manuals would also be destroyed.

"They are priceless—like an ancient song," the old man explained. "They ignite the spirit that has long since forgotten the melody and true lyrics of love." He stared intently at Jockim's dark features. "It is not by accident that you have been drawn here, young man. I sensed it before you even arrived. The Silver Stag has been wandering the shores of the lake for some nights now."

Jockim stared out across its glassy, mirrored expanse. "Yet, as always, he eludes me!"

"He will reveal himself when you are ready. Prepare yourself by preforming the task which has been allotted you. Secure the first of the three manuals, *The Tao of Trust*. You will find it in the possession of a peasant boy named Benjamin, along with another two manuals. The humble are afforded great privileges. Treating all things with reverence as they do, they are innocent of the great treasures entrusted to them and therefore cannot be puffed up in pride. You must take possession of the first volume and hide it at Doomeerie for safe keeping. The second and the third will be safeguarded by other souls whose identity is to remain unknown. That way it will be ensured that the location of all three manuals remains a mystery, should the Oge become victorious."

Jockim nodded, staring at Pover. She had become as white as the snow that was soon to fall. "Can I take Pover and Freedom back with me to Tal?"

"Indeed you should. She has been without the comfort of her spirit companion for too long now. Pover's presence will fill her with consolation, melt what remains of her stubborn ego, and soften her heart to true forgiveness."

He smiled knowingly at Jockim. "Do not be aggrieved by Talitha's seeming lack of trust in you when you finally return to Deerie Castle. She merely mirrors what you are afraid to look at within yourself. Deep down, you fear that you will never be really able to change, that somehow the ways that you have learned at Doomeerie from your youngest days are imprinted upon your soul and cannot be erased. But fear not, what has been promised will indeed be given to you. Rather rejoice that it will come to pass, for nothing is impossible to the Great One."

His voice became a whisper. "All things that speak of love are yours for the asking." The hollows in his face became deeper, the furrowed lines longer. "That you must believe and act upon, even if it is not made manifest to your human eyes."

With a sigh he momentarily closed his tired eyes, as the sun's energy spilt, lengthening the shadows upon his kindly countenance. "And now, it's time for an old man to retire. I know that you will leave soon, so I will say goodbye. Fear not, Jockim. My spirit remains with you always." Silently, he made his way into the stone hut.

Jockim did not tarry. He was used to travelling at night, and there was no further need to stay. Besides, there was fear of being caught in approaching snow storms which years of experience instinctively told him were not far off in these northern lands. His sadness was hollow and brittle, easily cracked open by the sound of babbling brooks, the lonely call of wolves, and the free falling leaves that spiralled to the earth, gracefully surrendering their well-spent time. For weeks it remained so, nature's signs of the approaching winter travelling with him, reminding him of his loneliness.

Finally, he found himself amongst the crowds that listened to Kyriedor. Like the others around him, he hung on his every word. Nourished with renewed life and hope, he headed into the coastal hinterland, in search of a boy named Benjamin.

✳ ✳ ✳

Within a few weeks of Jockim's departure, Rose and the general returned to the castle. There was talk of travels, sights, and adventures which spilled over the hours of dinnertime, becoming increasingly embellished as the wine flowed more and more freely.

Despite the excitement of their arrival, Talitha could not shrug off her sadness. Loneliness had become her constant companion. It was a heavy, brooding feeling, sitting stonily inside. In the midst of frivolity and laughter, it refused to budge, but instead lodged, sullen and dejected. It hid behind the pretence of her eyes that feigned interest and her mouth that faked smiles. It murmured all kinds of polite and pat responses to questions and requests, hardly knowing what it was speaking.

Late one evening, she made her way across the courtyard. Her solitude pressed down heavily. Like a great, sunken stone lodged deep within her throat, it swelled painfully, begging to be released. She longed for Jockim, but equally for Pover. She had been separated from the little bird's counsel for too long. Pulling her cloak tightly around her shoulders, she quickened her pace. She was about to ascend the stone stairwell when Rose appeared before her.

"Tal," she addressed her softly, "might I have a word with you?"

Despite her dejection, Talitha nodded. "Come up to my room." She smiled wearily. It was less exhausting to simply go along with Rose's request, than it was to advocate her own need for rest.

They entered the tiny space and she lit a lantern. It immediately captured Rose's flaxen locks in a blaze of silken shimmers. Talitha gazed admiringly, awe struck yet again at her incredible beauty.

"I wanted to thank you, Tal," Rose said softly. "You have been a great friend to Raybet. Father and I stayed with Kyriedor sometime after you had gone, and he told us how you had helped him. Raybet has been able to share his sorrow about unwittingly putting Father in the front line of battle with us, and the love between us all has been strengthened by his honesty."

She hesitated, her golden flax falling into the light as she lowered her head. "I am so sorry for the trouble that I caused between you and Jockim before the war. How foolish I was not to listen to my true feelings. I spent too long denying them so that I could please Father, and in the end it only made things worse for all concerned."

"It is all in the past now Rose, think no more of it. Besides you were not alone in the deception. Do not take all the blame on yourself." Talitha took her hand in a gesture of gratitude.

"I know, but I feel that I have a greater portion of the blame than Jockim. Father forced him into a corner. He had a lot to lose: the castle, the safety of its occupants, and his self-belief. Jockhein always favoured Raybet when the boys were growing up. Jockim was treated with contempt. He sowed seeds which must have made Jockim doubt if he would ever be capable of being master of this castle. I'm sure that he would have felt a failure as a man if he had not been able to hold onto it."

Talihta nodded her head sadly. "Yes, I understand what you are saying."

"I only say it in the hope that it gives you some inner peace. I sense you are struggling, and that things did not finish in a good way between you and Jockim when he left. I know that it is not my business," again the golden locks swayed softly, "but should Jockim return, my words may help you to forgive him, just as you have forgiven Raybet, Father and I."

"Thank you, Rose." Talitha smiled genuinely at her. "That is very kind of you."

Rose stood up to leave. At the door, she turned and looked back. "I do hope with all my heart that things work out for the best for you and Jockim, Tal. I am very fond of you both." She flashed a pretty smile and quickly exited the room.

Talitha wearily laid her head on the pillow and finally permitted the stone in her throat to rise and express itself in heaving sobs. Eventually, when the rawness of her emotion had settled, she stood to pull the curtains back. A full moon was lodged just above the cliffs and for a moment she thought she saw the silhouette of a stag outlined grandly against the brilliant disc. Immediately, her eyes filled again and the moon metamorphosed into a thousand silver splinters, like pieces from an ancient, cracked mirror. She quickly brushed her tears away. Once more it shone softly down at her, as if bemused by her fancifulness, but this time there was no stag.

Oh, Shiloh, have you come to haunt me too, or is my mind beginning to shatter with sadness? Her thoughts grappled with the reality of what she believed that she had witnessed. With a sigh she laid her tired limbs upon the bed once again and was soon asleep.

Morning brought with it an explosion of excitement. There was a light in Rose's eyes that had not shone before, and Raybet was like a man with a new spirit. At breakfast they looked lovingly at each other. Raybet cleared his throat.

"Rose and I have some news that we would like to share with everyone," he announced, brimming with excitement. "We have decided to marry. Rose has agreed to become mistress of my half of Deerie Castle. This is now officially to be our new home. However, we are not broadcasting this news to the rest of the castle until Jockim returns."

There was a chorus of congratulations amidst embracing, smiles, and acclamations of approval all around. The old general beamed with pride and hugged them both as if they were his bear cubs.

"At long last I have lived to see my children, all three of them, happy!" Contentment mellowed his strong features. "Doomeerie has now become our home and there is only one thing that could make me happier ..." he stood up and put his arm on Talitha's shoulder, looking down fondly upon her, "that you, little lass, will always be here to share it with us."

CHAPTER 3

The Stag Man and Boy

Jockim hid behind the clump of trees, furtively watching the small lad. The boy at the inn had called the lad the 'stag kid', when he had inquired if he knew a boy call Benjamin.

"Yep, mista, he's the stag kid. He lives in a farm hut in the forest, just north of here. His dad's been missin' since the fightin' at Doomeerie Castle," the boy asserted, eyeing Jockim up and down.

"You're one of them folk from the castle, aren't ya?" he said. "I heard 'em talking about ya. They say ya'r the master of the castle. Them maids at the inn, they're always giggling about ya and prettin' themselves up in the mirror before they go in to do yer room." He smirked. "I reckon they hope that ya'd take a fancy to one of 'em"

Jockim ignored his remarks. "Why do they call him the stag kid?" he asked, his interest heightened.

"'Cause he loves stags and does! Always feeding 'em and playing with the fawns. They let him come near to 'em too. They trust him. Even the great Silver Stag does!"

Jockim could not control his eagerness. "The Silver Stag, you say?"

"Yes, sir, that's right!" The boy eyed him suspiciously. "But I wouldn't try to catch him. He's faster than lightning, that one. Many have tried but they never can. They say that the Great Spirit has made him swifter and wiser than any other stag. That's because he has suffered at the hands of man, and now he has risen above man to the spirit world."

Jockim looked at the lad strangely.

"I donno, that's just what they say. Anyway, I gotta go." He started to head off.

"How do I find the stag kid?" Jockim called after him.

"Just follow the path by the river to the north. You'll see 'im in the forest. He'll be there saving the deer from hunters and poachers." His scraggy body disappeared around the corner out of sight.

The 'stag kid' was younger than he had expected. He looked to be about the same age as Tobias, possibly only five at the most. He was sitting beside a trap, which had imprisoned a leggy, unsuspecting fawn. Despite his determined efforts, he did not have the strength to open it, and he had sunk into a dejected, little bundle beside it.

"Don't worry, Bess, I'm gonna free him!"

Jockim watched keenly as a doe approached forlornly. She sniffed at her fawn, moaned softly and raising her right, front foot stamped the ground a couple of times. The boy raised his hand and patted her neck trying to comfort her. Suddenly, Pover and

Freedom flew out from the trees and landed on the trap, chirping. The doe lifted her head and looked in his direction intently, ears flickering, nostrils quivering.

"What is it, Bess?" The stag kid jumped up. "Is someone there?"

Knowing his presence was no longer a secret, Jockim emerged. "Don't be frightened, Benjamin," he said. "I will free the fawn for you." The boy watched him with wide eyes as if he had seen a ghost.

Jockim wrenched the trap apart, and the little fawn awkwardly hobbled out, legs tumbling over legs. He nuzzled his mother and then Benjamin and Jockim.

"Son of Silver Stag, you're free!" the boy exclaimed in delight, hugging the fawn.

Jockim looked down at the lad. "Why did you call him that? Does the Silver Stag live around here?"

"Sometimes he does. Bess' fawn is his son. I know 'cause I've seen 'em running together. The doe only stays with the father of her young 'uns. Anyway, how did you know my name?"

"A wise, old man told me." Jockim playfully messed the boy's dark hair with his hand. It hung wavy and unkempt, not unlike his. Maybe it was the fact that this boy liked stags, but somehow Jockim felt himself to be immediately drawn to him.

Dark eyes looked up at him knowingly. "Kyriedor … yeah he said you'd come for the book. He said the man who saves the fawn is the one to give the first book to. But Kyriedor isn't old!"

Jockim laughed. "Indeed, he is not. No, this man was a friend of Kyriedor's. He was a lot older. Shall we take the fawn home?" He reached out his hand to the boy. "Fix her leg where she has been hurt … that's if Bess will let us."

"Oh, she'll be fine. She always comes to the farm and brings Son of Silver Stag."

Jockim nodded, picking the fawn up in his arms. "Are your mum and dad at the farm?" he asked.

"My mum is … my dad went away to fight for the castle. He never came back. My mum, she really misses him."

"I'm sure she does!" A wave of guilt washed over Jockim. "What is your mum's name?"

"Bess … same name as the doe."

Jockim went rigid. A shifting mixture of dread and excitement swirled in the pit of his stomach. No, he mustn't jump to conclusions. That would be thinking the worst.

"How old are you, son?" He tried to keep his voice light.

"Almost five … soon be able to ride the big horses."

Silence fell between them. Jockim's mind was racing. The boy said his mother's name was Bess. That was the name of the maidservant who had been employed at the castle before Talitha. The boy certainly had the same dark eyes and hair as her and could possibly pass as her child. But, she was not with child when she had gone, and surely this boy would have been born not long after that. He ran his fingers through his dark hair. *Oh God,* he thought, *surely not.*

The pain of Bess' departure was like an old wound, lashed open. Over the months of her employment they had grown close and had eventually become lovers, but she had mysteriously left one night stealing a necklace that had belonged to his mother. His grief had been hardened into wrath at her deception. She had never been found, and after some time he had thought that it was better that she was just gone; out of his life forever. The necklace meant little to him, save the fact that it had belonged to his mother. Then Talitha had come into his life and erased all memory of her from his heart. She had softened the anger. It had broken apart, allowing the grief to seep out of his heart. In her presence, he no longer even thought of Bess. But no, it was a common name. He was allowing ghosts from the past to haunt him yet again. He shrugged off the uneasiness that had drifted mist like across his thoughts. The trees began to thin.

"Here's our place, hey Bess!" Benjamin said, stroking the doe.

Ahead of them a homely, little cottage nestled in amongst the tall, willowy grass with a backdrop of oaks guarding it. It was whitewashed with a thatched roof and a red door. Its A-framed roof was divided in the front by a tall, stately chimney that stretched its way up into the sky. Surrounding it, an old, wooden fence barely held together, determined not to fail in its responsibility of protecting the occupants. Benjamin broke into a run, and the doe accompanied him.

"Mum, Mum," he yelled. "He's here—the stag man—he's here for the book!"

The door opened and she gracefully glided into the breeze, hair flowing wildly as he had always remembered it. The shawl around her shoulders struggled to free itself from her grasp, as her dark eyes watched her son and the doe trot up the pathway towards the cottage. Following them, she saw him; a tall, lean figure of a man with dark eyes and windswept hair, holding a fawn tenderly in his arms. Her heart missed a beat. All too soon he was there beside her. The air seemed to have been sapped from around her. Breathless, she stared at him.

"Hello, Jockim, this is not what I expected."

"Bess ..." He stared at her.

Benjamin looked up at his mother. She looked frightened like the doe had been when its fawn had been trapped. Her dark eyes were wide and wild. He glanced towards Jockim. What was wrong? Had he made a mistake? Surely this was the stag man. The man whom Kyriedor said would come.

Jockim looked down at the fawn and then back up at her. "The fawn ... his leg is injured. It will need to be attended to." The air around them was heavy. It shifted uncomfortably.

"Aye!" She glanced at the blood soaked twig of a leg and sprung into action. "Bring him in. I'll attend to him. Ben, give the doe some water and hay. She must be fair near spent after seeing her young one so." She gestured for Jockim to enter the house, while the boy went off to attend to the doe.

Jockim glanced around him at the humble, yet comfortable surroundings.

"Put him on the table," she said, trying to focus on the task at hand.

He did as she asked. She pulled out a chair and gestured for him to sit. Placing an apron over her head and tying it around her fine waist, she stared at him. He had not changed much. He could still take a woman's breath away. He met her gaze, and she quickly moved away to collect water, rags and ointment to attend to the fawn. Her movements were confident, yet gentle. Her pale, soft hands and the curve of her face lowered in concentration brought back bitter and tender memories. He brushed them aside roughly.

"You are well?" He didn't know what else to say.

"Aye and you …?" She continued with her task.

"The same," he replied. "The boy's father …" He faltered. "I'm sorry … How long have you been here on your own? Benjamin told me that he has not returned."

She began hastily throwing the used rags together, cleaning up in an agitated fashion. "He's dead or maybe imprisoned within the walls of Doomeerie." Her eyes did not meet his. The water was pitched out the door in a gust of frantic hostility.

"Benjamin!" The lad came running.

"Have you fixed the doe?"

"Yes, Mum. She's in the back stable," he replied, breathless.

"Alright then, take the fawn out to her and stay there with them both until I call you. Watch over them. I will make tea for the stag man, and then I'll call you in for some lunch. Don't come in until I call you. The stag man and I need to talk. Do you understand?"

"Yes, Mum." Benjamin walked into the kitchen sombrely. She was upset but he didn't know why. This was the stag man and he seemed so kind. He picked the fawn up in his arms and carried him to the door. He glanced fleeting at Jockim as he passed and whispered, "Thank you for saving Son of Silver Stag."

Jockim smiled and nodded. The pot on the stove began to splutter and bubble.

"Will you be having tea then sir?"

"Thank you," he replied, feeling awkward. Her words caused warm memories to flood over him.

"What is your husband's name, Bess?" he asked tenderly, staring at her fine, straight back, partly hidden behind the thick, dark hair that tumbled over it.

The tea landed heavily on the table before him.

"He's not my husband, nor is he the boy's father."

Jockim shifted uncomfortably on the chair. His eyes met hers. "Go on." Her eyes were dark and foreboding.

"His name is Tyrone, younger son of Brody Deerie. He's your cousin. Some say he died in the war, others that he was taken prisoner." She looked pleadingly up at him, waiting for him to unlock the mystery that had kept her awake so often at night.

Jockim swallowed hard. "He is well; a prisoner at the castle." He watched her eyes, relief followed by sadness. "And the boy's father … is he still alive?" Jockim stared at her fixedly.

She returned the stare unflinchingly. "You know more of him and his wellbeing than I do, sir."

She watched as the sadness that had been in her eyes now drifted into his. A heavy silence descended upon the little room. He stared down at his tea and then back into her eyes. They confirmed his suspicions. The boy was his. He stood up impatiently, pushing the chair back.

"Why didn't you tell me?" His voice was unsteady. "How could you leave without saying?"

She watched him begin to pace around like a lion, muscles tightening under his swarthy arms. She remembered how they had felt so strong, yet so tender when they held her in embrace.

"I … I … couldn't say … You might not have let me go."

"I thought that we loved each other. But obviously, it was something different to you. Just a tumble in the hay, I suspect." He glared over at her, eyes like dark caves under his furrowed brows.

"I did love you once, Jockim, but not enough to die for you.

I couldn't stay at the castle." She stopped, searching for a glimmer of understanding from the black coals that were glowing so fiercely. "How could I? The curse of the Doomeerie maidservant—you must know it. Konfra showed it to me. He must have overheard me telling Madame Avileaux that I was with child. How could I stay, knowing it?"

Jockim stared at her. "What rubbish is this you would have me believe?" His tea remained untouched on the table, steaming hot vapour into the tense air.

She rose and walked into an adjoining room. His glare followed her, demanding an explanation. Sounds of a chest groaning and then rustling filtered into the room. Re-entering she handed him a script of rolled paper. Simultaneously, she threw a small parcel wrapped in cloth onto the table. "Your sapphires … I don't want them. Konfra gave them to me, so I would shut my mouth about the baby. Said if I didn't, he would track the child down and have it killed."

Jockim undid the scroll and scanned it contents. A series of curses scrawled their ominous warnings to the reader. Midway down the page, someone had underlined words in ink. He read them quickly. *A maidservant who gives birth to a child within the castle's territory shall be doomed to be killed by the first born son.*

He looked up in disgust. "Surely you don't believe this superstition?"

"Why shouldn't I, Jockim?" she replied, empathically. "Konfra said that your father had had a mistress, a maidservant that they hustled out of the castle before she gave birth, so that she did not fall to the curse, and that your mother had died giving birth to you, and that Jockhein's mother had died giving birth to him, and that

Clare had been a maidservant—"

"Stop this nonsense! My mother was not a maidservant and neither was my grandmother, Sarai. You lie." He threw the script on the table. "You had just had enough of me and wanted to go on to fairer fields—to Tyrone." He paused and ran his hand through his hair. "Does he know the boy is mine?"

"No, only Konfra and Madame Avileaux know, and I have heard that Madame Avileaux is now dead." She started to sob. "I told Tyrone that the father had been killed, drowned at sea. A storm had brewed up when he was fishing, and he was never seen again. I was working at the *Swinging Lantern* when we met. The folk there had been kind to me. They took me in to work and then let me stay on to have the baby there." She wiped her eyes, and her voice settled a little.

"I hated Doomeerie and so did he. It was that which brought us together in the beginning ... our mutual hatred of the castle and its folks. I needed to get away before those that think they are doing good, decided that I had no right to keep my baby. I knew they would take Benjamin off me and send him to St Auburn's orphanage, so Tyrone said he'd help me escape. We left together one night. I knew he had a wife, but he'd said that he couldn't go back to her, that he'd been away too long. It wouldn't be fair, he reckoned. He said she would have had someone else by now, and that it would only make things hard for her."

She began to roll up the discarded scroll tightly. "He never spoke about her again, and I did not speak of Benjamin's father. Tyrone was good to the boy—treated him like his own. We were happy, and then Andor wanted him to fight for the castle. I begged him not to, but it is in his blood, being a descendent and all. Well, the rest you know." She looked up at him, dark eyes pleading. "Will you not set him free Jockim, if not for what we once had together, for your son?"

Jockim ignored her plea. "How does the boy come to have the holy books?"

"The Oge ..." She fiddled with the script in her hands. "They came here pretending to help a single woman all alone. I trusted them. They took over the house and bundled me off to Edgewater where Kyriedor was preaching."

She lowered her head and the tears began to spill from her eyes. "They dragged me before the crowds, proclaiming to all that I was an adulterous, an unmarried woman with a child, and that I had been living with a married man who was not the child's father. They wanted to kill me; throw me over the cliff to be dashed against the rocks. He stopped them. Kyriedor, he stopped them." She started to sob. "I have never met a man such as him!" The sobbing continued and Jockim waited for it to subside.

"Later, he came to me under cover. He said that some of his followers would take me back home, and that the Oge would not trouble me again while he was alive. He told me that these people would give Benjamin some books which we were to hide. A stag man would come for the first ..." she faltered momentarily, "and others would come for the second and third."

"I'm sorry, Bess." Jockim sank to the table. He ran his hand through his hair. "God knows, I'm sorry." His voice choked. "I didn't know about the child. I can understand that Konfra would have spooked a young girl in your predicament with this nonsense, but why didn't you come to me about it?" His hand reached out and touched hers.

She raised her head to look at him, eyes shining with sadness, but remained silent.

He sighed. "I can't promise you that I can give Tyrone his freedom yet. I will need to think about it. I must ensure the safety of those at the castle, but if it puts your mind at rest, he is well and in comfortable quarters. He is locked in a room in the castle, not the dudgeon."

"Thank you." She smiled, grateful to know that he was alive and not suffering.

"Do you think that you can persuade him not to raise arms against Doomeerie again if I send him back to you?"

"Oh Jockim, I will promise you that I will do my utmost if you could only allow him to return."

"Keep the sapphires. You may need them. I will bring you provisions under the cover of dark every few weeks, and the boy ..." He stopped. A look of horror stole onto her face.

"Oh no, please don't take him from me. He is all that I have on this earth. I cannot be separated from him. I will do whatever you ask of me."

Her frantic face assured him that her love for the boy was upmost in her heart. "I will not ask anything of you, only that Tyrone should never know that he is my son, and if he is ever cruel to either of you, you will leave with the boy."

She nodded. "Of course, but he loves the boy. He would never harm him. He treats him like his own."

Darkness crossed Jockim's face. She bit her lip. "I'm sorry, I shouldn't have said that. It was thoughtless and cruel of me."

He stood up. "The boy must be hungry. We should eat, and then I should head off with the book before it is too late. No one must know that I have been here."

She nodded. "I will prepare something. Perhaps you would like to tell Benjamin." Their eyes met over the boy's name.

"Something inside told me that he was mine … when I first saw him with the fawn."

"Oh Jockim, I'm so sorry," she whispered. "I never intended—"

"I know it's alright … I know."

He raised the palm of his hand gesturing for her to be silent. Words could never suffice. Somehow he made his way to the rear of the cottage. His head was reeling—a son—he had a son these past five years, and he had never known. In fact, he may never had found the boy if Sanctusis had not sent him to protect the sacred sutra.

The little lad was curled up beside the fawn, making patterns in the dirt. He bolted upright as Jockim entered the stable. He smiled down at him.

"How is Son of Silver Stag going?"

The boy's face lit up. "He has fallen asleep. It's been a scary morning for him."

"Indeed, it has …" Jockim crouched beside him, "and it's been a big one for you too, Benjamin." He placed his hand on the boy's shoulder. "Are you hungry? Your mother is preparing some lunch."

"Yes." He jumped to his feet. "Is she alright?'

"Of course," Jockim answered quickly. "Why?"

"She looked scared." He glanced at Jockim again. "I didn't think that you were an Oge. A stag man couldn't be an Oge."

Jockim shook his head and smiled. "No, us stag folk could never be Oges." They both laughed. Jockim placed his arms around the boy. It felt good to hold his son—if only for a minute!

CHAPTER 4

Careless Comments

It was Bess who suggested that Jockim spend the night with Benjamin in the stable. The boy wanted to watch over Son of Silver Stag throughout the night. Jockim didn't need convincing. He longed to be with him. Hence, he decided to prolong his stay, at least for a few more hours.

It was an unsettling night. The Silver Stag had bellowed outside the stables at some point, presumably calling the doe. She had lifted her head nervously, gone to the door, stood and waited for a minute, but when there was no further sound, returned to the fawn. Jockim got up and went outside. He peered into the night but there was no sign of him. The sound had been so hauntingly mournful, opening up some lost space in his soul. He settled Benjamin back to sleep, only to toss and turn for hours.

Morning brought hot porridge and scrambled eggs, as well as Benjamin's wide, toothy grin as he produced the holy book. Jockim eyed him proudly. "When did you get that, son? You must have been up before dawn."

"You was sleeping. We crept into the forest. Freedom came too. Son of Silver Stag is doing really good now. Him and Bess are back in the forest again," he announced excitedly.

"That's good to hear, Benjamin. Did Freedom come back with you?" He looked concerned.

Benjamin was too elated to pick up on the edge in his voice. "No, she stayed in the forest with the others."

Bess lent forward to collect the plates. "Did you have to take the hummingbird back with you, Jockim?"

"No, I suppose not, if the bird wants to be free and go her way then I cannot stop her. Pover is still with me. That's the main thing."

The little, white bird looked up at him from her position on the window sill. She was watching out for her companion's return, but in her heart she knew that she would not come.

"Who knows … Freedom may meet up with us in the forest on our way back to the castle?" He stood to help her clear the table.

"Did you hear the Silver Stag last night, Mum?" Benjamin asked eagerly.

"No, I can't say I did. Was he bellowing outside the stables? He must have been calling his doe."

"He sounded angry. Do you think he was mad at Bess 'cause his son got caught in a trap?"

She laughed a little nervously and glanced fleetingly at Jockim. "No, I don't think so Benjamin. He knows that she did her best. She can't see every trap in the undergrowth and those that lay them are very cunning."

Jockim cleared his throat. "I think he was wishing that he had been there to save her and the fawn. Maybe that's why he sounded so mournful. He is sad that he failed his love."

The plates clattered into the wash bowl. "He must not be so. She understands that he didn't know what happened to her and the fawn. She knows that he would have helped her. He was busy protecting his territory and looking after all the others that he had responsibility for. She knows that he would never have intentionally let her down, and that even now he must return to his territory."

"I bet that's why Jockim was sent to save the fawn mum, because the Silver Stag couldn't." Benjamin beamed brightly at them both.

She threw the tea towel towards him. "Come and help us, wise one." She laughed playfully. "Yes, Jockim helped the stag, and the stag will help Jockim find his way home."

"Don't you know the way home, Jockim?" Benjamin looked shocked.

Jockim messed the boy's hair playfully again. "I've been lost many a time Benjamin. Your mother is an astute woman."

Their eyes met momentarily, and she hastily glanced away. Benjamin felt happy. He didn't know what 'astute' meant, but they seemed so much better this morning. It was like they really cared about each other.

"Can I help with any chores before I leave? This farm must be a lot of work for a woman."

She smiled. "Why thank you, Jockim, but we manage. However, I could do with a little firewood chopped for the winter."

"Is the axe in the stable?" He peered out the window at the ramshackled, wooden building where he had spent the night.

"Yes, I'll come with you." She removed the final plate from the soapy water and headed out after him. "Benjamin, when you finish drying up can you feed the chooks please? I'm going to help Jockim with the firewood."

"Okay, Mum. Can I go into the forest when I finish?"

"Yes, but mind you keep an eye out for traps too and be back for lunch!"

Jockim had already started chopping when she joined him in the stables. He looked up and smiled but continued working. After a good half hour he stopped, wiped his brow and stared at her.

"Thank you for what you said in there. Your forgiveness means a lot to me."

"And yours to me, Jockim. You need to be forgivin' yourself ... Things will sort themselves out with others, if you do that first." She glanced at him out of the corner of her eye and crouched to collect more firewood.

"It's not quite that simple," he replied stoically.

She rose and placing her hands on her hips, laughed heartily. "Well now, the master of Doomeerie wouldn't be fishin' for some feminine advice, would he?"

He grinned sheepishly and ran his fingers through his hair. "I admit I don't understand women much, but it seems to me that a man thinks in a straight line from A to B. He knows what he wants and goes out to get it, but with a woman, well it all becomes mighty complicated, the line of reasoning is never straight forward ..."

Her laughter tinkled freely. "Ah Jockim ... she has you under her spell, doesn't she?"

His dark eyes shot up quickly. *Just how much did she know about Talitha?*

She instinctively read his thoughts. "Folk talk you know. I've heard she's young and pretty, and very brave and very foolish, and hardworking and dutiful. She's kind and likes to save animals and people, but I'd be thinking that the poor girl needs to save herself."

"What do you mean by that?" Jockim sounded wounded. Did she think that he would destroy Talitha if she stayed on at the castle?

"Well I'd be thinking that from a young age she's been taught in the ways of being a woman. She's compassionate and caring to others, but I bet she hasn't thought too much about what she wants. It's all about others needs and what's the noble thing to do."

"Mmm ... that makes sense." He spoke his thoughts out loud. It sounded like Talitha. He crashed the axe down again. The wood groaned and snapped. "I really want to believe that deep down she loves me, but every time I get close to talking about us and the possibility of a future together, she changes the topic on to bloody Raybet." Again the axe landed heavily.

"Mmm ... Konfra's son, I wonder what he symbolises for her."

He sighed. "Okay, so now we're into the realm of feminine mystique, I assume." He stood the axe upright on the ground for a minute and leaned upon it, a slight frown crossing his face.

"Think about it, Jockim ... Assuming that she really does love you, which sounds like a distinct possibility after all that I've heard that you've put the poor girl through," she grinned cheekily at him, "something about your treatment of Raybet must upset her. Maybe you are treating her the same way. She probably isn't even aware of it herself ... only something just isn't quite right for her, and the sorting of whatever it is with Raybet will make her feel better."

He went quiet. *Raybet … he thought, I've been kind to him, forgiven him. I set him free when I left the castle. I told her she was free to go if she wanted to. No, that's not it.*

"Well, I'm all done here," Bess announced. "I'm going to prepare lunch." She smiled at Jockim kindly, placing her hand on his shoulder. "Thank you for your help. I'll send Benjamin out to get you when it's ready."

He watched her walk away. *Just what does she mean? Something about the way I'm treating Raybet? What more can I do for him? I've offered him half share in the castle, equal standing and respect to me!* He stopped. His heart quickened. *That's it! Talitha didn't know that when she took Raybet the note. She wanted me to give him equality, respect. She craves the same for herself. I wanted to relinquish her of her maid duties and ask her to stay as a guest that day in the study, only she spoke about Raybet first, and with all the upset that morning I never did tell her.*

He laid the axe down and wiped the moisture that was trickling down his forehead. Things were beginning to make a lot more sense!

✳ ✳ ✳

"Here Jockim, take this." Bess handed him a package of provisions for the journey after they had finished lunch.

"Thank you Bess, for your hospitality and for sharing your wonderful son." He lifted Benjamin, tossing him playfully in the air before returning him back to the floor.

"Look after your mother, son." He crouched down beside the

boy hugging him goodbye. "She's a very brave lady." He smiled up at Bess. "And she's a fine mother. You are very lucky to have her."

Bess beamed. "Thank you Jockim, for your kindness and understanding." She ran her open palms down the sides of her apron, a little nervously. "You are welcome back anytime you want to return." She lifted a dainty, right hand and he took it in his, meeting her dark eyes with genuine gratitude.

"Thank you, I hope to do so. Remember if you should ever need me, you know where I am."

He looked away quickly and grabbed his belongings. They walked to the door and she put her arm around the boy's shoulders as they waved good bye. He headed down the stony pathway; the little, white bird fluttering around him. At the gate, he stopped and waved once, before turning his face north. It was a wrench to leave but even more so to stay.

Early the next morning, he reached the castle. Physically tired and hungry, his first stop became the kitchen. He was grateful that he had returned under the cover of night so that he would be unnoticed. Even so, he did not account for Fanny's early rise to bake for the remaining soldiers. He startled the poor woman fair out of her wits.

"Hush, Fanny," he whispered urgently as she let out a yell at his presence. "It's only me!"

"Good grief, sir," she gasped, "you fair startled me. I didn't expect to see anybody down here at this hour of the morning."

"I gathered that much." He flashed a grin to assure her that he was not annoyed.

"What is there to eat?' he demanded, scavenging around the

shelves and pouring himself a drink.

"I'll boil you up some soup, sir, if you can wait until I get the wood fire started." She stared at his tired and dishevelled state.

"Here, I'll get started on the fire and you start on the food."

She chuckled. "Just like you were as a lad when Avie would bring you down here for supper, you couldn't wait a minute; anyone would have thought you were fair starving."

"Well believe it or not, I am Fanny. I've travelled a long way and by God it's beginning to get bitterly cold out there. We're in for a heavy winter." He lit the fire easily as she sat the soup upon the stove.

"So, tell me, what's the gossip upstairs? What has everyone been doing since I left? How is the lad coming along?"

"Listen to you," she said, "asking the likes of me a servant about your own folk, or are you more interested in the servants in the house, especially one particular, young maidservant?" She ventured cheekily, sensing that he was dependent upon her for a good feed.

"Alright, you've had your fun … Yes, how is Talitha?"

"Oh, she's okay, sir. Been fair moping around since you left like a lost puppy, but I've got to say that she has been attending to her duties without fail."

"Well, that's good to hear."

"What's good to hear, the fact that she's been down in the dumps since you left, or the fact that she has attended to her duties well?" Fanny stirred the pot, looking very matronly in her starched, white apron that fitted tightly across her large breasts.

Jockim chose to ignore the question and pressed for further news about the others.

"Well, actually quite a lot has happened since you left. General

Konfra and his daughter Rose have returned, and Raybet and Rose have announced to a select few that they are to be married." She scrutinised him carefully, observing his reaction.

"Is that so?" he replied, biting into his half eaten apple. A sense of relief flowed over him. Nothing had eventuated between Raybet and Talitha. Raybet's affections really were for Rose. Thank God he had left when he did. Otherwise, he would have definitely made a fool of himself.

"Well, that's good for them! I bet that the general is beside himself—having all of his offspring living in the castle now." A sudden surge of anger filled his belly. He would deal with Konfra, but first he must set things right with Talitha.

"That he is sir … that he is. Ah, but the old man is starting to fail a little I think. He uses a walking stick now and his appetite is nowhere like it used to be. I swear that some days he pecks at food like that bird there." She gestured towards Pover. "That white bird looks mighty like the brown one that Miss Tally used to have. Is it for her, sir?"

"That white bird *is* Pover. By some freak of nature, her plumage has changed to a brilliant white. There is only a tiny patch of brown remaining under her belly. Maybe it's changing colour for the winter." He looked at Pover strangely, as he had many times since he had observed her new, feathery covering.

She smiled and continued, "My, that is unusual. Speaking of strange things, the young lad, Tobias, well, I'd thought that he wouldn't pull through, but he is doing just fine. The women folk, Angie and Tally, had him riding the donkey around the other day. I saw them down there in the animal fighting compound walking around and around with Tobias on Balaamine's back. Well at least Angie and Tobias were going around. Young Tally got upset and went to sit under the pine trees. I daresay it probably bought back memories of that time you had to teach her a lesson, sir."

He stopped eating suddenly and pitched the core angrily in a nearby bin.

"Now don't you go upsetting yourself over that, sir? She's a lot more able to take orders now than she was in the early days. She needed to know that you're boss, and she can't get away with anything she wants, just because you're a little fond of her, so to speak."

Fanny began to feel uncomfortable, as if she had raised a sore topic that she shouldn't have. She continued blustering on, trying to make up for her mistake. "Na, the whipping was just what she needed, brought her back down to size. I know it must have been hard losing the stag and—"

"Fanny," Jockim interrupted sharply, "is that damned soup ready yet? I'm tired and cold."

Fanny nervously began to ladle the soup into a bowl. "Yes, of course. Here it is," she replied hastily, placing the food before him.

"Thank you."

He gulped it down. "The soup is good, Fanny. What time do the others arise?"

"Well, Miss Tally is up early to help with the baking. The men arise about six, and the ladies dine with them at seven in the breakfast room."

"Can you let them know that I'm back?" he said, placing his bowl into the washing up container. "I will sleep through until midmorning, and then I'd like to see Talitha in my study. Can you tell her?"

He turned to face her. "Thank you, Fanny. It was delicious, and it is good to be back." He smiled at her gratefully, and she beamed back, happy that she had not caused any damage by her careless comments.

He was about to head out the door when he stopped and held his hand out for Pover to alight upon it. "By the way," he looked over at Fanny, who was watching him closely, amazed at the way the usually timid creature had taken to him, "don't let Talitha know about the bird. I want to surprise her. A kind of … gift for her." He rubbed his fingers through his hair in a gesture of confusion.

"You have my word, sir. I'll not say a thing," she replied, starting to knead the bread. "I can't think of a better way to win back that one's heart." She tossed the dough effortlessly.

"Win back her heart?" Jockim said quietly to his little companion, as he ascended the shadowy staircase. "Have I lost it, Pover?"

CHAPTER 5

Dismantling Lesser Dreams

The door swung open. There she stood. He felt breathless. She looked so beautiful. Her petite frame was clad in an emerald green gown which fitted her snugly to the waist and then fell away in sensual folds that hugged the curves of her feminine hips. Her cheeks were slightly flushed from hurrying. Strands of her auburn, brown hair that had been tied back in soft, long waves at the nape of her neck, had fought their way free of their black, velvet restraint. Defying the ribbon to hide their beauty, they fell in soft, wispy waves around her oval face. She looked up at him with those great, doe-like eyes that wrenched at his heart. Her pretty lips remained closed, determined not to give away any hint of emotion.

"Hello, Tal," he said, holding out his hand and feeling decidedly awkward like a young, adolescent boy again.

She took his hand and curtsied ever so politely. "Sir, welcome back."

"Please, call me Jockim; we are more friends than master and servant surely?"

"As you wish, sir—Jockim, however I think that whatever relationship we've had in the past is exactly that … in the past."

"Please, come and sit down," he said, gesturing towards the great, brocaded chairs by the fire. *Things have not got off to a good start*, he thought. *Remain calm. Be kind. She may come around yet.*

"Can I get you something to drink?" He walked towards the whisky decanter.

"No, thank you," the pretty, porcelain figurine replied politely.

He shuffled nervously for a second. Offering a drink hadn't worked last time either.

"How are you?" He looked directly into her large, doe eyes.

"I'm well thank you, and yourself?"

"I'm good, now that I'm home again. It's been damned cold out there at nights."

He walked towards the great, bay window and stared down at the grey River Styx tumbling along on its never ending journey. He thought of Benjamin many miles south along the river's course. What might the lad be doing now? Silence settled uneasily. She began to feel uncomfortable, wondering if he had even remembered that she was in the room.

Clearing his throat, he turned to face her again. "I wanted to thank you for what you have done while I have been away. Fanny has told me that you have been most attentive to your duties."

"And what else has Fanny told you about me?" she asked, tilting her pert, little chin defiantly.

"Nothing," he said, a frown beginning to slightly crease his forehead. He looked questioningly at her, wondering what she could mean. "Is there something that I should know?" He hoped that she was not going to tell him that she had decided to go.

"Not at all, only that I have asked Padyah to find some different employment for me. I will be leaving as soon as he does, unless of course I hear back from him over the next couple of days, in which case I will give you the usual two weeks service until you are able to find a replacement. The others can let you know their own business."

"I didn't ask you here to catch up on the castle gossip," he replied, becoming a little frustrated at her detached manner. Her words weighed heavily. She *was* going! He sunk into the chair opposite her.

"Then why did you ask me here, sir?"

"Look Tal, I'm sorry, I'm very sorry about the way I acted the last couple of times that we were together," he blurted out abruptly, running his fingers through his dark, unkempt hair.

She said nothing and merely stared at him; sculptured, unyielding loveliness.

"I see you are having problems remembering." He was annoyed that her silence remained. "We met shortly after midnight. You were pretending to assist Jeremiah in his duties as a way of getting into Raybet's room to give him Cathy's note to my father."

Her stare got frostier. "I mistakenly accused you both of being lovers. I'm sorry, that was inappropriate of me. Raybet had every right to know his parentage. He has no doubt told you that I intended to give him half share of the castle, if that is what he and

Rose should want." He hesitated. Still, no reply came. He cleared his throat.

"And the incident with Jeremiah … well I was upset and angry that such a fine horse as Noble should die from a lad's attempt to boost his self-pride. I had fully intended to tell you that I loved you that morning and ask you to be my guest at the castle. I wanted to relieve you of your duties as a maid, but I lost my senses grieving about Noble. I felt ashamed of my treatment of the boy and then when you said that you had important feelings to share with me," his head lowered, and he rubbed his brow with his long fingers, "I was incredibly let down that you didn't express any feeling towards me, instead you spoke of Raybet yet again."

He looked up at her, desperately hoping for some gesture of understanding, but she remained unmoved by his words. Instead, she replied haughtily, "You told me to go back to the kitchen and laundry. How do you think that felt after you had just kissed me? I had spoken no words of judgement about your abhorrent whipping of the boy. I tried to give you compassion and understanding. You snatched it from me and then nonchalantly ordered me back to Fanny as if I was some object of pleasure to be used by you."

He knelt on one knee before her. Taking her hand tenderly in his, he earnestly held her eyes captive. "I understand that for a long time I have been insensitive to your needs. I have used your kindness to add balm to my wounds, without considering your feelings and needs. Tal, I am truly ashamed of my selfish behaviour. I can only ask that you will consider forgiving me. I will do my utmost never to repeat it. I want you to stay, to be a guest in my home. Please, consider it."

She looked away into the flames, trying to assess his honesty. Her heart wanted to believe him capable of change, but her head cautioned any rash response. He looked at her a little quizzically. Leaning forward, he gently lifted her lowered chin. Their eyes locked. He smiled, amused at her wide eyed, childlike stare. She felt the blood rush to her face. Annoyed that he also had seen it, she pulled away. *How dare he*, she thought, brushing aside her feelings of discomfort. *Does he think that he can causally come back after being away for weeks and expect me to believe that he is capable of such change?* Anger and resentment welled within her.

"Yes, you're right. Your actions were abhorrent, even for a master to a servant, let alone between friends, which I foolishly believed us to be. And what's more, it's not just what you said, Jockim," she replied, a heated passion rising in her voice, "it's what you didn't say!" Again, her chin tilted a fraction higher.

"What do you mean?" He was genuinely perplexed by her sudden, zealous reply.

"You left without apologising or even saying goodbye, without telling me that you were going. Everybody else in this castle knew except me. I looked like a fool asking for them to wait for you at breakfast. Then, I was the object of their pity as Vadio explained to me that you had left and might not be back for years."

Her voice became more and more agitated as the hurt that she had bottled up for weeks tumbled out, a cascade of suppressed rage. "And you had the gall to accuse me of not trusting you that night and of holding information back from you!"

She rose and straightened herself to her full height, facing him in all of her raging splendour. He looked up, not knowing what to say. He had expected her forgiveness and understanding, always so freely given, not her fury.

"I'm sorry, Jockim, I would like to believe you capable of change, but it's too late, and it's all words. As I said, I will be here until Padyah finds me other work. Maybe if I can see some evidence of real change, I will reconsider my plans. In the meantime, I will take you at your word, and I will not be reporting back to Fanny!" She strode towards the door and then stopped, turning sharply. "And, if you think that I've been waiting around this doomed castle for you to return, you are mistaken. The only reason that I am still here is that I honour my word, and I have a contract to finish." She gathered her skirts around her and swept towards the door. "And that maybe I might eventually find Shiloh—if he is still alive!"

"Wait, Tal please!" he called after her, but she was gone in a flash of cold wrath; blazoning, brilliant green loveliness, slamming the door after her.

He sunk into the large armchair, thinking, *What happened? What the hell?* His spirits plummeted. *Have I lost her?* Brooding, he watched the flames leap and dance before him, tantalising him with their sensuous beauty. Their heat filled him with heaviness. Mesmerised by their movement, his mind drifted lazily back, his body lost in the inertia of hopeless disappointment. Suddenly, Sanctusis' wisdom seeped through the haze of hollow, brittle thoughts that held him captive. *'All things that speak of love are yours for the asking and it will begin to come to pass. That you must believe and act upon, even if it is not made manifest to your human eyes.'*

He forced himself up. What good was wisdom without action? Trudging outside into the biting wind, he dispiritedly pulled his coat about him and made his way along the stony path to the tool shed. Grabbing some implements, he headed straight for the animal fighting compound. There it stood, stark and black against a bleak, forgotten sky; a lasting testament to his superstition and cruelty! The mighty doors creaked open with a whine. *Destroy the stag, the woman and your soul, and you will save Doomeerie for yourself for all time!* The evil whine echoed hauntingly, clutching to the guilt shackled memories of his tormented mind.

With one mighty heave, he lifted the axe and landed it down hard upon an ancient wooden trestle, splitting open the pain that had settled deep within his skull. Bang! Creeek! Crack! Again and again, he hammered upon the trembling timber. With each blow, he begged that the unending agony would somehow be destroyed— released from her, from him, and from the stag, wherever it was. The wind picked up and thrust the great oak doors in and out, battering them back and forth as they wailed in objection. *You have chosen Doomeerie for your soul ... Nothing can erase the past ... The curse is upon you forever.* He brushed aside the moisture that seeped from his eyes. Its sting blurred the shadows before him.

On and on he went, attacking trestle after trestle until his strength depleted. Dropping the axe, he slumped onto the hard, cold earth. *Take me,* he inwardly raged, *take me Doomeerie, with your accursed past, if it will somehow save her and the stag.* The wind battered him in gusts; mighty squalls blasted in upon his aching body with the incessant swinging of the great oak doors.

Finally, he pulled himself to standing; his task barely started. Stumbling out, he bolted the ominous doors behind him. Talitha must not know. Not until he had removed every last shred of evidence that a killing compound had ever existed. Yet, he could never erase his memory, no matter how brutally he wrenched at it. He trudged on through the barren loneliness which shrouded the compound's exterior. Ahead of him, the stately elms swayed wildly, releasing their swirling leaves gracefully into the spirited river. Somehow the barrenness about him juxtaposed their beauty, breathtakingly, mysteriously. Might it be the same for him? If only this memory wasn't just a wasteland. The thoughts flurried in his mind, gathering momentum. Maybe, just maybe, they could be the force that was needed to relinquish his past, to use its pain to propel him to a new place, a gentler place, a place that had somehow been prematurely snatched from him, long before he was ever able to claim it as his own.

CHAPTER 6

What Changed Your Mind?

Fanny awoke Jockim several hours later. "Dinner is served, sir and everyone's waiting."

"Thank you, Fanny," he muttered, dragging his exhausted, limp body up and trudging to the basin.

"Ah, sir …"

He stopped and looked at her solid frame, sensing her distress. "Yes, Fanny … what is it?"

"I understand that you have relieved Miss Tally of her maid duties, and that she is now a guest at the castle. However, I just thought that you should know that she is refusing to dine in the great hall with the others. She has told me that she will eat in her room. She is in such an obstinate state of mind that I fear no amount of persuasion on my part will convince her otherwise." Irritation was firmly plastered across Fanny's features. "What would you have me do, sir?"

Jockim dried his wet face and smiled at the older lady. "Nothing … nothing at all, Fanny … She may dine in her room if she so chooses. Will you be right to serve at the table or would you like some assistance?"

"Thanking you, sir. I shall be alright." She bustled out of the room just as quickly as she had entered into it.

The meal was a little awkward, especially when anything slightly related to Talitha arose in the conversation. Everyone knew of their dissention. Vadio and Anya felt sorry for both Jockim and Talitha, however Raybet believed that the former had received his just desserts. Still, as night after night wore on with no sign of the stubborn young woman, sympathy for Jockim began to mount. The women talked with Talitha during the day. They could see that in attempting to hurt him, she was in fact hurting herself even more. However, her pain ran too deep. Past wounds that could not be easily healed were festering.

During the following days, Vadio and Raybet helped Jockim complete the dismantlement of the compound. They worked solidly day after day, from morning to evening. On the third day, the ominous, grey skies turned white and released the soft snow that they had been promising. The men were so close to finishing that Jockim stayed on to complete the final section alone, determined to have the job done before the heavy snow set in. Eventually, all that remained was a large, walled enclosure.

Jockim's hands were blistered and red raw from the heavy labour. He looked physically exhausted and worn from the events of the past weeks. Slowly, he dressed for dinner, wondering when he should try and approach Talitha and show her the now bare compound.

The others were already seated and discussing the first snows when he arrived at the table. He took his seat and looked up to see Talitha and Fanny bringing in the hot soup. Fanny appeared flustered and bothered, Talitha subdued.

"What is going on?" Jockim rose from the table, frowning and taking the plates from Talitha. "My guests do not wait on tables in this castle. Please, take a seat Talitha. If Fanny requires help, I am capable of assisting."

"No sir, definitely not," the stout woman replied. She glanced down at Jockim's swollen and blistered hands. "Good God, sir! What in heaven's name have you been doing to yourself? Your hands will need immediate attention before they get infected."

"Yes, perhaps so, Fanny … Talitha would you be able to assist me?"

She looked taken aback but rose without speaking and followed him out of the room. They walked silently towards the laundry area of the castle where the medical bandages were kept. Taking care not to meet his gaze, she quickly filled a basin with warm, salty water while he took off his coat and rolled up his sleeves. Placing his hands over the basin, he watched her gentle, graceful motions as she carefully washed his cuts and blisters. Not a word was spoken, neither quite knowing what to say. She began to sniffle. Tears trickled down her cheeks. No amount of resolve could stop them. In fact, her efforts to control them seemed only to make them burst forth in a fresh flood of abundance.

Eventually, he spoke, "If you cry any more tears the basin could overflow. I'm quite sure that my hands haven't earned that much sympathy." Pulling a handkerchief from his coat pocket, he gave it to her.

"I'm sorry …" She sniffed, wiping them away. "I've been an idiot—such an arrogant fool. I came back to the castle to complete my contract." She took a deep breath between sobs. "I loved you and wanted to be with you again, but when I saw that you were still struggling with your old, selfish ways, I was disgusted at your wretchedness. You see I was very smug and self-satisfied with the progress that I had made on my journey."

Again, she sniffled. "I had conquered my fear. I had softened my resentment towards Raybet's betrayal and even yours, but I hadn't conquered my pride. I was determined to show you that I had changed … that I was strong and emotionally superior to you." She glanced at him quickly. "You are a slave to your temper … You are fiery one minute and then icy cold the next! I would never allow my emotions to become so undisciplined, so I pushed them down, buried them under a mound of fear and false pride."

She twisted the handkerchief, unable to meet his gaze. "But, from our very first meeting you disarmed me. I lost control of my temper, and I felt like a naughty child once again. Around you alone, I seemed unable to control myself, so I removed myself from you, not wanting to face my weaknesses. And then my sprained leg forced us together again and all of my old feelings towards you returned. You were so kind and loving to me. That day in the study with Jeremiah … I hated you for sending me back to Fanny. I was angry at you, and I guess that was part of my motivation for taking the note to Raybet, even though I convinced myself that my motives were only altruistic. I realise that for all this time, I have been stuffing my emotions down because I couldn't face their pain."

She stopped and sighed. "If only I had tried to understand myself better, things may have been different. Instead I was always striving to be there for others. I have become so damned self-righteous." He said nothing, grateful that she was finally opening up to him. Now was the time for listening, even though he inwardly squirmed at her harsh self-condemnation.

"I no longer know what to do." She gazed up at him fleetingly. "What is best for us? I love you, and I want to accept your apology, but I don't think that I can be around you. Part of me is fighting to maintain my soul around your all-consuming power, while another part of me loves you desperately. I know that it has been wrong of me to refuse to dine at the table, but I don't know where to go from here. I am so confused. I cannot forgive either you or myself. I have long since forgotten the meaning of the reeds and the ripples that I confided to you when I returned to the castle. There is too much pain for me now. I am too frightened to open my Pandora's Box of shame. It will surely destroy me!"

"Now, now, Tal," he replied, drawing her to him. "That's enough of this kind of talk! It doesn't sound like you at all. You're always the first to forgive. This time you have finally given me the opportunity to repay you for all of your understanding ways. Would you deny me the chance of making up to the love of my life?"

He placed his hand under her chin, drawing it up to look him in the eyes. "There will be no more talk of punishment at Doomeerie. The old ways are behind us, and to prove it I have something to show you. Help me fix these wounds so we can go and see."

They bandaged his hands and then strode out into the crisp, stinging air. The stars were brilliant, the moon crystalline, suspended over the castle. They neared the animal fighting compound. She drew back, her eyes wide and pleading.

"Oh, let's not go in there Jockim … of all places, let's not go there."

Her throat was constricting. It was hard to breathe in the cold, biting air. Her mind was spinning, a downward spiral driven by panic.

"Trust me, please, Tal. I think we need to."

"Why drag the past up again. It's over!" It was an effort to get the words out.

"Is it? I not so sure about that! I think that it keeps meeting up with us in the present under a multitude of guises. Just stay with me … please."

He pulled at the heavy bolt of the door. It clanged loudly. She sensed that something was different. The old stone wall remained, but the wooden enclosure inside it had been removed. Stepping through the great, oaken doors, the area looked barren with no seats or fences, just a void of clean, freshly fallen snow, encased in a circular, stone wall. Her eyes immediately began to fill again.

"I didn't think it would make you cry." He watched her fumbling with her handkerchief once more. "I'd hoped that it would make you happy. Erase some of those painful memories for you. I thought that in the spring we could plant gardens in here. We could call it the 'Garden of Awakening'. I feel a new spirit awakening within me. I'd hoped that it would awaken new love between us too, but if that's too painful—"

"No, the garden is a beautiful idea," she interrupted. "It's just that it is so kind of you, so very kind of you." She faltered not knowing how to express the depth of her emotion.

He drew her to him. "Oh Tal, I am so very sorry that I caused you so much pain. If I could live a thousand lives giving you nothing but perfect love, I would still feel that I had not made up for my mistakes."

He searched deep into her eyes trying to convince her of the depth of his remorse. "Can you not look at the gains that I have made: the freed animals, the healing of Tobias, the freeing and forgiveness of Raybet, the removal of the prisoners from the dungeons, sharing the castle with Raybet and Rose? I am striving towards greater change. It is you who is inspiring me, saving me from myself. Please do not abandon me midstream. A beast cannot become a man instantaneously, and it is love alone that draws him on."

"Yes, I know you have tried to change, and I no longer hold what happened here at the animal compound against you. For some strange reason it was meant to happen, I feel sure of it, to show me how to love. Not just to love you, but also to love myself. To see beyond the broken woman that the world beholds, to trust that I am so much more than what I believe myself to be."

"Would you walk with me, just once, around the circumference?"

She hesitated, her stomach constricting. Her voice sounded breathless. "I don't know Jockim, there are too many memories. I don't want to go back there."

"It would help me too, you know. I feel a lot of shame about this place as well. I think we need to face it together, walk into it and embrace it."

She looked frantically around like she was contemplating escape. He knelt before her, taking her hand in his.

"Tal … you are a guest at my home. You have seen inside my shabby soul. Allow me to enter into yours … if just for a few moments."

She crouched down beside him, distressed. "Jockim, you humble me … bowing before a maid!" A rush of heat drenched her face.

He rose and drew her up with him, smiling at her discomfort. "A guest remember, not a maid, and at Deerie Castle, not Doomeerie. Come, walk with me."

They proceeded around the ancient pathway, where life had been spilled so cruelly and carelessly. About a third of the way along, he stopped. Staring into her eyes, he asked, "What do you feel, my love?"

She looked away, fighting the moisture that was welling. "Unimportant, overlooked, misunderstood, the least and lowliest of all. I am so very sad." She whispered into the cold, unfeeling air.

He drew her to him, holding her close. "Stay with it, just for a little." A deep silence cloaked them. "Now, listen again. Can you hear it? The voice of your soul, it's saying, 'You are important. Your feelings are important. Your needs are significant. Enter the stillness and try to understand them.'"

He felt her body begin to tremble slightly as the tears erupted. He held her close; safe and secure in his arms. They stayed entwined for a few minutes, and then he drew her on again. Stopping further around the arena, he asked again, "What do you feel now, Tal?"

The rotten eggs smelled putrid; the stench, the spoiled fruit and vegetables splattered over her. The stickiness clung to her skin, wet and clammy.

"I am worthless, defiled, dishonoured and despoiled." He drew her to him again. She hid her face in his coat. It was burning with memories. "I am sinking into my shame."

"Stay with it. Embrace it!" The wind rustled the silhouettes that surrounded the compound. A few leaves danced amidst the dirt at their feet. "Now listen again to your soul. It is saying, 'I am worthy. I esteem my holiness. I treat myself with respect regardless of how the world treats me.'"

Her breath gently slid into the rhythm of his, slow and steady, calm and comforting. They remained still—content to be momentarily woven into its spell.

"Only a little further now." He broke the silence. "We are almost there." They returned to the entrance.

"Where are your thoughts now, my love? What do you feel?"

"The sting of the whip, red heat swelling my face … I am less than human. I want to be annihilated! I feel only fear and hopelessness." Again, she sought the refuge of his coat, burying herself like a child who had been caught doing something disgraceful. He sighed deeply; the shame of remembering her looking up helplessly at him as Matthais struck her gripped his heart, twisting it mercilessly. He tightened his hold around her.

"Stay with it. It's only your false sense of self that needs to be destroyed." He stared up into the sky in desperation. The stars were a shimmering haze. How could he have done this to them? His gaze shifted towards the moon. Its soft light seemed unperturbed by his inner pain. He listened carefully. There was no sound in the still, night air. Then suddenly, the words came clearly, breaking through his barren mind. He felt a wave of release wash over him.

He allowed himself the luxury of wading in it for but a minute, and then wanting to share it, he whispered the words to her. "You are my beloved."

The wave lifted her up, propelling her on to a new place. She was drifting on the serenest sea, floating in the folds of the sacred breeze, igniting with an explosion of ecstasy. They stood together, holding each other. The silence extended on, broken occasionally by the gentle tremor of the wind.

Finally, he drew her gently to him, kissing her lightly on the forehead. "Thank you for staying with me and completing the walk … I know it would have been hard for you."

"Thank you Jockim, for the walk, the words, and the promised garden." She smiled at him contentedly, her face afire with love.

He nodded. Sharpness had stealthily crept into the night air. It whispered of winter's advance. *She must be emotionally exhausted,* he thought, *and freezing.*

"I guess we should be heading back in before it gets any colder." They walked towards the castle in silence. "Have you heard from Padyah?"

"Yes, he has found me a place to work … looking after a child … a little girl who has lost her parents."

His heart plummeted. A leaden stone lodged itself firmly in his throat. His legs felt heavy.

"So you'll be leaving then … in about a fortnight?"

There was silence. Her head was swimming. It had seemed like the right thing to do, but now she was filling up with sorrow. What was going on? Her anger had dissipated leaving behind a great, empty void. Waves of sadness were surging in, quickly filling it.

"Well …" she stammered, "well, I'm just not quite sure. I had planned … but …" Her words trailed off, lost in the mist of her confusion.

"Would you not reconsider? Could we not try a little longer?"

"Perhaps, I could." She smiled up at him. "Padyah indicated that there was no urgency in starting, that the child was well cared for and loved by an elderly couple. It's just that they thought that she needed someone younger as well, someone who could play with her and take her into the forest … Apparently she yearns to be with the animals." She went quiet. "Yes, I guess I could stay a little."

"That sounds like employment that you would love, but not something that you need to rush into. Good, I'm happy that you will stay for a while as my guest."

His step lightened a little. There was still time. He would prove to her that he had changed. Placing his arms around her shivering shoulders, he asked, "What changed your mind? Why did you decide to wait on the tables? Did Fanny bully you in to it?"

"Not at all." She laughed. "Although she has been telling me how bold and ungracious I was for not dining at the table for the last few days. Pover visited me. It was wonderful to be reunited with my spirit companion again. Everything seemed so much clearer to me, like I had been graced with new insights! I have so enjoyed the last few days. Thank you for bringing her back to me." She beamed up at him.

"Hmm … that cheeky, little bird … she was meant to be a surprise. Now she has stolen my trump card! I ought to take the whip to her." He chuckled and pulled her close towards him, hugging her.

"Come on, I wonder if we can salvage some food from the kitchen for dinner without Fanny knowing. We can have it in the study together."

"Sounds like a brilliant idea." Her mirth tinkled across the night air.

The snow began to fall lightly. Jockim watched it with a growing sense of wonder. Talitha felt soft and warm. He thought of Shiloh, of Son of Silver Stag, and of Benjamin. How was he going to tell her? Would it create a rift between them again now that they were closer than they had ever been? No, he couldn't do it. He just couldn't shatter the magic of the present moment. There was time. He would do it later, sometime that seemed to be the right moment, sometime down the track.

The tiny, frozen, star shaped droplets began to fall with greater ferocity, veil upon veil of white lace descending gracefully out of oblivion. They hurried towards the castle entrance, stopping briefly to watch before entering. The flakes slowly swallowed up all evidence of other existence. They stood watching, gazing into the void. The world looked clean and new, like a blank canvas waiting for the caress of new and softer strokes.

CHAPTER 7

The Tide Begins to Turn

Jockim watched his soldiers and servants shuffle into the great hall. A long chain of misery bonded by human cells droned past him exuding listless sorrow. Why had *he* of all people been given power over them? Shame surged over his body. What a mess he had made of his time as master of Doomeerie. He had contributed so much misery to their already difficult lives.

They looked nervous. Many kept their eyes averted from him. He searched the motley crowd for Talitha. Where was she? How could he possibly address them? Surely, they must despise him. Behind him sat Raybet, Rose, Anya, Vadio, and Konfra. Did they secretly despise him too? What an ass he was, an absolute ass!

The room went silent. The last of them had closed the door, and they stood before him like puppets, waiting for him to pull their strings. He swallowed hard. *Oh God, give me courage,* he inwardly pleaded. Pushing down hard upon his nervousness, he stood to address them. He was in command. He had to believe in himself. If he didn't believe in himself, how could he possibly ask them to believe in him?

"Good morning, everyone … I have summoned you here this morning for a few announcements." An element of sterness disguised his nervousness.

Hollow, expressionless faces stared back at him. *What has happened? Who has transgressed?* Most of them had already noticed the *Doomeerie Code of Conduct* on the table.

"Thank you for assembling so promptly."

Why wouldn't they? An ugly, accusing voice spitefully crept into his thoughts. *After all, they're all terrified of what might happen if they were late.* He dismissed it uneasily and continued.

"As you know, I have been absent for forty days. During that period I have done some serious reflection. I also spent some of my time with Sanctusis in the lake country and with Kyriedor in the south. The Oge are spreading rapidly over the island, and the time will soon come when folk must pledge their allegiance to either Kyriedor or the Oge. I have chosen the former. Those of you who are not happy with my decision are free to leave. There will be no reprisals, and of course you will be fairly paid for your services."

He hesitated for a minute endeavouring to take in the response on their faces, but only a sea of stony, coldness confronted him. Clearing his throat, he continued. "In making this choice I have come to the realisation that I have, in the past, been a very cruel master. I could blame my upbringing, my father Jockhein's example, but to do so would be fooling both you and me. I am a man and responsible for my own decisions. I regret to say that I have failed you all miserably, and for that I can only say that I am deeply sorry. Over the coming weeks I will endeavour to meet with each of you personally, to thank you for your on-going service to Deerie Castle. To those whom I have treated unjustly, I will try and make recompense. I am only a man, and hence I am sure to make mistakes again." He paused and ran his fingers through his black hair. "But I do promise that there will be no more punishment at the castle."

He lifted the *Doomeerie Code of Conduct* and threw it into the fire. Hundreds of tiny sparks exploded within the dark, stone cavity to be followed by an intense blaze of light.

"As a group we have believed that evil will befall us if we didn't carry out this code, but now as your master I urge you to change your thoughts. We must practise some compassion, before we all fall. By casting blame and repaying mistakes with further suffering and pain, we are only compounding our doom, digging our own graves of hate and self-condemnation. The outer world will repay us with what we believe is our due. The Oge will be only too eager to step in and feed upon our guilt, turning us into mindless drones. Of course I will ask each of you to take responsibility for your actions and to accept the consequences for your behaviour, as I myself am trying to do, however there will be no further need of punishment to enforce this."

Some of the soldiers shuffled nervously, uncomfortable with witnessing this change from one whom they had known to be so harsh and unrelenting. Silence held the room tightly. Noah stepped forward. The man whom he had always believed Jockim to be was there waiting to take command. He, for one, would offer him support. It was either forwards or back to the same, old ways. The choice was obvious.

"Thank you sir, we will continue to support and work for you. Many of us feared that we would starve when you stopped the animal fighting, but now we have more to eat than we ever had then. The animals are coming back in abundance to Night Forest, and we take only what we need, treating them with reverence. I am sure that your desire for a change in the castle's code of conduct will also bring good fortune to us. My men will be happy to work for you. What say you, men?"

A loud cheer resounded in the room. Thunderous clapping followed. As it began to subside, Fanny stepped forward.

"And the castle servants, sir, we too will be pleased to follow your plans." The words came out of a sense of loyalty towards him whom she had always cared for. Again a cheer erupted from the servants. Broad smiles contagiously spread across the human mass. Jockim breathed a sigh of relief. Kyriedor was right. They did accept it. They would change. His eyes looked tired but grateful as he spoke again.

"All I can say is thank you, from the deepest part of my being. I hope that this day will be the start of a new era for us all, an era of peace!" Again the cheers resounded around the hall. He cleared his throat as they subsided. "And now Raybet has an announcement to make."

Anya looked over at him smiling lovingly. *Thank you,* she mouthed. *I'm so proud of you.*

Raybet addressed the group with his usual ease and charm, announcing his and Rose's engagement, his relationship to Jockim as half-brother, and his subsequent ownership of half of the castle after his and Rose's wedding. There were further cheers and applause. A buzz of excitement hummed busily over the room as everyone nattered in amazement about the strange turn of events. Many held reservations that Jockim's plan would work, but none could deny that he was a man of his word. It had certainly paid off to stop the animal fighting, maybe this would work too. At the very least, it was a relief not to have the thought of the lash hanging over one's head.

Finally, Raybet dismissed the assembly. Jockim watched keenly, noting the expressions on the soldiers and servants faces, imagining what they were saying to one another. They filed out of the room enlivened with enough gossip to last a lifetime. Never before had folk at Doomeerie witnessed such a radicle change of events.

When the hall was finally empty, Raybet turned to his half-brother. "You've travelled a long way, little brother." He slapped him on the back. "I must admit that I doubted if I would ever see this day."

"Aye, that is so," remarked Konfra. "It's not an easy road, Jockim. I'm still travelling down it; one step forward and two backward most of the time."

"I know," Jockim replied soberly. "I'm well aware of my weaknesses."

"Not the least of which is your frustrating, elder brother, hey!" Raybet's smile was its usual, charming curve.

"Oh, I think I conquered you back there in the forest when I made the decision not to shoot you."

"Maybe," Raybet replied knowingly, "however I think that I would still be quite capable of ruffling a few feathers where a certain, young lady is concerned. Don't think you're out of the woods yet,

Jockim!"

"Where is Tal anyway?" Jockim remembered that he had not been able to locate her in the crowd.

Konfra's face creased with concern. "We need to talk Jockim. She was not at the assembly, and I'm worried for her safety."

Jockim stared at the old general. Just what had he done now? "Yes, you're right. We *do* need to talk." His voice was suddenly tense.

Raybet stared at his half-brother and then at the man whom adoption had decreed to be his father. Jockim's face had reverted to a stony grimness. Konfra's eyes widened, opening to some new insight. *Just what is going on here?* Raybet thought. *Something new has come to light between these two ... I wonder ...*

"You'll accompany me to the study then, Konfra. We can discuss matters in private there." Jockim's voice sounded more like a command than a request.

They entered the room and he closed the door, gesturing for Konfra to sit. The old gentleman settled into an armchair beside the fire, while Jockim poured them a brandy. He needed to find out about Talitha first, and then he would raise matters concerning Bess.

"So what do you know about Tal? Where is she?" He handed Konfra the brandy.

"I know very little Jockim ... only what Fanny has told me. She was working on the spinning wheel, talking with Talitha. I believe that Fanny wanted to apologise for her past, overbearing ways. The needle broke. Talitha went off to fetch a new one from the chest in Miriam's room, but she never returned. No one has seen her since very early this morning."

Jockim stared at the old general. "You're telling me the truth

I hope, Konfra. You know I can verify your story with Fanny. I'm well aware of your lying and scheming. If you've done anything to interfere with Tal, I'll—"

"I've done nothing ..." He looked the younger man squarely in the eyes. "Believe it or not, I am fond of that slip of a girl. She saved Raybet's sanity, and she has been mighty kind to Rose and I, considering how we treated her prior to the war. If you ask me she's the best thing that ever happened to this place."

"Why didn't you tell me sooner?" Jockim snapped.

"I only found out myself prior to the assembly. Fanny took me to the side and asked me if I had seen her."

"Alright, I'll have a thorough search of the castle done. If she's not here I think I've got an idea how I might find her."

"Good." Konfra began to rise. "I hope that you find her quickly. There may be no need for alarm. She could just be down with that donkey or wandering in the forest, looking for the stag."

"Not quite so fast, Konfra ... I haven't finished with you yet!"

Konfra slumped back into the chair, a sudden sensation of overwhelming lethargy taking hold of his body.

"There's another matter that came to my attention while I was away concerning Bess and Benjamin!"

Konfra nodded in a resigned fashion, seemingly unsurprised. "So you located the girl and her son. I knew it would only be a matter of time."

"MY SON!" Jockim's voice rose in anger. He stared in rage at the old man. He held a tight grip upon himself. Every muscle in his body wanted to spring into action, drag him to his feet and then knock him down again. *It's hardly the way I need to behave. It will set a poor example in the castle. Steady on.* He tried desperately to remain in control.

"I'm sorry, Jockim. There were many times that I wanted to be honest with you about the situation, but I knew that you would be furious; that you'd go tearing out and find that girl and try and reclaim her as your own. I suppose she has told you that she has been with your cousin, Tyrone, over the past few years. You would have brought Andor and him, and their forces down upon you long before you were ready to defend yourself. Doomeerie would have been lost."

Jockim stared at the old man incredulously. "I wouldn't have had to go tearing after her if you hadn't taken it unto yourself to scare the poor thing out of her wits and bustle her off into the wilderness—just to pave the way for Rose. And to think that you had me believing that she was a thief! What kind of a man are you anyway?" He eyed him with disgust.

"A very, poor one, Jockim, I'll make no bones about that. I'm sorry. Somewhere, sometime over the years of my loyalty to Jockhein and yourself, I lost my way. I raised Raybet for Jockhein. I fought for him as I did for you, laying my life on the line for Doomeerie, but you see there was never any reward in it for me. I could see that Jockhein only wanted me to save the castle. He knew I was the most powerful man in the country and he paid me well, but power comes to an end, era's come and go. I needed some lasting legacy. I wanted Doomeerie for my children, and God forgive me I schemed to get it. And now I'm an old man, and I regret my ways. All I can say is that I am sorry. Throw me out on the streets if you want, lock me up in your dungeons. God knows I will accept it. You see I've been with the Oge. I've paid harshly for my greed and deception, but I've also been with Kyriedor and I've made amends with my soul, so do with me what you will."

The old man looked frail and worn. Jockim sighed. He was beginning to sound like Raybet. Still, they all had their demons and he certainly couldn't claim innocence. He had been happy enough to believe him rather than trusting in Bess. Now he too would have to deal with the pain of his actions; living apart from Benjamin and having Tyrone raise his son. He rose and walked over to the table.

"I'll be using your men to take provisions secretly to Bess and Benjamin in the future, that is, when I am unable to go myself. As far as I am concerned, you're an old man. You've served Deerie Castle well over the years. You can stay on here. This castle is big enough for the both of us and with time, I might be able to stomach you a little better than I can at the moment." His eyes flashed hot coals of anger towards Konfra.

"However, I'll not be fooled again. There is to be no more interference in the castle's and my personal concerns. As you know I have promised half of this dwelling to Raybet after he marries Rose!" Konfra nodded. "If there is any interference in castle affairs on your part then this contract will become null and void." He opened the drawer pulling out a document. "You are to sign this now. I will explain the situation to Raybet, and he will also sign. If either of you don't sign then the arrangement falls through."

Konfra rose and hobbled towards the table. Jockim handed him the quill, looking him straight in the eyes. The old man sighed.

"Thank you, Jockim. There will be no interference. You are a finer man than your father." He signed and placing the quill down, nodded sadly at Jockim. "I wish you had been my son. You would make any father proud."

Jockim swallowed hard. How long he had wanted to hear those words from Jockhein, but they had never come.

"Thank you, I will do my very best to put what is past behind us."

Flight by Fiery Night

Talitha watched Anita with fondness. The little girl darted in and out of the bushes chasing her beloved hummingbird. She was a mysterious child; dark eyed and solemn at times, yet brimming with gaiety and mischievousness at others. Perhaps it was her past that drew the solemn moments over her, like a heavy curtain that shut in the window of her heart. She had certainly been through difficult times, having her mother die when she was born and her father remarry such a harsh woman. Then, the beloved hummingbird had been taken from her, and she had been lost in the forest.

She remembered when she had first heard her story from Angie. How she had shivered at the gypsy woman's description of the Oge and the strange events at White Cliff Castle. And now, here she was, nanny to the child in this delightful, little cottage, nestled just inside the leafy confines of the southernmost end of

Nightmare Forest. Few dared to live in this forest, which made it a perfect hiding spot for the child. The couple who had taken her in were kindly but old. Talitha was fortunate that Padyah had arranged for her to gain lodging there, as well as a little payment for caring for the child.

Still, she missed Jockim enormously. It broke her spirit to leave him without saying goodbye. But what else could she have done once she knew the truth? Sometimes she wished she had been more watchful of Kyriedor's warning about staying awake to her soul and not being caught into indiscriminately helping others. She would never have taken the letter to Raybet if she had been astute enough to realise that he was what Kyriedor had warned against, a dead man imprisoned. Then, she had been too keen to secure Fanny's approval. Was it because she always failed to esteem herself that she was drawn to search for other's approval? She recalled vividly how she had jumped to assist her when she had broken the spinning wheel's needle, saying that she would collect a new one from the chest in Miriam's room. That's where she had found it. The Sacred Sutra! *The Tao of Trust*!

Immediately, she opened it and read the brief notes about Benjamin and Bess that Jockim had scrawled inside the front cover. How could she have any future with him if he already had a son to a past mistress? His duty lay in caring for them. It was too distressing to speak with him about it. She couldn't bear the pain of parting, as she knew that he would try and convince her otherwise. That wouldn't be fair to Benjamin and Bess! No, she must steal away and make a new life for herself where he could not locate her.

The forest shadows were beginning to lengthen. "Anita," she called. "We'd better start back."

The little girl ran eagerly towards her. Behind her Freedom and Pover glided through the gathering gloom. They rounded the corner and came to the familiar crossroads. The wider, dirt track led into the nearby township of Woodlark, the other to their cottage. A podgy man was sitting on a log beside his donkey and cart, puffing a pipe. He tipped his hat.

"Afternoon ladies!" He smiled at Talitha and Anita.

"Hello!" Talitha nodded.

"I'd be looking for directions, miss." The words drifted out amongst puffs of smoke, coiling around his discoloured teeth. "Which track do I take to Woodlark?"

"That is the one, sir!" Talitha pointed. "The bridge into the town is about five mile south."

"Thank ya, miss."

Talitha smiled and kept walking. Her eyes were drawn to the old, grey donkey. It looked to be a pitiable creature.

"You look like ya gotta kind heart, miss!" The chubby man jumped up and started hobbling towards her. "Me donkey's fair spent. Don't suppose ya'd be able to bed us down for the night."

Talitha stopped and patted the donkey's weathered forehead. "I'm sorry, sir. I'd like to help. We live not far, just down that track, but I can't invite strangers into my master's home."

"We'd repay ya handsomely with firewood." The old man's eyes gleamed as he pulled an old blanket off the top of the cart, revealing a huge pile of sticks.

Panic gripped Talitha as the image floated hauntingly into her memory. Kyriedor's final warning was like a beckon searing into her foggy mind. "I'm sorry, sir, we have no room." Clutching Anita's hand, she hurried on not daring to look back.

"Shame on ya, miss!" he called after her. "The donkey may not make it through the night!"

* * *

Jockim paced the floor in agitation. "I'm going to head off immediately, Padyah. I have an uneasy sense. I can't wait till morning. I feel that she is in danger."

The old sage nodded knowingly. "Yes, I sense it too. The Oge will stop at nothing to kill the child. God speed …" He shook Jockim's hand and raised his other hand to pat him on the shoulder.

He barely had finished telling Jockim of her whereabouts, and now the young man was off again. Yet, he knew that he had done the right thing revealing her secret lodging. He too felt that something was amiss. He only hoped that he would reach her in time.

Jockim headed south through the forest. The nervousness of the animals alerted him first, then the stale smell of smoke, and finally the sight of its sinister coil, swirling chalklike into the night sky. He hastened his pace, breaking into a run as the smoke thickened, eventually displaying its fiery source. Fortunately, the land surrounding the little hut and stable had been cleared so the surrounding trees had not caught alight.

The hut looked like it was gone. Frantically, he circled it, searching for some way of possibly entering. Again and again, he made to run through its ravenous heat but it was too consuming.

Finally, he forced his way through and into a small bedroom. Anita was asleep on the bed. He hastily scooped her up in his arms and fled for the door. The walls collapsed around him.

"Tally, Tally ... Nanna, Poppie!" She sobbed, awakening to the nightmare exploding about them.

"Where are they?" He prompted her for information, his eyes wild with fear. The little girl said nothing. Her tiny finger pointed towards the hut. It was all but devoured by the insatiable flames. It would be madness to attempt another entry!

He crouched down in despair, head lowered in his heads. Wait! The stable! It had only just caught alight. Maybe, just maybe she was in there asleep with the animals. He flung the door open and immediately heard Balaamine's bray.

"Steady on girl. You're alright!" He comforted the old jenny, while he frantically searched the animal pens.

"Where are they ... Talitha and the others?" he addressed Balaamine as he led her to safety. There was no other sign of life inside save a few chooks, which he herded out before him. Balaamine nervously pawed the ground as the hut collapsed in a mighty roar, sending sprays of amber sparks into the dark sky.

There was little that Jockim could do. He and Anita stared horror-struck. At any moment, the surrounding trees could catch alight. He must move the child and donkey on to safety. Tears blurred his vision as he hastened with his companions deeper into the forest, heading north in the opposite direction of the wind.

The world seemed surreal, like it was coming to an end and he was the only man left surviving; he and the child, and the donkey— the gentle donkey that saved his life all those years ago. Where had the years gone—forgotten fragments of feelings blown away like the ashes that he had left behind, scattered wind-blown, lost in time? Soot dust, black dust, haunting dust, it stung your eyes making them weep, but even weeping couldn't shift the hollow, brittle sadness that clung to his parched throat.

CHAPTER 9

The Door and the Dream That Was

For those who dare to watch into the night,
The darkness disappears in shafts of light.
Even the shadows are but a lesser love,
Held in reverence from high above!

Talitha awoke with a start. She had been dreaming. She had been in the study with Jockim and a small boy. The child was sobbing inconsolably. Jockim was coming towards her. "Help him!" she screamed. "If you don't help the boy we will be burned." She felt herself choking, suffocating …

She sat up, relieved to be awake. Beside her, Anita was sleeping soundly. She slipped silently from the bed and looked out of the window. Shafts of moonlight danced playfully about the trees.

She pulled a shawl across her shoulders and sat quietly watching. What was Jockim doing now she wondered? Agh ... brr ... The sound of the old couple snoring drifted softly into the stillness of her room. It was going to be difficult to get back to sleep. Perhaps she should just sit for a while and watch the shadows play tug o' war in the wind.

She hadn't been by the window long when she saw him—the majestic Silver Stag, enigmatically gliding through the patches of moonlight. He stepped proudly out of the shadows, holding his great antlers high and pawing the ground. He was staring straight at her. She held her breath. "Shiloh," she whispered, her voice quivering with awe.

Stealthily, she headed for the door. Pover followed. If only she could just touch him once more. They were in the clearing now. His hind quarters were slipping silently into the trees. She and Pover followed closely, as he led them on and on. Finally, he nestled down on the forest floor in a leafy grove. They crept in beside him. He lowered his head gracefully as Talitha gently stroked his coat. He looked into her eyes. Her heart began to melt. At last, they were together again!

✳ ✳ ✳

The soft rays of dawn's first light filtered through the leafy canopy. Talitha thought she could smell smoke. She sat up. She was in the forest. What had happened? Memories of the night tumbled back into her thoughts. Shiloh! She looked around. There was no sign of the stag. She jumped to her feet and hurried back in the direction of the hut.

The air was thick with stale smoke. A haunting sense of fear began to rattle her nerves. On and on she pressed until she came upon it: the burnt, charred remains of her past life. The wind swept around the haunted trees that were twisted into black, gnarled, knots of dry wood— standing bereft and stark, like tombstones. She crouched in the dust—nothing, nothing but scorched remains, where once there had been a kind old couple, a beautiful little girl, and a beloved donkey. But where were they? There was no sign that life had ever existed here. The wind scurried around in eerie eddies, scooping up the black soot and depositing it into her eyes, her nose, and her mouth. She was suffocating. Then she saw them: the charred bones of the old couple. She stared in horror. The air slowed. Heat rose and swam nauseating about her. The trees began to rotate, swallowing her up. The spinning, black whirlwind was taking her into oblivion.

✳ ✳ ✳

The townsfolk found her collapsed amongst the ashes. She said she wanted to be taken to the shepherd healer, and so they made the frightening journey through Nightmare Forest. By the time they reached Padyah's hut, Jockim had already left to take Anita to one of the old sage's trusted friends, who would transport her further to a hidden location.

Padyah had given Talitha something to help her sleep at first, and when she had awoken he had listened to her tale of grief—grief for the old couple, the little girl, the beloved donkey, but most of all for Jockim.

Then he had erased some of it. He had told her how Jockim had come for her, and how he had saved Anita and Balaamine. But he would not tell her where Anita had gone. That must remain a secret. Even Jockim didn't know. It was better that way. Especially as the Oge would be intent upon destroying her. She accepted it was for the best, even though her heart longed to see the child again. He softened her sadness by saying that Freedom had sung a melodious song the evening that they had secretly departed. It had echoed into the silence of the dark night, like a forgotten tune breaking through all the confusion that strangles hope's first rays.

Next, he had told her about Jockim: how distraught he had been when he had returned from the burnt hut with Anita and Ballamine, and how he had freed Tyrone so that he could return to Bess and Benjamin.

She went quiet thinking about Jockim. Why did he release his cousin? After a few minutes, she said, "Surely freeing Tyrone was not wise? Might he rise to take over the castle again?"

"Indeed, he may," Padyah replied, "but you more than anyone else must perceive the significance of what Jockim has done?"

She looked at him searchingly. "My dear Talitha, he has sent Tyrone back to care for Bess and Benjamin. He will willingly give away all that he can lay claim to—his castle, his heritage, his son— to have you with him."

A shadow of sadness shot through her eyes. He took her hand in his. "Do not fret. Tyrone is not a bad man. He just views life from a different level. He has been a good father to the boy and a good partner to Bess, and he will continue to be so. Life will keep moving him forward as it does all of us. We keep evolving. What we consider to be of value now is not what we thought to be so earlier. Perhaps in the future he will no longer desire the castle. You must trust."

She nodded. "Yes, I have seen Shiloh roaming free, and now I no longer feel I need to find him. I trust that he is where he is meant to be."

"And what about you, Talitha? … Where are you meant to be?"

She pondered his questions for some days until Jockim, having heard of her whereabouts, returned. A week of rejoicing in their reunion passed too quickly. Eventually, he stated that he must return to the castle. She had not yet made her plans clear to either him or Padyah.

She watched him saddle up his horse. Speaking softly to it, as he had always done to Noble, he turned to look at her, his gaze gently admiring her familiar features.

"Well, my little maidservant, are you ready to return home? Shall I saddle up Balaamine?"

"I don't know if Doomeerie is my home, Jockim." She struggled for the right words.

"No, you're right, it isn't. It never was. But perhaps you might consider Deerie Castle to be. Doomeerie is a spectre of the past, Tal. I have created something new, something wonderful that you have shown me."

He took her hand, and they walked over to the tree line. Turning to face her, he lifted her chin up to search the doe-like eyes that shone serenely before him.

"I was hoping that I might take you back not as a guest, but as my betrothed."

He dug into his pocket, pulling out a simple gold band. Gently, he opened the palm of her hand and placed the ring in it. She hesitated and his heart trembled anxiously. Suddenly, Pover swept from behind them in a flurry. She was flying directly towards the castle.

"Well at least she knows her mind." Jockim laughed nervously.

"That she does, and she has never been wrong before."

He smiled and drawing her to him, kissed her tenderly. "Then I take it the answer would be yes."

"Yes, Jockim," she smiled contentedly, "of course it is yes. Uncertainty doesn't cause me to falter … it's just …"

"Just what …?"

"I don't think that the folk at Doomeerie are quite ready to see a past maidservant become their mistress. Surely, they will believe that something dreadful will befall the castle?" She looked concerned.

He threw his head back, laughing heartily. "What does it matter what they think? You are always too concerned for the welfare of others, Talitha. That's what gets us into such predicaments. You need to become a little selfish. Self-nurturing is just as holy as selflessness when one's intent is pure."

He took the ring from her palm and placed it on the chain about her neck. "Why didn't you trust me enough to speak with me about your plans before you left the castle to martyr yourself for the sake of Bess and Benjamin?"

She stared silently at him. He gently lowered the ring under her bodice. "Maybe you need a little more time to see yourself as mistress. Part of your soul is still lost to you … like that Hidden Garden that you search for … but when you find it you will love your shadow as much as your sanctity, for light draws new life from darkness." He gently traced his finger down the curve of her smile. "Your vision will come when the time is right, but for now we will keep our intentions hidden, if that is easier for you." He smiled tenderly.

A breeze rustled about them bringing down a flutter of leaves. They walked a little into the forest. A shaft of light penetrated the swaying, green canopy; soft, trickling, gold dust. She sighed, her breath becoming one with the sacred space.

"Like the leaves, we tremble at the thought of our own potential."

"Look," he pointed towards it, "it's so pure." Her gaze alighted upon the loveliness that gently spilled into their surrounds. She felt his embrace draw her close as together they walked into the shaft of sunlight. The soft glow bathed them in its gentle warmth.

"The whole of creation is suspended in love," she whispered, "but mostly we fail to see it because we do not trust that we are worthy enough to lay claim to it!"

✳ ✳ ✳

It was dark by the time they neared the castle. Jockim's lantern flickered playfully amongst the shadows. They approached the remnants of the old, killing compound. The wind strengthened in a sudden, frenzied burst of excitement causing the black branches to ripple against the mirrored sky. A faint moan echoed from behind the great oak doors. They stared at each other simultaneously, in shock.

"What is that?" Jockim sounded alarmed. "Something must be bolted behind the doors." He eased down from his mare, but Talitha was already fumbling at the bolt. Her hands were still clasping the only possession that she had left from the fire—the map of the Hidden Garden. For some reason she had tucked it in her bodice that night when she had followed Shiloh. The heavy bolt held fast. Fearful that she would tear the map trying to force it free, she lowered it to the ground.

"Yes, it's tight," said Jockim. "It's impossible to open with anything clasped in your hands."

A sudden whirlwind flurried about them, lifting the map. Silently, it carried it into the night sky. She watched it floating serenely towards the River Styx. With a cry of dismay, she took off after it. Too late! It landed softly on the shimmering surface. Speedily, with an air of excited abandonment, it was propelled forward towards the great falls.

Her heart sank! Wearily, she wiped the tears from her eyes. Her dream to return to the Hidden Garden was gone forever, swept away in a whimsical, passing breeze. What was the point of life—of dreams—of anything?

Jockim read her despair as she approached him dispiritedly. "I'm sorry, Tal." He cradled her in his arms as she broke down. "I know it meant so much to you."

"My first dream … my earliest memory of a warm and tender place." She sobbed.

"We are forced to put everything down when we open new doors." He smiled at her, wiping away her tears. "Just trust! I'm sure that you still have something to guide you—maybe something different to what you expected."

He pulled at the now unlocked door, and they entered the compound. There stood Shiloh! Raising his noble head, he stared directly at them. The moon surrendered its light to the gathering clouds and darkness enveloped them. They felt his presence move stealthily past like a sacred spectre.

"Shiloh!" she whispered.

"Yes my love, he has returned. Despite everything, our trust has somehow made us worthy of his spirit. Perhaps he will lead us to your Hidden Garden!"

Peering intently, Jockim watched into the night. His gaze alighted upon a single wildflower trembling softly under the light of the surfacing moon. He bent down and tenderly picked it.

"Lucky we didn't trample it in our ignorance. Some miracle has enabled it to withstand the approaching winter." He handed it to her.

She smiled. "And an even greater one has allowed us to behold its beauty."

"Mmm … maybe we have entered your Hidden Garden without even knowing it!"

She pulled the golden band out from under her bodice. It felt warm. Tenderly, she entwined the stem of the tiny wildflower around its curve. Its fragile thread met full circle. Then she allowed it to fall ever so softly on top of her bodice. It rose up and down almost imperceptibly, in harmony with her breath, reflecting a circle of soft, unending light.